STOLEN
DAUGHTERS

BOOKS BY CAROLYN ARNOLD

DETECTIVE
AMANDA STEELE SERIES

The Little Grave
Stolen Daughters

BRANDON FISHER FBI SERIES

Eleven
Silent Graves
The Defenseless
Blue Baby
Violated
Remnants
On the Count of Three
Past Deeds

DETECTIVE
MADISON KNIGHT SERIES

Ties That Bind
Justified
Sacrifice
Found innocent
Just Cause
Deadly Impulse
In the Line of Duty
Power Struggle
Shades of Justice
What We Bury
Life Sentence (prequel
romantic suspense)

McKINLEY MYSTERIES

The Day Job is Murder
Vacation is Murder
Money is Murder
Politics is Murder
Family is Murder
Shopping is Murder
Christmas is Murder
Valentine's Day is Murder
Coffee is Murder
Skiing is Murder
Halloween is Murder
Exercise is Murder

MATTHEW CONNOR
ADVENTURE SERIES

City of Gold
The Secret of the Lost Pharaoh
*The Legend of Gasparilla and
His Treasure*

STANDALONE

Assassination of a Dignitary
Pearls of Deception

STOLEN
DAUGHTERS

CAROLYN ARNOLD

bookouture

Published by Bookouture in 2021

An imprint of Storyfire Ltd.
Carmelite House
50 Victoria Embankment
London EC4Y 0DZ

www.bookouture.com

ISBN: 978-1-80019-020-7
eBook ISBN: 978-1-80019-019-1

To survivors of abuse…

PROLOGUE

Her lifeless eyes stared up at him. All was quiet. The struggle gone.

His rage had subsided, replaced by tranquility and bliss. He had risen above his past and shown mercy when the world had shown none to him.

Inspired, he tapped a kiss to his fingers and pressed them to her forehead. "Rest in peace."

He closed her eyelids and got to his feet.

His gaze still upon her, he felt himself to be the very embodiment of love and forgiveness. He was... The Merciful.

Yes, he liked that.

Excitement vibrated through his entire body, but he had to move. There was more work to do.

He took the jerry can and soaked her body with fuel. Satisfied he was finished with her, he continued pouring as he walked down the hall, then stairs, to the main level.

He stopped in the middle of the house, a few feet from the puddle of fuel, his gas can now empty. He pulled a matchbook and struck one to flame. He watched it dance on the tip for a second or two before tossing it onto the accelerant. It ignited with a blast of heat.

He hustled through the door into the backyard, a smile on his face. The darkness of early morning and his black clothing were his cover. The neighborhood, too, was one in which people saw and heard nothing—and they certainly didn't talk to the police. Besides, most people would still be in bed.

And by the time anyone smelled smoke, the place would be ash. The girl along with it.

CHAPTER ONE

Washington, DC
Thursday, April 1st, 10:00 AM

Amanda Steele's phone rang, and she looked down at it on the conference table in front of her. She was seated in a room at a prestigious Washington law firm with her mother, and her mother's lawyer, Hannah Byrd.

Hannah stopped talking mid-sentence and looked at Amanda.

Caller ID told her it was her boss, Sergeant Malone. When Malone called, it often meant someone was dead. She looked apologetically at her mother and Hannah. "I'm sorry, but I need to take this."

"No problem," Hannah assured her with a smile.

"Thanks." Amanda answered and listened as Malone told her she was needed back in Dumfries immediately. A young woman had been pulled from a house fire in the east end, and the circumstances looked suspicious.

"Sorry, I know that you're probably in Washington right now..." Also a family friend, Malone knew about the meeting and the reason for it.

"No, don't mention it. I think we're almost finished anyway." She sought out Hannah's gaze, and the lawyer nodded. "I'll get there as soon as I can." She hung up and looked at her mother, feeling swamped with guilt. "I'm sorry, Mom."

"You've got a case." A conclusion, not a question. But her mother was familiar with the demands on those in law enforcement, and it was one reason Amanda and her mother had driven there separately. If something came up, then it would free Amanda to leave.

"I do." Amanda was torn. She wanted to get out of there but couldn't quite get herself to move.

"Go," her mother prompted.

"Will you be all right if I…?" Amanda pointed to the door.

"I'm a grown-ass woman, so, yes. Go. Besides, Hannah will take care of me."

Amanda hesitated a few seconds longer, then stood and tapped a kiss on her mother's forehead. She thanked her and Hannah for their understanding and left.

Stepping outside, she appreciated the warm, fresh air and the freedom—not that it could erase the reality that her mother was facing a murder charge. *A murder charge*, the thought repeated in her head.

She'd had a few months to come to terms with it and still hadn't. Maybe it was really because she didn't want to accept it. After all, Julie—Jules—Steele had been an upstanding citizen all her life… well, until this point.

She'd raised Amanda and her siblings—a brother and four sisters—and was now a grandmother to four. She was also the wife of the former police chief of the Prince William County Police Department.

Amanda got into her Honda Civic and headed to the Dumfries address Malone had given her. It would take about forty minutes, give or take depending on traffic, to get there from Washington. But she didn't need a GPS to tell her that. She knew the route and every backstreet in Dumfries, where she'd grown up. It was a small town of under six thousand—not exactly a booming metropolis—but it was a desirable place to live given its close vicinity to Washington, DC. The flipside was that crime levels were probably higher than what other small and more isolated communities might see.

While her father had been police chief for the PWCPD until his retirement five years ago, Amanda was currently a detective with Homicide stationed out of Central District Station in Woodbridge—another small town about ten minutes from Dumfries. Maybe one day she'd reach the position of chief, but given the trajectory of her life during the past six years, it might be a while before that happened.

She pulled down a side street, headed toward 532 Bill Drive, and had to park a block away. Dumfries PD had the area cordoned off to allow the firefighters room to work. She didn't see any sign of her partner, Trent Stenson, who Malone had told her would meet her on scene. She did see her friend, Becky Tulson, who worked with the Dumfries PD, though.

The same age as Amanda at thirty-five, Becky had her shoulder-length brown hair pulled back into a ponytail, which accentuated her heart-shaped face.

Amanda parked and got out of the car. The smell of smoke clung heavy in the air and tickled her throat.

She looked down the street at the mangle of emergency response vehicles. There were a few fire engines with the Dumfries Triangle Volunteer Fire Department, a medic's truck, an ambulance, and a police cruiser. They were all parked haphazardly in front of a two-story house that didn't look like it was in too bad of shape, considering it had been on fire.

She approached Becky, who was guarding this end of the scene. There would be another officer posted at the other side.

"Hey," Becky said, "how did everything go?" Amanda had told her about the planned meeting with Hannah this morning to discuss her mother's defense strategy.

Amanda let out a deep sigh. "Honestly? It's a long road ahead, and there are no guarantees."

Becky put a hand on Amanda's forearm. "I'm here. You know that?"

"Always." Amanda smiled. "You haven't seen Trent, have you?" She looked around again, but it was possible that Trent had parked at the opposite end of the scene.

"Not yet."

As if on cue, a PWCPD department car pulled up near Becky's cruiser, and Trent shut off the engine and got out.

"Ladies." He smiled at them both. He was a couple of years younger than Amanda, with blond hair and blue eyes. She imagined he might be a charmer when off the clock, but she had no romantic interest in him. One, having a partner on the job was complicated enough without making it personal; and two, she was seeing someone else. Logan Hunter. Their relationship was rather new, sometimes awkward, and entirely casual. Probably all because he was the first man she'd dated since her husband died in a tragic car accident almost six years ago, along with their six-year-old daughter.

"About time you got here," Amanda said. "I came from Washington and still beat you."

"Hey." Trent shrugged. "Got here as soon as I could."

"Primping takes time?" she teased.

"Well, I can't be showing up looking like riffraff."

She waved goodbye to Becky and started down the sidewalk with Trent toward 532, looking at the neighboring houses as she went. Most of them were in need of maintenance with sagging porches, chipped and peeling paint, and curled shingles. This part of town was where dreams came to die.

Two doors down from the scene, they ran into Officer Deacon with the Dumfries PD.

"I got the call," Amanda said, holding up her detective badge more out of habit than necessity. Both she and Trent had met Deacon before. He simply gestured for them to carry on.

Amanda took in 532 Bill Drive in more detail. A two-story century-old clapboard home. It was pretty much intact from what she could see from the outside, but the windows were boarded. She'd guess that was the case before the fire. The front door appeared to be lying on the grass, leaving a gaping hole in the structure where it used to be.

"Whoa, whoa. Hold up there." A man in dress shirt, tie, and slacks approached. He reminded Amanda of an old dog with his hooded eyes. He had a ruddy complexion but was trim and had an obvious exercise regimen, given the lay of his shirt across his chest and his thick arms. His hair was mostly gray with some cracked pepper.

Amanda held up her badge, and Trent followed suit. "Prince William County PD, Homicide Unit," she said. "And you are?"

"Fire Marshal Craig Sullivan. I'm in charge of this scene, ma'am."

He was older than she was, but she didn't take offense to the term *ma'am* like some women. It did sting a little today, though, with her thirty-sixth birthday only five days away.

Fire marshals were essentially arson investigators, but they were also a bit law enforcement. Some even carried guns, but they focused on their area of expertise—the cause of fires and gathering all pertinent evidence to that end. Amanda and Trent's relationship with Sullivan would be somewhat of a unified command structure. He'd stick to matters pertaining to the fire, and she and Trent would focus on the victim.

She shouldn't have to point all this out to Sullivan, though. "We're here about the dead girl," she countered, not about to get into any battle over jurisdiction, and her stomach souring at the word *girl*. It brought back her more recent encounter with a local sex-trafficking ring.

"She's in there." Sullivan pointed toward the medic's vehicle. "Firefighters found her when clearing and hauled her out for medical attention. The medic attempted CPR but was given permission to call time of death by the attending doctor at the hospital. Hence, the body's still here—and now an ME is on his or her way from Manassas."

Manassas, about thirty minutes north of Dumfries, was where the Office of the Chief Medical Examiner was located.

Amanda nodded and stepped toward the vehicle but turned back to Sullivan. "When did the fire start?"

"I'd estimate around five thirty, give or take. It was called into nine-one-one at five fifty by a neighbor a few doors down and across the street. We had it out by six twenty."

It was going on eleven now, but it would have taken time for the fire marshal to do his thing and for the death to be called. Then she and Trent had to arrive, along with the ME—who still hadn't shown up. Two things stood out to her. "You guys have a fast response time."

"On the high end, we can be on scene within five minutes. We strive to get out of the firehouse within forty-five to sixty seconds from the time of alarm. When it's residential, well, our drivers might press a little heavier on the gas. We know we're dealing with people's homes and lives are at stake."

That might have been a little more information than she needed, but it was interesting. Now for the second thing she'd noted. "The person who placed the call to nine-one-one did so rather quickly after the fire was estimated to have started?"

"Yep."

"Do you have this person's information?"

"I can get that for you."

"Thanks." She also wanted to get her hands on the 911 tape.

"Do you figure it was arson?" Trent asked.

Sullivan seemed to acknowledge Trent for the first time. "I'm trained to look at the evidence without any preconceived notions about intention or foul play. As homicide detectives, you'd look at everything with an eye to murder. But, with all that said, from what I see so far, I have no doubt in my mind the fire was set on purpose. Evidence is still being gathered from inside the home, but my initial impression is that accelerant was used. I'll still need to confirm what that was, but the girl is wet and smells of gasoline. The medic noticed it when performing life-saving endeavors."

She turned to Trent. "We'll need to speak to the person who called nine-one-one. They could have seen the firebug, maybe even *been* the firebug."

"Nah." Sullivan winced and shook his head. "Not to tramp on toes here, but a firebug, by their very nature, loves to watch the fires they set. They're not going to call and have them put out."

Amanda glanced over a shoulder to some people crowded across the street. Could one of them be the arsonist?

"Before you ask, we got pictures of everyone," Sullivan said.

She slowly drew her attention back to the fire marshal. The person who called in the fire may not have started it, but they could have seen the person responsible. She gestured to the boarded windows. "Did you do that or—"

"No, it was like that."

"But not the front door?" Trent flicked the tip of his pen toward the discarded door on the lawn.

"No."

They'd have to look up the property records, but Amanda would assume it had defaulted to the bank, given the boarded windows. If so, the previous owner might have set the fire to spite the bank—the girl an unexpected casualty—but then that didn't explain the gasoline on the body. "Do you know how long the home sat unoccupied?"

"Can't say I've gotten that far." Sullivan's eyes darkened. "I can tell you that it seems squatters used the place. Not much garbage, but there are a few mattresses upstairs. The girl was found on one."

Amanda took in the property, its long grass and the gate at the end of the driveway. "Guessing there's a back door?"

"Yeah, and it's definitely the access point they would have used—the people crashing here and likely the firebug. A large padlock was found on the back porch, and there's evidence it was cut off. Now, the seed of the fire—"

"The seed?" Amanda queried, not quite sure what he meant by that terminology.

"The *origin* of the fire, where it started," Trent jumped in to answer, shrugged under their gazes. "My uncle was a firefighter before he retired."

"Huh." Sullivan regarded Trent, this time with respect lighting his otherwise dull-gray eyes. "As I was about to say, the seed of the fire was in the middle of the main level and seemed to follow a trail toward the stairs. That's what the burn marks are telling me anyway."

Amanda nodded to acknowledge Sullivan's conclusion and said, "Could you take us to the victim now?"

"Sure." Sullivan led the way down the walk toward the medic's vehicle.

As they moved, Amanda's heart thumped a little off rhythm as she prepared herself to see the burnt remains of a young woman. Her mind was also churning with what exactly had taken place at 532 Bill Drive. A body doused with gasoline, left in a house set ablaze… that sounded like murder to her.

CHAPTER TWO

"Hey, Marshal Sullivan." A uniformed firefighter came over just as they reached the medic's vehicle. He was dressed in full gear, his helmet in hand. Soot was smeared on his cheeks and forehead. He gave Amanda and Trent a brief look but focused on Sullivan. "Is it good for us to head out?"

Sullivan gave a small bob of his head, then said, "Actually, I'd rather you stick around for a bit."

A small pulse tapped in the firefighter's cheek.

"These are Detectives Steele and Stenson with the PWCPD." Sullivan gestured toward them.

The man leveled a cool gaze at her, but he removed a glove and held out a hand. "Spencer Blair."

He had a strong grip, not surprising, but the way he was staring through her made the seventy-degree weather feel like a cold front was moving in. "Blair?" she asked to ensure she heard him right. She knew someone else with that last name.

"Uh-huh." He then shook hands with Trent, though he barely gave him a glance.

Amanda studied the firefighter. He was in his mid-to-late twenties. "Is your mother Emma Blair, a crime scene investigator, by chance?"

"The one and only." Spencer kept his gaze locked on her, and it would seem he had some sort of issue with her, just like his mother did. Her interactions with Amanda were always curt and cool.

"Small world." Sullivan gripped Spencer's shoulder. "Spencer here is one of the firefighters who pulled the young lady out of the house."

"You thought she was alive?" Amanda said.

"Not my call. We see a body, we clear it from the structure, hand it over to the medic."

Sullivan clarified, "The only reason we wouldn't is if it was obvious the victim was dead or had been murdered. Think a knife sticking out of a chest or a body riddled with bullets."

"Or burned very badly," she said.

Sullivan shook his head. "We'd still remove them. That is unless it was very evident survival was impossible. In the case of an obvious murder, we'd do our best to defend the area... That just means we'd preserve it or protect it from the fire."

Amanda nodded and turned to Spencer. "Sullivan told us she was found on a mattress. Did she have any personal belongings with her?"

Spencer raked a hand through his hair, looked around. "Not that I saw, but my focus was on clearing the house of victims—and keeping myself safe." He glanced away from her to look at another fireman who was gesturing for him. Spencer turned to the marshal. "I gave you my statement already, so I'm not sure what else you could want."

"I'd like to walk through the scene with you again." Sullivan's voice was firm.

"Well, I'll be over there." He joined his colleague, and they engaged in a spirited conversation that had Spencer's arms gesturing wildly.

"Gave you his statement?" Amanda asked Sullivan.

"Standard procedure. Everyone who had contact with the victim needs to help me rebuild what happened. How the fire looked at the time, where the body was found, how it was positioned, etcetera. In an empty house, we're at least not dealing with the possibility of furniture being moved around, but still the conditions change due to the fire."

She could appreciate all of what the marshal had said. "We'll want to read those statements."

"Of course. I'll get them to you. I'll also get you sketches and photos of the interior and where the body was found." Sullivan knocked on the back of the medic's van, and the doors swung open.

The smell of gasoline wafted out of the vehicle and had Amanda taking a few steps back.

"I'm not too late, I hope," a man's voice said behind her.

Amanda turned to find Hans Rideout. He was one of her favorite medical examiners. He was in his late forties and had a passion for working with the dead—as wrong as that might sound. But he never let his macabre job darken his spirits. More the opposite. He was quick with light humor and possessed a contagious smile. Rideout flashed one now and accompanied it with a small salute.

"Oh no, not you." The medic, a forty-something man himself, groaned, but his expression quickly gave way to a large smile.

"You son of bitch," Rideout countered, and the medic jumped out of the vehicle and gave the ME a huge hug. "How have you been?"

"Good, good. You?" Back pats and shoulder squeezes.

"Doing good."

Amanda glanced at Trent, then Sullivan. It would seem the medic and Rideout were longtime friends who hadn't seen each other in a while.

"Something tells me you're acquainted," she said, smiling.

"Very astute, Detective." Rideout grinned at her. "Jimmy Wood and I go back to childhood. He married my high-school sweetheart."

"And you're still talking to him?" Sullivan asked. "Better man than me."

Rideout laughed. "Turns out he did me a favor."

Jimmy nudged Rideout in the arm and hopped back into the vehicle.

Rideout went in after him, then Amanda and Trent. It was a tight squeeze, but they made it work. The ME and medic were on the victim's right, Amanda and Trent on her left. Sullivan stayed outside and left the back doors open.

The deceased was on a stretcher, and Amanda's chest ached at the sight of how young she looked. Was she even eighteen?

She had a round, cherubic face, and her hair was long and blond and fanned around her head like a halo. Her skin was a bluish gray from decomposition, but she'd had a fair complexion that would have stood in contrast to her black eye makeup. She didn't appear to have even been touched by the fire.

She was clothed in a black, short-sleeved shirt with a crew neck, blue jeans, and a matching jean jacket. On its collar was a dragonfly pin. It was gold, about an inch and a half in height and two inches wide, and its wings were iridescent teals and purples. It seemed like quite a nice piece of jewelry for a person her age and contradicted the gold stud in her nostril.

Rideout leaned over the girl, angling his head left and right.

"Something you're noticing?" Amanda asked him.

"She was doused with gasoline." He paused his inspection and looked at Amanda with a sardonic smile. "I'm sure you can smell that."

"Yes."

"No evidence she was stabbed or shot that I can see. There is petechiae in her eyes." He snapped on some gloves, pulled a camera from his bag, and took some pictures of her. Afterward, he returned the camera to the sack and grabbed a flashlight. He opened her mouth and shined the beam inside. "Some petechiae on her gums too. She was deprived of oxygen. What time was the fire believed to have been started?"

Amanda glanced over a shoulder at the marshal but answered for him. "We were told in the neighborhood of five thirty."

Rideout studied the girl and looked at his wristwatch. "It's eleven thirty now, and based on the amount of rigor present, and that it's beginning in her face, I'd say somewhere between five and seven hours ago. Factoring in the estimated time that the fire began, I'd say she died anytime between four and five thirty this morning."

"So before the fire?" Amanda couldn't help but think that was a small mercy compared to being alive and suffering the excruciating pain of flames snacking on her flesh.

Rideout nodded. "Absolutely. I'm not seeing anything to make me assume she died due to the fire or from smoke inhalation." He proceeded to lower the collar of her shirt and pointed to light bruising on her neck. "And I'm quite sure I just found out how she was starved of oxygen."

"She was strangled to death," Trent said.

"Well, at the very least, someone squeezed her neck pretty hard and cut off her air for a while." Rideout turned off his flashlight and tucked it into a pocket.

She recalled how Sullivan had said that she and Trent were wired to think murder first, and he'd been correct. But the evidence in this case—coincidental or otherwise—was indeed stacking up in support of homicide. An abandoned house set on fire, this girl, presumably a runaway, doused with gasoline, bruising on her neck indicative of a chokehold… "So what is your initial response here? Are we looking at murder?"

Rideout glanced once more at the girl. "I'd say it's quite likely given the circumstances, but before I rule manner and cause of death, I want her on an autopsy table."

Trent tapped his pen against his notepad, and everyone looked at him.

Rideout arched his brows. "Penny for your thoughts?"

"Often fire is used to destroy the body and evidence…" Trent was starting to get a good rhythm going, mapping out his own musical beat. She put her hand over his to still his movements.

"Sorry," he said.

"Don't be, but what else? I have a feeling you have more to say…"

"Well, if that was the point here, why pour accelerant on her and then start the fire elsewhere? Why not ensure that her body was destroyed?"

"Setting the fire where they had would have allowed the person time to get out." It was Sullivan who suggested this; he must have overheard Trent's question. "Remember I said it's looking like a trail was leading straight to the stairs, likely to the room she was in, though I have yet to confirm that latter bit. But the person who set this fire might not have expected that we would arrive so quickly. Probably figured the fire had time to reach her. They might not have known that old houses burn slower. Also gasoline doesn't burn as fast as people believe."

Amanda turned her attention back to the medic and Rideout. "Is there any ID on her?"

Jimmy shook his head and responded. "No, I checked all her pockets after I pronounced. Sad, too, because the poor girl can't be much more than sixteen."

Amanda's gaze fell upon the adolescent Jane Doe, her heart aching. *Who are you, sweetheart?*

CHAPTER THREE

Amanda and Trent left Rideout and Jimmy. She took some deep breaths as she stepped out of the van. The outdoor air was still tainted with the smell of smoke, but it was a welcome relief from the gas fumes she'd been inhaling inside the vehicle for the last while.

She headed down the driveway and stepped through the gate into the backyard. A six-foot-tall privacy fence lined the property. The seclusion would make it easy for trespassers to go unnoticed.

"Sixteen," Sullivan mumbled from behind her. She turned, and he appeared like he'd spent time in a boxing ring and had the wind knocked out of him.

"It's always worse when it's a kid." Amanda's own statement drilled an ache in her chest as her thoughts first went to her sweet, beautiful Lindsey, then to the young girls she'd rescued recently from a sex-trafficking ring.

"You've had cases like this before?" Sullivan asked.

Amanda glanced at Trent, back at Sullivan. Three months ago, she and her family's tragedy had been regurgitated publicly—as well as the fact she'd saved those girls. It had made front-page news in the *Prince William Times*. She was surprised he hadn't heard. Usually word got around in a small town.

"I have," she eventually said, her throat tight and her mouth suddenly dry. The flashbacks were attempting to align into focus with color and clarity, but she refused to allow them to take hold.

She squeezed the memories from mind; it was best they remain fuzzy. "Well, not exactly like this, but…"

"With young people?"

"Yeah."

Trent cleared his throat and prompted Sullivan, "You said you had the info on the person who called nine-one-one."

"Yeah, let me get that for you. It's in my truck."

They followed Sullivan to an SUV. He ducked in the passenger door and pulled a notebook out of the glove box. He flipped pages and said, "Shannon Fox."

"Address?" Amanda asked.

"Six-oh-two." He nudged his head, drawing their attention across the street and down a few houses.

They'd pay Fox a visit, but Amanda would prefer to hear the call first. "Thanks," she told Sullivan and pulled out her business card and handed it to him. "Everything's on there. Phone, email…"

Sullivan smiled and gave her his card from the front of his notebook. "I'll get everything over once I get it compiled, Detective."

"Thank you." She started toward the sidewalk, turned, and shrugged. "Actually, if you wanted to send it in chunks that would work for me."

He held up her card as if to show he'd heard her but didn't make any promises.

She proceeded to take out her phone and, with it, captured pictures of the crowd across the street as discreetly as possible. She knew Sullivan had taken photos, too, but there could never be enough. "Sullivan mentioned there were a few mattresses upstairs. Sounds like more than Doe was squatting there—and that's assuming she was."

"You don't think she was?"

"Too early to say yet. What I do want to know is where the other squatters are now." She flicked a finger toward the gawkers. "Maybe one of them will know."

"There has to be thirty people or so."

"You have something better to do?" she deadpanned. His complexion was pale, and his mouth opened, shut, opened, shut. She smiled. "I'll call in for backup to help, but we need to get started."

"Sure."

She motioned for him to get moving while she called Malone. "Hey, we need unis down here for canvassing and to question onlookers."

"I'll get on it."

"Thanks, Sarge. Oh, could you also get me the recording of the nine-one-one call?"

"Consider it done."

She thanked him again, hung up, pocketed her phone, and set off across the street. Trent was talking to an older man, but it was a man in his twenties who caught her eye. He was wearing a navy-blue hoodie and avoiding eye contact. She held up her badge. "Prince William County PD, Detective Steele."

He was twitchy and kept looking at the ground. He was either high or nervous—maybe both.

"What's your name?" She pulled her notepad from a back pocket. She often went back and forth between using an app on her phone to the old-school method of pen and paper.

"Simon."

"Well, Simon, how long have you been standing here?" She pulled the pen out of the book's coils.

"Dunno."

"Since the fire started?"

He met her eyes now. "After I heard the sirens."

"So since early this morning?"

"Yeah." He glanced away again.

He must not have a job to get to during the day. "Do you live along here?" She pointed down the street with her pen.

"Next block over." He pushed back his hoodie and revealed spiky, teal-colored hair. "I'm a light sleeper."

"Can anyone confirm that you were at home and in bed before coming here?"

"My girlfriend, Cindy." He looked around the crowd. "She just went to get us coffee."

Amanda nodded. It would seem neither of them held a day job. "So why have you been here all this time? Do you like watching fires?" The comment Sullivan had made about firebugs loving to watch their creations wasn't far from her mind.

"Not particularly. Suppose I'm still here because... well, someone died in there, right?" He swallowed roughly, his Adam's apple heaving. "I watched the medic get the body from the firefighters, and now you're here asking all these questions. Was the person murdered?"

"It's an open investigation." She was about to ask if he'd seen anyone around the house, particularly any squatters, when a woman called out Simon's name.

She looked to be about the same age as Simon. She wore large dark-lensed sunglasses, and her hair was blond with teal highlights. To match her boyfriend's hair? She stepped through the crowd holding two coffee cups. She handed one to Simon and, with a bit of a scowl, faced Amanda. "Who are you?"

"Detective Steele with Prince William County Police. And you are?"

"Cindy."

"Where do you live?" Amanda asked.

Simon's brow scrunched up. "I told you—"

Amanda held up a hand. "If Cindy could answer..."

"Just a block over." Cindy slurped back some coffee.

"An address?"

Simon rattled it off, and Amanda noted it in her book, then looked at Cindy. "Where were you when you heard the sirens?"

"I just—"

Amanda leveled a glare at Simon, and he stopped talking. She wanted to hear Cindy's response.

"In bed." Cindy nestled into Simon's side, and he put an arm around her.

"Are you familiar with the house at all, maybe the people who squatted here?" Amanda flicked a finger toward 532.

"Not really," Cindy replied and put her lips to her coffee cup.

"You ever see anyone go into the house or around it?"

She shook her head. "No reason. I mean, we don't live on this street."

"And you, Simon?"

"Nope."

"All right, then. Before I leave, I'll just need your full names and a number to reach you in case I have any more questions."

"Sure." Cindy provided the information, and Amanda recorded it in her notepad.

She left the young couple and went on to interview several more in the crowd. Most weren't that interesting. Everyone was curious. One or two waxed philosophical on how all humankind was connected and thereby affected by the loss of anyone—stranger, friend, or foe.

When two uniformed officers arrived to assume responsibility for interviewing those in the crowd, Trent came over to her.

"I want to go speak with the immediate neighbors," she said to him. "I want to hear firsthand if any of them witnessed any activity around that house."

"You got it."

She led the way to number 534, the house next to their crime scene, and knocked on the door.

"Hey!" a man called out.

Amanda and Trent turned, and a forty-something man with a bad comb-over was headed toward them. They held up their badges, and the man groaned.

"Detectives Steele and Stenson with the Prince William County PD," Amanda said. "And you are?"

"Ted Dixon."

"You live here, Mr. Dixon?" She jacked a thumb over her shoulder.

"Uh-huh." He chewed on his bottom lip, and she expected to see blood drawn.

He was clearly uncomfortable, and she'd get to the root of why that was, but first she had some procedural questions to ask. "How long have you lived here?"

"Ah, five years."

"Did you know your neighbors next door?"

"Not by name. But they've been gone a while now."

Between the boarded windows and now this, she was really leaning toward the likelihood the bank had repossessed the property. "Was it a family or a couple or…?"

"Just a couple. Say, in their forties. No kids that I saw."

"And when did they leave?"

"Several months ago."

That surprised her. Amanda had expected it would have been longer ago than that given the boarded windows. It would seem something kept it from going on the market. She scribbled in her notepad, *Why not for sale?*

"Hey, whatcha writing there?" Ted jabbed a finger toward the page, and Amanda held it toward her chest to take it out of his view.

"Nothing you need to worry about." She offered him a small smile.

"Okay," he said, not that he sounded convinced.

"You ever see anyone hanging around the place after that couple moved out?" Trent interjected.

Ted looked at him. "Yeah. Maybe. I don't know."

"You don't know?" Amanda asked, skeptical. "It's a *yes* or *no* type of question, Mr. Dixon."

Ted glanced over a shoulder, then back at her, and stiffened. "No. I never saw anyone."

She didn't have to spend any time studying him to tell he was lying. He just wasn't about to talk to the police, and she couldn't force him to—yet. She handed him her card. "Call me if your memory returns." She turned and left.

Trent matched her stride. "I think he saw something."

"Makes two of us." She faced him. "People were squatting at five thirty-two. We know that because of the mattresses, but who are they and where are they now?"

"And did they kill Jane Doe?"

Amanda considered this and shook her head. "You know what? Probably not. Why burn down their shelter?" She glanced at a cruiser posted in front of 532. The place would have surveillance on it for a while, and if anyone suspicious came around, they'd be brought in and questioned. She had faith in that. Just as she trusted canvassing officers to talk to all the neighbors. "I'm thinking we head back to the station, pull the property records, and see if we can get our hands on that nine-one-one recording. Then we'll come back and talk to the person who placed the call."

"Works for me."

"I've got my car here, so I'll meet you back there, but I may be a little delayed. I'm dying for a coffee and something to eat. Want me to grab you anything?"

Trent gave her his order and went on his way, leaving her with her thoughts, which were focused on Jane Doe. Someone out there was probably missing their daughter, but she'd been stolen from them, her life wiped out before it really began. Amanda would do everything in her power to make the person responsible for that pay.

CHAPTER FOUR

It was going on two in the afternoon when Amanda stopped at Hannah's Diner on the way out of Dumfries. She and Trent had spent more time on site than she would have guessed. No wonder her stomach was growling. While Hannah's had tasty food, Amanda mostly gravitated there for the coffee, which was the best, bar none, that Amanda had ever tasted.

The place was owned by May Byrd and named after her daughter, Hannah—the same Hannah who was Amanda's mother's defense attorney.

Amanda went inside and found May standing behind the counter. She was in her sixties but still worked as a server. Today, empathy flooded her facial features. "Hey, sweetheart. How ya holdin' up?"

Amanda knew how to read May. The question was in reference to the situation with Amanda's mother. "We'll get through this." She spoke with far more confidence than she felt. After all, her mother was guilty despite her plea, and Amanda feared some judge would want to make an example out of her.

May put a hand on Amanda's forearm. "I have no doubt ya will. You Steeles are strong, but you've had to deal with an awful lot in your lives."

"I'm not going to argue with that."

"Hannah doesn't tell me any details on account of attorney-client privilege, but I get the impression there's reason to hold out some hope." May leaned across the counter, peered into Amanda's eyes. "Am I right?"

"Too soon to say, but Hannah's working to build a solid defense to get a lighter sentence." It was another topic that sent Amanda into a moral debate. The man who had driven drunk and killed her family got a measly five years in prison. Hannah was striving to get Amanda's mother's sentence down to fifteen years with parole in seven and a half. Thinking of her mother in prison for all that time was unbearable. To the victim's sole surviving relative, it wouldn't feel like enough. It was strange how perspective changed everything.

"Well, if my Hannah can sort something out, she will. I'm rooting for your mother, Mandy." She straightened out and asked, "So what can I get ya?"

Amanda was relieved that the chitchat had ended. Talking about her mother's crime just made it more real. She ordered two large black coffees, a ham and cheese on wholewheat for herself, and a chicken-salad sandwich on white bread for Trent.

As May prepared everything, Amanda lost herself in her thoughts. She used to hold out so much hope for the future, but life had taught her not to be so foolish.

A few minutes later, May was putting the wrapped sandwiches into a brown bag and shoving the coffee cups into a take-out tray.

"Thanks," Amanda said and headed for the door.

A man was on his way in and backtracked to hold the door for her.

"Thanks," she told him.

He didn't say anything, and she continued to her car and got behind the wheel.

Once there, she unwrapped her sandwich and took a bite, letting her thoughts drift again. So often she'd just tell people she was doing fine. She'd put on a brave and confident front like she truly believed everything with her mother would work out okay. Of course, she'd face prison; it was just a question of how long.

Hannah planned to use Amanda's dad's character in her mother's defense. Amanda wasn't entirely sure if that would work. While she had faith in her father, she also knew that he wasn't perfect and above reproach. Many years ago, rumors had circulated that called his integrity into question, but they likely had their origins in the murmurings of ungrateful underlings who wanted to smudge his name. But she couldn't just dismiss everything that was whispered about him either. While she preferred to believe the best of her father, she also didn't view him through rose-colored glasses.

She finished her sandwich and drove to Central deep in thought.

CHAPTER FIVE

Central was one of Prince William County PD's three stations, and one of two located in Woodbridge. The Homicide Unit was housed at Central, along with some other specialized departments and administration.

Once inside, Amanda headed to the warren of cubicles where Homicide was located. She and Trent had their own office spaces next to each other. The dividers were high enough to afford some privacy and dampen sound, but low enough to talk over.

Homicide was currently down one detective. She glanced over at where Detective Bishop, a.k.a. Cud, used to sit and wondered who would take his place and what they'd be like. She typically played well with others—unless they were partnered with her. Trent had been the only one to stick for this long, and there were still days she was amazed at how he'd wormed his way in. But he'd shown loyalty on several occasions—even when the circumstances wouldn't have made it easy.

She found Trent at his desk and handed him his coffee and sandwich.

"Thanks," he said, his gaze taking in her cup, but otherwise empty hands. "You're not eating?"

"I couldn't wait. Have you pulled the property records on five thirty-two Bill Drive yet?" she asked, switching tracks from the mindless banter.

"Just about to."

"Okay, good. I have a feeling a bank owns it, but just find out. If so, then get us someone to talk to."

"Sure."

"I'm going to follow up with the sergeant and see if he has an update on the status of the nine-one-one recording." She set off down the hall toward Malone's office. His door was shut, but she could see him through the window in the door. He waved her in.

She entered but didn't bother to close the door or make herself comfortable. She wasn't planning to be there for long.

"Why don't you sit." The way he presented the offer made it more a command. There was no doubt when he added, "Close the door first."

She did, then dropped into the chair across from his desk. "What's up?"

He pointed to the coffee in her hand. "Where's mine?"

"Next time."

"All right. You came to me, so you start."

"Just following up on the nine-one-one recording." She sipped her coffee.

"It should be in your inbox soon." He leaned forward, clasped his hands on the desk, and let out a loud sigh.

"What's going on?" Given his body language, she wasn't sure she wanted to press him.

He let out another sigh and shuffled some papers around on his desk. She held out a hand to stop him.

"Whatever it is, I can handle it." She appreciated that he seemed to be trying to protect her from something, but she'd been through hell in this life and survived. "Sergeant?" Maybe using his title would jar him to speak.

"The lieutenant is moving to have you demoted."

Amanda came close to jumping out of the chair. "What? Why?" She was aware the woman hated her, but as far as she knew she hadn't given her any fresh reason to go after her. In fact, the last time she had an audience with the woman, Hill had thanked her for her work.

"She's been keeping a close eye on your performance..."

"Then she'll notice my close rate has been a hundred percent."

He loosened his tie and unbuttoned his collar. "She's more concerned with—or should I say *interested in*—the fact your mother has been charged with murder."

"What does that have to do with me, and the job I'm doing?" It felt like little electric currents were running through her body.

"She believes that you could easily lose focus."

She and Trent had worked two homicides since her mother was arrested, and the killers were now awaiting their day in court. "Regardless of what my close rate shows? Unbelievable." Amanda gritted her teeth.

He held up a hand. "I know your close rate is incredible."

She flailed her hands as if to say, *Yep.*

"If it was based on that alone—"

"It should be," she burst out. Her heart was racing, and she was burning up. How dare this woman hold her mother's actions against her? But Amanda instantly felt hypocritical. After all, she blamed herself. She asked herself the what-ifs, including *what if* she'd never pulled away from her family in their time of grief? Would her mother still have done what she had? "I know you're on my side, but that woman—" She clamped her mouth shut, too angry to continue.

"She pisses the hell out of me too, but for now we're stuck with her."

"For now?" That was enough to make her sit straighter and give her some hope for the future.

"Didn't mean to get you excited, and I probably shouldn't say anything."

"Please do."

"Rumor's going around that she may be transferring to—"

"She's leaving the PWCPD? There is a God."

"Amanda Steele," he reprimanded, sounding more like a father or an uncle than her sergeant.

She should have known better than to bring God into any of this. Malone was far more religious than she could ever claim to be, but she couldn't bring herself to apologize. Her faith in a greater being had been shaken when her husband and daughter died. Also wiped out that day had been her unborn baby and her ability to have children in the future—collateral damage only she knew about.

Malone's cheeks were flushed. "She's not leaving the PWCPD. She just might not be in our face as much."

Why doesn't that make me feel better? "Where's she transferring?" Dread balled up and kneaded in her gut.

"She's looking to take over for Chief Paxton." He clasped his hands again.

"You've got to be kidding." Ernie Paxton had become chief after her father had left the department. Paxton was four years older than her father, and she had never expected he'd stay at the post forever, but a little longer would have been nice. "She doesn't deserve to be police chief. Please tell me there's no chance in hell." For some reason he never objected to mention of the fiery abyss; just don't speak about God in vain.

"I wish I could. She has supporters on the county's board of supervisors."

Officially known as the Prince William County Board of Supervisors—the ones with the power to appoint the police chief.

"Surely someone else wants to be considered." She groaned.

"Not that I know of." He slowly raised his eyes to meet hers.

"Son of a bitch."

"Yeah. But you don't even need to worry about her promotion so much as the fact she's determined to get you demoted before she leaves her role as LT."

She narrowed her eyes and clenched her jaw. "She's really threatened by me that much?"

"Seems so."

She knew Sherry Hill and Nathan Steele had never gotten along—neither had respect for the other one. But now that rivalry threatened Amanda's career. "I'll get my lawyer involved if she comes after me, Scott. I will." She rarely pulled out Malone's first name, but it tumbled from her lips now.

"I am going to do all in my power to get her to back off, but you need to leave her alone, keep your nose clean, your head down."

"I'll tell you what I should do. Go after police chief myself." An obvious stretch at this point, given that she was still working to get her mind straight.

"One day. Just trust me, Amanda." His use of her first name was reassuring and comforting.

"I do, and I appreciate the heads-up on her plans. Thank you." She stood, and her phone chimed notice of a new email. She opened it, saw the attachment, and read the subject: *911 Recording—532 Bill Drive, House Fire.* She held up her phone. "Got the recording."

"Good. Keep me posted on the case."

"Will do."

Amanda headed back to her desk, no longer interested in what was left of her coffee, and tossed it into the first garbage can she passed. All she was in the mood for was to strangle the life out of the lieutenant. Who the hell did that woman think she was, and did she really expect that Amanda would go down without a fight? Her mind catapulted her to a future in which she knocked Hill from the position of police chief. Just imagining that day brought a smile to Amanda's face. Maybe Hill's promotion was exactly the motivation that Amanda needed to pursue the appointment for herself.

CHAPTER SIX

It had taken a while for his heart to calm down. Detective Amanda Steele had been right there. He'd held the door for her! He'd seen her briefly at the scene of the fire, but he had left before anyone had a chance to question him.

He knew about her accomplishments in cleaning up the county. She would understand him. She worked with a badge, he on his own terms. But still. Kindred spirits.

He tapped his foot under the table. Jittery from the two coffees he'd downed in the last half hour or because of the murder? He was terrified by how quickly the fire had been put out and wondered if the body had been sufficiently destroyed. He'd seen it hauled out of the house but hadn't gotten a good look. He tried to set his doubts aside and bask in what he'd done.

He lifted his cup, now topped up with a third refill, and his hand shook the entire way to his mouth.

"Can I get ya something to eat, love?"

Coffee sloshed over the rim and onto the table. He set his mug down with a thud and looked into the eyes of the older woman. She was far too generous in dishing out sentiments such as *sweetheart*, *dearie*, and *love* to everyone who came into the place. She also kept coming around and checking on him, and it was driving him crazy.

"I'm good." He glanced away from her. He wasn't in the mood for conversation, and she was standing there like her legs were anchored to the floor. He raised his cup again, his hand shaking.

"Maybe I should cut you off." She smiled at him, but it chafed. He took a sip and hissed, "I'm fine."

She narrowed her eyes and pointed a finger toward the table, drawing his eyes down to the pool of coffee. "You sure don't look like you are."

"Just leave me alone." He looked away from her now, placing his gaze across the diner, his focus on nothing. He needed her to go away, or he couldn't be to blame for what he might do. The rage was building inside of him to a boil.

"You got a problem with me, you leave. This is my diner." She crossed her arms, and the motion hoisted her bosom.

He made eye contact and attempted to soften his expression. "No problem, ma'am." He wanted to flash a smile, but his lips wouldn't move. "I don't want to be any trouble."

"Good. I wouldn't want to be calling the cops." Her eyes narrowed as she seemed to study him, trying to place him, but she wouldn't recognize him after all this time. He hadn't been into this place for many years.

Someone came in the door, and she padded off to see to them. *Finally, some peace and quiet!*

He grabbed his phone off the table—thankfully, it was outside the spill zone—and brought up the internet app to see if any news of the fire had hit the worldwide web.

And... *Nothing?*

Not one word about the fire. Not even on the wagging tongues of the townspeople entering the diner. It was like the fire had never happened.

Again, he was invisible. He and the girl, but he didn't feel sorry for her. She didn't deserve the attention like he did.

She had lived her life oblivious to others and their feelings. A selfish heart who deserved no better than to be punished. Yet, in the final moments, he had shown mercy. Why, he still wasn't sure. A testament to his character, The Merciful?

She had begged for life, release, redemption—all three? He had delivered them all.

He pinched his eyes shut and felt the warmth of a tear on his cheek. He swiped it away and looked at his wet fingertips. After all these years, he finally felt complete and on track, making a difference, no longer flitting about meaninglessly.

The fact the world hadn't yet acknowledged him made him feel cheated and vengeful. But his mother, in one of her better moods, had told him, "Focus on the good."

He'd dwell on how killing made him feel powerful, in control, visible.

He looked down at his phone again and refreshed the search—and finally!

The headline read: "Arson Suspected in House Fire that Claimed One Victim."

No! They'd gotten it all wrong. He had killed her, not the fire. When would the truth come out?

His phone pinged a reminder. It was time for him to go and do the job he was paid to do. Then he'd head home and plan his next act as The Merciful. He couldn't take them all out, but now that he was awakened to his real purpose in life, he would kill as many girls as he could.

CHAPTER SEVEN

Amanda retrieved Trent from his desk, telling him she'd received the 911 recording, and they headed for the conference room.

"How did you make out on the property records?" She glanced over a shoulder at him as they made their way down the hall.

"The property was repossessed last August by Woodbridge Bank. It used to belong to a Glenn and Susan Burke. He's living in an apartment in town. Susan's in Madison, Wisconsin, where she's been since September. Regardless, I pulled her background and his. No record on either of them."

"Did you get a contact name at the bank?"

"Aiden Adkins is the one in charge of the property, and we have an appointment with him tomorrow morning at nine o'clock. That was the soonest I could get."

She pulled out her phone and checked the time. It was half past three in the afternoon, and most banks around there closed at five. "Why not today?"

"Mr. Adkins is off."

"All right." Not that she was pleased.

They reached the conference room, and she entered first.

She proceeded to bring up the email with the 911 recording.

She turned her media volume up all the way and hit Play.

The house across the street is on fire."

"Please tell me who I'm talking to," the dispatcher replies.

"Shannon Fox. Please get the fire department here."

"I see you're calling from six-oh-two Bill Drive. Is that right, ma'am?"

"Yes."

The dispatcher verifies Fox's phone number, then asks, *"What are you seeing?"*

"I told you. The place is on fire. You going to get someone here to help?"

"When did you see the fire?"

"Just a minute ago."

"What's the address on the burning house?"

"Five thirty-two Bill Drive."

"Is anyone in the house that you know of?"

"I don't know. I don't think so."

"I've dispatched local firefighters and emergency response units to that location. Please keep your distance from the house, ma'am."

Amanda noted that the dispatcher had been calm and professional, asking the necessary questions, such as where, what, when, and who. Fox had sounded more annoyed than panicked, but Amanda picked up on something else. "When the dispatcher asked if anyone was in the house, Fox said she didn't think so. Makes me wonder if she had seen people go into the place before."

"She could give us a lead on the squatters, which could possibly end up getting us Doe's identity and some insight into who may have killed her. Just one thing, though. If Fox was aware of their existence, why not warn the dispatcher that people could be inside?"

"Let's go ask her."

CHAPTER EIGHT

The emergency vehicles were gone except for a police cruiser parked at the curb. But the pall of death was energetically tangible, and a small memorial on the front lawn of 532 Bill Drive was a visual testimony to the loss of life. Bouquets, candles, and cards were set with care. *Rest in Peace* was scrawled with black marker on poster board.

They'd need to have it all photographed and cataloged just in case their killer had decided to leave a message. But that didn't mean the thought felt right. It would be like they were desecrating a sanctuary.

The memorial was still on Amanda's mind several minutes later when she and Trent were seated across from Shannon Fox in her living room. Shannon was a trim and petite brunette with short-cropped hair, brown eyes, and sculpted brows. Her background, which they'd checked before coming, told them Shannon was forty-three, single, rented the house she was living in, had no criminal record, and worked at Prince William Medical Center in Manassas.

"I never saw anything." Shannon had been adamant about that fact and repeated her claim several times since she'd let them into her house.

"You obviously saw fire to call it in," Amanda said.

"Ah, sure. I saw flames through the window in the front door."

"We listened to your nine-one-one call, Ms. Fox," Amanda began. "You sounded rather calm."

"I work as a nurse at Prince William Medical Center. I see worse things most days." Shannon rubbed her cheek against her shoulder.

"Okay, fair enough," Amanda conceded. "What had you up this morning?"

"I was getting home from a night shift. I got off work at five, but by the time I actually left, it was about quarter after or so. I also stopped for a coffee and a donut on the way home."

That would explain the passing of fifty minutes, even though the driving distance was thirty minutes at most—and in the early morning, probably less. Out of due diligence, they'd confirm Shannon's statement about working. Amanda would keep in mind, though, that Sullivan had said firebugs don't usually call to have their fires put out. And what would have a nurse deciding to kill a young woman? Amanda was about to ask a question when Shannon spoke.

"Did someone die? I saw the..."

"The memorial? And yes." Amanda wasn't going to tell Shannon outright they were approaching the death as murder, but no doubt the woman could piece that together.

Shannon got to her feet and looked out her front window to the street. "I'm happy that I don't have to go to work again until Sunday night. I need time to process what happened... right across from me."

Yet, she'd claimed to have seen worse in her job as a nurse. Amanda joined her at the window. They'd covered that Shannon hadn't seen anyone suspicious that morning. That had led to the repeated, "I didn't see anything." Amanda would try another angle.

"We understand the couple who used to own the house moved out last August. Have you seen anyone going in and out of the house since then?"

Shannon rubbed her arms. "Yeah, kids hung around the place. They probably crashed there sometimes, but I haven't seen them in a few days. And I swear that I didn't know anyone was in there at the time of the fire." Her eyes beaded with tears.

"You couldn't have known for certain." Amanda felt the desire to ease Shannon's guilt, and she highly doubted the woman before her was a murderer. "The fire isn't what killed the victim."

"What did?"

"I can't get into details, but I'd like to know why you didn't at least mention the possibility of squatters to the nine-one-one dispatcher?"

"I should have, I guess. I just didn't want to get anyone in trouble. And, now, that's all I'm saying."

Amanda studied the woman. Given the faraway look in her eyes, she would guess Shannon may have spent time on the street herself. She thanked her, and Amanda and Trent saw themselves out.

She felt drawn to the memorial and went toward it. The closer she got, the heavier her legs became. She could handle murders—even the grisly ones. But when the victims were young, it was much harder to compartmentalize and remain detached. It was one thing to do this at a crime scene, but when faced with something like this memorial, it was even tougher. Looking at it made death much more real. Visceral. Choking. Suffocating.

She became engulfed in a wave of emotions and imagery. Of her husband's casket and her daughter's tiny coffin being lowered into the ground... She stopped on the sidewalk in front of the makeshift altar, Trent beside her.

Before she'd lost Kevin and Lindsey, Amanda had found it strange how people liked to commemorate the location of a tragedy. In the months following the accident, she'd found herself returning to where it had happened, as if by being there she could find out why they had to leave her. But she'd come to realize how ridiculous that was, how foolish. They weren't there, and their spirits weren't there—even if they had survived death in some form. She still wasn't sure where she stood on the matter of the big man—or woman—upstairs, and the concept of an afterlife was wrapped up with it.

Trent was taking photos of the items. He was quiet and solemn, likely feeling the impact of loss himself. It would be impossible not to.

She looked up at the house, thinking of the girl, intending to find her justice while being plagued by uncertainties. They didn't even know who she was. How could they ascertain suspects or pin down a motive for murder?

Her phone pinged with a text message. She read it and shared the gist with Trent. "Rideout's conducting the autopsy at six thirty." That gave them less than two hours. It would have been nice to have a little more notice, but they had time to make another stop first. "We'll swing by and have a talk with the former homeowner, Glenn Burke, and then we'll head up."

As she spoke, Trent hadn't made eye contact with her. He was staring at a bouquet of daisies like he was locked in a memory. She'd ask, but they weren't *that* close, or at least she didn't want to be. There was an advantage to maintaining a distinction between the personal and professional worlds. Blur that line and trouble followed. People got comfortable, *too* comfortable.

She returned her attention to the memorial, and her gaze landed on a card without an envelope. It was simple with a dragonfly on the front. She gloved up and cracked it open. All that was inside was a drawn heart, followed by "Always," signed off by *C* and a doodle. "Trent, what does that look like to you?"

He put his phone away and studied the drawing. It took him less than a second to make a conclusion. "A dragonfly."

"Looks like that to me too." She flipped it closed and pointed out the image on the front. "Our Jane Doe had a dragonfly pin. Seems a little too coincidental to me. Whoever left this card, I'd bet they knew our victim well."

"Killer or friend?"

"Too soon to know, but we're taking this with us."

CHAPTER NINE

The next stop was Glenn Burke. While Trent drove, Amanda called Prince William Medical Center and confirmed Shannon's shift. They should probably check with the coffee shop to verify that part of her story, but Amanda doubted Shannon was really behind the fire or the murder.

Glenn Burke, on the other hand, may have more motive than she'd originally thought. He'd managed to downgrade from the rundown Bill Drive—and that was saying something. He kept his apartment tidy, but an air diffuser pumped a floral perfume into the room periodically, and it battled with a musty smell. He was in his early forties and in good shape, about six foot on the mark, with black hair and thick eyebrows.

Amanda and Trent were at his kitchen table, a round pine number with enough seating for four. The introductions behind them, she went for the meat.

"Your old house on Bill Drive was set on fire. Would you happen to know anything about that?"

"No." Glenn looked from her to Trent and back to her, his brow furrowed up. "Why should I know something? I haven't lived there in months." He got up and went into the kitchen, which was right next to the dining area and visible from where Amanda and Trent sat. Glenn stuck a pod in a coffee machine and set it to brewing.

To Amanda, it felt like a strange time to get up and start a coffee, like he wanted to avoid the conversation. Was it because he was uncomfortable and embarrassed over losing his house, or something more sinister?

"We understand that you lost the property to the bank," she laid out, exploring the first option.

"Yep." He paused as the machine gurgled. "I lost my job of ten years, and I was already in hock with credit card bills. The bank worked with me for as long as they could, but they probably told you that."

"We still need to speak with your banker, Mr. Burke. When did the bank reclaim the property?" She liked to hear things straight from the source when possible.

"Six months ago."

She counted back in her head. August was closer to eight months ago, but Glenn could have lost track of time. He also could be trying to make them think losing his home hadn't been a big deal. She'd poke and see if there was a scab to pull. "That must have been hard, losing your home."

"Yes and no, but in the end it was just a house, ya know." He opened the fridge and pulled out a carton of cream, dolloped some in his cup, and stirred in two teaspoons of sugar. He returned to the table and sat down. "It was much harder on Susan. That's my soon-to-be ex-wife. She's filed for divorce."

Amanda was planning to bring up Susan, but Glenn had beaten her to it. "Sorry to hear that."

"Nah, don't be. It was a long time coming even before we lost the house. But things have a way of working out. It took me a bit to realize it, but I'm better off without her."

His admission seemed sincere, but Amanda was still interested in getting a better feel for the couple. "She lives in Madison, Wisconsin. Has been there since September, right?"

"That's right. It's where her folks are, but she nested up with some dentist out there. Apparently, they used to be high-school sweethearts. He's got lots of family money too. She's not looking back. Trust me."

It would seem Susan Burke was off the suspect list, but Glenn Burke remained, even if not at the top. He was holed up in some horrible apartment, in debt, with a marriage about to be dissolved. It was time for Amanda to be a little more direct. "There was a young woman found in the house. She had been murdered." She watched him for a reaction but didn't get any. She wished she had a picture of Jane Doe to show him, but typically it was frowned upon to show photos taken at a crime scene to civilians—even if they were suspects. "Could you tell us anything about her?"

"No, how could I— Oooh." His eyes widened as the implication sank in. "You think that I... that I—" He rubbed his jaw.

"You could have been angry with the bank, the direction of your life," Amanda put out there. "You could have finally had enough."

He swallowed roughly, and his facial expression soured. "And what? Killed some random girl? And tell me, do killers usually vomit in their mouths?"

She made a show of considering, even though she had to admit that the likelihood Glenn was the person they were after was slim.

"They do?" Glenn blanched, seeming to jump to a conclusion from the silence.

"Uh, maybe you could just tell us where you were this morning from, say, four until six?" Trent asked, covering the time-of-death window and then some.

"I was in bed."

"Can anyone verify that?" Trent looked ready to write down a name and number.

Glenn shook his head and frowned. "Unfortunately not. My date last night didn't exactly go according to plan."

She gave Glenn her card and said, "Call me once you solidify your alibi."

"How am I supposed to do that?"

"Just speak with your neighbors, Mr. Burke. Maybe someone can confirm you were home." She got up and stepped into the hallway with Trent.

He closed the door behind them. "I don't think he did it."

"Me neither, but sometimes we need more than our gut feelings."

"What we need is to make some headway," he mumbled. "So far, we're not making much at all."

"That's how it works sometimes, but we keep asking questions and talking to people, and if we're doing it right, eventually we get to the truth and we catch a killer."

They got into the department car, and the clock on the dash told them it was quarter to six. The autopsy was in forty-five minutes, and they had a thirty-minute drive to get there.

"Take us through a drive-thru for something to eat. We'll chow down on the way, but you'll need to step on it if we're going to make it to Manassas in time." Her phone rang and caller ID came up as *Alibi*. Otherwise known as Logan Hunter. Long story made short, he'd been her alibi in a previous murder case. Someday she'd get around to renaming the contact. "Detective Steele."

"*Detective.* I'll never get tired of hearing you say that."

Her belly fluttered, and her core flushed hot at the sound of his voice. Logan was her new… Whatever he was, he was good in bed. "I'm working a case. Is there something I can help you with?"

"Ouch. So cold."

She laughed at his mocked offense. "Don't be so sensitive."

"Easy for you to say, you're a bad-ass cop."

Trent glanced over at her, and she pushed closer toward the door, as if the extra half inch would give her the privacy she wanted. "I can't talk right now."

"Okay, well, I'll figure out what to do with this prime rib steak all on my own, then."

All on my own… Then her mind cleared. It was Thursday night, and he was supposed to be cooking them dinner at her place. "Oh! I'm so sorry. I completely forgot."

"It's okay. Really. You got a case. It happens." He talked like he was a cop and understood the job, but he worked in construction.

"I really am sorry." Her stomach was grumbling. She'd only been seeing Logan for the last few months, but he was an amazing cook. "I'll take a rain check if you're handing them out."

"For you, I'll make an exception."

"Thank you. Again, I'm sorry about this."

"I'll make sure you make up for it." He chuckled and hung up.

Trent looked over at her. "Logan?"

"Just watch the road." She pointed out the windshield. She could tell that Trent was just expressing interest, but she didn't exactly want to chat with her partner about her lover. She was uncomfortable enough with the situation she'd found herself in with Logan. It was somewhere between dating and the one-night stand where they had begun. After losing the love of her life, she didn't believe it would come again. That kind of romance only happened once in a lifetime. While Logan was fun to hang out with, easy to talk with, had culinary skills to rival a gourmet chef, and an incredible sense of humor, what they had was casual at best. That's really all she wanted out of life at this point. But life had taught her before just how unpredictable it could be.

CHAPTER TEN

He'd been so busy he had missed seeing his work on the six o'clock news. It was about six thirty now, and all the headline stories would be over and done. But he had good reason for being late. Besides client appointments, he had taken care of a personal matter. He smiled thinking about what he had done. It might have been risky, but it had felt right.

He let himself into his mother's farmhouse. She was puttering around in the kitchen, wearing an apron and singing some Louis Armstrong song that tried to pitch the lie that the world was a wonderful place. She must have been in one of her good moods. He loved her like this.

"I'm home, Ma." He hung his light jacket on a hook near the door and entered the room. She said nothing to him, didn't give any indication she'd seen him. He was still invisible. All the time, invisible. Yet he was determined to win her approval before she left him.

She'd been sick for a long time, if the doctors were to be believed. To him, she looked just fine, though she was prone to violent mood swings and sometimes isolation. But through her ups and downs, he was always there for her, even if she didn't see him.

He got himself a cup of coffee. "I grabbed something to eat on the way home. Hope you don't mind. Figure you would have eaten earlier."

She wiped her hands on her apron and took it off, hung it on a hook by the door, and went into the living room. He followed, and she sat in her favorite rocking chair. She collected her ball of yarn and her knitting needles from a sack on the floor and got to work.

"Whatcha making, Ma?" He hunched on the floor near her feet.

She started whistling the tune she'd been singing earlier. She looked in his direction, but it was like she was seeing through him. Maybe she didn't know how she made him feel so worthless, so less-than. After all, she looked so harmless sitting there, rocking, doing what she enjoyed. Would she continue to look that way if he told her what he'd done? Would she be proud or angry? Would she finally *see* him?

He took her hands into his, stopping her from knitting. "There's something I want to tell you. You'll be proud of me. You will. What I did, I did it for us—for you and me, Ma."

She ceased rocking, met his eyes, and pulled her hands free of his. She started to move the needles again, and rage balled in his chest along with frustration.

"I need you to listen to me." He put his hands on hers.

She freed one and touched his cheek, tenderly. "Talk to me, sweetheart. You can tell me anything."

Her contact and her words made him well up with pride. She was finally listening; she would hear him, and she would understand. "I helped a girl see how selfish she had been, and now she'll never hurt anyone again." The words spilled out, and they felt right, though they were a little off base. He'd done what he had due to the hatred festering in his soul that needed an outlet. He recognized that now, just by how much he had enjoyed taking that girl's last breath.

His mother returned her needles and the yarn to the sack.

He held his breath, waiting for her response.

She asked him, "You did this for me?"

"That's right." *And for more reasons than you know.*

She grinned, the expression lighting her eyes. "I'm so very proud of you, my boy. Come here." She motioned for him to lean in, and she kissed his forehead.

"Thank you, Ma." Tears wet his eyes, and he palmed them dry as he got to his feet. "Sleep well."

"You too. You earned it." She rocked again, the wood floor groaning beneath the chair's rails.

He headed for the loft in the horse barn. While his mother lived in the main house, he'd favored the loft since he was a teenager.

He went to a desk where he had his laptop and brought up the internet, looking for the latest on the fire and the girl. He searched the local TV station's site and found a link to watch a replay of the night's news.

He started the video, waited out two annoying ads he couldn't skip, and prepared to hear the anchorwoman, some Diana Wesson, talk about the fire and his work. All the story got was a thirty-second recap geared toward a Good Samaritan who had called 911.

He opened another internet tab, hoping the newspaper had done him more justice. He did a search and clicked on an article by Fraser Reyes. He scanned its length and thought, *More like it.* He read and savored the spotlight. Included was a quote from Sergeant Topez with the PWCPD's Public Information Office: *"I can confirm that the body of a young woman was found in the house, and an investigation into her identity and her death is underway."*

He smiled, pleased that the police were taking him seriously. But they'd never figure out who the girl was or trace her to him. Surely, even though the fire was put out far earlier than he would have liked, it must have obscured some evidence.

He kept reading.

"The body was in fairly good condition thanks to a heroic citizen who called 911."

Fraser had briefly interviewed the caller, Shannon Fox, a nurse at Prince William Medical Center. She said she did what anyone in her place would have done.

He balled his hands so tightly that his nails pierced his palms. So she was why the fire was put out so soon! His mother, if she knew how botched up this was, would be disgusted by his failure. And she'd blame him.

That Fox lady should have minded her own business. Then the story would have read quite differently. He had to set this right the best way he knew how and since there was no going back, he had to look ahead. But first, one little unexpected detour. He'd take care of that Shannon Fox lady and make his message clear.

People needed to mind their own business, and more importantly, he had no plans to stop—ever.

CHAPTER ELEVEN

There were several stations in the morgue, and another autopsy was underway. Rideout waved Amanda and Trent over from the corner of the room. Next to him was a steel gurney with the body of Jane Doe covered with a white sheet.

"Good evening," Rideout offered in greeting once they got close to him.

"Hi, Hans." Amanda's gaze went to the draped body. She glanced at a nearby table where there was a bulging paper evidence bag. It probably held the girl's clothing as paper didn't degrade DNA like plastic did. "Tell me we have a better idea of what happened to her."

"We'll get to all that, but there are a few things I'd like to discuss first." He grabbed a small, sealed plastic bag and handed it to her. It contained the dragonfly pin. She looked from it to Rideout. He went on. "There's an engraving on the back."

She flipped the bag over. "'To our dear Crystal,'" she read aloud, then passed it to Trent for him to have a closer look. "It could be her name, or she could have come into possession of the pin from someone named Crystal."

"By stealing it, even," Trent suggested. "It looks like real gold, and possibly mother-of-pearl in its wings?" He regarded Rideout, obviously seeking an answer, and gave the bag back to him.

Rideout took it and set it back on the table. "I'm not a jeweler, Detective."

"I'd like to get the piece appraised," Amanda inserted, "to find out its makeup and value."

"I'll make sure someone in the lab gets that done," the ME assured her.

"Thanks." She could use the dragonfly pin as a parameter for searching reported missing persons, but additional markers would certainly aid the endeavor. "Anything stand out about the body? Birthmarks or tattoos?"

"I'll get to that." Rideout's voice was firm and didn't allow room for negotiation, and Amanda found that strange given his normal easygoing nature. He went on. "I will be taking a dental mold that can be run through Missing Persons. But depending on when—and assuming *if*—a report was made, it might not be that useful to us. I'll also be running her DNA through the system. I should have a computer-rendered photo of her for you by tomorrow afternoon."

"Sounds good." That would be something that she and Trent could use during their inquiries instead of showing people the face of a corpse.

"Now, I X-rayed the body," Rideout continued, "and was able to determine the hyoid was broken. Sometimes it doesn't show up that way. Regardless, I'll still be conducting a neck dissection to get a better look."

"So she was strangled," Trent surmised.

Rideout met his gaze and nodded. "I've conducted more tests to confirm TOD and stand by my original assessment. The victim was dead by the time the fire was started. A closer look at the contusions on her neck tells me she was likely strangled by a man. Though I guess it could have been a woman with large hands. Whoever it was, it's not easy to break the hyoid bone. It takes strength and determination."

"Whoever killed her really hated her," Trent chimed in.

"They were determined anyhow," Amanda corrected, sticking closer to the heart of what Rideout had said. "Strangulation and choking are often involved in domestic violence cases. The abuser uses it to display their power and control over their mate. It doesn't always need to be fatal. It's often in the moment, considered to be a crime of passion. But she was so young..." Amanda let her words taper off, then asked, "Was she raped?"

Rideout shook his head. "No sign of recent sexual intercourse—consensual or otherwise—which is surprising." He paused for a second, then added, "But I'll get to that. There is something else that the X-rays revealed. She suffered numerous breaks and bone fractures throughout her short life. The oldest—a broken ulna in her left arm—probably dates back to when she was nine, given her current age approximation as sixteen. The latest injury shows no signs of healing. It was a hairline fracture to her right wrist."

If their Jane Doe was a runaway, maybe it had been because of an abusive home life. She might have figured she'd be safer on the streets. "What could have hurt her wrist?"

"A struggle with her killer, possibly. He could have gripped her wrist and twisted. But there are no obvious signs that she defended herself. No abraded knuckles, for example. I have, of course, scraped under her nails, and the trace will be sent to the lab for analysis. I'll also require a full tox workup to see if she was on anything."

Amanda glanced down at the young girl, feeling sad for the short and troubled life she'd led. "Is there any sign of drug use?"

"Not that I see, but I just want to cover all the bases. There are no signs of injection sites, but that doesn't mean she wasn't on anything. She could have ingested a drug in liquid or pill form. Either something she took herself or was given to her... possibly in her food or drink."

"You think her killer subdued her with something?" Amanda asked.

"Only one way to know."

"The tox run."

He nodded. "Now, I must tell you, in addition to the internal injuries, she has some bruising on her body, in various stages of healing. And there's more..."

"Still more?" It was hard for Amanda to imagine that was possible. She looked down at Doe's face again, and her heart pinched. Her lifeless eyes really stamped home the finality of the situation. This young woman would have had dreams and aspirations she'd never get to fulfill.

Rideout slowly peeled back the sheet, and Amanda watched as he bared Doe's chest. She gasped as her gaze landed on a black-and-white tattoo just above the girl's left breast. It was about three inches in diameter. The depiction of a crown entwined in thorny vines with the letters *DC* scrolled over them.

"She was a..." She gripped her throat, where the rest of her sentence had become lodged.

The images were hurtling back with fierce tenacity. Fifteen young girls in four cells. All barely dressed and living in filth and violation. Their young, angelic faces, their tearstained cheeks, their wide eyes, their terrified expressions—and most of them with this marking.

"Amanda?"

She heard her name as if it were being said from across the room at a whisper. Then she felt a hand on her shoulder. She shrugged it off and stepped back.

Trent was watching her with wide eyes. "Sorry, I shouldn't have..."

Her heart was hammering, and her palms were clammy. She put her attention back on the girl and stiffened her posture, trying to find the strength inside to face the undeniable truth. "She was a victim of sex trafficking before she was a murder victim."

CHAPTER TWELVE

"They brand them like cattle," Amanda said through clenched teeth, as she loaded into the department car with Trent. Her new friend, Patty Glover, from Sex Crimes had told her that. But it was only part of what had her popping antiacids for weeks after rescuing those girls. She couldn't get their flesh-and-blood faces out of her head, or the illicit images she'd seen of young victims in a database created by the sex-trafficking ring that she'd uncovered. Though it was more catalog than database. The girls were inventoried like merchandise. There was also a spreadsheet of buyers and payment confirmations, which Amanda knew Patty was still working through. Patty had explained that sex trafficking could take various forms. Some girls were sold directly to an end user, and others were pimped out as prostitutes.

"Do you think one of the people in the ring killed her?" Trent asked as he started the car.

"I don't know." She felt numb, an old, familiar feeling. The way she'd mostly gone through life since the loss of her family. "Maybe she ran away, and they caught up with her… But why strangulation? Why not a gunshot? And why the fire?"

"The fire could have been to hide evidence and destroy the body."

She looked over at him, not really wanting to verbalize what she was thinking. If they found the girl, they'd just recapture her and force her compliance. All the bone breaks and fractures, the bruising, testified to the fact they took no issue with physical coercion. And to kill her on such a stage risked drawing attention to the ring.

It was more likely that Jane Doe had been sold to some psychopath who liked to strangle young girls and set their bodies on fire. She pulled out her phone and called Patty Glover on speaker.

She picked up before the second ring finished. "Detective Glover."

"Patty? It's Amanda." There was no need for formality.

"Oh, hi there. How are you?"

"Not good. I'm here with my partner, Trent."

"Hi, Trent."

"Hi."

Pleasantries out of the way, Amanda said, "There was a house fire in Dumfries, a young woman inside…" She was trying to build herself up to handle this conversation.

"I read about it online."

"She was branded, Patty. With the tattoo we saw a few months ago. The crown and the letters *DC*."

Patty's end of the line fell silent.

"Tell me we've gotten somewhere with tracking more people in this organization."

"I wish that I could…" Patty sighed loudly. "Unfortunately, we're still working on running down bank transfers."

"Do you think it's possible that those people—the ones in charge—had her killed?"

"There's no way to know without you following the evidence, but I don't see it as something they'd do unless they had no other recourse. They'd probably just have hauled her back and put her to work."

Amanda glanced over at Trent. "I had a bad feeling you'd say that." Her stomach lurched. "She was only about sixteen, Patty."

"It never gets easier. Was there any evidence of rape?"

"No. Not even consensual sex." Which on saying out loud, Amanda found surprising.

"Then I'd definitely say you're looking at another motive here. I must say, though, when these people find out one of their girls was taken and killed, they're not going to be too happy, and they might seek revenge."

"Scary thought." But she didn't find the concept hard to imagine. "Okay, keep me updated if anything comes to light."

"I will." There was a brief pause, then, "Find who did this to her."

"You can bet on it." She ended the call and faced Trent. "We need to start by tracking Jane Doe's movements. Find out who she was." What Amanda really wanted to do was knock down some doors—but so far, they didn't have any to barge through. The clock on the dash told her it was ten thirty. They could work a little more before calling it a day. "Let's go back to the station and give Missing Persons a try."

"You got it." He put the car into gear and took them in the direction of Central.

"We could also read interviews from the canvassing officers. All I know is her loved ones deserve some closure." But did Doe's parents? They could well have been the reason she took to the streets. A couple of things ratcheted Amanda's red-headed temper: drunk driving and those who abused women, children, or animals.

About thirty minutes later, Trent pulled into the station lot and parked. They went inside—her to her desk, Trent to the break room for a coffee. The fact their victim had been caught up in sex trafficking was enough to jolt her wide awake.

She found a folder on her desk and looked inside. It contained the interviews from the canvassing officers.

She put her light jacket on the back of her chair and dropped down.

Amanda shuffled through a few of them but didn't find anyone's statements particularly helpful at quick glance. She closed the folder and brought up Missing Persons on the computer. She keyed in the little they had in the way of narrowing things down. The butterfly pin, the name Crystal, her approximate age at time of death, her height, and her hair and eye color.

Trent returned and settled in at his desk. She handed him the folder over the partition. "Officer interviews," was all she said as an explanation.

She clicked enter on her search and tapped her fingers and toes while she waited on the results. Nada.

They needed more. Her DNA profile, which Rideout was handling, and the girl's dental impression—just in case it came in useful. She didn't want to consider that no one was missing Jane Doe.

She logged into her email, and there was a message with attachments from Fire Marshal Sullivan. She opened it and read his brief message. He was still compiling his sketches and the photographs of the house's interior, but he sent photos he had taken of the crowd across the street at different points throughout the day. She opened them, looking at one after the other, scanning for anything that might seem obviously out of the ordinary. Nothing struck her, and the direness of their reality sank in.

It was starting to feel like their only option for ID'ing the girl was waiting on Rideout and hoping that Jane Doe was actually in the Missing Persons database.

She glanced over at Trent and could only see the top of his head. "How are you making out over there?"

"Nothing yet, but I just got a coffee. I'm good to keep at this."

She got up and grabbed her jacket. "I need a break."

"Sure. You okay?"

She just waved and left. She was far from okay, but she wasn't in the mood to get into it right now. There was one place she wanted to be. Whether it was healthy or advisable would remain to be seen.

CHAPTER THIRTEEN

Amanda stopped by 532 Bill Drive on the way to her intended destination, just to feel like she was doing something to move the case along. A quick conversation with the officer on scene only emphasized the slow progress with this case. He hadn't seen anyone who stood out to him, but the memorial had grown significantly from earlier in the day. Amanda knew it would only blossom further once the news of the fire and death reached more people. Then throngs would come to pay their respects. She found hypocrisy in how some would show support to a stranger in tragedy but snubbed those they didn't know in daily life. But death had a way of changing people and the way they looked at the world. Amanda knew for a fact she viewed everything differently after being personally impacted by the work of the Grim Reaper.

She gave the memorial another look and realized she didn't want to show up where she was going empty-handed. She got back into her car and drove to a convenience store that she knew sold bouquets and bought two. Then she headed to the graveyard.

She pulled in through the gates of Eagle Cemetery and followed the winding roads to a parking lot. Getting out, flowers in hand, she noted how once again she was here at night. Above her, an almost fully formed *egg moon* hung in the sky—a British term she'd learned from her maternal grandmother for a full moon in April. Its glow illuminated her path as she walked up the hill toward an oak tree that was perched at the top. Kevin's and Lindsey's plots were just over the crest.

For a while, she'd stopped coming here. It just felt too awkward, uncomfortable. It never got any easier to speak out loud to her dead husband and child as if they could hear her when she wasn't sure they could. But she'd persisted, and over the last few months, she actually felt like she'd bonded with them. She had sensed the touch of her daughter's spirit—or her memory anyway—affect her and help her. She hadn't yet told Kevin she was seeing someone, and she wouldn't unless things with Logan became serious. And she had no plans of that happening.

But with the case of Jane Doe and the nightmarish images resurfacing of those poor sex-trafficking victims, she didn't know who else to talk to. She probably could have gone to Becky's and chatted with her, but she didn't want to burden her friend, and the hour was rather late. And, even if it was earlier in the day, she certainly wasn't about to pour her heart out to a shrink. She'd tried that after Kevin and Lindsey had died, but it hadn't lasted long. Besides, she just wanted to talk without being interrupted or offered advice. That was one strong advantage of talking to the dead. Though Rideout would disagree and say the dead talked *a lot*. She supposed they did, in their own way.

She reached the top of the hill, stopped, and breathed in the warm night air. It had her wishing she'd just left her jacket in the car. She took it off now, though, juggling the bouquets from one hand to the other as she pulled her arms out of the sleeves. She tied the coat around her waist and continued toward their graves.

She rounded the stones and noted there were already flowers in each of the holders. Probably from her mother, who visited religiously.

Amanda squeezed a new bouquet in with the one already at Kevin's stone. Her gaze landed on the inscription as she straightened back up. *Beloved Husband and Father, Kevin James.*

There were so many times since his death when she'd wished she'd taken his surname and not stuck with her maiden one. It had purely been strategic when she'd made the decision. Her father was the police chief, and his recognizable name would go a long way as she climbed the ranks. At least that had been her reasoning.

She moved her daughter's bouquet around to make room for the additional blooms she'd brought for her. As she was fussing with the flowers, a small envelope came out of the older arrangement, wedged between her fingers. She smiled, thinking that it was just like her mother to leave a note for her granddaughter.

Amanda gathered the two bunches of flowers in hand, the card temporarily set aside on her thigh as she crouched down. She fed the two bouquets into the holder and went to replace the card. But she stopped cold. The moonlight spilled over the envelope just enough to make out the person to whom it was addressed.

It was Amanda's name—in type.

A chill tore through her, and she looked over her shoulders, left and right, right and left, left and right again. Suddenly it felt like the night carried eyes.

She rubbed her arms. Maybe she was making too much out of this, but there was a nattering voice in her brain cautioning her. Anyone who knew her and had something to say to her could pick up a phone or show up at her door. Who would have the audacity to leave a message for her here—and why?

She let go of the envelope, and it fell to the grass. She never should have touched the thing. What if it was evidence? A feeling of dread pricked her skin, but as she stared down at it, her curiosity had to be satisfied.

She pulled out her cell phone and turned on the flashlight.

"Here goes," she said out loud. As if it wasn't creepy enough that she was haunting a graveyard at night, now she was receiving mail at her daughter's grave…

She set her phone on her thigh as she picked up the envelope again, resolute, but her fingers were working slowly to peel back the seal. Once the lip was lifted, she withdrew what was inside, and with her other hand, she aimed the flashlight on it. Just a piece of regular copy paper folded in half.

A typed message read, "*We're on the same team. Be grateful that your angel will always stay innocent.*"

She dropped the card and her phone. *What the hell?* She fumbled to pick up both quickly, now concerned about the dew destroying the note and her phone.

She read the letter again as she stood, and her legs quaked unsteadily beneath her.

The card's sender had to be Jane Doe's killer, but for what purpose? Suddenly, she wasn't feeling much like talking to anyone. It was time to leave.

CHAPTER FOURTEEN

His adrenaline was pumping, and he felt so very alive. He'd take that as further confirmation he was on the right path. Getting the address for Shannon Fox had been easy, thanks to the internet. Maybe he was being reckless or stupid returning to the same street in less than twenty-four hours.

It was about five thirty in the morning when he parked along a side street a block away. The closer he got to the nurse's house, and by extension 532 Bill Drive, where he'd killed that girl, the more his hands started to shake. So much for being at complete peace with what he had done. But, for once, he had his mother's understanding and attention. Possibly even approval. That spurred him forward and helped him focus.

He was dressed in jogging pants and a sweatshirt, and he trotted along the sidewalk toward Fox's house. Or *the* Fox... Ah, he liked thinking of her as that. Because that's what she was. Cunning and scheming, hiding her true intentions behind a good act.

He kept an even pace, not too fast, not too slow. If any curious neighbor saw him, they'd just conclude he was out getting some exercise in the early morning.

He looked at the cop car in front of 532. Even the officer wouldn't think anything of him if he noticed him. But the sight of the house again, just how untouched it was, had rage blistering within him. But all he could do was move forward, perfect, and get things right this time.

He stopped at the end of Fox's driveway, running in place and checking his watch, probably appearing as if he was consulting one of those gadgets that tracked heart rate, distance, and calories burned. In his peripheral, he looked at the four-door sedan in the drive, but he also saw a light coming through a second-story window. Someone was certainly home and, by the looks of it, awake. That could prove to be a problem. Did he wait, or come back and try another time?

He jogged in a circle. He didn't want to put this off. A message needed to be sent, and he had to redeem himself.

He ducked up the driveway with one more furtive glance at 532, this time thinking of the girl who had been inside. He was doing this because of her, because of what she represented.

The end of the driveway butted against a chain-link fence and tall shrubbery. He found a gate, which he unlatched and slipped through. The backyard was banked by large bushes and trees. The branches overhung the space, filling it with shadows like outreaching fingers. The moon was the only source of illumination back here, but that was a good sign. And maybe the light in the house was also a positive omen. It would give him a place to target.

He slipped across the back of the house to a deck and a sliding patio door. Closed vertical blinds took away the possibility of catching a glimpse of the interior, but he'd been in houses that looked similar to this one, and the layout here was likely the same.

He considered the door as a point of entry. He put on a pair of gloves and tugged on the handle. The slider didn't budge. The security bar was probably in place. He could break the glass, but that would make a racket and draw attention.

He moved farther along the rear of the house and found a window at the far west end near the fence line. It was only about four feet above the deck, and it was aluminum cased and opened vertically. Given the age of the home, he'd be surprised if the latch even caught anymore.

He smiled. This just might work.

He pulled a knife from a pocket in his jogging pants. He took the blade and sliced the screen out of its frame, and it fell to the ground like crumpled silk.

Next, he lifted the pane and smiled as he met with no resistance.

He made his way through the opening and closed the window behind him.

He was in a small, dated bathroom that smelled of vanilla. Through the door there would be a hallway that went left to a room. Right would lead to the other living areas of the home, and he'd find the staircase near the front door—if the floorplan was as he imagined.

He walked slowly, thankful for numerous nightlights placed in outlets throughout Fox's home. But one unfortunate placement of his foot, and a floorboard let out a loud groan. He froze in place, listened. Nothing—just his heartbeat pounding in his ears.

He proceeded until he came to the staircase, positioned just to the left of the front door, as he had guessed. He looked up. A faint light spilled across the landing, and he guessed it was probably another nightlight.

He treaded slowly, cringing to think of another misplaced footstep that could expose him. After all, it was crucial that he keep the element of surprise.

He made his way up, sliding his back against the wall as he went. At the top, he confirmed that it was just a nightlight. There wasn't any light trickling out from under any of the closed doors.

He scanned his surroundings—three rooms, two on the right and one on the left. Then he slinked down the hall and confirmed the first room on the left was a bathroom—facing the front of the house. It had probably been the source of the light he'd seen from outside, but it was dark now. Maybe Fox had just used the toilet and gone back to bed.

He strained to hear anything or detect movement. Next to the second room on the right, he heard heavy breathing coming from inside. He slipped a hand into his pocket, wrapped it around the needle, and twisted the door handle.

It was a bedroom, and there was a form in the bed, likely Fox. He stepped inside, but immediately felt something was wrong. Fear curdled through him. The deep breathing was now coming from behind him.

Before he could turn, he was struck. A blinding pain pierced his skull, and he roared. As his vision cleared, he made out Fox in a bathrobe, holding a bat over her head, poised to hit a home run.

But the form on the bed... He rubbed at his head and advanced on Fox.

"You come near me, I swear to God, I'll—"

He pulled his knife and arched it in the air. It stopped her midsentence. Her eyes were darting around the room and behind him. *Is somebody else here?*

He glanced quickly over a shoulder. The form hadn't moved at all, and he pieced it together. Fox was indeed a sly one. She must have heard him enter the house and positioned her pillows to make it look like she was in bed. *As long as she didn't call 911...*

"Get out of my house!" Fox yelled.

He lunged toward her, and she juked left, swinging the bat at him, but he ducked. The bat bit into the drywall above his head, and dust rained down. He coughed but kept his focus on her. The bat had gotten stuck somehow in the wall, and she was struggling to reel it back.

"Well, well." He grinned as he closed in on her. *Trapped little fox.*

"Help!" Fox screamed, her voice ringing in the otherwise silent house. She reached out and swiped at him. Her long nails bit into his arms, and pain fired through him. He howled, but adrenaline swiftly minimalized the sting.

He thrust the knife into her gut, and she wailed. He felt the blade tear through tissue and bank in bone.

Not his intended use for the knife. It was an impulsive act, but it had disabled her. If only she'd shut the hell up! He removed the loaded syringe from his pocket and plunged it into her neck. It would deliver a heavy dose, and she'd become a lifeless puppet.

Almost immediately, her eyelids lowered. Then they lifted slowly, but it was obvious she was having a hard time keeping them open. Her body crumpled against the wall, then down to the floor in a heap.

He crouched next to her. She was still breathing. He lifted one of her arms and let it go. It fell beside her. Good, she was completely incapacitated. She probably wouldn't feel much. He truly was The Merciful.

He cupped her chin in one hand, forcing her to look into his eyes. "You should really learn to keep your mouth shut."

CHAPTER FIFTEEN

Amanda had hardly slept last night after finding that note at the grave. It had to be from Doe's killer—or did it? She teetered back and forth on the matter. But it was the wording that chilled her. *"The same team… happy your angel will always stay innocent."*

What team? Did it refer to values and beliefs? Something more? If it was the killer, did that mean he saw himself on the same side as law enforcement? And, really, the only possible thread connecting Amanda and the killer would be sex trafficking. But he had killed a victim of sex trafficking, while she had rescued them. The last tidbit wedged in her mind. *She'd rescued them…*

Had the killer seen the articles earlier this year about the girls she'd found? If so, that would indicate he was a local. Another shiver ripped through her.

But what had truly prompted the note? Was there an enclosed threat—that he could get to her whenever he wanted? He had, after all, violated her daughter's resting place. Or was he simply delusional, really believing that she was an equal with a man who had strangled a young woman and intended to burn her body to ash?

She tapped the steering wheel of her Honda Civic. She was sitting in the parking lot of the Department of Forensic Science in Manassas waiting for the place to open at eight. Only a couple more minutes to go.

Her plan was to turn over the note to investigators and rush back to Woodbridge for the appointment at the bank. Hopefully, Forensics would get somewhere with fingerprints or touch DNA.

The clock told her it was time, and she got out of the car and entered the building. She was going to request CSI Isabelle Donnelly, whom she rather liked, but another CSI she knew was to the left of the counter. Amanda smiled and lifted her index finger to the receptionist and took one step toward CSI Emma Blair just as she withdrew from an embrace with her son—the fireman, Spencer Blair.

Amanda's instinct was to glance away—even walk away—like she'd interrupted an intimate moment between the two of them simply by being there. Instead, she signaled to the CSI that she was coming over, but Amanda's legs felt weighed down as she started to walk. Both Blairs were leveling glares and scowls at her. She was tempted to just conclude the family was miserable, but she'd seen them be nice to other people. It would seem their hostility was aimed at her. Not that she had a clue as to why.

"Hello," Amanda said, as an inclusive greeting for the two of them.

"Detective Steele," Emma said coolly. "What can I do for you?" Given the way she'd delivered the question, whatever would come from Amanda's mouth was presumed an imposition.

Spencer had yet to say anything; he just kept his gaze fixed on her.

"Detective?" Emma prompted.

"I need you to analyze something for me." Amanda extended the note, which she had sealed in a plastic evidence bag taken from the trunk of her car. Before putting it in there, she had taken photographs with her phone just to have on her person if she ever wanted to refer back to it. Not that she imagined forgetting the message anytime soon.

Emma turned to her son. "Guess I have to get to work."

"Have a good one, Mom." Spencer left, but not without first firing off another glare missile in Amanda's direction.

Emma snatched the bag. "What is it? Which case is it associated with?"

"I believe it's related to the arson and murder at five thirty-two Bill Drive."

Emma narrowed her eyes. "You *believe*? I'm going to need more than that to facilitate this request, Detective."

Amanda clenched her jaw. She should have known she could hit a wall with the request. She hadn't even informed Malone, fearing the news would somehow result in her getting benched from the case. But of all the people to come clean to about the note first, it was Emma Blair?

"I found it at my daughter's grave," she said softly, just hating that whoever had left it had the nerve to go there. *Same team?* Utter crap. "You'll need to eliminate my prints as I didn't think to put gloves on before handling it. But you'll see it was addressed—"

"To you." Emma looked up from the envelope.

"Uh-huh. I think—and this might be a stretch—that it's from the person who killed Jane Doe."

"What does it say inside?"

"'We're on the same team. Be grateful that your angel will always stay innocent.'" Recited verbatim.

"Huh." Emma chewed her bottom lip, met Amanda's gaze. "I'll see what I can find, but no promises."

"All I ask… Except…" Amanda extended another sealed evidence bag. This one included the card taken from the memorial. She'd gone past the station and got it before heading out here. "I was also hoping you could test this for prints and DNA, see if it gets you anywhere."

Emma looked down at the bag but made no move to take it. Amanda practically stuffed it into her hands.

"Where did this one come from?"

Amanda told her.

"Again, I'll see what I can do."

"Thank you." Amanda was about to turn and leave, but she was drawn to say something else. Maybe if she took a stab at showing an interest in the CSI's personal life, it would improve their working relationship. She smiled and said, "I just met Spencer yesterday. I didn't know you had a son."

Emma's face hardened to granite. Even the light that had been in her eyes flickered off. Her posture stiffened. "Well, it's not really like we socialize, Detective, so why would you know?"

Amanda stood frozen for a few seconds, trying to make sense of the CSI's harsh response. Eventually, when she could get her mouth to open, she said, "Suppose that's true." With that, she left, now chewing on another mystery but with a little insight. Given the shut-off body language, she'd wager whatever the CSI had against her was personal, but Amanda had no idea what that could be.

CHAPTER SIXTEEN

The woman at the front counter of Woodbridge Bank directed Amanda and Trent to a grouping of chairs in the middle of the lobby. Amanda sat in one that put her back to the line of tellers and had her facing the front doors.

Offices lined each side of the room. Aiden Adkins had his to Amanda's left. Currently his door was shut, but she could see through a window that a fifty-something man was in there on the phone— Oh, he was just hanging up.

The door opened, and he exited, scanned the space, and settled his gaze on Amanda and Trent. She was already to her feet when he reached them.

Aiden held out his hand to her. "Detective...?"

She took his hand. "Detectives Steele and Stenson. You're Aiden Adkins?"

"That's me." He shook Trent's hand, too, then said, "Come, let's talk in private." He took them to his office and closed the door behind them.

Amanda and Trent sat in chairs facing his desk.

"Looks like you're a busy man." She gestured to a heap of paperwork in a tray.

"Even more now with the fire." Aiden sighed deeply and raked a hand through his hair.

"Insurance claims?" Trent queried.

Aiden clasped his hands on his desk and leaned toward them. "The bank insured it, so really it's just out of one pot and into another. Any external insurance companies wouldn't touch the property."

Amanda angled her head. "Why's that? People had been living in it…"

"Sure, but at the time they insured it, the structure had been sound."

"That changed?"

He nodded. "It wasn't up to code. Mr. Burke, that's the man who we reclaimed the property from, had added a bathroom under the stairs without a permit—not that he would have gotten one."

"Is that why the house isn't for sale?" Trent asked.

"Uh-huh. County Services reserves the right to request that the house be returned to its previous state. They can even levy a fine, but thankfully, I was able to negotiate that away. I got the contractor in about two months ago to do the work, but I'm still waiting for a county inspector to give us the all-clear. Then I'll get the real estate agent back on it and insure the property with an outside firm."

When she and Kevin had renovated their house, he'd handled everything. Hopefully, he got the necessary permits, and it wouldn't come back to haunt her. "Could you run us through what happens when the bank reclaims a property? I'm mostly interested in how many people would have been involved and may have known it was sitting empty."

"The bank always tries to help the homeowner retain their property, but once efforts to secure credit have been exhausted, legal notices are served. Upon foreclosure, we commission a third-party inspector and an estimator to go in. We also line up a real estate agent."

The list of people was growing. "We won't take up much more of your time, Mr. Adkins, but we do have one other question about the property: why were the windows boarded?"

"The neighborhood's not the best, and we wanted to discourage squatters."

"Yet there were," she said with some empathy for the spot the banker found himself in.

Aiden frowned and rubbed his jaw. "Yeah, I read that there was a girl who died in the fire." His gaze made his statement a question.

"The body of a young woman was found," Amanda confirmed.

"Murdered?"

"It's an open investigation."

"Oy vey, so that's a yes. I might as well just hand in my resignation. That house is cursed, I tell you. Who's going to buy it now?"

"A young woman is dead," Trent said firmly.

Aiden met his gaze and massaged his forehead. "I'm sorry… It's just this property has been a nightmare from the start."

While Amanda felt for Aiden's position, she wasn't about to become influenced by emotion. She drew one of her business cards and extended it to him, and she took one of his from a holder on his desk. She pointed to hers in his hand. "Please shoot me over the names of everyone involved with this property. The inspector, estimator, real estate agent, contractor, and whoever you dealt with at County Services. My email's on there."

Aiden looked at her card. "I can do that."

Amanda thanked the banker, and she and Trent left his office.

Stepping into the parking lot, she said to Trent, "We just got a few more potential suspects."

"A few? I'd say a lot more than that."

Her phone rang, and she answered as she got into the department car. "Detective Steele… We'll be right there."

"Who was that?" Trent said, glancing over as he clicked his seat belt into place.

"Malone." She met his gaze, an ache burrowing into her heart. "Shannon Fox is dead. Found murdered in her bedroom."

CHAPTER SEVENTEEN

Becky Tulson was standing outside her patrol car, which was at the curb in front of Shannon Fox's residence. She was talking to a woman who was crying and holding a yoga mat rolled under one arm. Trent parked behind the cruiser, and he and Amanda got out and headed for the house.

Amanda caught Becky's eye as she walked past. The woman was probably the one who had found the victim. They'd get back to her, but first Amanda wanted to look at the scene.

She and Trent started up the walkway when the sound of a vehicle had her turning. The forensics van had arrived with two CSIs—Emma Blair behind the wheel. Amanda would have been happy to have a little more time before seeing Blair again.

Amanda and Trent signed in with the officer at the front door, and he stepped aside for them to enter. He told them to go up the stairs and down the hall to the second door on the right.

Up there, they found Becky's new sergeant, Lisa Greer, in the hall with Malone. Now that the PWCPD detectives were on scene, Sergeant Greer would move out, along with the other Dumfries PD officers.

"It's not pretty in there," Malone said to Amanda.

"I'm going to go before we all start tripping on each other." Greer excused herself and passed Amanda and Trent with a subtle nod before she headed down the stairs.

Amanda edged closer to Malone. "What are we looking at?" He hadn't given her any details on the phone. He'd just told her to get her butt over there quick.

He moved aside to allow her and Trent the space to get past him.

She held eye contact with him as she brushed by him into the room. She saw the body immediately.

Shannon Fox was slumped on the floor and against the wall, like a puppet whose puppeteer had let go of her strings. One arm lay at her side; the other was folded into her lap, her hand closed. Her head was arched back so far that it was unnatural. Given the angle of her body, it would have made more sense if her head had fallen forward, chin to chest. It was like her eyes were looking upward.

Blood had dried around her mouth and on her chin. A trail led down her neck and stained the front of her white bathrobe like a macabre bib. Farther down her torso another red bloom soaked through and around a hole in the cotton.

Amanda pointed that out to Trent and said, "She was stabbed or shot." She continued to scan the room. A wooden baseball bat was lodged in the wall, and she gestured to it. "Doesn't look like she was beaten, but she may have tried to defend herself."

"Let's hope she got some good hits in before her killer got the upper hand."

She felt the same way. A good beating might do the man some good. But had Jane Doe's killer returned for Shannon? If so, why?

Malone shadowed the doorway. "You take a close look at her mouth?"

"No... I..." She couldn't get too close to the body for risk of disturbing evidence, but she bent over and peered into the bloody cavern at Malone's prompting. "He cut out—" she paused, recoiling in disgust "—her tongue."

"Yep." Malone smacked his lips together.

"That is so wrong." Trent blew out a mouthful of air and glanced at the ceiling for a second.

She was surprised by his reaction. Sure, it was a grotesque display, but Trent handled autopsies like a pro and they were far messier than this. "You going to be all right there?"

"Yeah, it's just not something you see every day."

"Thank God for that," Malone lamented.

"I'll be fine." Trent cleared his throat. "So are we looking at the same bastard who killed the girl and set the fire, or someone else? It's a different MO."

Shannon's killer had indeed used a different method of operation, but it was hard to ignore the fact her house was just a few down from 532 and hard to dismiss another truth. "She's the one who called nine-one-one. Maybe the killer found out somehow and decided to silence her?" She motioned toward Shannon's mouth, indicating the absence of a tongue.

"Her name was in the newspaper," Trent said, "along with the fact she was a nurse at Prince William Medical Center."

"Wow," Amanda said. "Apparently, the media doesn't hold anything back."

"It would have been easy for the killer to find out where she lived." Trent's voice held a sour note.

"We need to keep in mind that we could be looking at someone else, possibly within Shannon's circle." As soon as they pigeonholed an investigation, they risked sabotaging the case. Regardless of where the evidence took them, she felt for Shannon Fox. She would have thought she'd done a good deed, but it hadn't exactly netted a reward worth receiving. Even the intrinsic feeling of knowing she'd done an honorable thing had been short-lived.

"I read the article on the fire last night," Trent volunteered. "The reporter played up Fox as a hero, but Fox herself was quoted as saying that she did what anyone would have done in her place."

Maybe it hadn't just been the call to 911 that had made Shannon a target. It wasn't a leap that this killer might see himself as having done a good thing with the fire and killing of Jane Doe—and wanted the glory all for himself. Again, that was assuming that Shannon's killer was also Jane Doe's.

"Excuse me." Paula Jeffery ducked her head into the room. She was another ME from the Office of the Chief Medical Examiner in Manassas, and not Amanda's favorite person. She took herself too seriously, in Amanda's opinion, and fared better in relationships with the dead than the living.

At her heels were CSIs Blair and Donnelly.

"We're going to need the room," Jeffery said.

"We'll get out of your way." Malone smiled cordially and was the first to leave.

Amanda and Trent followed him down the stairs and out the front door. They gathered in a circle.

Trent was the first to speak. "Doe's killer had doused her body with gasoline, likely for the purpose of destroying it and making identification impossible. But the fire was put out before that could happen. I think the killer blamed Fox and her call to nine-one-one for ruining his plan. He thought he'd teach her a lesson."

Malone latched a hand onto Trent's shoulder. "Let's just slow down before we start jumping to conclusions."

Amanda turned away and settled her gaze on the woman who had been with Becky earlier. She was now in the passenger seat of the cruiser with the door open and her legs outside the vehicle. The yoga mat rested in her lap, and she was dabbing her cheeks with a tissue. Amanda nodded her head toward her and said to Malone, "That who found her?"

"Yeah. You should go talk to her." With that, Malone was off across the yard in the opposite direction from Becky and the woman.

"Before we head over there…" She reached out and caught Trent by the crook of his elbow. "Just remember that we need to go into this investigation with an open mind. You understand that?"

He scanned her eyes but said nothing.

She continued. "We can't just run on the assumption that the same killer is involved. We could blind ourselves to the actual evidence. We approach this like any other murder, looking first at the people in Fox's life." She was saying this just as much for herself as she was for him.

Trent angled his head. "You don't think it's the same killer?"

"An. Open. Mind." She started toward the woman, Trent at her side.

As they approached, Becky helped close the distance and said, "You're a busy woman."

"You too. So who is she?"

"Name's Bethany Greene, and she was the victim's best friend, according to her anyway. She arrived here at nine thirty. She and Shannon were to go to yoga together at ten."

That explained the mat. "How did she get inside the house?"

"Short answer, she has a key. Long answer, she knocked on the front door and called her friend's cell phone, and when she got no answer, she let herself in."

Amanda glanced past Becky to Bethany and, at this distance, noted her cheeks were puffy, her eyes bloodshot, and her mascara smeared.

"Did she touch anything in the house?"

"She says no. She's real shaken up, though."

"I can understand that. Okay, we'll go talk to her." She brushed Becky's arm on the way past. "Ms. Greene?" Amanda called out.

The woman looked up from where she'd been staring at the sidewalk, but there was nothing behind her eyes—like she was in some distant world, avoiding reality.

"I'm Detective Amanda Steele, and this is my partner, Detective Trent Stenson."

Bethany barely blinked.

"We're very sorry for your loss," Amanda offered softly. She paused, giving Bethany ample time to insert something, but she didn't. "It must have been quite the shock finding your friend that way."

"I— I don't have...the words." Bethany's voice cracked like thin ice.

"We understand that you gave your statement to Officer Tulson, but we have some questions for you. Some may be ones you've already answered, but bear with me, okay?" Amanda thought she'd get in front of an objection that always came.

"I'll do whatever I can to help." Bethany rolled her mat across her lap as if seeking a mindless distraction from her grief, her fear, whatever other emotions were swirling through her.

"Do you know if Shannon was on the outs with anyone? Someone she didn't get along with?" Amanda had told Trent they needed to examine Fox's personal life, and she'd been serious about that endeavor.

"I can't imagine anyone doing that... *that*... to her. They cut out her—" She cupped her mouth.

It obviously hadn't escaped Bethany's notice, even in the horror of the bloodshed, that her friend had been mutilated. "Did you touch her, or anything in the house?"

"No." She sniffled.

"How long were you two friends?" Trent asked.

"A few years, but we got close fast. Had a lot in common." She added the last bit with a shrug.

"It's awesome when you find someone like that. What similar interests did you share?" Amanda wanted to set Bethany at ease as much as possible, given the circumstances, so she'd continue to open up.

"We're both in our forties, single, never married. We like to do yoga and eat healthy. We're also members of a singing group out of Washington." Bethany rattled off everything in present tense, which was completely normal in the immediate aftermath of loss—even for some time after.

"Sounds like a great friendship." Amanda offered a gentle smile. "Was she dating anyone?"

"Ah, no. You get to be our age, and the dating pool's smaller than a kiddie pool. They're either married and cheating scum, pot-bellied, or liars. Sometimes all three. Most have so much baggage, they'd need to pay extra to travel by plane."

Hearing Bethany's bleak view of dating was depressing, possibly true. Amanda hadn't really given it much of a shot. One-night stands were much simpler. No names, no questions, no emotional connection. But as they added up, they took a toll.

"What about family?" Trent interjected. "Does she have any in the area?"

Bethany gave a small bob of her head. "Her sister lives in town. Her dad? No one knows where he is. He ran off when she was a girl. The mom died of a drug overdose several years ago. She never was much of a mom."

"Doesn't sound like it..." Amanda recalled how Shannon had given the impression she could relate to the squatters at 532. Had Shannon ever taken to the streets? She'd ask but wasn't sure if it would be relevant to the case. Then again... Her eyes widened, considering. What if Fox was somehow linked to sex trafficking like they knew Jane Doe had been? Maybe even a victim at one time who had escaped. If Fox was somehow wrapped up in the ugly mess, that could be another thing linking her murder to Jane Doe's. But she talked herself down. She was getting ahead of herself.

"We'll need to get her sister's information," she said to Bethany.

"Sure." She fumbled in one of her pants pockets and took out her phone.

Amanda happened to look up and see Malone coming toward her. "You got this?" she said to Trent, and he nodded.

Amanda stepped away, putting about ten feet between herself and Bethany and Trent. "What is it?"

"I just spoke with the officer posted outside five thirty-two," Malone said. "He's been there since midnight. Didn't see anything all night. I know we don't have TOD yet, though I'd expect sometime between then and now."

"Huh. I would think he'd have seen something that might help us." If this was the same killer back a second time, he might as well have been the invisible man. "The officer was awake, though? Eyes open?" She knew from personal experience just how boring and mind-numbing surveillance could be.

"I sure hope so."

"But you're not sure?"

Malone angled his head and pressed his lips. "It's entirely possible he saw nothing."

"He confirmed that he hadn't left his post?"

Malone clenched his jaw. "Why are you being so stubborn about this? If we can't take the word of one of our own, then we might as well give up now."

She realized she might be coming across just as Malone had accused, but she was feeling frustrated. Maybe taking it out on the faceless officer. Then again, if a badge told Malone he saw nothing, then Malone would believe him. His brothers in blue had to give Malone strong reason not to trust them.

Malone snapped his fingers. "I can see it on your face, Steele. But let it go."

When he pulled out her surname, it was hard to feel like she had much choice but to submit.

"So how did it go with—" He nudged his head toward Bethany.

"She's the vic's best friend. No leads on who had a beef with Shannon, but Trent's getting info on the next of kin now."

"I can take care of delivering the notification."

"Actually, I'd prefer to do it," she said. "We might get a lead on someone in Fox's circle. As you said to Trent we need to slow down, and that means considering all the angles on this case. It appears on the surface like Jane Doe's killer might have motive, but what's to say someone with a vendetta against Shannon didn't take advantage of that? Her name, after all, was in the paper."

Malone seemed to consider her words, then grinned and wagged his finger. "See, that's why the LT can't knock you down, Amanda. You're an amazing cop. Just keep that up." Malone's gaze went beyond her. "And speaking of good cops." He waved someone over. She turned and saw a male PWCPD officer headed their way.

"This is Officer Tucker," Malone said once he got to them. "This is Detective Amanda Steele."

Trent joined them and held up his notepad to Amanda, likely to communicate he had the sister's information.

"And Detective Trent Stenson." Malone swept an arm toward Trent. "Officer Tucker here found where the killer gained entry to the residence. You go ahead, Tucker."

Tucker was in his early twenties but, based on the shining pride in Malone's eyes, held a lot of promise. He had a willow-reed frame and brown hair. He smiled, or rather twitched, uncomfortably as Amanda looked at him. "It appears like he may have accessed the property through a window in the back. It's shut, but the screen was cut. There's also a sliding patio door back there. It was unlocked."

Amanda glanced at Malone, then Trent. "Then why enter through the window? Surely he would have tried the door first."

"I'm thinking that's likely the way he left, ma'am," Tucker said. "It would have been much easier than crawling back out the window."

"I agree. Good observations. Make sure to pass this information along to the CSIs. They should dust the windowsill for prints. Also, the inside handle on the patio door." She offered a smile at the rookie, though she wasn't entirely sure what had Malone so enraptured with him. Now wasn't the time to ask, but she was interested in popping into the backyard. While she and Trent looked around, it would also give the CSIs and ME more time to work.

She walked to the rear of Shannon's house. Trent came with her, but Malone didn't.

Like at 532, there was a gate at the end of the driveway. She went through, not even knowing exactly what she was looking for. But she was interested in seeing where Shannon's killer had gained entry with her own eyes.

She noted the overgrown bushes, large trees, and the relative seclusion. Windows in the houses butting against Fox's property would have offered an exceptional line of sight, though. Amanda pointed them out to Trent. "Someone might have seen something." She'd make sure that canvassing officers visited the residents. Depending on Shannon's time of death, most people likely would have been sleeping, but they still needed to ask. "If we're looking at the same killer," she added, "his killing Fox was a brazen move." She hated that her mind was going to the dark place where serial killers lurked. But even if the same person was behind the murders, didn't a serial killer by definition have more than two victims? She really didn't want to think about that.

"That's for sure. Striking twice in two days, and on the same street? I'd definitely say he wanted to make a statement."

"The mutilation tells us that, no matter who killed her. But what are you thinking?" she asked.

"Pretty much the same. And, if it's the same killer, he's willing to take out anyone who interferes with his plans."

The picture of a true psychopath... "Okay, well, if it is him," she began, "let's hope his impulsiveness caused him to screw up and leave us evidence we can work with."

"We can hope. Also, *if* it is the same guy—just continue to hear me out—I don't think we're looking for someone who wants to hide their actions. Rather, he wants to draw attention to them. Otherwise, why kill Jane Doe in an abandoned house and proceed to set it on fire? If he just wanted to dispose of the body, why not burn it a field? I'd say he wants his fifteen minutes of fame."

She regarded him, smirking. "You a profiler now?"

"I worked a case involving a serial killer before."

"Yes. *One.*" She arched her brows. She'd found out all about Trent's fifteen minutes of fame years ago at a barbecue that Becky had held at her house. He'd helped the FBI track down a serial rapist and murderer and almost got a one-way ticket to the white light.

"Just trust me. The last thing I want is for some serial killer to be on the loose."

"I'm with you there. Let's just explore it being an isolated incident before we get carried away." The message from the note at the grave screamed at her, despite her words, and made her feel hypocritical. Whether the sender was Fox's killer or not, just the fact that he said she was on the same team as him made her determined to prove him wrong. She should probably tell Trent about it, but then he might lose all objectivity.

"True enough, and I hope we're getting ahead of ourselves." Trent hopped up on a narrow deck that ran along the backside of the house and went toward a window with a pile of screen on the boards beneath it. "The entry point Officer Tucker mentioned."

She nodded. "Let's go back upstairs and see if the ME and CSIs have anything to tell us." She'd seen enough, and it was time to get some answers.

CHAPTER EIGHTEEN

Amanda and Trent headed back inside Shannon's house and passed the CSIs, who were leaving. She heard Officer Tucker calling to the investigators just as the front door closed behind them. Upstairs, they found Paula Jeffery crouched near the body, her booty-covered shoes straddling the pool of blood.

Jeffery pressed a hand to the side of Shannon's neck, her index finger and thumb spreading out and indicating the space between them. "There's a prick in her skin. It's possible she was pierced with a needle."

"She was drugged," Amanda concluded. "You'll have a full tox panel run on her?"

"You can count on it."

"Cause of death?" Amanda crossed her arms so tight, she had to release a little to expand her chest.

Jeffery didn't respond.

All righty then…

Amanda took in all the blood on Shannon's robe and pooled on the floor near her. "Was she alive when her tongue was severed?"

Jeffery kept her gaze on the body as she spoke. "She had a heartbeat, yes. As for how much she was 'with it,' though, would depend on the drug in her system."

"Our killer may have shown some mercy. That's if he used a type of paralytic," Trent reasoned.

Jeffery glanced over her shoulder. "*If.*"

"Did she bleed out?" Trent asked, and Amanda winced at him. He had every right to ask whatever question he liked, but Jeffery didn't seem to be in the mood to answer many.

"You mean did she die due to exsanguination?" Jeffery paused, as if to let the technical term sink in and prove herself intellectually superior. "I wouldn't think so, given the volume of blood loss I'm seeing, but it's too early to conclude." She proceeded to open the robe, and Amanda held her breath as she let her gaze go over the woman's chest.

No tattoo.

A relief, but it still didn't excuse Doe's killer from committing this murder. Even the different MOs should steer her suspicions in another direction, but her instinct was screaming they were looking at the same man.

Jeffery paused movement, her eyes on Shannon's torso. "Umm."

Now that Amanda could see the wound, she could tell it had been caused by a stabbing, not a shooting. She waited for Jeffery to elaborate on her *Umm.*

"Stab to her abdomen, and it appears to be rather deep, but it must have avoided the arteries in the region, or we'd be looking at more blood."

Rather deep… Amanda contemplated the meaning behind that. Perhaps whoever killed Shannon had been driven by rage, but then that didn't explain the restraint. Why just one stabbing? Why not several?

Amanda studied Shannon, searching her mind for similarities between the Jane Doe and Shannon Fox murders. After all, if they were looking at a serial killer, there would likely be something that would irrefutably link the two murders. Something beyond the coincidental. Something beyond a gut feeling. The murder methods had been different, and there was no obvious attempt to set a fire at Fox's house. Jeffery said that Shannon had been drugged. Did that apply to Jane Doe too? Or was their killer not only impulsive but also versatile? The questions were plentiful, the answers not so much. And she had something else she needed to ask. "Could you estimate TOD?"

"Her body has started into rigor..." Jeffery got up, rummaged in her kit, and pulled out a thermometer, which she pierced into Shannon's liver. A few seconds later, she noted something in a small book, looked at Trent. "What's the temperature in the house?"

Trent glanced at Amanda as if looking for permission to go check. Amanda nodded her head. He left the room and came back seconds later.

"It's seventy-two degrees," he told Jeffery.

She tapped the tip of her pen into the air, and her mouth moved as she made some calculations. "I'd say the victim died anywhere between four and six this morning."

Basically the same hours estimated for Jane Doe. It still would have been dark, but it wasn't an absolutely ungodly hour like two or three. Assuming Shannon's killer didn't spend hours with her, someone in the neighborhood might have been up and seen something, especially if she was killed closer to six. By then, people would be waking up to get ready for work.

Jeffery put her items aside, then opened Shannon's hand, which had been closed, resting on her thigh. "Well, I found her tongue."

"Oh." Trent turned away.

Amanda wasn't sure if she'd even heard the ME correctly, and she couldn't make out what the mound of flesh was. "You found her tongue... in her hand?"

"That's what I said." Blunt, tactless, without patience.

Amanda gave her a hard stare and headed for the door. She'd had enough of Ego ME. "Keep me posted on when you'll be conducting the autopsy."

Jeffery grumbled something in Amanda's wake, but Amanda just shook her head and went down the stairs and outside. She sensed Trent right behind her.

Malone was on the front step. "Get any answers?"

"Not much," Amanda said. "Jeffery put TOD between four and six this morning. She won't conclude cause of death until she has the body on a slab, but there was a needle mark in Shannon's neck."

"The same for Doe?"

Amanda shook her head. "No injection sites that Rideout found, but he was having a tox panel run on her. She could have consumed a drug in her food or drink."

"If Doe was drugged, that could be something else that connects the two murders." Malone rubbed the top of his head. "Do you think the same guy is behind both?"

"Hey, you said to slow down with assumptions. In that vein, we're going to speak with Shannon's sister and see if she knows of anyone who may have had a problem with Shannon. The friend didn't." Amanda glanced over the front lawn. It would seem Bethany Greene had been sent on her way.

"Whatever you do, wrap this up quickly. Last thing we need is another body."

More to the point, it was the last thing *she* needed. Not to sound unsympathetic to the victims, but if Amanda missed clues and the bodies continued to pile up, the lieutenant would only use it as ammunition against her. "I'm with you there. Did you hear Doe was branded by a sex-trafficking ring?"

"Not from you, but dear God." Malone made the sign of the cross and looked heavenward. "Poor girl suffers like that and then she's murdered. What the hell is the world coming to?"

"Let me know when you figure it out," she kicked back.

"Please keep me posted, and if you need anything…"

"Actually, can you make sure officers talk to the people who live behind the property? Some of the windows overlook Shannon's backyard."

"Will do." With that Malone walked off.

"Do you really think we're looking at an isolated incident?" Trent pierced her with his gaze.

"All I can say is, I hope the killing stops here."

"Guess we'll find out soon enough."

Her partner had a point, but it wasn't one she liked, and it wasn't as if they were discussing something of no importance—they were talking about *lives*. "It's our jobs to determine what's going on before the body count increases, and that's exactly what I intend to do."

CHAPTER NINETEEN

Amanda looked across the street at the crowd. It didn't matter how many times she witnessed people gathering in the aftermath of tragedy, it was always unsettling. She scanned everyone's faces. Some were familiar from the day before, but it was the same street, so the same neighbors. A couple of officers were already making the rounds and speaking with people.

"Trent," she started, leaning toward him and speaking in a low voice, "without causing much fuss, pull out your phone and take pictures of the crowd."

He did as she asked without a word.

While he did that, she called Rideout's cell number. He answered on the second ring. "It's Detective Steele." After asking him how he was, out of courtesy, she got to the meat of her call. "Any way to rush the tox panel on Jane Doe from five thirty-two Bill Drive? We might be looking at another victim."

"Oh. Do you suspect the same killer?"

"Honestly, undecided, but it's entirely possible."

"I'll see what I can do."

"All I can ask— Oh, actually, since I have you, are you getting closer to forwarding Doe's photo to me?" He had said that he should have it to her by the end of today. Hopefully by asking early afternoon she wasn't pushing too much.

"Should be soon. All I can say. I have sent the DNA sample to the lab and taken the dental impression. I'll let you know if either one gets us anywhere. Though you know DNA takes forever."

"I do, but I appreciate whatever you can do." With that she hung up and found Trent had finished taking pictures and was watching her. "Just called Rideout. He's going to try and rush the lab on Doe's tox panel. No photo of her yet. Soon, he says."

"Some good news."

A *PWC News* van pulled up, and Amanda groaned. "And there's the bad news."

There was no honor or sanctity in murder—none. The poor victim, in a way, continued to suffer. The person they once were became inventoried as a catalog of parts on the autopsy table while their lives were dissected by investigators and the media.

"Let's get out of here." She marched toward the department car. Her hand was on her door handle when the reporter's words made their way to Amanda's ears.

"This is Diana Wesson with *PWC News*. I'm here on location where a woman has been discovered murdered in her home. This comes just one day after the body of a young woman was pulled from a house fire a few doors down. Prince William County Police Department is on scene."

There was a lull in the reporter's speaking, and Amanda could sense what was coming. She flung the door open, but the twentysomething, blond reporter wedged herself between Amanda and the car.

"Excuse me. Are you the lead detective on the case? Do you think the incidents are related?" The reporter thrust a microphone in her face.

Amanda pushed the mike aside. She had little tolerance for reporters and journalists—even less when they were in her personal bubble. "No comment."

"But it is correct? There was a murder?" Her blue eyes were wide and blinking.

With her gaze locked on Diana's, Amanda flushed with rage. Doe's killer might want his fifteen minutes of fame, but if this was his work, she wasn't giving it to him. "You need to leave. And you—" Amanda glared at the cameraman "—need to turn that off. Now."

"Di?" the cameraman appealed to the reporter.

Diana leveled a glare at Amanda. "You really can't expect us to leave. This is a breaking news story."

"A break—" Amanda took a few breaths. "A breaking news story? A woman was murdered."

"The public has a right to know," Diana seethed.

"You want a story? You contact the Prince William County Police Department's Public Information Office. Get your facts in order." The second Diana Wesson left, Amanda would be calling the supervisor at the PIO and telling him to hold back everything.

Diana stood there for a good thirty seconds before grounding the heel of one of her stilettos into the pavement. "Fine." She lassoed her arm over her head, a gesture to *wrap it up*. The camera-man followed her back to the news van.

"Gah, I hate reporters," Amanda griped and pulled out her phone. Ronald Topez at the PIO answered on the second ring. "You might be hearing from a Diana Wesson with *PWC News* about the murder at six-oh-two Bill Drive. Don't give her anything."

"I don't have much, so that will be easy."

She detected a smile in Ronald's voice. "Thank you."

"Don't mention it." He hung up first, and she joined Trent in the department car.

"Notification of kin?"

"Yep." As Trent pulled away, she took in the madness around her—all the people milling about, both civilian and law enforce-ment—drawn together because of a horrid crime. Some might see this as evidence of humanity, but that wasn't what Amanda saw. Most people were there because misery loved company and knowing that a calamity had befallen someone else made them feel better about their own lives. They also wanted to feel important, like they mattered.

Like they mattered…

Was that also the case with their killer—assuming the same man had killed both women? Did he want to feel like his journey on this planet was of consequence? In addition, did he require that reassurance from others, possibly long for approval? Was that why he'd left that note for her, to initiate a bond?

She glanced over at Trent. She should tell him about the note on her daughter's grave in case everything got out of control. As if two bodies in twenty-four hours, on the same street, wasn't already an indication of that. "There's something you should know…"

CHAPTER TWENTY

Amanda made Trent stop at Hannah's for a coffee before laying out everything about the note. She needed the caffeine to think straight, for one thing. After a few long draws, and with the diner in the rearview mirror, she told him.

"I really don't like the sound of that." Trent was splitting his attention between looking out the windshield and glancing at Amanda in the passenger seat.

They were on the way to give notification to Keira Norris, Shannon Fox's sister. Amanda couldn't respond to Trent as she had a mouthful of muffin—something else she'd picked up from the diner.

Trent continued. "It sounds like he's taunting you. He obviously wants you to know that he can get to you. A threat? Also, to put it on Lindsey's grave…" Trent winced. "That's like him saying he knows your darkest secrets."

She highly doubted that. She harbored some doozies.

"And I know how you feel about investigating the people in Fox's life," he added, "but what would make a one-off killer leave a note like that? I mean, it seems obvious it's from him, and he sounds like someone who intends to kill again."

"Just striving to keep an open mind." Maybe if she said it enough, she'd sincerely view Shannon's murder from a broader perspective.

"How do you think he found out where your daughter's grave is?"

"Don't know. I do know that I was in the news back in January, and what happened to my family was made public knowledge—again. He could have found their obits."

"So he's a local."

"I'd say that's a safe bet."

Trent pulled into the driveway of a townhouse that was one of many on a string.

"Before we go to Keira's door, bring up her basic info." Amanda gestured to the onboard laptop.

Trent clicked away, leaving the car—and the AC running. It was turning out to be a warmer day than yesterday.

A few seconds later, he said, "Pretty straightforward. Thirty-nine, married, no record."

"All right. And is she Shannon's only sibling?" She hadn't had a chance to ask before now.

"Yeah."

They got out of the vehicle and knocked on the door.

A woman answered. She had long, brown hair, a high forehead, and a round face. "Can I help you?"

What was about to follow was the worst part of the job. Telling people that their loved one had died had been a painful exercise before she'd lost her husband and daughter. After, even worse. There were times it felt like she was reliving that horrid day.

"Mrs. Keira Norris?" Amanda asked.

"Yes."

"I'm Detective Amanda Steele, and this is Detective Trent Stenson, with the Prince William County PD. We need to talk with you for a moment about your sister, Shannon. Would we be able to come in and sit down?"

Tears sprang to Keira's eyes. "Tell me she's okay. Please, tell me."

"If we could please come inside," Amanda petitioned. Informing a person while they were sitting was easier on everyone. Shock had been known to cause people to faint or collapse.

Keira licked her lips and let them enter. She dropped on a couch in the living room.

Amanda and Trent followed her there and sat in a couple of chairs.

"We're sorry to inform you that your sister, Shannon Fox, was found murdered in her home this morning." Normally, at this point, Amanda would say how the person died, but they didn't know the exact cause yet.

"Murdered?" Her voice was small, and she blinked rapidly, her eyelashes wet. "How, and who would…?"

"We were hoping that you might be able to tell us if your sister had any enemies," Amanda said.

She sniffled, tears streaming down her face, and her eyes blanked over. "Who, ah, who found her?"

It wasn't uncommon for the notified to drift, and Amanda would honor the woman's feelings by answering her question. She'd return to hers shortly. "A friend of hers named Bethany Greene. Apparently, Bethany was there to pick your sister up for a yoga class they do together. Did you know your sister did yoga?"

"Oh, yeah. Shannon loved it, not that I ever got the appeal. I know Beth too. She's a good lady and was good for Shannon."

She'd answered Amanda's next question without knowing it.

Keira went on. "You think it was a home invasion? A robbery? Shannon never had anything worth stealing. How did she—" She gripped the collar of her shirt.

"We don't know exactly how yet, but we're still investigating. We'd like to know if you're aware of anyone who might have wanted to hurt her." She was finally able to circle back to her initial question.

Keira pinched her nose, and Trent grabbed the tissue box next to him and took it to Keira.

"Thanks."

"Don't mention it." Trent returned to his chair.

Keira sniffled and blew her nose a few times.

Amanda joined her on the couch. "Did you know of anyone?" she prompted gently.

"I never..." Fresh tears fell, and Keira dabbed her nose. "I never would have thought it would come to this."

Amanda straightened up and leaned toward Keira. "What, Mrs. Norris?"

"She, uh..." Keira twisted the tissue in her hand. "She got messed up with some nutjob a few years ago. It began with mental games, then he got more and more controlling and aggressive. When he started hitting her, that's when she left."

Amanda had a bad feeling where this was going. Abusive men didn't typically let their women go without a fight. "Did he come after her?"

"Oh, yeah. Repeatedly. He threatened to kill her. Also repeatedly."

Amanda glanced at Trent. This was why they had to keep an open mind. Bethany Greene hadn't mentioned anything about this relationship, but it was possible that Shannon had kept it from her. Maybe due to shame, like she felt she deserved the abuse for some reason. It could also be as simple as Shannon believing the guy was in her past. She was just about to ask for this guy's name when Keira spoke again.

"Maybe he did this to her?" Another bout of crying. "He's still around."

Amanda's skin tingled. "As in recently?"

Keira nodded. "Last week."

"We're going to need his information."

"No worries there. If he killed my sister, you nail that son of a bitch!" Her anger toward her sister's abuser—possible killer—burned hot but morphed quickly back to grief for her sister. Her face became shadows, and her eyes vacant. "He was freaking obsessed with her, even though he'd apparently hooked up with some other woman. Not that it stopped him from showing up at Shannon's door from time to time. She told me I was making too much out of it, and that she had it under control." Keira bit her bottom lip.

"Did she get a restraining order against him?" Trent asked.

Keira shook her head and picked at the soaked tissue in her hand. "As I said, she didn't think he was anything she couldn't handle. Besides, a restraining order wouldn't have stopped the bastard. He did whatever he liked."

"Well, if she had gotten one, it would have given police authorization to put him in jail if he broke the terms." Amanda hated that her words made it sound like Shannon was to blame for the harassment.

"Sure, okay, but then he'd just get out and return to the streets angrier than before."

Amanda had nothing to say to that. The system wasn't perfect. She watched as Keira turned the tissues into shreds. "You and your sister were close," she said kindly in offer of support.

"Very. We were all we had. Our parents weren't any type of role models."

As they'd learned from Bethany... "Sorry to hear that, and so very sorry for your loss. Is there someone that we could call to come be with you? Your husband?"

Keira dabbed her nose. "We separated last month. He was a cheating piece of shit."

"Anyone else?" Amanda's heart broke for this woman.

"Nah, I'll make some calls myself."

"If you're sure." Amanda inched forward on the couch. "Before we go, we'll need that man's information."

"Not really a man in my opinion, but his name's Sean Fitzgerald. He lives in town." Keira proceeded to give them his address, which Trent recorded in his notebook.

They said their goodbyes, and once back in the car, Trent brought up the ex's background in the computer.

"He's forty-eight, and he's a piece of work all right," Trent said. "Guy's got a record. Drug possession, and charges of domestic abuse and assault."

"Let's go meet him."

CHAPTER TWENTY-ONE

"What the f—" The door swung open, mid-knock and mid-sentence.

The man standing in the doorway, with his large gut and wide girth, would have intimidated a lot of people. Not Amanda. Not given what Keira had told them. Not with what his criminal record had revealed.

She held up her badge. "Detective Amanda Steele with the Prince William County PD. My partner, Detective Trent Stenson, and I would like to talk to you about Shannon Fox."

"Oh, yeah." He crossed his arms, which were like tree trunks and heavily tattooed.

She stepped to within a few inches of him. "She was found murdered this morning. You have something to do with that?" She was primed to drag his ass to the station. She just needed him to give her one teeny reason.

He started to laugh. "She's, ah, what now?"

"Murdered," Amanda hissed. "We understand that you—"

"Threatened to kill her? Yeah, I'd admit to that."

She should be appalled by his blatant audacity, but guys like Sean lacked the ability to shock her. "Okay… Did you act on your threat?"

Another laugh. "Bitch wasn't worth my time. Can't say I'm surprised she drove someone to it, though."

With every word from the man's mouth, Amanda's temper ratcheted.

He arrogantly carried on. "It was fun toying with her. Making her a little loco." He spun a finger in a circle next to his ear and grinned.

She curled her hands into fists but coaxed herself into relaxing them. She didn't need this loser viewing it as a threat from the police. "We're going to need to know where you were between four and six this morning."

He turned around to the inside of the house and yelled, "Tara!"

There was some thumping, then obvious padding of footsteps heading toward the door.

Sean stepped to the side, leaving room for this small woman to stand next to him in the doorway. He draped his arm over her, hanging it on her like a treacherous vine. "Tell this detective where I was this morning between four and six."

The woman had dark circles under her eyes, and it looked like she had a fresh cut on her chin. Amanda imagined that this asshole had struck her not long before their arrival.

"Tell them." He nudged Tara in her side, and she winced.

Amanda guessed he might have hit her in the ribs. It was usually best in suspected abuse cases like this to play it cool, but it was taking all of her control not to haul off and hit the guy. Maybe give him a taste of his own medicine.

"Ah, Sean was in bed with me." Tara's voice was weak and unsure.

"Uh-huh, that's right." The baboon was grinning. "We was—" He mimed the rest by thrusting his hips forward and back.

"For two hours? You? I highly doubt it. Less than two *minutes*, that I'd believe." She knew she was antagonizing him, but that was the least of what she wanted to do.

Sean grimaced. "No, lady, I'm just that good at pleasuring the ladies."

Trent stepped closer to the man. "What you think and what you are—likely two very different things."

His smile faded, and he scowled at Trent, but he looked back at Amanda. "When I wasn't giving it to her, I was sleeping. Ain't that right, baby?" Again, he nudged her.

"That's right." Tara's gaze was on the ground.

"Okay. You need anything, call me." Amanda extended her card to Tara, but Sean swatted it out of the way, and it fluttered to the front step.

Trent picked it up and pressed it to Sean's chest. "You dropped something."

Sean stared at him. "She don't need your deets. Get outta here."

Trent didn't budge.

Amanda pried her eyes from her partner and Sean to look at Tara, but she was gone. She must have returned inside. "Let's go, Detective Stenson."

"You heard her." Sean smiled smugly. "Do as the bitch tells you."

Trent lunged forward, but Amanda grabbed his arm and shook her head. "It's not worth it."

Trent huffed but relented and returned to the car. She caught up with him.

In the vehicle, she stated the obvious, "The guy got under your skin."

"You could say that."

Amanda could tell that what they'd just witnessed struck close for Trent. "Guys like that piss me off too, but I learned a long time ago you can't help everyone. The women who get caught up with these losers get themselves locked in a cycle of abuse. It's really hard to break them free, and there's no chance if they don't want to help themselves."

"I'm well aware."

She usually tried to avoid getting too personal with Trent but... *Screw it!* "Someone you cared about was abused?"

"Yeah."

"Want to talk about it?"

"Not really."

She pulled out her phone and checked her email. She wasn't going to pressure him to talk; she knew what it felt like to be on the receiving end of such an endeavor. It was shit.

"Tara probably just lied to cover for him," Trent eventually said.

"She could have."

"But he just gets away with being an ass."

"For now."

"It was my aunt... After my uncle's death, she met this guy. She really thought she'd found love again. At first, it seemed she had, but that quickly changed. He ended up breaking her arm and three ribs." He paused but didn't meet her gaze, seeming lost in his own thoughts. "The shithead ended up getting away with it too. My aunt was too afraid to turn him in."

"Sorry to hear that. Did she ever get away from him?"

Trent slowly shook his head. "Still with him, as far as I know. But, as you said, they have to want to help themselves. Sadly, my aunt lost her confidence and started to believe she deserved the way this guy treated her."

"Jeez."

"Yeah, there's nothing much to say." He looked over at her now, pressed his lips. "But now you know why I go off when I run into assholes like Sean Fitzgerald."

"Understandable." She knew she should have discouraged his behavior, but she couldn't find it within herself. Sometimes, people just brought out the nasty side. It was human, badge or not.

"Hey, I know we have no real choice but to take Tara's word. Doesn't mean it doesn't piss me off."

"Just take a few deep breaths," she encouraged without sounding patronizing. Her red-headed temper had gotten her into trouble more times than she could count, so she wasn't qualified to stand as anyone's judge.

Trent just sat there and breathed for a few seconds.

"Feel better?"

"Yeah. No. Not really. But thanks for trying." He smiled at her.

"Anytime. Let's just focus on what we got out of this visit. With Fitzgerald off the list, we can assume that the same person killed Jane Doe and Shannon Fox."

"A serial killer? Not feeling all warm yet."

She laughed. "I'm not concluding it's a serial killer yet."

"Okay, I can live with that."

You will; the victims might not...

She glanced down at her phone. No email from Rideout, but there was one from Aiden Adkins. Seeing his name stamped home how talking with him had felt like another lifetime ago with everything that happened since.

She opened the banker's email and scanned it. "We've got the names and contact numbers for the bank's inspector, estimator, real estate agent, and contractor. Looks like the estimator is in Mexico on vacation and has been since last week. One person we can rule out. Aiden said he's been dealing with Ester Hansen at County Services. Gives us someone to ask for."

Trent started the car and pointed to the clock on the dash. *3:20 PM.* "We have plenty of time to make it over there. They probably close at five."

"Let's do it."

As Trent drove away, Amanda looked at Sean and Tara's house. She wished she could just storm inside the place, snatch Tara, and get her to see the light. But her efforts would likely be useless. She just wished the same couldn't be said for their list of potential suspects. Surely, their killer had to be on there somewhere.

CHAPTER TWENTY-TWO

It was three thirty when Trent pulled into the lot for County Services. The sign posted on the door confirmed they closed at five, but that left Amanda and Trent plenty of time to ask the questions they needed.

The woman at the front desk greeted them as she shuffled a stack of papers from one side of her desk to the other.

"Hi." Amanda offered a kind smile and pulled her badge. "I'm Detective Steele, and this is Detective Stenson with the Prince William County PD. We'd like to speak with Ester Hansen if she's in."

"Ah, that's me, but I'm not sure why the police would want to speak with me."

"Your name came up during an investigation. There was a house fire in east Dumfries yesterday morning, and a body was found inside the home. You might have heard about it on the local news." Amanda hated giving any glory to the media, but it was an easy way to establish a foundation for the conversation.

"Yeah, I did." Ester's shoulders sagged, and her face went blank. "Why are you interested in me?"

"Woodbridge Bank owned the property and has informed us that they were waiting for approval from this office before they could put the place on the market. You're the bank's contact."

"What's the address?" Ester poised her fingers over her keyboard.

"Five thirty-two Bill Drive."

"Oh, I'm familiar with that address." She sank back in her chair. "Let me guess. It was Aiden Adkins who sent you."

"He gave us your name."

"Mr. Adkins… He's, um, persistent, always asserting himself and applying pressure on me to get things moving faster. He doesn't seem to grasp there's a procedure and a queue."

Amanda could imagine Aiden being that way, but she couldn't blame the man with the way he'd painted management hanging over his head. "We're just trying to determine everyone who may have been aware the property was sitting empty. I assume you were?"

"Yes, of course, but…" Ester's voice trickled off into nothingness.

Amanda didn't see anything in Ester's demeanor that spoke to her being a heartless killer who took out a teenage girl. Her hands were also small and feminine, not large enough to match the bruising on Doe's neck. "Who goes out and does the inspections? Is it someone within this office?"

"No, third parties are used."

"Who was assigned to inspect the work done at five thirty-two Bill Drive?"

"I might be able to find out."

"Might?" Amanda pressed.

"Well, depending on how far out it is in the schedule, it may not have been assigned to anyone yet. I'll check." Ester tapped away on the keyboard. "Okay, so that property isn't booked for inspection yet so that means the wait is longer than two weeks. Usually that's how far in advance appointments are firmed up."

"Who has access to the calendar?" Trent asked.

"Pretty much everyone in this office, but they'd have no reason to look."

Unless they are a psychopathic killer looking for a place to dump a body and burn down… But she and Trent couldn't exactly pull records or speak with everyone who worked in the county's office. Maybe Ester could point them in someone's direction. "Is there anyone in this office who has been a little 'off' maybe, or who has shown an interest in that property recently?"

Ester held up a hand, and her mouth was twitching, like she was fending off laughter. "Sorry, I know none of this is funny." She sought out Amanda's eyes as if to stamp home the apology. Amanda saw a woman battling with shock, and levity being her defense against it. The clerk continued. "It's just the entire bunch here is a little 'off,' me excluded, of course." She paused to insert a small chuckle. "But no one stands out and fits what you'd be after. At least not that I've noticed."

Amanda nodded, disappointed, and handed Ester one of her cards. "Call if you think of anyone after we leave."

"All right, but don't be waiting by the phone. We might all be nuts, but I don't think anyone here is a killer."

Amanda wasn't going to terrify the woman by saying that murderers were usually the person one least suspected. "Thank you for your help, Ms. Hansen."

Ester nodded, and Amanda and Trent saw themselves out.

Back in the car, she did up her seat belt and leaned against the headrest. "Well, we can't exactly pull backgrounds and visit everyone who works as county inspectors or has access to that database." She was sulking, and she heard it in her voice, but she was frustrated. Fox was dead because she'd dropped the ball with the Doe murder—or at least it felt like it. Not that she'd had a lot of time to work the case.

"We just need to keep moving forward and exhaust the leads we have. It makes sense that the killer knew the house was empty, and it's too soon for us to rule out anyone on our list."

She looked over at him. Trent, her cheerleader. "Look at you. All right, Mr. Positive, what's next?"

"To talk to the bank's inspector?"

"Sure." She pulled up the information the banker had sent them, and said, "Turns out he lives just a few blocks over."

Trent nodded but didn't put the car into drive.

"What are you waiting for?" She pointed out the windshield in much the same fashion Captain Picard did on *Star Trek: The Next Generation*, one of Kevin's favorite television shows. Only Picard would say, "Engage." She found herself smiling.

"The address would be helpful." He was laughing.

"Oh, that?"

*

Over the next few hours, Amanda and Trent ruled out the bank's inspector, the real estate agent, and the contractor. None of them looked good for Doe's murder, but visiting all of them had eaten up time. It was going on eight at night, and they were headed back to Central with full stomachs. They'd stopped for something to eat at a chicken place in Woodbridge.

Otherwise, they were in need of some leads. Even her email inbox wasn't providing anything useful. Rideout hadn't come through with Doe's picture, and there was zero news about the girl's dental records scoring a hit in Missing Persons. Was it too much to hope that they could give the young woman a name after being objectified most of her life?

She looked over at Trent. "What if we're making too much out of the killer knowing the property was empty? And really, how could we even narrow that down? Anyone passing by could have noticed."

"Quite a chance for the killer to take, though, if he didn't know it was going to be left alone for a certain time period."

"Maybe not. The windows were boarded up. That sort of screams it's uninhabited and probably will be for a while. Our killer was likely quite confident no one would be showing up in the early hours of the morning either. But I definitely think he wanted to make a statement by killing her there, or transporting her there…"

"What are you thinking? Something about the history of the home?"

"Not sure."

"It's interesting he returned about twenty-four hours later," he said, "to the same street, no less. He could be drawn there geographically."

She looked over at him. Impressed with him again.

He continued. "I picked that up when I worked with the FBI. Some serial killers can select an area for a reason, such as personal attachment. He could have lived there when he was younger." He pulled into the lot for Central. "Then again, maybe the location doesn't mean anything."

"Don't know, but I'm quite sure our killer has brass balls and an ego the size of a Mack truck."

"Wouldn't doubt that."

Just what they needed—a killer with an inflated sense of self. If so, she'd happily give him a reality check.

CHAPTER TWENTY-THREE

Amanda and Trent spent a couple of hours slogging away at their desks, reading police interviews from both crime scenes, and studying photos of the crowd. Nothing was standing out. By ten thirty, her vision was starting to blur, but it probably didn't help that she'd hardly slept last night. Still, she felt by going home she was giving up on both Doe and Fox. But sometimes calling it a day and getting a fresh start was the most productive thing to do.

"I'm heading out," she told Trent as she stood. "You can, too, if you want. We can get an early start."

"Works for me. I'm beat." He hadn't needed to say it; his cheeks were red, as they often got when he was tired.

He left ahead of her, and she got in her car to go home. She could really handle popping a sleeping pill, climbing into bed, and shutting out the world. She honestly needed a break from everything—the investigations and the matter with her mother, and how it made her feel so damn responsible.

She thrummed her fingers on the steering wheel as she drove, trying to shove the murders from her mind but having a difficult time doing so. It was always frustrating when leads seemed to dry up. It also left her feeling like she was missing something that was right there, but just out of reach.

She was approaching Becky's house, and it was lit all up. Amanda could use some mindless chitchat with her best friend and to maybe veg out on the couch in front of the TV. As she got closer, Amanda noticed there were two cars in her driveway. Only one was Becky's, so she had company. Amanda should probably just keep going, but she found herself pulling in.

She turned off the ignition and looked at her friend's bungalow, which was much like her own. She was just about to restart the car when the front light flicked on.

The door opened, and Becky stepped out. "Amanda? That you?"

Amanda got out of her vehicle. "Yeah, it's me."

Another figure stood behind Becky, but it wasn't much more than a shadow until the person stepped into the light. Brandon Fisher, Becky's FBI boyfriend. Amanda groaned a little internally. It wasn't that Amanda didn't like him—okay, maybe it was. He could have treated Becky a lot better, and even though they seemed to be in a good place right now, they'd had their rough patches. Becky had shared it all with her, including that Brandon had been romantically involved with a member on his team and the two still worked together.

"I should go." Amanda jacked a thumb over her shoulder. "Leave you guys alone."

"Just get in here." Becky rolled her arm in a big, welcoming wave.

Amanda felt her heart lift, and she locked her car doors with her fob and jogged up the front walk.

Becky hugged her. "Everything all right?"

"Why wouldn't it be?" Amanda drew out of the embrace.

"Ah, let's see. You're at my door at almost eleven at night, unannounced."

"I thought we were close enough that a heads-up call wasn't necessary, no matter the time of day."

"Never is. Doesn't mean it isn't suspicious." Becky smiled at her. "Come in."

Brandon shuffled back to allow them more room. He pressed his lips and dipped his head as a greeting.

"Hi, Brandon," Amanda said. She sometimes forgot that he had red hair too. It still didn't mean she had to like him.

"I'll just go turn off the TV." He headed for the living room, which was visible from the front door.

He sounded pleasant enough and not irritated by the interruption to his evening with Becky. Maybe he wasn't that bad. Her friend seemed to love him, so he had to possess good qualities. Also in the "pro" column was his career in law enforcement. Although, if she bought into her father's criticism of feds, that would add a mark in Brandon's "con" column. According to her father, feds were a bunch of conceited jackasses.

"As long as you're sure I'm not messing up your night."

"Nonsense," Becky shot out. "Something's obviously bothering you, and Brandon doesn't mind."

He was fiddling with remotes and didn't say anything.

"Want something to drink?" Becky asked. "We're drinking wine, but I know I won't be talking you into that."

Tonight, it did sound tempting, but she hadn't had a sip of booze since the drunk driver had wiped out her family. She'd patronized several bars in the last few years, but only to pick up her one-night stands. "I'll have some water."

"You got it. Just sit where you'd like." Becky headed for the kitchen, and Amanda slipped out of her shoes and sat in an overstuffed chair, which was her favorite piece of furniture in the home. A person could lose themselves in the hug of foam and suede.

Brandon dropped onto the couch and took a sip of his wine. As he lowered the glass, he met Amanda's gaze and smiled.

They'd never exactly bonded, but in fairness, they hadn't spent a lot of time around each other.

"How's everything going in your world? FBI, right?" She put it out there like she was clueless.

"Yep. Profiler with the Behavioral Analysis Unit." Short and blunt.

She'd guess he didn't really like her a lot either, but they didn't need to be friends. They just needed to tolerate each other for Becky's sake. Still, there was something in the way his eyes darkened when he mentioned his job that sparked a thought. That's if she bought into things happening for a reason. As an FBI profiler, he might be able to lend some ideas on her current investigations. She'd opened her mouth, about to ask him a question, when Becky stepped in front of her with her drink.

"Thank you." Amanda took the glass from her friend and guzzled back some water.

Becky sat on the opposite end of the couch from Brandon, moving a throw blanket aside.

"Is this one of those times you just want to watch TV with me, or do you want to talk about what's bothering you?" Becky asked.

Amanda glanced at Brandon, back at Becky. "I had just wanted to hang out, but now that I see Brandon's here, maybe I could run the cases I'm working past him." She realized how she was talking to Becky, as if seeking her permission and implying Brandon didn't have a say. "I mean if you're okay with it?" she said to him.

It was Becky who groaned softly, then did her best to cover her dissatisfaction.

Amanda met her friend's gaze. "We don't have to. It is Friday night, and no one's on the clock. You—" she gestured toward Brandon "—especially would probably prefer to talk about anything else but murder. You track serial killers all day, and now here I am wanting to talk about the killer I'm after."

Brandon's posture stiffened, but he leaned slightly forward, showing an interest. "I wouldn't say *all* day."

Amanda cleared her throat. "What is a serial killer anyway… by definition?"

"Not a textbook definition," Brandon started, "but serial killers usually kill over a span of time. They often have a signature—something that makes them unique, though not always. They typically adhere to a murder method—then again, not always."

Amanda caught Becky's eye, and they smirked at each other.

"There's obviously a little flexibility with the *definition*." Becky attributed finger quotes to the last word and chuckled.

"Yeah," Brandon admitted, "but normally more than three victims. Many of them have a type too, so you'll notice similarities in victimology. Do you think you have a serial killer?"

Becky's eyes widened at Amanda. "Do you?"

"I don't know," Amanda admitted, feeling defeated yet again. "What I do know is I've had two murders fall into my lap within twenty-four hours, and there is a connection between the victims."

"Oh," Brandon said.

She took in his facial expression. His mouth had tightened, and the corners angled down. Not quite a frown but smacking of one. "What?" she asked.

"Tell me some details."

She had a bad feeling, given his grim countenance, that he was already thinking *serial killer*. "The first victim was a teenage girl pulled from a house fire. We still don't know her identity."

"Really?" This from Becky as she curled her legs beneath her and leaned against the arm of the couch.

Amanda shook her head. "And I'm still waiting on a photo I can use."

"Were her remains badly affected?" Brandon asked.

"No. The fire was stopped before it could damage the body. She'd been strangled before the fire was started."

"And the other murder you feel is connected?"

"A woman in her forties, killed in her home on the same street. Cause of death is not confirmed yet, but it seems she was drugged and stabbed. The second victim was the person who called nine-one-one about the fire. Her tongue had been cut out and left in her palm. We're waiting on toxicology results, but it's possible both victims were drugged."

"Oh." Brandon glanced at Becky, back to Amanda.

A second *oh* in about as many minutes didn't bode well. She pressed on. "We've looked into the second woman's life, but no one is standing out with motive to kill her. My partner and I—"

"Hey, do you remember Trent Stenson?" Becky interjected, posing the question to Brandon.

"Do I remember Trent? Ah, yeah. Kind of hard to forget that guy."

Amanda wasn't sure how to read Brandon's reaction. Was it in favor of Trent or against?

"Tell me, is he still gung-ho?" he asked. "When he helped us with a case, he had lots of fire and zeal but lacked control. Got himself shot. Twice. Interesting how he wound up with the Prince William County PD and landed in Homicide."

Amanda shouldn't be surprised that Brandon knew exactly where she worked and for what department. "Interesting in what way?"

"I got the feeling he wanted to advance rank and work for a bigger police department. Looks like that's exactly what he accomplished."

"Yep. Living the dream." She chuckled. "He came on as my partner back in January."

"Huh." Brandon took another drink of his wine, then turned serious again. "As you were saying, you have considered a serial killer?"

"We discussed the possibility, but we figured to qualify as such there would be more victims involved."

"Could be ones you don't know about."

"That's a chilling thought."

"He could also just be getting started. I must admit I'm concerned by how fast he moved on to his next victim."

"Yeah. I was also thinking it was disturbing that—assuming it's the same killer for both victims—he's demonstrated versatility."

"He's also shown that he's not going to let anyone get in his way and stop him," Brandon added. "By cutting out that woman's tongue, it sounds to me like he's definitely sending a message. Same with putting the house on fire with the girl inside."

"Trent and I thought that too. Why burn her rather publicly? And does the location factor in?"

"Good questions. As for the fire, it's often associated with cleansing and purification. The location... Well, it could be that your killer is making a statement with that too. It could also be that he's recreating something from his own life. Besides the nine-one-one call, is there anything else that connects the victims?"

"Not that we've discovered. The young girl was tattooed with the mark of a sex-trafficking ring."

Brandon's eyes darkened. "Can you connect the second victim to that world?"

She shook her head. "Not from anything we've found out so far."

Brandon pursed his lips, in obvious thought. "I don't have a lot of information to go on here, but often killers who take out prostitutes and the like—"

"We're talking about a sixteen-year-old girl," Amanda snapped. She might be a little touchy, given the girl's age—and how dare the killer proclaim himself on the same team as her? She amended her outburst with a calmer summary. "It's not like it was her choice. She would have been manipulated and coerced into that lifestyle."

"You and I know that, but the killer may see it differently." Brandon's cool demeanor in the face of the victim's stated age surprised Amanda, but then again, he probably faced the worst murders imaginable. He went on. "There are four different types of serial killers: thrill seekers, visionaries, power or control seekers, and mission-oriented killers. It's very early yet to determine which category your killer falls into. Given the girl's history, though, perhaps he sees it as his duty to clean up society. He may see the world as a better place without certain types in it."

"She was just a child." Her heart was aching with rage and grief.

"He may have still held her accountable. Remember I'm going on the little I'm being given here, and it usually takes a lot more to build a profile. But one thing with mission-oriented serial killers is they can be easier to track down because they have a specific type. The second victim could have been killed simply because he saw her as blocking his mission. This type of killer is also rarely clinically insane. They often hold jobs and have stable and reliable lives. They are typically native to the geographical area in which they kill. They are organized and usually plan meticulously for their crimes."

Trent might have been on to something when he'd brought up geography, but it didn't help Amanda to think their killer was in his right mind. And there was that taunting note...

"The killer left me a message," she said.

Brandon's gaze flicked to Becky, then back to Amanda. Becky's eyes were on Amanda as well, her mouth agape.

"What do you mean, a message?" he asked.

Amanda got to her feet and walked around the back of the chair, then stood there bracing herself on it. "I found a note at Lindsey's grave." She glanced at Becky. "It was addressed to me."

"You never said anything to me about that." Becky sounded almost wounded.

"I've been busy." Truth was, she didn't want to go around sharing that news with everyone—not even her best friend.

Brandon inched forward on the couch. "What did it say?"

"That we're on the same team, and to be thankful that my angel—Lindsey—would always stay innocent."

"Huh. He definitely wants acknowledgment and credit for his murders."

"That thought had occurred to me."

"This note could tell us that he lacked approval and acceptance in his own life. Possibly childhood abuse or neglect. The note could be seen as a cry for attention and approval, but don't dismiss that there's definitely a threat enclosed. See, as long as he considers you an ally and you're not hindering his actions, he's fine with you. Do you have any idea what put you on his radar to begin with?"

"I have my thoughts… The first girl was branded, as I told you. I was in the local news back in January for rescuing fifteen girls from a sex trafficker. Still not sure how that puts us on the same team. I helped them. He killed one."

"Yeah, it's hard to know where his head's at exactly. But it would seem apparent he justifies his actions, even sees them as necessary to achieve his end goal, whatever that turns out to be. I still say there may be some connection in his personal history that will intersect with human trafficking. Possibly just sexual abuse. And it is possible that he saw that article you mentioned, and it served as a trigger for him. He could have been drawn to you, figuring you'd understand him. Hence the note."

Her legs buckled, but she retained her composure as far as they would see. It was one thing for her to consider that possibility and another to hear it coming back at her. But how could her doing a good thing have potentially set a psychopath on a killing spree?

"He could also idolize you in a way," Brandon said. "But don't miss the message that he's giving you. He wants you to know that he can get to you." His face went very somber. "He's demonstrating a very volatile and fragile psyche, Amanda. You should watch your back."

"Wow. So happy I stopped by." She laughed stiffly, trying to make light of what Brandon had said, but her attempt fell heavy in the room. "Maybe we're just getting ahead of ourselves. The killing could stop here."

Brandon locked eye contact with her. "I hope so, but I don't think it will until you stop him."

She gripped tighter on the back of the chair, then flailed her arms. "I'm open to any suggestions. I've never hunted a serial killer before."

"Well, serial killers don't become such overnight. There are contributing factors."

"Like childhood abuse, which you've mentioned." Amanda kicked that back with a smile. She really wanted to make light of this conversation because honestly it was scaring the shit out of her. This guy had been at her daughter's grave. He knew that he could reach Amanda there. What else did he know? Where she lived?

Becky smiled awkwardly, as if to support Amanda.

"Not always. That was just one possibility I mentioned. He could have been affected by something else during his childhood or teenage years. This could have made him feel invisible, something that greatly hurt him. He could have witnessed something or had a loved one who wounded him by becoming a prostitute, maybe even a victim of sex trafficking."

"That would be crazy if that's the case. These girls don't exactly sign up for it."

Brandon angled his head. "What we call crazy, serial killers justify in their minds. They're not wired like the rest of us."

"Not disputing that." She sat back down.

"You might want to look up previous cases that involved some of the parameters from these two cases. It doesn't have to be all of them. Say, young women who were victims of arson and/or strangulation, and so on. I could have my go-to analyst run a search in ViCAP for you."

Amanda was familiar with the FBI's Violent Criminal Apprehension Program. It was a database that housed unsolved crimes, but any searches needed to be handled through the FBI. "I'd have to get something like that approved by my sergeant."

"If you end up deciding you want to go ahead, let me know. But you could very well find your killer by looking at closed cases too. He may have served time and recently gotten out. I would recommend getting a media ban in place. Sounds like this guy wants the spotlight, and you'd be further ahead not to shine it on him."

At least she'd sort of done something right. She had sent Diana Wesson away in her *PWC News* van.

"More importantly, and I can't stress this enough—" Brandon let those words hang for a minute, his voice sullen, before continuing "—really watch your back with this one."

Goosebumps pricked her flesh. They were after a monster and had no idea which closet to find him in.

CHAPTER TWENTY-FOUR

It was midnight, the fresh start of a new day. Nothing yet had hit the news about Fox's murder. Probably all because Detective Steele had shut them down. He'd seen her turn that reporter away. How could she be so obtuse? His message needed to get out, and she had stopped that from happening. She had made herself his enemy, and he felt betrayed. Just like all those years ago when he'd been stung by the same emotions—the rejection, the abandonment, the utter helplessness. The invisibility. The detective would pay for what she'd done. He just had to figure out the best way to hit her. Because when he did, he wanted it to be such a blindside, she'd be spinning. That thought brought a smile to his face.

He looked down at his arm where Fox had clawed him. The skin had welted from her attack. He just hoped she hadn't infected him with something.

He grabbed a bottle of hydrogen peroxide from the medicine cabinet over the sink. It was probably expired, but it would have to do. He grabbed a tissue from his pocket and dabbed at the wound. No sting. He swiped the area, cleaning it yet again. Still feeling nothing but emotional angst. Rage, heartbreak, and confusion whirled like a tornado within him.

How could the detective turn on him like she had? Had she not received his message at the grave? Did she not appreciate how important his work was? No one ever seemed to understand him.

He caught his eyes in the mirror. They were dark and clouded, unlike his mind and soul, which were, in a lot of ways, clearer than ever.

He returned to the sitting area in his loft and logged into his laptop. He checked online again to see if anything had hit the news about Fox, and there was nothing. He balled his hands into fists. Detective Steele would pay for this. The public had a right to know about his work, and couldn't the detective see how meaningless Fox's death was without the message getting out?

He brought up an article on the fire, from two days before, and settled on the reporter's name. Fraser Reyes. He should just call this Fraser guy and get him to tell the story. He could keep his anonymity, block his number, and say he was a neighbor—or even a friend of Fox's friend. He'd seen the woman hugging the yoga mat and sobbing. She was the one who had found Fox, and she must have been close to her.

But he had to think this through. Did he want to make the call? Was there any way it could be traced back to him? But from what he understood, reporters protected their sources. It could work out blessedly.

The contact page on the newspaper's website took him to an online form.

He'd pass. That wasn't what he wanted.

He dug around the internet and found Fraser Reyes's LinkedIn page. There was a phone number listed on his profile—out in the open for anyone to see.

He went into his phone's settings and chose to hide his number. Then he entered Fraser's digits into his phone and stared at it, his finger poised over the call button.

It was time the public knew what was going on in Prince William County and also what Fox's so-called heroic act had brought her.

He placed the call, and it rang to voicemail. He hung up immediately. He'd try again in a few minutes. What kind of journalist wasn't sitting by their phone, regardless of the hour?

More anger whirled through him, his leg bouncing wildly. *Now what?*

He'd consider how to get even with the detective, while staying focused on his mission. Should he kill her or toy with her?

He took his laptop and went into the farmhouse. There was no sign of his mother. She must have been puttering around the place somewhere, but he was happy for the solitude right now. Though that wasn't always the case. He used to be a people person. He preferred team sports to solitary ones. The deer hunts his father took him on were some of the most horrible days of his childhood. There was no bonding, just his father's desire to groom his son into a skilled archer, which had failed—though he was good at the gutting and skinning of the animal.

But when it came to baseball, he was part of a team. He became so good at the sport that he'd received a college baseball scholarship. Not that the gift had led anywhere. He was still invisible to the people who should have loved him the most. His grades suffered, and so did his game. No baseball scout wanted him.

Even if he'd taken up bronc riding like his mother had wanted, that probably wouldn't have been enough for her to really notice him. He was invisible because of *her.*

He sniffled and clenched his jaw. *She* could do nothing wrong—even when she did. But enough of that! He was finally taking hold of the reins of his life and seizing control. No wonder his mother was proud of him now and finally paying attention.

He made himself a coffee and set his laptop on the kitchen table as he waited for it to brew. He also took out his phone and tried that journalist again.

"Hello. Reyes here."

Fraser had answered, and the shock of it rendered him momentarily mute.

"Hello?" Fraser repeated.

"Hi." The one word scraped from his throat.

"Who is this?"

He felt on the spot and panicked. "I know something you need to know."

"Let's start with names. Yours would be?"

"No names, but I think there might be a serial killer in Prince William County."

There was a long pause on the other end of the line, then, "What makes you say that?" There was hesitation and trepidation in Fraser's voice.

He tried to suppress his amusement. He didn't want his smile to travel the line. "My friend's friend was murdered."

"Keep talking."

And that's what he did. He told the journalist probably more than he should have. He mentioned the severed tongue, but surely Fox's friend would have noted that little touch, so it wasn't a far stretch that she'd, in turn, tell another friend. That's why he went with "friend" not "neighbor."

When he'd finished with the reporter, his coffee was cold, but he couldn't stop smiling. He retrieved his cup and sat with it at the kitchen table.

His spirit felt lighter now, and there was a grace to his steps. To think he hadn't been too sure he could murder a person at first, but it had come so naturally to him. In fact, he wished he'd started killing sooner. But there wasn't anything he could do about that. All he could control was the future.

He'd read that when you were doing something purposeful to your soul, people and circumstances lined up for you and everything progressed smoothly. He was finally experiencing the truth of that.

He cracked his knuckles and got to work on his keyboard. It was time to select his next victim.

CHAPTER TWENTY-FIVE

Amanda had left Becky's around one in the morning. So much for getting a good night's sleep. Brandon's warning kept repeating in her head, along with his conviction that they were very likely looking for a serial killer. There was no room for emotion. She needed to remain grounded and detached. At the same time, she couldn't dismiss the way things were looking and the fact there had been at least one active serial killer in the area before. Trent's bullet scars were a testament to that.

She was at Central now in front of her computer, a black coffee within easy reach of her left hand. The clock on the wall told her it was just approaching eight o'clock, and she had been there for an hour already. It was Saturday morning, so there weren't too many other people milling about, and the room felt peaceful. She'd texted Trent to meet her at the station when he got the message.

Rideout still hadn't come through with Doe's picture, but she had received a message from Sullivan. The fire marshal had forwarded over some sketches and photos of inside 532 Bill Drive. He also confirmed that gasoline was the accelerant used to start the fire. Included in his packet were transcribed interviews with a few firefighters who had removed Jane Doe from the room and house. Spencer Blair was one of them.

His statement was straightforward. He went upstairs, found the bedroom door open, and the victim lying on the mattress. She was on her back and appeared to be staring at the ceiling. He tried to rouse her, but there was no response. He made the call to remove her from the house and hand her over to a medic.

Amanda brought up the photo of the room where Doe had been found. The head of the mattress was against the back wall. It and the drywall didn't even look touched by the fire. There also didn't appear to be any personal possessions in the area.

Her cell phone rang, and she answered without consulting the caller ID.

"Detective Steele?" It was a woman's voice, and she was very guarded.

Amanda held out her phone. *P Jeffery.* The ME. "It is. Paula Jeffery?"

"I'm calling to let you know I've scheduled Fox's autopsy for this afternoon at one o'clock."

"Thank—" She never got the full expression of gratitude out before Jeffery hung up. The woman wasn't exactly Miss Congeniality.

Amanda was getting ready to read more interviews when her phone rang again. *H Rideout.* She answered formally.

"Detective, you'll be happy to know that I've just emailed you Jane Doe's picture."

She was happy but also felt it was about time. "Good news."

"I ran her dental impression through Missing Persons but no hits. I have forwarded a sampling of her DNA to Forensics to be analyzed and entered into the system. As you know it will take time for them to process that, though."

It could take months, but she didn't want to dwell on the limitations of science, technology, and administrative backlogs. Results could come faster if a law enforcement agency was willing to foot the bill for a private lab, but that expense was rarely approved. Now, maybe if they proved there was an active serial killer and other lives were in immediate danger, they'd be able to get the go-ahead. Until then, she'd have to wait it out. There was nothing like the feeling of having your hands tied.

"I heard back about the dragonfly pin," Rideout continued. "It's worth five thousand dollars. Apparently, it's handcrafted, made of gold and mother-of-pearl. As Trent had thought."

"Whoever the true owner was had money." Whether that was Doe or someone she had taken it from, Amanda would need to determine, and she had an idea just how to do that. "What about expediting the tox?"

"I've put in the request to have it moved along. I'll keep you posted."

"Thanks."

"Don't mention it."

She ended the call. A pin worth five grand... Someone had to be missing it. When she'd tried searching Missing Persons with the pin as a parameter, she'd netted nothing. But there was another route they could try. Given the high value of the pin, maybe it had been reported stolen—and that would get them closer to an ID on Doe.

She saw Rideout's email filter in and clicked on the attachment just as Trent came toward her holding two cups from a shop in Woodbridge. Their coffee wasn't as good as Hannah's Diner, but up there.

"Jabba for you." He handed her a cup.

On their first case together, he'd told her about his little sister, who as a kid had gotten *java* confused with *Jabba the Hutt*. And every now and then Trent dropped the expression.

"Thanks."

"Don't mention it. When did you get in?" Trent took a sip of his coffee.

"Early." She went on to fill him in about Fox's autopsy, Rideout's call, and her thinking that the dragonfly pin might have been reported as stolen.

He perched against the edge of her desk. "I can check with Property Crimes."

"Sounds good." She felt the need to come forward with what she'd learned last night too. "I'm not jumping to the conclusion we have a serial killer, but I spoke with an FBI profiler yesterday."

Trent stood. "You're bringing in the FBI?"

Amanda smirked. "Not exactly. But an agent happened to be at Becky's when I went for a visit."

"Brandon Fisher." A conclusion, not a question, and Amanda wasn't sure what to make of Trent's tone—excitement or distaste.

"Good guess."

"Well, it's not a secret that Becky's seeing him. You talked to him about our investigations?"

"I did, and he thinks it might be the work of a—"

Natalie Ryan, a.k.a. Cougar, another homicide detective, walked past Amanda's cubicle, and smiled in greeting. They smiled back.

When Cougar was out of earshot, Amanda finished her statement. "Brandon thinks we should seriously consider a serial killer is at work here."

Trent had this expression on his face that was a mix of fear and excitement. "I told you."

"No, you don't get to do that."

Her chastisement didn't stop him from smirking his I-told-you-so smirk.

"I'm still keeping an open mind," she said, clinging stiffly to the idea.

"Uh-huh. So what did he suggest?"

She told him that Brandon thought their killer might have murdered before and that he also might have been affected by something similar earlier in his life. Possibly something involving a loved one.

"Perfect. I can get behind that."

"We only have two bodies, but his analysis was persuasive. We should look at similar closed cases. He could have served time, gotten out. I might be able to start searching if you stop interrupting me," she teased.

"Surely you're not complaining that I brought you a coffee."

"Would never dream of it." She laughed. When they'd first been partnered, Trent had been an easygoing guy—so easygoing that it had rubbed her the wrong way. As she'd come to discover in the last three months, he could return sass just as easy as she could dish it out. "Don't you have a phone call to make?"

"Fine. I'll reach out to my contact in Property Crimes and see what he says." He went over to his cubicle.

"You do that." She was smiling as she turned her gaze to her monitor again. The expression faded at the sight of the windows she had up. One was Spencer's interview, one was a picture of the room where Doe had been found, and the other was Doe's computer-rendered photo.

Amanda took in Doe's round face, milky complexion, blond hair, and brown eyes. So young, and to have known so much evil. All the bruises to her body and the pummeling of her spirit—the girl hadn't stood a chance in this life. There was something far more heartbreaking seeing her this way than in the back of the medic's vehicle or even on the slab at the morgue. Here she was, a combination of pixels, like she had never been real. The face looking back at Amanda was not only lifeless, but cold and sterile.

She heard Trent on the phone and held out hope the call would get them somewhere in identifying her.

"Uh-huh… Just repeat that one more time?" A few seconds later, Trent proceeded to rattle off an address that presumably his caller had given him. "Thanks." He shot to his feet and ran around to her cubicle. "A dragonfly pin matching the description of the one with Jane Doe was reported stolen three years ago by Leila and Henry Foster out of Washington."

She pulled a background on the Fosters. "They have a daughter named Crystal…" She opened the Missing Persons database and keyed in Crystal Foster, and the report popped up immediately. There was a photo attached, and it could have been their Jane Doe.

"Foster was reported missing three years ago. She was thirteen. That means if she's our victim, she *was* only sixteen when she died." Amanda mulled on that. "Just a child." She scanned the personal effects section for any mention of the pin. She found gobbledygook that might have been meant to spell "dragonfly pin." Likely a bad case of fat-finger syndrome.

She looked at the photo again, impossible to tell for certain if it was their Jane Doe, but they should speak to the Fosters. She got to her feet. "Time for a road trip."

"Okay," he dragged. "But you know who they are, right?"

"You mean besides possibly being the parents of a murdered girl?"

"They own Protect It, a publicly traded security firm. One of the largest in North America."

"Am I supposed to be impressed?"

"No, but you might not be able to just go up to their door and get an audience."

"Do they put their pants on one leg at a time like the rest of us?" She raised an eyebrow.

"Yes."

"Then, they're human, and their daughter may be lying in the morgue. Trust me, they'll want to speak with us."

CHAPTER TWENTY-SIX

By the time Amanda and Trent had briefed Malone and made it to Washington, it was nearing eleven in the morning. They arrived at the Fosters' house, which was regal and spoke of money. Hired help answered the door and saw Amanda and Trent to a parlor. High ceilings, large windows, and wainscoting accentuated the space, and the morning sun drenched the room with light and warmth.

"Mrs. Foster will be with you shortly," the woman said.

"Thanks," Amanda told her.

The woman left, but neither Amanda nor Trent sat down on the high-end furniture that looked like it should be observed rather than used. Crystal wouldn't have lacked for anything financially, but that didn't mean she wasn't neglected in other ways. Amanda couldn't brush aside Doe's childhood broken bones and that they could mean possible abuse. But was Jane Doe Crystal Foster?

"Detectives?" A blond woman with blue eyes, dressed meticulously in a white silk crepe pantsuit, entered the room.

Amanda bridged the gap. "I'm Detective Amanda Steele."

"Yes, and you?" The woman looked past her to Trent, who stepped forward, holding out a hand to accompany his introduction.

The woman disregarded his proffered hand and crossed her arms loosely. "I am Leila Foster, though I'm sure you know that. Henry should be joining us shortly." Leila lowered herself gracefully into a rose-patterned wingback chair. She sat with her legs tight together and clasped her hands in her lap. "Please. Sit."

Amanda and Trent did as she asked.

"On the phone you said you may have news about Crystal." Leila tilted out her chin.

Trent had convinced Amanda to call ahead on their way there.

"We believe—" Amanda was interrupted by a tuneful chime that started playing throughout the house.

"Never mind that," Leila said. "It's just the doorbell, and Tonya will get it. Henry's likely here now. Please continue."

It would seem the couple lived separately. "Let's just wait a minute for him." She smiled politely at Mrs. Foster and got the feeling she wasn't used to being told what to do.

The woman pursed her lips and stared blankly across the room.

"Mr. Foster to see you," Tonya announced at the entrance to the parlor.

At her side was a forty-something man dressed in suit and tie—both of which probably cost more than Amanda's car—with gray hair and brown eyes.

"Hello," he said to those in the room and settled his gaze on his wife.

Her eyes were ablaze, and it was obvious that the couple was in a rough patch—may have been for a while.

Henry sat down in a chair farthest from his wife. "When Leila called, she said you'd found Crystal?"

Amanda hadn't exactly said that. Instead she'd kept things very vague and simply said she wanted to speak with them about their daughter. "Too soon to know yet, but we have questions we'd like to ask." She paused there to take in the Fosters' reactions. Leila was stoic, but Henry's eyes were watery.

He cleared his throat. "What unit are you with?"

"Homicide."

Leila gasped slightly and paled.

Henry gulped. "Then you believe she was, uh, murdered?"

"Let's not jump ahead quite yet." She smiled kindly at him. People like Henry always made her uncomfortable with how they wanted bad news delivered without delay, as if that would somehow make it easier to absorb. It was a "get it done and out of the way" mentality. But it was usually those people who had the hardest time processing loss. Amanda should know; she was one of those people. "I have a photo I'd like to show you. Now, please keep in mind that this girl was estimated to be sixteen. We understand that your daughter went missing three years ago, so if it is her, you may notice some differences." Amanda pulled up the picture on her phone and did the rounds, holding the screen for each in turn. "Does that look like your daughter?"

Henry was biting his bottom lip while Leila's expression lacked emotion, like she'd barricaded herself behind a wall to avoid feeling anything.

"It could be." Henry looked at his wife, but she wouldn't meet his gaze. "Leila," he prompted.

She looked at him now, but like before, there was a fire that burned in her eyes when she met her husband's gaze. "It could be her, but it's hard to say for sure. Where did you get that?" She flicked a finger toward Amanda's phone, indicating the picture. "It looks computer rendered."

Henry glanced over at Leila again, and his shoulders sagged. He turned to Amanda. "Is she dead?"

There'd be no more putting it off. "The girl pictured is, yes, but we need to determine if she was, in fact, your daughter," Amanda started. "There was a dragonfly pin found with her, and it had the engraving 'to our dear Crystal' on the back. You had reported it—"

"I told you it would get our girl back," Leila burst out and faced her husband.

Henry clenched his jaw, and tapped the arm of his chair, but said nothing.

Amanda thought she might have figured out what was going on here. "You reported the pin as stolen in the hopes that it would be found and, in turn, deliver your daughter to you?"

"That's right." Leila picked at something on her pant leg.

"The pin was a gift for her thirteenth birthday," Henry volunteered. "That was four months before she disappeared. I can't imagine her letting it out of her sight." His eyes darkened as if he may be giving himself over to accepting that his daughter was dead. He added, "She loved dragonflies, always had a fascination with them since she was really little. That's why Leila and I decided to get her the pin."

Amanda could tell that Henry hadn't truly let his daughter go, and she could understand the difficulty in that all too well. Letting go was more than a matter of release; it meant acceptance, which was even harder. "Do you know why she ran away?"

"She left us a note saying that she'd be better off on her own," Leila stated.

Amanda wasn't seeing evil in the Fosters, but if the girl in the morgue was, indeed, their daughter, the numerous broken bones and fractures were hard to ignore entirely.

"Did she say why?" Trent interjected.

A few seconds of silence passed before Leila spoke.

"You're probably aware that my husband is the founder and CEO of Protect It."

"We are," Trent replied.

"Well, that kept him busy," Leila added. "It also kept me occupied. The business grew fast, and we were left trying to catch up with everything that was happening. Crystal was three at the time we started the company. Before that, I was often at home. After, I just didn't have the same amount of time. We employed a full-time nanny, and she basically replaced us—only she didn't. Not really. Crystal started acting out and doing things to get our attention. We responded by buying her anything she wanted."

And by doing so, they had rewarded bad behavior and became guilty of neglect. All this by the two people who should have made Crystal the priority in their lives. And maybe the physical abuse hadn't come from the parents, but rather the nanny. Before she could ask about the woman, Henry spoke.

"Crystal got in with some kids at school who loved doing drugs and drinking. At twelve." Henry stopped there and rubbed his jaw. "Who would have thought they'd start so young? I used to criticize the other kids' parents, but after Crystal disappeared, I realized how hypocritical I had been. After all, as Leila said, it wasn't like we were around for our girl. Crystal even got herself hauled in by the cops. I talked them out of laying any charges."

"Like you're a hero." Leila rolled her eyes.

Again, Amanda noted how he'd used the word "disappeared." It was like he still wasn't willing to accept responsibility for his role in Crystal running away. "Why did the cops bring her in?"

"She was caught smoking weed. It could have been worse," Leila said.

"Worse?" Henry snapped back. "She was twelve, Leila."

Leila shook her head. The tension in the room was tangible.

"You mentioned that Crystal had started acting out once the nanny came into the picture?" Amanda asked, hoping to regain control of the conversation.

"It started with her talking back to her teachers and picking fights with other kids," Henry said.

"Was that how she broke her left arm?" Amanda asked.

Leila looked at Henry. Her brows down, lips pressed.

"Crystal never broke any bones," Leila said. "I would have remembered that. Does that mean that this girl you found isn't Crystal?" Her voice cracked.

"But why would this girl—if it's not Crystal—have her pin?" Henry's forehead compressed, and a deep groove formed between his eyes as he looked at Amanda for an explanation.

Amanda found herself discouraged. It seemed their Jane Doe wasn't Crystal Foster, and now they had to figure out how she came into possession of Crystal's pin. Not to mention, by their involving the Fosters, Amanda felt an obligation to find out Crystal's fate. "Mr. Foster, I can't say yet—I don't know. But I'm so sorry we weren't able to give you an update on your daughter."

"No. You can't just leave. You need to find out what happened to her... where she is." Henry's eyes filled with tears as he pleaded.

"We'll do all we can to find Crystal." Amanda refrained from making a promise, but she'd do whatever she could to deliver closure to the Fosters. And she was feeling a touch hopeful. After all, if the pin had made its way to Dumfries, it was possible Crystal had as well. But now, in addition to stopping a potential serial killer, they had another missing girl to find.

CHAPTER TWENTY-SEVEN

Amanda and Trent left the Fosters considering where their new knowledge left them. Crystal had, it seemed, crossed paths with Jane Doe at some point. But when and where?

"How did she get the pin?" Amanda's question tumbled out, and Trent glanced over at her as he drove. "It just seems that our victim and the Fosters' daughter have to be connected..." Her words tapered off, but her mind was spinning like mad. It was as if the link was right there, but she couldn't quite grasp it. She thought about what little she knew about Crystal. It appeared she'd run away because of the all-too-common teenage longing for freedom and thinking she could do better on her own. Physical abuse couldn't be confirmed as they didn't have Crystal's body in the morgue, but her parents had been too busy to be a part of her life. She had acted out, a well-known ploy for getting attention. *Acted out...* Crystal had also fallen in with a bad bunch of kids. Probably associates who understood her, who were close to her—"The card at the memorial," she blurted out. "The one signed off with *C* and the doodle of the dragonfly. The Fosters said that Crystal loved dragonflies. Was Crystal a friend of Doe's? And, if so, did Crystal give Doe her pin? And were they friends for a long time? It's a long shot, but maybe a friend she also ran away with?"

"You think so? The pin was worth a lot. Why would she give it away? And don't you think the Fosters would have said something if their daughter's friend ran away too?"

"Who knows what happened on the streets? But the Fosters were too busy to notice their own daughter, let alone know her friends. Probably." The tiny crack of doubt sank in her gut like a boulder. Either way, she wouldn't forgive herself if she didn't try. "Turn us around. Take us back to the Fosters."

They'd only gotten a couple blocks away, so hopefully Henry would still be there.

She twisted and looked out the back window as if that would get them there faster.

Trent turned them around and pulled into the Fosters' drive just as Henry was getting into his Jag. He stopped, one leg in his car, and stepped back out when he saw them. His brow was furrowed, and he had his cell phone to an ear.

Amanda got out of the department car and went to him, Trent in step with her.

"I'll call you back." Henry pocketed his phone. "Detectives? I thought you said it wasn't Crystal. Did you change your mind?"

Amanda shook her head. "I've got a question for you."

"Sure."

"At the time Crystal ran away, did any of her friends also go missing?" It was a shot in the dark, but one worth taking. As her father always told her, it was better to ask the questions and get nowhere than fail to ask and miss the mark.

The front door opened, and Leila stepped onto the landing. "What's going on?" Her body language was stiff, and she crossed her arms.

Amanda walked to her, and Henry followed, though it felt to Amanda like she was leading him to the execution chair. But this wasn't a conversation she wanted to have the neighbors overhearing.

"I'm just wondering if any of Crystal's friends also ran away around the same time she did?" Amanda said.

"The Lynches," Leila said.

Amanda had expected some denial and protest. "The Lynches? And they are…?" She looked from Leila to Henry, who wore a quizzical expression, like he had no idea.

Leila leveled at glare at Henry. "You really that out of touch?" She turned to Amanda. "The Lynches lived a few doors down. They had a daughter named Ashley. Two nights after Crystal ran away, Ashley's mother came to our door looking for her daughter. She said her daughter was here for a sleepover. First time I'd heard of it. And she certainly wasn't here. Before that night, I'd never met Mrs. Lynch. I've never met their daughter."

"But you'd seen them around before?" Trent asked.

"Sure. I'm not blind, but it's not like I ever paid them any real attention." Leila huffed out a deep breath as if agitated she had been placed in a position in which she felt the need to defend herself. She looked at her husband and jutted out her chin. "Detective Robbins asked us about Ashley Lynch. You really don't remember?"

He flushed but said nothing.

Robbins must have been the detective assigned the missing person cases. They hadn't gotten that far before heading to Washington. Amanda pulled up the picture of Jane Doe on her phone again and held it for Leila to see. "Do you think that could be their daughter?"

She shook her head. "Honestly, as I said, I never met her or paid the family any real attention."

"Did Crystal ever mention having a friend named Ashley?" Trent asked.

Leila looked at him. "No."

Amanda wasn't taking that as confirmation. From the picture the couple had painted of their family life, she'd probably been optimistic that they could have named any of their daughter's friends. But Amanda's gut instinct about returning to the Fosters' seemed like it might pay off. "Do the Lynches still live just down the street?" Amanda looked left and right, taking in the other gorgeous houses around them, but would guess, based on Leila's use of the past tense, the Lynches had moved on.

"They live in Michigan now." Leila shrugged and added, "From what I've heard."

"Which house did they live in?" Amanda asked, and Leila flicked a finger down the street and described the house. "Okay, thank you for your time." Amanda turned back toward the department car, and as she and Trent were walking away, the Fosters were in a heated conversation with arms flailing wildly in the air. It ended with a slammed door in Henry's face at about the same time Amanda and Trent got into their vehicle.

"They obviously hate each other," Trent said as he pulled out of the driveway.

"There's a lot of rage, that's for sure. And blame."

"What made you think that Crystal ran away with a friend?"

She thought she'd explained it already, but she'd elaborate anyhow. "Crystal was thirteen. She could have run away alone, sure, but her father mentioned that she was involved with the wrong crowd at school. She got pulled in for smoking weed. These kids probably also felt like they were on the outskirts of society for some reason, not understood. I just don't see Crystal leaving solo. She was looking for someplace to belong."

She gestured toward the dash. It was going on eleven thirty. It would take them an hour to get from Washington to Manassas for Fox's autopsy, but they had a little time. "Just pull over, and let's see if we can find the Lynches in the system."

Trent parked at the curb and keyed into the onboard laptop. "The Lynches, Hugh and Sabrina, and, yep, I've got a Michigan address."

"Pull up Missing Persons. Search Ashley Lynch." She could hardly wait for Trent to do that and for the results.

"She's here all right. Thirteen at the time, and the report was filed within a couple of days of the one the Fosters submitted on Crystal."

"The time it took the Lynches to know their daughter was missing and not just at a friend's for a sleepover," Amanda concluded. "Is there a picture?" She leaned over to get a better view of the screen. Trent angled it more toward her.

Staring back at her was a younger version of their Jane Doe. It was in the eyes and unmistakable. "It's her." She sank deep into her seat. She thought that once she had a name, there'd be a level of relief, but it only made her feel more determined to find the girl justice. "We need to get on the road, but when we finish up at Fox's autopsy, we'll dig into Ashley's Missing Persons report and see what the investigating detective had to say. Then we'll go from there."

After the situation with the Fosters, there was no way she'd be reaching out to the Lynches until she was absolutely positive the body of the young woman lying in the morgue was indeed their daughter.

CHAPTER TWENTY-EIGHT

Amanda and Trent stepped into the morgue and found Paula Jeffery in a smock, wearing a helmet—the face shield down—and a bone saw in hand.

"You started without us." Not a question. If Jeffery was getting ready to cut, she'd already conducted an external examination. Amanda was appalled. An ME of Jeffery's experience would know that detectives preferred to be present from the very start of an autopsy. This was just one more indication that Jeffery thought herself above law enforcement.

The ME gestured a hand toward a clock on the wall that was housed behind a metal cage. "You are late."

Amanda read the time. "You said you'd be starting at one. It's five minutes after." They'd grabbed a quick bite to eat, but then ran into an accident on the highway that had resulted in lane closures, delaying them.

"Yes. Late." Jeffery pursed her lips.

"What have you already found out?" Amanda went the diplomatic route. The ME would have started earlier than one to be at this stage of the autopsy, but accusing her wouldn't do Amanda or Trent any favors.

Jeffery lifted the face shield and set the saw aside. "I scraped under the deceased's fingernails and found epithelia."

"I want that fast-tracked at the lab." If it went through the process and garnered a hit, they could be reaching the finish line faster than expected.

"Yes, it is all a priority," Jeffery said drily, and Amanda wasn't sure if she was being snide and sarcastic or serious. The ME added, "And it only helps if the killer is in the system. However, if the skin cells are from her killer, he would probably have obvious scratches on his face, neck, arms, or hands. Think any possible exposed skin. That could help you ID him. Well, once you find him." The ME opened Fox's jaw. "I also took a close look at the mutilation. The edge is clean, not jagged."

"So the killer didn't hesitate?" Trent asked.

"It could also mean that the victim didn't fight the killer while he was cutting out her tongue."

Amanda leaned a little closer to the body. "Then she was dead at that time?"

"No," Jeffery dragged out. "You may recall me saying at the scene that, given the amount of blood loss, her heart would have been pumping. No doubt in my mind she was alive."

"Then, she was given a type of paralytic," Amanda concluded.

"Not necessarily, but something that would have subdued her."

Amanda's phone rang, and the ME pinned her with a nasty glare. Amanda checked caller ID, and it was Malone. "I've got to take this." She stepped away and answered.

"It looks like one of the canvassing officers yesterday might have gotten you a lead," he said.

"Why so late coming in?"

"Just listen to me."

"I'm listening." And she was, but she was also watching Jeffery rolling her eyes. When Malone finished sharing his news, she updated him on the Fosters and told him that there was reason to believe Jane Doe was Ashley Lynch, originally from Washington.

"Nice work. She has a name now."

"Seems so, but I better go. I'm at Fox's autopsy and getting stink eyes from the ME." She ended the call and returned to Jeffery and Trent. "Do you have any more observations to share about the mutilation? Do you think the clean cut is also the result of the killer knowing what he was doing with a knife?"

Jeffery stared at her like she was waiting for an apology for her interruption. She'd be waiting forever. Eventually, the ME said, "Most certainly. Cool under pressure, if nothing else. The victim may not have been able to move, but she likely would have been conscious and watching him."

That thought sent chills through her. Brandon was probably spot-on when he warned her about this killer. He was a true psychopath. Cutting out Shannon's tongue while she watched him… She couldn't imagine the horror that poor woman had experienced in the last few moments of her life. Seeing a man come at her mouth with a knife and feeling—

Amanda stopped her musing there. Hopefully, the drug's effects also numbed pain. Regardless, Shannon would have been powerless, trapped. Amanda swallowed roughly. "Do you know what kind of knife was used?"

The slightest of nods. "Based on the stab wound, I'd say it was a Bowie knife with an eight-inch blade. The same weapon was likely used to sever the tongue."

"A Bowie." Trent stepped closer to the table. "Very sharp. Very large. Commonly used by hunters."

Amanda regarded Trent. Was her partner one? But this revelation was telling about their killer.

"For fear of repeating myself, that's not a small knife," Trent said. "It would have taken skill not to slice into her cheeks."

Jeffery leveled her gaze at him. "Well, based on where the tongue was severed, the killer would have pulled it outside of the mouth, then cut."

"Yeah, I guess that would have made it easier." Trent looked away from the ME.

Amanda pointed toward the stab wound in Fox's abdomen. "At the scene, you weren't sure if this was the cause of death. Now?"

Jeffery moved down the body and held her gloved hands around the wound. "I'm still of the same line of thought. While the penetration of the knife had been deep, I don't believe it was fatal."

Amanda gazed upon Shannon's face and spoke to the ME. "Was it the drug she was given that killed her?"

"In probability and why I'm going to rush the lab on tox results. Hopefully, we'll end up looking at a matter of hours rather than days before we get results."

"Please let me know the findings the minute you do."

"You'll be the third to know. After the lab and me."

"Just one more thing before you start," Amanda said. "Is there any indication that Shannon Fox was raped?"

"No evidence of any sexual activity." Without another word, Jeffery lowered the face shield of her helmet again and retrieved the bone saw from the table. She got to work on the cadaver. Amanda and Trent hung back as Jeffery proceeded with the Y-incision, cutting into the rib cage, and then prying it open. She collected samples of tissue and blood and put them in vials. They stayed until about three thirty before heading out.

On the way back to the car, Amanda turned to Trent. "We've really got to stop this son of a bitch."

"Goes without saying." He smiled softly at her, but the expression didn't reach his eyes.

"Rideout told us that it took a lot of determination for the killer to strangle Doe—I mean, Ashley Lynch." She'd gotten in such a habit of calling her Jane Doe, now her real name was having a hard time sticking. Or maybe it was because as long as she was assigned a label, Amanda could better handle her emotions. "Possibly a lot of hatred," she amended. "Now Jeffery has described Fox's wound as deep—so without restraint. Did he feel hatred toward her? He did mutilate her."

"I'm telling you. He was angry she called nine-one-one."

"Right. Now Jeffery also described the killer as cool under pressure. And he cut out her tongue while she watched." The thought was horrifying, but some light came with the second murder. "Our killer has shown versatility in murder methods and also that he can act quickly. Two people in two days. In the same neighborhood no less. And I bet that's where he really messed up."

"Now you're losing me."

"That was Malone who called me. One of Fox's neighbors, a Chris Ingram, told Officer Wyatt that he saw a jogger the morning of her murder. It might be nothing, but it's a lead we need to follow." She proceeded to tell him the man's address. "Malone's forwarding over a copy of the interview. We'll read it and pull Ingram's background before we knock on his door. But you get us there."

They got into the car, and she read the interview while they drove the thirty minutes back to Dumfries. At least there were no delays this time.

CHAPTER TWENTY-NINE

Amanda was probably starting to hinge too much hope on this eyewitness account about an early-morning jogger panning out, but a detective couldn't be picky as to what leads to follow. Every one needed attention like loose threads on a sweater. Though when applied to an investigation, one wished for a string that, when tugged, ripped apart an entire seam. Real effect and consequence. Sadly, finding them was the tricky part.

When Amanda and Trent got out of the department car at Chris Ingram's house, located at 603 Bill Drive, it was going on four o'clock in the afternoon.

Across the street, a piece of yellow crime scene tape had snagged on a bush in Fox's front yard and flapped in the breeze. She looked toward 532 and saw a growing memorial, but there was no police car.

"Just a minute," she said to Trent as she pulled out her phone and called Malone. Received voicemail. "On Bill Drive following up that lead you gave me and noticed there's no uniform on five thirty-two. Why? Please call me back." Once she finished leaving the message, she noticed a man standing in the front window of Ingram's house.

She and Trent headed up the walk, and the front door was opened before they climbed the stairs and reached the landing.

A man in his forties was studying them.

Amanda held up her badge, as did Trent. She announced them. "Detectives Amanda Steele and Trent Stenson. Are you Chris Ingram?" He looked just like his DMV photo, but it was always best to confirm identification.

"That's me."

"You provided a statement to Officer Wyatt. We have a few follow-up questions we'd like to ask."

"Come in." The offer was extended on a sigh, but Chris stepped back to allow them room to enter.

The house smelled strongly of pine cleaner and gave Amanda an immediate headache.

"Do you have somewhere we could sit?" Trent asked.

Her pounding head was making it hard to fully concentrate. She did note a living room to the immediate right of the entry, though. Zero clutter and the basics: a couch, a chair, a couple of coffee tables, and an entertainment stand. But in place of a TV, there was a fish tank. Maybe that's what the cleaner was trying to cover. Fish could be peaceful—or boring—to watch, but their tanks could stink if they weren't cleaned regularly.

"Here fine?" Chris gestured toward the sitting area.

"Perfect." Trent smiled politely.

Chris sat on the chair, and Amanda and Trent shared the couch.

"You told Officer Wyatt that you saw a man jogging across the street around five thirty yesterday morning." Amanda knew that from reading the officer's interview on the way here.

"That's right."

"I know you provided a description of the man to Officer Wyatt, but could you tell us again, in your own words?" Amanda asked.

"In his thirties, early forties maybe. He had dark hair, trimmed short. Average build and height."

That matched the statement the officer took and was generic as hell. "Had you ever seen him before?" Again, she was aware of what the interview had said but wanted to hear it for herself.

"I don't think so."

Amanda glanced briefly at Trent, as if to instill a teaching moment, but said to Chris, "You told Officer Wyatt that you hadn't seen him before." Changing stories or memories that resurfaced were why she always questioned things that came from a third party.

Chris's gaze flickered just slightly, as if annoyed. "If you know everything I told him, why ask me?"

"Just now, you said that you didn't *think* you'd seen him before. A lot less definitive than you were with Officer Wyatt," she pointed out. "I'll ask again."

"I might have. I'm not sure. He wasn't jogging the other time, though."

Trent and Amanda both inched forward on the couch. He asked, "When and where?"

"Just walking down the street… with a woman?"

She hated it when eyewitnesses responded with a question like they were unsure, but she had to take what she was given. "He was with a woman? Can you describe her?"

Chris took a deep breath, let out a funky moan, and said, "She was blond. Probably about your height."

Amanda was five nine. "Did you get a good look at her face?"

"Nah, it was dark out."

"Early morning or night?" A valid question as the sun didn't rise until closer to seven these days.

Chris rubbed a hand down his face. "I'd been drinking, so it must have been night. Don't ask me the time. Heck, probably why I'm not even sure if I saw him."

She was just going to ignore his self-doubt. "When was this? Recently? A while back?"

"I'd say recently."

"Within the last couple of days?" She was really hoping to narrow the timeline down a tad.

"Yeah, I'd say so."

And there was the gold nugget that Amanda had been looking for—a possible connection to Ashley Lynch. She had been murdered two days ago and was about Amanda's height. Was she the woman Chris was talking about? There was the matter of Chris saying that he saw them at night, and Ashley's time of death was pegged between four and five thirty in the morning. Did that mean the killer had spent time with Ashley before killing her—and doing what? It hadn't been sex because Rideout had found zero evidence of that—consensual or otherwise. But maybe Amanda was getting carried away to think it was Ashley and her killer that Chris had seen. "How old would you say she was?"

"I didn't get a good look."

Amanda continued to mull over the implications of the woman being Ashley and the man her killer. Had he walked with her to 532 Bill Drive? How had he gotten her cooperation? Drugs? Maybe something different than he'd given Shannon Fox, or a smaller, non-lethal dosage? And if the killer had chosen the house, did the geography mean something to him? Was he from this neighborhood? It would allow him to blend in more.

"How did they seem to you?" Trent asked. "Like were they friendly with each other or did she look in distress?"

"She was fine, I guess. Laughing a bit. Unsteady on her feet."

That could be the result of drugs. Whatever the case, Amanda had this strong feeling in her gut that the woman was Ashley. She considered showing him Ashley's computer-rendered photo, but feared he'd easily fall prey to the suggestion and jump on Ashley being who he'd seen with the man. Besides, he had said he didn't get a good look. She was curious, though, why Chris hadn't said anything about the duo when officers would have gone to his house after the fire. Had he simply minimized the importance of a man and woman walking down the sidewalk? She supposed it wouldn't have stood out at the time. But then, when he saw that same man again, jogging on the morning of—and in the vicinity of—a second murder, it came back to his mind. That was plausible.

"You seem awfully interested in this man and the woman from the other day…" Chris eyed them studiously. "Do you think this man is a murderer?"

"Far too soon to say."

"Well, there was a young woman found in the fire," he said. "Then Ms. Fox and what happened to her. I read an article that she's the one who called the fire department. Is that why the killer targeted her?"

"These are open investigations, Mr. Ingram, and I'm not at liberty to discuss them with you." Goosebumps spread across her flesh. People liked to play detective, but she was getting a bad feeling about Chris.

"It had to be because she called nine-one-one." Chris mentioned the call again, sounding quite confident it was what had gotten Shannon Fox murdered.

Tingles spilled over the back of Amanda's neck and down her arms. Their killer wanted attention, and he'd sought her out… What if the story of a jogger had been a ruse to lure them here? Then the additional story of a man and woman to toy with them? Could they be sitting across from the killer they hunted?

"How can you be so sure Ms. Fox was killed for placing the nine-one-one call?" Amanda pushed out.

Chris's gaze flicked to her, to Trent, then to the floor. "I heard her tongue was cut out."

His words didn't relax her. He could claim he'd heard it when he'd actually been responsible. But his soft, almost timid demeanor, calmed her. "Who told you that?"

He tugged on the sleeves of his shirt. "Everyone around here knows."

"Not a direct answer to my question, Mr. Ingram." She leveled a glare at him.

He turned a deeper shade of crimson. "It's just the scuttlebutt in the hood."

"Who did you hear it from?" She was one step away from hauling his butt to the station if he didn't start talking.

"Uh, some guy down the street, lives next to the house that was burned down."

"Name? Number?" Trent inserted, probably sensing her impatience.

"I dunno. He's in his forties and has a bad comb-over. That help more?"

"That it does." She got to her feet and pressed one of her cards into Chris's hand. "See anything suspicious, call me anytime." Depending on how things shook out, they might be back for his alibi just for due diligence.

"Ah, sure."

She left the house and trudged down the sidewalk.

Trent caught up. "Ted Dixon?"

"Sounds like it, but I'd like to know how he found out."

She walked up Ted's path and banged on his front door like his place was on fire. She was mid-knock when he answered. She lowered her hand. "We need to talk to you, Mr. Dixon." She made a move past him into his house.

"Hey, what the— What are you doing?"

"You don't want anyone to see you talking to the cops," she said. "Just honoring your wish and saving us some time."

Trent came inside, too, and Ted closed the door.

"You better have a good explanation for barging in like this." He thrust out his chin and put his hands on his hips.

"We've heard you're spreading rumors about Ms. Fox's murder." She laid out the more innocent explanation, giving him the benefit of the doubt that he was just a gossip.

"You're going to have to give me more to go on here." He swallowed, his throat bulging like a whole rat was going down.

"Really?" She angled her head. "I think you know exactly what I'm talking about."

His peacocked stance started to crumble apart; his shoulders sagged, and his head bowed slightly forward. "I might have heard that her tongue was cut out."

"You heard it, or you did it?"

"What? No!" he burst out. "I swear to you. I just heard about it."

"Who told you?" She hadn't exactly confirmed the mutilation had happened in so many words, but the subtext of the conversation was serving to unnerve Ted.

He rubbed at the back of his neck and worried his lip.

"Mr. Dixon, if you don't start talking, I'm going to assume that you killed Ms. Fox, maybe even the girl from next door. Did you?" she pressed.

"I'd swear on the Bible, no."

"Then where did you hear that Ms. Fox was mutilated?"

"I shouldn't say."

"You absolutely should." She pulled her cuffs out, the threat of arrest implied.

Ted held up his hands and waved. "No, I'll talk. I heard it from a friend of mine."

"You're going to need to get far more specific than that." She snapped the cuffs, and Ted twitched.

"Fraser Reyes," he rushed out.

That name was one she was very familiar with. He was the journalist who wrote a piece a couple of months ago that had gotten her in shit with the LT. "Where did he hear it?"

Chris's forehead beaded with sweat, and he swiped it. "I dunno. Some source. You know how journalists are about things like that."

Source… Her heart was racing. No one outside of law enforcement should have had access to that information—although there was the neighborhood rumor mill and Bethany Greene. But what motive would she have to disclose tidbits from her friend's murder to strangers or the press? It had to be their killer behind this. Had he wanted his story out so badly that he did what he could to make that happen? She hadn't seen the news or read any, but surely if the mutilation had gone public, she would have heard. "Someone told Mr. Reyes?"

"Ah, yeah."

She was ready to hunt down Fraser Reyes, but she couldn't leave without asking Ted another question. She pulled up the photo of Ashley Lynch, justifying this move because he'd mentioned squatters and maybe he could put to rest whether Ashley had stayed at 532 Bill Drive or was randomly taken there. She angled her screen for Ted to see. "Does she look familiar to you?"

Ted leaned in, his eyes squinting. Then he shrugged. "Maybe."

"That's how you want to play this?" she slapped back.

"I'm not just going to say something because you want to hear it, Detective."

"This girl is dead, Mr. Dixon." She stamped home the somber reality.

"Fine, yeah, I saw her around before."

"Squatting in the neighboring house?"

"Maybe."

Amanda took a deep, staggering breath and put her phone back in her pocket. She swung the front door open and spun to say, "Just do us a favor. Stop spreading rumors, and if you hear anything, use the number on the card I gave you." She didn't speak the threat, but if she had to see him again, she'd be taking him in.

Ted mumbled something argumentative, but she didn't have time to deal with him.

She and Trent left. Once they reached the sidewalk, she turned to him. "We're going to talk to Fraser Reyes."

"I had a feeling you were going to say that."

CHAPTER THIRTY

Fraser answered his door in dress pants and a collared shirt, no tie. "Can I help you, Detective Steele?" He danced his gaze over the two of them.

Smug and cocky, and Amanda despised both qualities, but she'd adhere to the adage of getting "more flies with honey." Instead of bulldozing him and accusing him of withholding information from the police, she'd go about matters slightly more diplomatically. "We need to ask you some questions about Ted Dixon. We understand he's a friend of yours."

"All right, but I was just getting ready to go out, though."

"We won't be long." She smiled as genuinely as she could muster, and it had the reporter welcoming them into his home.

A simple apartment but tastefully appointed. He led them to a seating area with six chairs laid out in a basic circle, no couch in sight. He dropped into one wingback, and she and Trent into two others.

"How can I help the PWCPD?" Fraser asked, clasping his hands in his lap.

Interesting question. He hadn't helped them back in January when he'd accused the PWCPD of playing favorites in a murder investigation. All the finger-pointing had landed in her direction and had her facing off with Lieutenant Hill. In response, Amanda's temper had flared, and she'd almost walked away from being a cop for good.

"We understand that you may have come into some information about a recent murder case." She scanned his face, curious if he'd volunteer his knowledge or make her dredge it from him.

"I'm not sure what this has to do with Ted. You said you had questions about him."

Amanda shrugged. "It got us in your door, and Ted's really how we came to be here talking to you."

"I'm not understanding."

"I think you do, but I'll make it clearer for you. A woman, more specifically Shannon Fox, was murdered in her home on Bill Drive," she said.

"Okay." His face was stoic.

She was ready to abandon the whole "flies with honey" thing. It hadn't lasted long, but at least she'd given it a shot. "We know that you found out that her tongue was severed."

"Ah, sure. You read my article?"

"What article?" Her core rushed with molten lava.

He grabbed a tablet from a side table and swept his finger across the screen. "This one." He held it up for Amanda and Trent to see.

The headline read: "Murder and Mutilation in Dumfries."

She shot to her feet and grabbed the device from him and scanned the article. Shannon Fox's name was there, along with the details of the mutilation. She took a few minutes to compose herself and cool her anger, then said in an even voice, "Where did you get this information?"

Fraser glanced from her to Trent, then rubbed his chin. "Ah, a source." Stated calmly with no shame or remorse.

"The PWCPD's Public Information Office is the only source you should be listening to right now. And they aren't saying anything."

"Uh-huh, exactly." Fraser was the epitome of put-togetherness.

"Let me see if I understand your point," she began. "The police aren't talking to you, so you wrote your own story based on some source?"

"Yeah."

"Who's your source?"

"I'm not going to tell you that," he scoffed. "The press has constitutional rights, and the public deserves to know what's happening in their city."

"The police have rights, too, just as Ms. Fox has the right to justice. No one but the victim's friend, the police, investigators, the medical examiner, and the killer knew about the dismemberment. Do you gather where I'm headed with this?"

He sighed dramatically.

Amanda pressed on. "You're hiding behind your *source*." She added finger quotes. She longed to jolt him into speaking. "But maybe you're the source. Did you kill Ms. Fox?"

"That's absurd!" he exclaimed.

"Where were you between four and six Friday morning?" she asked. Fox's time-of-death window.

"I submitted a piece to a newspaper around five that day. I can get you proof of the submission."

"We're going to need that," Trent chimed in and stole Fraser's gaze.

The reporter shrugged. "Hey, I didn't know it was a huge secret."

"Sure you did. That's why you put it in the paper. You wanted admiration for providing that tidbit before anyone else." She paused and scanned his face, and he showed no signs of being bothered by what she was saying. "You need to take that article down immediately." She nudged her head toward the tablet in his hands.

"That's not going to happen."

"You will," she said firmly.

"I won't, and I couldn't if I wanted to. It's with the paper now."

"Let me put it to you this way. I'll make it crystal clear so there's no room for misinterpretation. If you didn't kill Ms. Fox, then your 'source' did." She felt confident in saying that. After all, it seemed apparent that their killer wanted attention for his actions. He'd be the most interested in making sure his story got out there. "Did this person give you their name?"

He shook his head. "He said no names. Many sources prefer anonymity."

"Especially killers or those with something to hide or protect," Amanda rebutted, and she flopped into the chair she'd been in before.

Trent glanced at her and must have sensed she was too angry to continue, so he picked up for her. "It was a guy… Can you give us anything else?"

"All I can tell you is that he was a friend of Ms. Fox's friend."

"Okay," Trent dragged out. "And the name of your source's friend?"

"No names," Fraser repeated. "He just said that she's the one who discovered Ms. Fox."

Amanda shot up straight. That meant the killer had been right there—probably in the crowd—and seen Bethany Greene talking to the police. That would excuse the lack of a name. He wouldn't have known it. "No names at all. That probably should have been a clue right there. And let me guess, no phone number either?"

"No."

"We're going to need to know exactly when he called and the number he reached you on." She'd get a contact of hers in Digital Crimes to track the call. He had a way of unlocking even blocked numbers.

"I'm not going to do that for you."

"You are, or we—" she gestured between herself and Trent "—are going to arrest you for interfering in an active murder investigation."

Fraser wiped his brow. "Fine. I'll give you what you want. But it's not because I respond to threats—" he shot a sour glare her way "—but because of Ms. Fox and her family and friends." Fraser pulled his cell phone and scrolled through his log. Then he proceeded to give her the time and date of the call, along with his number.

Trent recorded it all in his notebook.

Amanda stood, and Trent followed her lead. She said to Fraser, "I still want you to get that article taken down."

Fraser just stared at her blankly.

"You said that you were giving us the call information because of Ms. Fox and her family and friends? Well, her killer is feeding on the story of her murder getting out in fine detail. Do you really want to be his puppet and by doing so cause those people more pain?"

Fraser scowled. "I'm struggling because the public has a right to know there's a serial killer in Prince William County."

"You put that in your article too?" She felt nauseous. Start tossing out "serial killer" and people lost all common sense.

"No, but I'm thinking about a follow-up piece."

She narrowed her eyes, really detesting the guy and what he represented. "Don't." Fraser shrugged, and her core temperature went up a few notches. "I'd also like to ask that you stop running your mouth all over town, starting with your friends, including Ted Dixon. He's been spreading the rumor about Ms. Fox's severed tongue around Bill Drive."

"Is it rumor, though, when it's the truth?"

She stiffened. "I never said it was."

He smirked. "Everything about your visit here tells me it is."

She left his apartment and closed his door just a little lighter than a slam. She turned to Trent, fuming. "He can't get away with this. The information about Shannon's severed tongue has no place in the mainstream media. None."

"I agree with you, but what are we supposed to do?"

It took her less than two seconds to come up with the answer. "We have to get a media ban put in place. Simple as that." Though there probably wasn't anything simple about it. She'd have to convince Malone it was a good idea.

She called him on the way back to the car. Malone told her he was stuck at home for the night, and, yeah, he knew it was only six o'clock, but it was also a Saturday and his wife would kill him if he left. He welcomed her to come over, though.

"Malone's at home," she told Trent, "and I'm headed there to plead our case about a media ban. Hopefully, he sees the logic." She'd never asked Malone for this type of thing before, so she really didn't know how he'd respond.

"Okay, and while you're doing that, how about I pop by and see Bethany Greene? I could see if she mentioned the severed tongue to any of her friends. After that, I can go back to Central and find out what I can about Ashley Lynch."

"Great plan. I'm going to loop in Jacob Briggs over at Digital Crimes and get him tracking the call to Fraser's phone. Maybe we'll get lucky."

CHAPTER THIRTY-ONE

Amanda was on the doorstep of Malone's two-story house in Woodbridge. Located just ten minutes from Central, he could probably walk to work—not that she'd ever known him to.

She rang the doorbell and waited.

The front door cracked open at first, but when Ida, Malone's wife, saw Amanda, she grinned and flung it wide.

"Hey, Amanda, it's been a long time since I've seen you." Ida touched Amanda's arm affectionately. She was a warm woman but not a hugger. "Come in. Scott's in the backyard manning the barbecue, because heaven help us if I decided to cook on the thing."

Amanda laughed. Malone was particular—or *peculiar*, hard to say—when it came to his food. "How are you?"

Ida sighed deeply and smirked. "Doing good. But that man might drive me crazy yet." Amanda went to slip off her shoes, but Iva waved a hand. "Don't you worry about that. Just follow me to the back."

Amanda had been in the house many times and knew the layout by heart. In almost a straight line from the front was a sliding patio door that led to a backyard oasis. It consisted of a groomed green space and a flagstone patio, complete with a shelter for their barbecue, elevating it into more of an altar. They also had a beautiful wicker furniture set that would have cost a small fortune.

Ida slid the door open and gestured for Amanda to go out first.

"Ah, there she is." Malone smiled at her as if she'd been an expected guest and not a last-minute intrusion at the dinner hour. He took a beer bottle off the ledge of the "altar" and took a long swig from it, wiping his mouth with the back of his hand afterward.

The smell coming off the barbecue was intoxicating, and she inhaled appreciatively as her stomach grumbled and her mouth salivated. She should have grabbed something to eat before heading over. Sizzling on the grill were two potatoes in foil and a large T-bone steak about an inch thick with a large tenderloin piece. The entire thing must have weighed three pounds. Malone was in his late fifties and must not have received the memo that large amounts of red meat weren't healthy for a man his age. Then again, if he did know, he probably wouldn't care.

She opened her mouth and was about to speak, when he said, "I know you need to talk, and we'll do just that. But first we eat."

"Oh, I couldn't…"

On her way toward her husband with an empty platter, Ida put a hand on Amanda's shoulder. "Of course you can." She handed the plate to Malone just as a timer beeped.

"Off she comes." Malone's enthusiasm wasn't masked, and he removed the steak and potatoes, loading them onto the platter. "You never re-flip a steak." He eyed Amanda with all seriousness, and she quirked an eyebrow.

"Here we go," Ida mumbled and retrieved the food from her husband and took it into the house.

Amanda smiled. Malone had his share of stories, but his one weakness was talking his meals to death. It had been a while since she'd eaten a meal he'd cooked, but it was all coming back to her now. He loved to regale his guests with a breakdown of how the food came to be on their plate—the method of prep, including spices, how long he'd cooked it, at what temperature, and on it went. There were usually also little insights about why he did things one way as opposed to another.

Malone carried on like his wife hadn't expressed annoyance. "If you flip a steak more than once, it'll become tough."

Amanda played along. "Is that so?" She squirreled away the tip and wondered if Logan knew about that trick. Ah, Logan. She felt horrible about forgetting their dinner plans the other night, but she'd make it up to him. She smiled at the thought of *how* she'd do that.

"Uh-huh, young lady. It's a fact." He pointed the business end of a pair of tongs at her to emphasize his point.

They joined Ida in the house. She'd already set the table for three and portioned out the potatoes. Half of one each for her and Amanda, and a whole one for Malone. The steak was left untouched, though. Probably because there was an unwritten but adhered-to rule, that Malone divvied up the meat. And sure enough, he grabbed a large knife from the block on the counter and got to work.

Amanda said she wasn't very hungry, but she still got a sizable chunk of beef she wasn't quite sure she could finish. Ida had a small piece about the size of her palm, and Malone loaded the rest onto his plate, along with the bone. He was the first to dig in. As he sliced through the meat, pink juices oozed out and transported Amanda right back to Fox's crime scene.

"Dang it all, I forgot my beer outside." Malone dropped his utensils and started to slide his chair back.

Amanda shot to her feet and volunteered. A little separation was exactly what she needed to clear her mind.

She returned with his beer a moment later and was offered one by Ida. She declined, of course. Ida must have forgotten that she didn't drink.

Dinner went quickly with lighthearted conversation that only briefly turned to her love life. It was a subject she quickly steered away from.

As she was helping Ida clear the dishes, Malone said, "Okay, let's talk." He gestured toward the backyard. "I'll be out there when you're ready."

"Ah." Amanda looked at Ida, who was already watching her. She was torn. She wanted to help with the dishes, but her original purpose for coming here wasn't to get caught up in a personal evening. She checked her phone, but there was no update from Trent about how things had gone with Bethany Greene. She tucked her phone back in her pocket.

"Go on." Ida smiled at her as she turned on the hot water and pumped soap into the sink. "I've got this. I've been doing it for so long, I could do it with my eyes shut."

"Thank you." Amanda saw herself outside and sat on one of the wicker chairs that was adorned with bright-red cushions. She inhaled deeply, noticing for the first time that it was a pleasant evening to be outside. Birds were singing, heralding that spring was here, and the air smelled fresh and lush.

"So what is it that you wanted to talk to me about?" Malone snapped the cap off a fresh beer and took a draw.

"I need a media ban put in place."

"Am I missing something here?" He took another quick swig.

She'd thought about how she was going to present her case, and now face-to-face with him, her mind was blank. She didn't see Malone warming to the idea of a serial killer without some convincing.

"Amanda," he prompted.

"I'm not exactly sure what we're dealing with here." Safe, neutral ground. It would be far better if Malone came out with "serial killer" before she did.

"Regarding?"

"The person who killed Ashley Lynch and Shannon Fox."

"You sound confident they're the same person now."

She nodded. "There's no one in Fox's life who fits. She had her ex, who is a piece of work, but he's not her killer. I'm confident in saying that Fox was taken out because of her call to nine-one-one.

And if that's the case, it points to Lynch's killer." Her phone pinged with a message. *Trent, finally?*

"I'm still listening. Go on."

"The fire, the mutilation—both point to a killer who wants glory. He has something to say." She took out her phone and went to her messages as she spoke. It was Trent with bad news. She continued talking to Malone. "If we let the media continue to publish stories about these murders, we're giving the killer exactly what he wants. I don't agree with allowing that to happen." As she heard the words come back to her ears, she thought again of her mother. It was so strange that her mother was now technically a killer—though, in Amanda's eyes, her mother was nothing like the man they were after.

"Okay," Malone dragged out and set his beer on a side table. "But if we fail to give him what he wants, won't it make him more likely to kill again?" His eyes pierced through hers.

"I think he's planning that anyway."

"Oh, Amanda, I don't know. A serial killer? Doesn't there need to be more bodies to qualify?"

And there, he had said it. "I'm trying to prevent more victims. I don't even want to think there are others we don't yet know about."

"I can't request a media ban without more to go on. And the public has a right to know what's going on."

"Now you sound like Fraser Reyes." She crossed her arms and looked away.

"Fraser Reyes," Malone picked up. "Isn't that the journalist that almost had you throwing away your career?"

"In all fairness, that was more on Hill."

"Hmm. Whatever the case, this isn't what you need right now. Stay away from him."

She bit her bottom lip.

"Oh no. You spoke with him. You said I sound just like him. Tell me you didn't…"

"I did, but—"

"No buts, Amanda. I don't think it's really sunk in for you, so let me put it bluntly in words you'll understand: *Hill is gunning for your badge.*"

His warning sank in her chest and made her heart bump off rhythm, but she couldn't back down simply because she was afraid of the LT. She had to think of the bigger picture—the possibility that the killer would strike again. "If we let the news run with whatever they want, we're essentially letting the killer call the shots."

"And is that a bad thing if it keeps him from killing people?"

"We don't know that it will," she shot back. "It might whet his appetite to murder again."

Silence played out between them while they were entertained by the antics of a black squirrel juking this way and that as he ran through the yard.

"There's more you don't know," she began. Paused. The note flashed to mind, but she didn't want to tell him about it right now. She intended to stay focused on petitioning for a media ban. "Reyes just published an article on Fox's murder, and people on Bill Drive were already afraid to talk to us. We need that article taken down, for starters."

"What do you mean they're afraid?"

"The word about Fox's mutilation has spread." Amanda pulled up the piece on the newspaper site on her phone and handed it to Malone.

He skimmed the article and looked up at her. "How did he find this out?"

"The part I'm building to. A man called Reyes to tell him the story about Fox. He claimed he was a friend of Bethany Greene— that was Shannon Fox's best friend—the woman who found the body," she reminded him.

"You need to be following that lead."

"It's been done. I sent Trent to speak to her when I came here. That ping a moment ago was a text from him. Bethany didn't tell anyone."

Malone paled. "Can we track the call?"

"I have Detective Briggs in Digital Crimes on it." She'd reached out to him on her way to the Malones'.

Her boss's mouth was open like he was going to say something, but he shut it.

She said, "I don't know for sure if we've got a serial killer here, but I don't want more bodies to confirm it for me."

"Makes two of us." Malone took a sip of his beer. "You get anywhere with that eyewitness? The one who saw the jogger?"

"Yes. He thinks he also saw the same man another time with someone who could fit the description of Ashley Lynch."

Malone stiffened, and his gaze took on more intensity. "He's sure of this?"

"As much as possible. You know how eyewitnesses can hem and haw."

"I don't know what to say here, Amanda. But I feel my hands are tied."

"Two murders in two days, two different murder methods. He's organized and versatile. I'm sure he plans to kill again." She was presented with another opportunity to tell Malone about the note at the grave, but Brandon's warning flashed to mind. This killer could be especially dangerous. If she came forward with it to Malone, he might remove her from the case. He'd defend the decision as a precaution, but she wasn't willing to sit this investigation out. The killer had taunted her with saying they were on the same team, and she was past ready to prove how wrong he was.

Malone didn't say anything, but he stared at her for some time before breaking the silence. "I hate to say this—yet again—but there needs to be more victims before we can get carried away thinking this is a serial killer at work. This isn't some TV show, Amanda. This is real life."

"Yeah, and in real life serial killers exist."

"Still, I can't do anything about the media yet. My hands are tied. We both know Hill's on the warpath already. I need to consider your career, and my own."

It only proved how wise she'd been to keep the note from him. It also probably wasn't a good time to mention she'd booted the *PWC News* reporter from Fox's crime scene and told Ronald in the Public Information Office to withhold information. "Hey, it was worth a try." She got up and said, "Thanks for dinner."

"Anytime." Malone wasn't looking at her; he was draining his bottle dry.

She wished she had something to quench her thirst—only she wasn't thirsty; she was hungry. Not for food, but to put the killer she hunted behind bars.

CHAPTER THIRTY-TWO

Amanda had left the Malones' about seven forty-five and was still shaking with frustration when she walked into Central fifteen minutes later. She thought for sure she could have helped Malone see logic in implementing a media ban. Her failure to convince him rested on her shoulders. More lives were at stake because of her.

She found Trent at his desk. He got up and rounded the partition with a piece of paper in his hand.

"How did you make out?" he asked.

She shook her head.

"Oh. Well, we just keep working the case, doing what we can. Speaking of…" He handed her the sheet he'd carried over.

It was a color printout of Ashley Lynch as a thirteen-year-old girl. It was the one she'd seen briefly on the computer in the department car but much bigger. Amanda's heart splintered. "What did you find on her?"

Trent lurched in her doorway and leaned against the cubicle wall. "She was reported missing by her parents, Hugh and Sabrina, as you already know. What you don't know is the notes on the file say that Ashley had been quiet in the days leading up to her leaving. Spending a lot of time alone in her room, dressing in black."

Amanda sat in her chair and swiveled to face Trent. "What else?"

"She was easily irritated and snippy. Her behavior changed, and things she used to enjoy, such as playing the piano, she put aside. She made her parents cancel the lessons."

"A teenager wanting to be left alone, being moody, etcetera, that's pretty normal. But when it's abrupt and the crowd she hangs around with changes, along with her personality, that's reason for concern." Amanda's mind was spinning. After she'd rescued those girls in January, she did a bit of research on the red flags of sex trafficking. She'd discovered the victims weren't always snatched from the streets; some were coerced while living at home. The Fosters said that Crystal had changed and was getting into more trouble too. Had both girls gotten caught up in the DC ring?

"Did Ashley have new friends show up in her life?" she asked.

"Not that's noted in the file. I do have more, though."

"Go ahead."

"The parents had their suspicions Ashley was lured out by someone on social media."

If Amanda had any doubts as to when Ashley was caught in the web of sex trafficking, she was getting her answer. At the age of thirteen. The steak and potato Amanda had eaten earlier threatened a reappearance. "We'll need to speak to her parents at some point." She realized that was the truth, but there was a part of her that wanted to put that off as long as possible, given how things had turned out with the Fosters. "We should reach out to the investigating detective. Detective Robbins…?" She recalled Leila Foster mentioning his name and thought she had it right.

"Yeah, Chester Robbins with the Metropolitan Police in DC. Who names their kid Chester?"

"Number?" She grabbed her desk phone's handset.

Trent ran around to his cubicle and called it out to her, and she pushed each digit as he said it. The call rang over to voicemail, and Amanda left a message for the detective to call her back regarding Ashley Lynch as soon as possible. She hung up and sat back in her chair, discouraged. She hated feeling like she was on the losing end. "If they think Ashley was groomed on social media, then they must have messages. Were they included in the report?"

Trent shook his head.

"We definitely need to speak with Detective Robbins." More waiting. But they didn't have time to sit around—not if their killer was going to act again. They had to piece some of the nightmare together. "Ashley had been a victim of sex trafficking. We know that from the tattoo on her chest. Brandon told me there are different types of serial killers. In relation to our guy, we discussed those motivated by a mission." She paused and scanned Trent's eyes. He seemed to be following her thus far. She continued. "Shannon Fox only became a victim because she interfered with the killer's plans. He had to take her out, teach her a lesson."

"Sounds like the meting out of punishment."

She nodded. "I think so, and I say we put our focus on Ashley's case. She probably more accurately represents who he plans to target."

"All right, I get that."

She went on. "Brandon suggested that maybe the killer was affected by a similar crime when he was younger. He pointed out that our killer may have struck before. Let's look up cases similar to ours where the killer was caught and served time."

"Time to go fishing in the CCRE?"

The Central Criminal Records Exchange was a searchable database that cataloged closed cases, including a record of sentencing for the state of Virginia.

"We should. You focus on female victims and arson, and I'll look at female victims and strangulation." Her mind was also full of other possible angles they could try, such as revisiting the canvassing officer interviews and the photos of the crowds. She thought, too, of the card taken from the memorial that she'd passed over to Forensics. She'd follow up with CSI Blair on Monday to see if she got anywhere with it.

"As for geography?"

"Expand it statewide in case this guy has moved around." She remembered that Brandon suggested their killer was local, but he'd also added the caveat he was attempting to build a profile on the very little she'd provided him.

"Timewise?"

"I wouldn't think we should look any further back than thirty years." Chris Ingram estimated the man he saw as being in his thirties or early forties. If that man was the killer they were after, the parameter would make him ten, at the oldest, when he went to prison—which, obviously, wasn't realistic. But Chris had said he didn't get a good look, and the man could appear younger than his true age. Either way, the net was cast wide.

"I'm on it." Trent started clicking away.

She brought up the CCRE and entered her parameters. As she watched the various results fill her screen, she swelled with pride. Law enforcement in Virginia had taken these people off the streets and held them accountable for their crimes—though that same justice system would see her mother spending time behind bars. That thought reminded Amanda that she hadn't followed up with her mother. What had Hannah worked out, if anything? Amanda would just wait until the family dinner at her parents' tomorrow night and ask then. Her mother usually tucked in early, and at nine o'clock, she'd be getting ready for bed. Then again, that could have changed.

Her mother's personality obviously had. She'd gone from being a gentle spirit to one who exacted revenge. Her mother hadn't even taken the easy route and used a bullet to kill her victim. She'd chosen a murder method that had inflicted suffering and taken hours.

Amanda pinched her eyes shut and felt the warmth of unshed tears welling in them. If only she had been around for her mother after the accident. Then maybe she would have healed from the loss of her granddaughter and son-in-law and come to grips with her emotions. Maybe Amanda would have done better too. But who could really know? The circular thinking got Amanda nowhere. She shook aside her personal life and put her focus back on work.

She read through file after file, dismissing each one in turn. The arms on the clock were turning, the hours passing quickly. Then, finally, she found one of interest.

Samuel Booth. Served fifteen years. Was released three and a half years ago.

She went to the details of his crime and felt the goosebumps rise on her arms. "Ah, Trent."

"Yeah." He'd responded but sounded like he was concentrating on something.

"I think I found someone."

"Me too."

"Okay, I'll go first. Mine's a guy named Samuel Booth."

Trent glanced over at her. "Small world. I'm looking at him too. Served fifteen for killing a woman."

"A woman he strangled *and* stabbed," Amanda added.

"Yep. And did you get to this morsel yet? He lives only three blocks over from Bill Drive."

She felt herself go cold. "We've got to have a talk with Mr. Booth."

CHAPTER THIRTY-THREE

Amanda banged on Samuel Booth's door. It was just after midnight when she and Trent had arrived. They'd pulled a background on Samuel and found out he had been twenty-three when he went to prison and was now forty-one. That fell within the age range Ingram had assigned the jogger. Samuel's DMV photo showed a man who could pass for thirty-something. The hard time in prison didn't seem to have aged him beyond his years. Maybe he was one of those people who thrived behind bars and three squares a day. Their home away from home.

A year after getting out, Samuel had married a woman named Alesha, who was a couple of years younger than him.

Amanda knocked again. "Samuel Booth, Prince William County PD!"

Footsteps headed toward the door, and the deadbolt was unlatched.

A man stood on the other side of the threshold, matching the DMV photo for Samuel Booth. He was dressed like it was the middle of the day, not the middle of the night, in jeans and a T-shirt.

She held up her badge and so did Trent. "Samuel Booth?"

"Who wants to know?"

"We're Homicide Detectives Steele and Stenson. We're going to need you to come with us."

"Sam?" A woman called out from behind the man and joined everyone at the door. She was petite and had a nose that sat crooked on her face, like it was broken at one time, but it had never been set right. She was also dressed in casual clothes. "Who are you?"

"They're the police, Alesha." Samuel answered for them.

The woman gnarled up her face at Amanda and Trent. "He hasn't done anything wrong. What do you want with him?"

Samuel looked calmly at his wife, put a hand on her arm. "I'll just do as they ask and get this over with." He made eye contact with Amanda. "Yes, I'm Samuel Booth."

"What do you want with him?" Alesha squealed.

"We'd like to question your husband regarding the murders of Ashley Lynch and Shannon Fox."

"Murders?" Samuel's voice hitched. "I didn't—"

"No." Alesha stared at her husband. "Don't you let them do this to you. They're just targeting you because of your history." She met Amanda's gaze. "He didn't kill anybody. He was with me."

"You don't know the time of the murders, ma'am, and I ask that you move away from him." Amanda motioned with her hand for the woman to step aside.

"I can't let you do this to him," Alesha griped.

"We're just bringing Samuel in to talk to him. That's all." Amanda tried to assure the woman as best she could.

Samuel looked at Alesha. "This will work out. I didn't do anything. You know I didn't do anything. Just trust me."

"It's not you I have a problem trusting! It's them!" She thrust a finger to within a few inches of Amanda's face.

"I'm going to have to ask that you step back, ma'am," Amanda warned her.

"I'm not letting you take him." Alesha's eyes became wild, and she lunged toward Amanda.

Trent caught her and had her spun and in cuffs before she could blink.

"Looks like your lady friend got a ticket to the cells," Amanda said. "Are you going to join her?"

Samuel stepped outside. He proceeded to pull a key from his pocket and lock the front door. "I'm only going with you because I know I'm innocent."

We'll see about that…

*

They booked Alesha Booth for attempted assault on an officer, and they got Samuel into an interrogation room.

Amanda entered with Trent, and they both sat across from him.

She started. "It sure took you a while to answer the door, considering you and the missus were both up and dressed."

Samuel cracked his knuckles and clasped his hands on the table. "We were watching a movie and didn't hear you at first."

"I thought maybe you were considering running out the back door." She put it out there nonchalantly.

"No reason to. I have nothing to hide."

She opened a folder she'd brought in with her and consulted his background, though it was more for show than her needing a refresher. "You have a history of violence, Mr. Booth." She paused there, giving him a chance to defend himself, but he remained mute. She went on. "You have a sealed juvie record, but I'm going to guess it would support what I just said."

Samuel remained silent.

"Your wife's nose—"

He met her eyes. "What about it?"

"It's been broken and reset. Did you break it?"

"No, I'd never touch her."

They'd check hospital records and see if there was a history of domestic abuse in the Booth household. "But you did kill Joyce Summer."

"A matter of public record, and I served my time for that."

"Why did you kill her?"

Samuel clenched his jaw so hard a pulse tapped in his cheeks.

"Why don't you tell us what happened? Help us understand."

"Can't you look it up?"

"Hmph." Amanda glanced at Trent, back to Samuel. "You're not exactly being cooperative with us, Mr. Booth."

"I'm not? I could get a lawyer down here. I know my rights."

"Did you know Ms. Summer had a right to live? She'd be forty if she were still alive today."

"As I said, I did my time. Move on. I have."

Amanda leaned forward and angled her head. Samuel was questionable enough to bring in, but his attitude was rubbing her the wrong way. "Have you, though, or are you back to your old tricks? Why did you kill Joyce?"

"I was angry."

"Why?"

"She was a slut," he spat.

Amanda cringed at his reaction. "So what? She deserved to die?"

"She screwed my best friend."

"Yet, is he still alive?"

Samuel broke eye contact, dipping his gaze to his hands.

"It takes two to play. Why didn't you kill him too, Mr. Booth? Why just Joyce?" She had her reasons for pressing him and digging into his past.

He continued to avoid looking at their side of the table.

"Did you kill her because as the woman she deserved the punishment? To know what she'd done to you? Were you teaching her a lesson?" She wanted to see if she could get a telling reaction.

"I didn't…"

"Didn't what, Mr. Booth?"

"It wasn't about punishing her. She just got me so angry." Finally, some eye contact. His nostrils were flaring now, and his shoulders and chest heaving as he breathed heavily.

"So it was her fault?"

"Not what I meant, but, yeah, it was."

"You get angry again recently?" She pulled a photo the folder and put it on the table. "Ashley Lynch, sixteen. She was strangled, doused with gasoline."

He remained silent as he looked at the photo. His face was expressionless, giving nothing away.

"And Shannon Fox. Forty-three, stabbed, drugged, and mutilated." She slapped a printout of her picture down.

"I don't know who they are."

"Huh, and is this from you?" She set a picture of the note next to the ones of the victims. Her entire body quaked as she did so. "Did you think I'd understand what you did? And how, in any way, are we on the same team?"

Samuel's gaze lifted, though he remained mute.

Her heart was racing, and it was like she was watching herself, not really in possession of her faculties. "Answer me."

"I didn't kill either of those women."

"That's your story?"

"That's my *truth*. And I don't have any idea what this is…" He flicked a finger toward the note.

She shrugged. "Then you won't have a problem giving us your alibis for the times of their murders."

"None at all."

His confidence and demeanor had her second-guessing their decision to bring him in. Maybe they simply saw what they had wanted to see. She told him the times he needed to account for.

He paled and glanced up at the ceiling, let out a huff. "Doubt you'll believe me, but I was at home with my wife."

She sprung to her feet and went into the hall.

Trent joined her. "Do you think he killed them?"

She ran a hand through her hair. "I don't know… Probably not, but I'm not ready to let him go just yet."

"I know you want to close this case—so do I—but if Samuel Booth's not our killer, we need to release him."

"No, we have time to hold him without pressing charges. I can't ignore the fact he killed a woman for sleeping with his friend, and that he killed her because he saw her as a slut."

"You may have taken some liberty with that conclusion..." Trent winced.

"Nah." She shook her head. "What's to say he's not targeting women now for essentially the same reason? You know, cleaning up Prince William County."

Trent knotted up his face. "I think we need more."

She considered his words, and he was right. "We'll hold him overnight and do some more digging. If nothing turns up, we'll set him free."

"Sounds fair."

"I'm getting started right away." She headed to her desk and thought about what Brandon Fisher had said—that their killer may have been traumatized in his childhood. She'd just go rooting deep in Samuel Booth's closet to see what skeletons she could find.

CHAPTER THIRTY-FOUR

Amanda might have only gotten about five hours' sleep, but it had done her a world of good. She probably slept well because before heading home she'd been successful at finding potential evidence that could support Samuel Booth as their killer. However, his wife had denied any allegations that her husband beat or abused her in any way. There also wasn't any record of her receiving medical attention for unexplained injuries. Alesha was adamant that her nose had always sat crooked on her face, and she'd backed that up by showing them a childhood photo of herself.

It was eight o'clock Sunday morning and most of the county was still in bed, but she and Trent were at Central. They had Samuel shown to an interrogation room and would soon join him.

On their way there, Trent turned to her. "I'm not sure about this, Amanda."

"I know you have your doubts about him. Honestly, so do I."

"Open mind then?"

"Open mind," she agreed.

"We can't place him at either crime scene. I've looked at the photos again."

"Maybe he didn't watch, or he was good at avoiding having his picture taken." She realized she was convicting the man again, and that wasn't like her, but this case was making her a little crazy.

They entered the room, and Samuel barely lifted his head.

"Have a good night's sleep?" she asked.

"Yeah. The best," he responded sardonically.

She didn't say anything but pulled photos of Ashley and Shannon from the folder and laid them out.

He rolled his eyes. "Here we go again."

"What's that supposed to mean?"

"I was hoping you'd clue in that I didn't kill them."

"Not there quite yet. Ashley Lynch—" she pressed a fingertip to her photo "—was strangled, just like Joyce."

"As you told me yester—"

"She was stabbed, also just like Joyce," she interrupted him and pointed to Shannon Fox.

"But I don't know these women."

"You know that we'll get to the truth, Mr. Booth. You killed Joyce. In your words she was a slut. Ashley Lynch prostituted herself, but it wasn't because she had a choice. She was coerced and beaten into doing so. She was only sixteen." She could feel anxiety ratcheting in her chest. If Samuel had killed her, he deserved the heaviest sentence the law could give. "Did you see her as a slut, Mr. Booth? Is that why you killed her?"

He met her gaze, his eyes wide and wet.

She pushed on. "Did you kill Ms. Fox because she interfered in your plans?"

"You're losing me now."

Her heart was palpitating off rhythm. Maybe she was rather stubbornly latching onto Samuel being the killer because she wanted this case put to rest and get justice for two victims—one of which was only a young woman. She withdrew another photo from her folder. It was of Samuel's mother, and he visibly recoiled. "Just as I thought. You hate your mother, Mr. Booth."

"I, ah…" He rubbed his neck.

She was getting to the meat of what she'd uncovered. "She was a single parent, and she was a drunk all the time and slept around.

She brought strange men into your house. Maybe some of them even liked little Sam—"

"I want a lawyer, now!"

Her heart was pounding wildly. She felt a little out of control. Maybe she had taken her hypothetical too far, but she got a telling reaction. Brandon had mentioned the possibility of their killer being abused as a child, and Samuel's strong outburst just as much confirmed he had been. "The lawyer's probably a good idea." She got up and left with Trent. She faced him and said, "While he's waiting on his attorney, you and I are going to Washington."

"For?"

"We're going to talk to Detective Robbins in person and see what he has to say about Crystal Foster and Ashley Lynch. Maybe Booth even came up in his investigations?"

"I don't know about that..."

She could see her partner's doubt all over his face, and his expression served as a mirror for self-examination. She was the one having a hard time keeping an open mind, but all she could think about was the branding tattoo on Ashley's chest. That poor girl had lived in hell, and Amanda was determined to get her justice.

CHAPTER THIRTY-FIVE

Amanda tried reaching Detective Robbins several times before leaving Central as Trent drove them to Washington, but she kept landing in his voicemail. When they arrived at Robbins's police district station, they were told to wait in the seating area and that Detective Robbins would be out shortly.

"You looking for me?"

She raised her head to see a man with a stern demeanor bent down and waving a hand in front of her face. She'd hadn't even heard him approach.

"If you're Detective Robbins, we are," she said.

"I am. Who's asking?"

Amanda and Trent both stood. Chester Robbins was a giant of a man and had to be six four at least.

She was quite sure the person at the front desk would have told him who they were, but she'd play along. "Detectives Amanda Steele and Trent Stenson with the Prince William County PD." They held up their badges, and Chester immediately turned to leave. "Uh… we need to talk to you, and we're not leaving until we do. I left a message for you last night, and I've tried to reach you several times today."

Chester mumbled something that resembled "come with me" and set off down a hall. She and Trent followed.

"Did you get my message?"

"Uh-huh." He just kept walking.

She caught up to his side. "Okay, then you were going to call me back?"

Chester glanced over at her. "When I got a chance. I looked up the name. Ashley Lynch, right?"

"Uh-huh."

"She was reported missing three years ago. I've got fresh cases on my desk that need attention."

"Isn't that a coincidence? We have a fresh *homicide*, and we believe the victim may have been Ashley Lynch."

He stared at her but kept moving.

She couldn't understand why he was being so difficult. They were there with potential news about a case of his. Then again, maybe that explained the attitude—he didn't want to be shown up, and by a detective from another department no less. But shouldn't justice trump ego? "You heard what I just said?"

He stopped outside a door marked *Interview 2*. "You go in there and get comfortable. I'll be back in a minute."

"Ah, sure? Where are you—"

He was already down the hall. For a big man, he moved quickly and stealthily.

"Okay then," she said to Trent. Either Robbins was too proud to accept help from a fellow detective and/or he was having a bad day before they'd shown up.

Amanda and Trent sat at a table that would normally be used for questioning perps. Chester really wanted to remind them they were on his turf. Personally, she didn't have any interest in getting into a battle over jurisdiction. She just wanted a killer to go away.

A few minutes later, Chester returned with a laptop under his arm. He proceeded to put it on the table, then sat across from her and Trent. "Talk to me."

"The body of a young woman was pulled from a house fire in Dumfries, but her cause of death was strangulation."

"You're sure it was Lynch?"

Amanda pulled the computer-rendered photo of Lynch up on her phone and showed it to Chester.

Chester didn't give the screen much attention. "I don't remember what she looked like."

Amanda tucked her phone away and pointed to his laptop. "We'll wait if you want to bring her picture up. Keep in mind that she would have been three years younger at the time she went missing."

Chester seemed to debate whether he was going to do as Amanda suggested. He flipped the lid on the laptop open, clicked some keys, grunted. He was slower at typing than she was at texting—and that said a lot. "Could be her, I suppose."

"Do you remember much about the case?"

"What would you like to know?" He crossed his arms on the table, his body language closed off and rigid—defensive.

Maybe it wasn't so much that Chester didn't want to be shown up, but rather that he was feeling guilty about possibly missing something that led to the girl's death. "To start with, did a man by the name of Samuel Booth surface in your investigation?" He could have been the man to lure her away from home—and then been the one to take her out. She wasn't dismissing any possibilities at this point, though she also wasn't trying to convict him yet either—something she needed to keep reminding herself.

"Name doesn't sound familiar."

She pulled up a photo of Booth on her phone. "Look familiar?" She put her screen in front of him.

"Nope."

She put her phone back in her pocket. "We read that Ashley may have been groomed through social media."

"Is there a question in there?"

"Were there messages to support this?"

"Yes."

"And...?" she prompted.

"Lynch was communicating with a male—or perceived male—online. More specifically through social media, in the month proceeding her running away."

"A month?" That surprised her. Shouldn't her parents have noticed? But maybe they were much like the Fosters and only orbiting in the same vicinity of their child, not really a part of her life. Then there was the breaks and fractures. "What were the Lynches like?"

"Don't like to jump to conclusions about people, but I didn't like the dad. Pretty sure he was abusing the wife and daughter. I found out that she broke her arm when she was about nine. They said she fell, but I wasn't buying it."

Amanda and Trent met each other's gaze.

"Take it that means something to you?"

Amanda nodded. "The ME found a healed break like that in our victim." She was gaining more confidence that their Jane Doe was Ashley Lynch. "What was the name of the person contacting her?"

"Riley Sawyer. Definitely an alias. Most likely a pedophile. Sawyer approached Lynch and told her that he was a senior at Woodrow Wilson High School. She'd just started there that fall. He told her she was the most beautiful girl he'd ever seen."

Amanda hated to admit how easily flattery worked on most teenage girls—her younger self included.

Chester went on. "This guy filled her head with a bunch of nonsense. He also said she deserved a boyfriend who treated her right."

Whoever this Riley Sawyer really was, he would have had to know about her love life for the ruse to work. That could indicate someone within Ashley's circle, but it might also suggest that people in the sex-trafficking network were staking out the school. "This person was aware of her personal life to say that," Amanda concluded. "It also sounds like this guy she may have been seeing was abusive."

"You're not the only detective in the room," Chester said. "And we spoke with some of her friends at the high school. Even spoke to the boy she had been seeing. He was a senior and had already moved on with another girl."

Heartbreak alone could have explained a change in behavior, especially for an emotionally charged teenager. Amanda remembered sulking for months after she and her first boyfriend broke up. She'd only been sixteen, but it might as well have been the end of her life. After all, she'd thought she was going to marry the guy. Her father told her being in the house at the time had made him feel like he was in the elevator business—up and down.

"I take it you had no luck tracking this Sawyer guy down?" Trent asked.

"Dead end. Obviously, I got Cyber Crimes involved."

"We're sure you did all you could at the time. What came of questioning Ashley's friends and family?" Amanda asked.

Chester's posture softened at the flattery. "There was one uncle on the mother's side. A Ralph Field. He was one of those oddballs. A loner. Stuck to himself. He was forty-seven, never been married. And let's just say his looks and level of intelligence came from the shallow end of the gene pool."

"Was he involved in Ashley's life?" she volleyed back.

"Just during the holidays. The mother felt sorry for her brother and had him over that Easter—that was just days before the communication started with Riley Sawyer."

"Did the uncle know about the breakup?" Trent asked, beating Amanda to the question.

"Uh-huh. We searched his computers but didn't turn up anything."

"He could have just been good about deleting the evidence. Or used a computer you didn't know about." A bubble of frustration rose in Amanda's chest. "Anyone else fall under suspicion?"

"Nothing that led anywhere."

That doesn't exactly answer my question… "We're trying to solve this girl's murder. Any names you can give us would be appreciated."

"I can get you the list."

"How many were there?"

"Just three, but they were all cleared."

"Yes, please send me the names. Also send me the string of correspondence between Sawyer and Ashley," she requested.

"Sure, if you think it will help."

Amanda observed how much his attitude toward them had changed once he realized they weren't in any way blaming him for what happened to Ashley. "The day she ran away, did Ashley leave any note?"

"Don't remember that."

"We think she might have run away with a friend, Crystal Foster."

"Yes, I thought the same. Trust that I did everything I could think of to find those girls." With that statement Chester finally showed some emotion.

Her phone rang, and caller ID told her it was Malone, but she sent him to voicemail. "So this Sawyer groomed Ashley. I assume that this person arranged a meet. Where was that?"

"At the food court in City Center Mall here in Washington. We were able to find witnesses who saw Ashley and another young girl, who we concluded was Crystal. They spoke to an adult woman. We never tracked her down, and she was good at averting security cameras."

It sounded like the woman knew what she was doing. The fact a woman was involved in the recruiting didn't surprise Amanda at all. The sex-trafficking case from a couple of months ago had also led her to a woman, but she wouldn't be hurting anyone anymore.

"Now, if I remember right… Just give me a second." Chester proceeded to click on his laptop. After a few moments, he said,

"Here it is. There was an eyewitness—a male clerk at one of the burger joints. He said the woman got an order of fries, and he described a tattoo that went up the side of her neck."

Amanda felt a prick of dread. "What did it look like?"

Chester clicked on the laptop. "Like a bunch of entangled rose vines."

That would qualify as *thorny* vines. She inched forward on her chair. "Colored? Black and white?"

"Black and white."

"Any letters on it?" Her heart was racing.

"Not that the guy saw, but he said it continued under the collar of her shirt."

The DC ring tattoo was also black and white, though they typically placed it just above their girls' left breasts. Did this woman have hers extended up her neck?

"Is there something else I should know?" Chester asked. "You two are lookin' pale."

"Ashley was branded by a similar type of tattoo," Amanda began. "It's been linked to a sex-trafficking ring that goes by the name of DC."

"So it's one here in DC?"

"Unsure. One could assume there's a connection. All I know for sure is that's the name they go by, and they have a reach into Prince William County. We're going to need a copy of the case files on Ashley Lynch and Crystal Foster."

"I'll need to run it by my boss, but it shouldn't be a problem. You haven't found Crystal Foster, have you?"

Amanda shook her head. "Not yet, but it's entirely possible she ended up in the ring too." Her phone buzzed, and caller ID told her it was Malone again. "I need to get this." She answered, and Malone started talking right away. His words were hurling at her so fast she could hardly catch them all, but she did get the message, and it turned her cold. "We'll be right there."

"Hot lead?" Chester asked.

"Hot homicides. Two of 'em." She flicked a card across the table to Chester. "Email me the investigation files. Thanks." Next she looked at Trent. "We've gotta go."

CHAPTER THIRTY-SIX

Another fire. Two young women dead.

That was the recap Malone had given her. The timing of the incident meant that Samuel Booth was innocent. It was clear now that he likely never had anything to do with murdering Lynch or Fox either. She made the call to cut him loose, feeling just a touch of remorse for hauling him in and putting him through what she had. But she'd only been following what she had to go on.

The second blaze was in a higher-end neighborhood than Bill Drive. The houses were newer and bigger, and the vehicles in the driveways, luxury.

It was almost noon when she and Trent arrived. Officers had cordoned off the scene a few blocks back. Trent parked at the perimeter, and they walked toward 816 Clear Mountain Circle.

The air was heavy with smoke, and she coughed. She'd guess this fire was a lot worse than the first one and their killer hadn't left anything to chance this time around.

As they got closer, that thought was confirmed. Fire engines and other trucks from Dumfries Triangle Volunteer Fire Department were parked on the street in front of a burnt-out husk of a structure. A concrete foundation and some wood framing were all that was left. The bodies would be nothing but bones.

The gawkers were also there, gathered for the latest tragedy. Malone was standing on the lawn next to a For Sale sign. Did that mean this house had been sitting vacant too?

She hustled toward Malone, but a woman in yellow turnout gear played interference. "Before you go any further, I'm going to need to know who you are."

Amanda showed her badge, held it there as the woman diligently took her time reading it. "Detective Amanda Steele with the Prince William County PD. That's my sergeant over there." Amanda pointed toward Malone, who was now walking straight for them.

The woman let her gaze drift to Trent. "And you?"

Trent held up his badge. "Detective Trent Stenson."

"Now it's your turn," Amanda told her.

"I'm Mia Vaughn, fire marshal in charge here."

She had a commanding presence. Her hair was pulled back tightly in a bun like she meant business, and her sharp facial features only added to that image. And she was probably good at her job, but they could be looking at a serial killer, and Amanda didn't want to bring a new person up to speed. "Where's Sullivan?"

"Out sick, but don't worry, I've got this under control. I know all about the fire on Bill Drive."

Amanda met the marshal's gaze. "This one arson too?"

"It has the markings of it, but I'll need to conduct a full investigation to know for sure."

Amanda recalled Sullivan's words that they consider the evidence without a preconceived notion of foul play. She looked closer at the realty sign and noticed the agent's name was the same one they'd contacted after the Bill Drive fire. "Was the place lived in?" she asked Mia.

"Not currently, no."

"Is the place owned by Woodbridge Bank, by chance?" Trent asked.

Mia glanced at Trent. "It is and has been sitting on the market a couple of months."

Maybe they hadn't been far off to assume their killer was someone associated with the bank and aware of vacated homes. It was listed with the same real estate agent. Maybe the estimator and inspector involved with 532 Bill Drive were also pulled in to work on this property—even possibly the contractor and County Services. She'd call Aiden Aikens as soon as possible. It was Sunday, so she might have to hunt him down at his house, but she'd do what was necessary.

"Do we know what caused the fire?" Trent asked.

"My investigation should reveal that."

Amanda glanced again at the remains of the structure and let her gaze trail to the neighboring houses. Unscathed, except for some siding that was marked with soot. But whatever had been used to set the blaze had certainly done its damage quickly. "What can you tell us about the victims?"

"Not a lot at this point. I've called for an anthropologist." Mia twisted her mouth, and Amanda witnessed the first fracture in the woman's powerful demeanor. "There's not much there. Just some bones."

As Amanda had thought, but she looked quizzically at Malone, who was quietly taking in their conversation. When he'd called to tell her about the fire, he'd really made it sound like two casualties had been confirmed. "Then how do we know the remains belong to two people, both female?"

"Uh, we don't really," Malone said. "I was basing that on an eye-witness who came forward. He saw a man and two young women—as he described them—go up the driveway into the backyard."

Amanda battled with how to react—disappointed or encouraged. Someone else may have seen their killer, but they could have rushed in assuming the bones were the young women. "We'll obviously want to speak to this man. Before we do—" she addressed Mia "—when was the fire?"

"Neighbors said the explosion happened this morning at eight, and the fire was out at ten. It took a while to get the flames under control."

"An explosion?" The question scraped from her throat. "Are you suggesting a bomb?"

Mia shook her head. "Not necessarily in the typical sense. There are plenty of household items that can cause an explosion. Most common I'd say would be a propane tank with a cracked valve. All it takes is a spark."

"That the case here?" Amanda asked.

"Need time to investigate, Detective."

Amanda's thoughts returned to the time of the explosion—after sunrise. Did it take a while for the fire to build? She'd ask Mia but figured her answer would be she still needed time to investigate. She turned to Malone. "Where can we find this eyewitness?"

"In his house across the street with Officer Wyatt." Malone nudged his head in that direction.

Wyatt was the same officer who had interviewed Chris Ingram. Apparently, he knew whose doors to knock on. "Okay," she said, taking a step away, but then she walked back and handed Mia her card. "You have one?"

"I do, but…" Mia patted her hips, and it emphasized the bulky turnout gear. "I'll be around for a long while yet. Just pop back after you're done over there."

"Will do." Amanda briefly met Malone's gaze. "We've got more bodies. Tell me you're reconsidering that media ban. I know I had my reservations about thinking we have a serial killer, but I don't think we can ignore it anymore—not if two young women were killed in that house." When she'd finished talking, Malone was just staring blankly at her. "Well?" she prompted.

"I'm not considering the media ban."

"You still don't think we're looking at a serial killer?"

"Oh, I never said that." Malone ran a hand over his stomach. "But I think we need to do the opposite of a media ban."

"Now you've lost me."

"We've got four dead bodies now, potentially due to one man. Before victims continue to pile up, I want to open a tip line. It's time to reach out for the public's help. Someone might come forward."

"The ones who aren't afraid of their tongues being cut out, I guess."

"Amanda, consider the full picture. More deaths could prompt a brave soul to speak up. Someone out there might have gotten a good look at our killer, and just like that, the pieces will fall together."

She considered Malone's suggestion and weighed the options. When she'd wanted the ban, part of the reason was to deny the killer the attention he craved, and the other was she didn't want fear to shut people up. But Malone's viewpoint held some merit, too, and if it could help catch this bastard, she was for it. "It could work. Go ahead."

He smiled. "Glad you agree, though I didn't need your permission."

"I know." She rolled her eyes, teasingly, a flash of levity at a horrible crime scene.

"Get to work." He waved her off, but she didn't move.

"Just one thing… that real estate agent is the same person who was commissioned to sell five thirty-two Bill Drive. Trent and I cleared him for the first fire, but we should probably just get his alibi for this one too. Just in case there's a hole to be found. Whoever our killer is, he knows these houses were sitting empty."

"I'll get someone on it."

"Thanks."

She and Trent left Malone.

As she crossed the street, each step became heavier as it sank in that someone was targeting the young women of her town—again. Had these latest victims been caught up in a sex-trafficking ring too? There'd be no tattoos to find on their bodies as they were nothing but bone, but maybe the eyewitness noticed the marking on the girls.

She glanced over her shoulder at what remained of the house, finding it a tough balance between grief and pure rage.

CHAPTER THIRTY-SEVEN

The scene in front of him and around him was spectacular. The police may be able to barricade civilian vehicle traffic, but it didn't keep his audience away. He stood among a throng of people clustered on the sidewalk. They busied themselves chattering mindlessly—how they felt the explosion shake their houses, the rumors that it was set intentionally, that victims may be inside... All of it pleased him. They were, after all, talking about his work. This was his masterpiece, but far from his finale.

Everything had turned out perfectly and even better than he had planned. He wasn't a fire expert, but the internet was an endless resource. He'd looked up common household items that were highly flammable. Cotton balls coated with Vaseline were on the list. It was common among outdoorsy types to use for starting their campfires—who knew? The cotton sparked quickly while the petroleum in the jelly kept the fire burning longer, and it was waterproof. He'd paired it with a propane tank left on the property and opened its valve. Enough time for him to get out, and then it was *kaboom!* The place went up like a Roman candle, and it was a sight to see. And all that without collateral damage.

There'd also be no remains to cement an ID—not easily. Maybe some skilled anthropologist could piece together what was left and form an image, but that would take a very long time.

There was a subtle stench that lingered in the air, that of sickly sweet barbecued pork, and he imagined it to be burnt human flesh.

It had been easier to get the girls to the house than he'd played out in his mind beforehand. Sure, he had to help them into the van, but beyond that it would have just looked like three people taking a stroll after a night of drinking. It was unfortunate that the drugs had hit them a little harder than he'd anticipated, though, and they stumbled more than he would have liked. But overall, everything had gone smoothly. They were both stupid, naive, and gullible. All he had to do to convince them to go with him in the first place was say that he was taking them to a grand party. It had worked out gloriously that it was the one girl's birthday, and she believed the celebration was for her. Their names had been Candy and Sugar, but nothing was sweet about either of them except for their deaths.

After taking their lives, he returned to where he had parked a couple of blocks away and waited. The fire engines came, roaring their sirens, and he walked up like an innocent bystander and hadn't left the area since. Why would he want to? The view here was incredible, and he had the right to savor his accomplishment. All these people were here because of him. He'd finally be getting the attention he deserved!

He observed as more responders arrived, including some woman in a truck with a Prince William County seal on the door. She got out of the vehicle and carried herself with pride and determination. Her blond hair was pulled back into a tight bun, and he imagined that it fell well past her shoulders when she let it down. In his mind, he gave her soft curls to offset her otherwise jagged facial features—a small turned-up nose and pointed chin.

After the fire was extinguished, she'd suited up and gone inside what was left of the structure and moved around. When she reached the main area of the house where he'd put the girls, she'd signed the cross on her chest and looked out across the front yard. It felt like she was looking right at him, but it was probably all in his mind.

As pleasant as it was to witness all this, his intuition warned him that it was time to leave. But how badly he wanted to bear full witness to the investigation, maybe even become involved somehow. That thought caused him to smile, but the expression died quickly when a man bumped his elbow on his way toward some woman holding the leash of a teacup poodle. *Get a real dog, lady.*

When he'd turned his focus ahead again, he saw her. Detective Steele. Red hair, straight. Length to the top of her shoulders and parted to the right. She had a freckled face, but there was something about the way she carried herself that made her quite attractive. She was with a blond man, probably a couple years younger and immature; he had a little more bounce to his step, like working homicides excited him. Detective Steele by contrast had become hardened and all-business. She went toward the house, and the blond vixen in full turnout gear stopped her.

There was a conversation, and an older man joined in. He was pretty sure that was Steele's boss. Then there were gesturing arms and pointed fingers that seemed to indicate the house behind The Merciful. After they returned their attention to one another, he glanced over a shoulder casually as if he were just stretching his back or neck.

There was a person in the front window looking out, but they were far enough back that a glare across the glass obscured them. He couldn't make out if they were male or female, but he had a bad feeling they'd seen something.

He clenched his hands into fists at his sides. Had these do-gooders not learned anything from what had happened to Fox?

The detectives were crossing the street now, right toward him. His heart hammered. Maybe they hadn't been pointing to the house, but rather at him. But he couldn't let his paranoia trap him. He had to wait it out, if not just a little longer, to see where they were truly headed.

They stepped up the curb, Detective Steele's eyes skimming the crowd, though not in an obvious way. She seemed to look right over him—or through him—and kept going.

He took a deeper breath and caught a whiff of her perfume—floral and subtle—even over the pungent odors caused from the fire. But he couldn't let the detective's pleasant aroma influence him. He had to remain objective. She'd worked the other cases, and now she was back, obviously following some sort of lead.

Again, he looked at the house behind him. The figure in the window was gone, but the front door was cracking open, and the detectives were going inside.

His entire body thrummed with a vibrating energy, and his breathing became ragged. His nostrils flared as he drew in more oxygen, but a lungful of smoky air had him coughing. He started down the sidewalk toward the van, hands in pockets to hide the fact they were formed into fists. He tried to talk himself into staying calm, but it wasn't working. With each step, he fantasized about killing the detective and how wonderful it would feel. Maybe he should take her out. But killing a cop… Was he ready to go there, and wouldn't that be far too risky? After all, he still had work to do, and he didn't want anything standing in his way. They'd just intensify their efforts to find and stop him.

He may just have to figure something else out to send a message to the detective. He wanted it to sting and be incredibly personal. He also wanted it to be ingenious, something she'd never see coming.

CHAPTER THIRTY-EIGHT

Officer Wyatt introduced Amanda and Trent to the eyewitness, a man by the name of Justin Cooper, and left. Justin took them to his front sitting room, where he sat on a couch, and she and Trent on club chairs.

"It was absolutely terrifying." Justin said, rocking back and forth and rubbing his arms. He hadn't stopped doing that since letting them inside. "How it just went up like that… I've never seen anything like it."

"You were obviously already awake when it happened?" Amanda asked.

"Yeah, I was sitting where he is." He gestured at Trent sitting next to the window. "I was having a coffee and looking outside."

Justin had probably assumed it was going to be like every other lazy Sunday morning—until it literally went up in flames. "Tell us what you saw."

"I had just glanced away for a second. Then there was this loud boom and a blast of light. I could feel the heat inside my house." Tears filled his eyes. "I didn't know what I'd just seen. It's like my mind couldn't make sense of it."

"Understandable," she empathized.

"I kept thinking *people are hurt*, and I jumped to my feet." His eyes widened at the recollection. "Then I remembered the place wasn't lived in anymore. But there were those people I saw." He rocked more fervently, the couch moaning some in protest.

"Yes. Can you tell us about them? Also, when you saw them?" she asked.

"Well, I saw them on the sidewalk going toward the house, then into the yard. I thought it was the real estate agent at first, but it didn't make sense it would be him because of the hour, and the girls looked young."

"You mentioned the hour?" she pressed. "What time was it?"

"It was around midnight."

Mia said the explosion had happened at eight that morning. If the victims were the girls that Justin saw, again the question came up: what had their killer been doing with the girls all that time? Or maybe he'd killed them rather quickly and then hung out with their bodies. Amanda really didn't want to give any of it too much thought. "You're sure?"

"Yeah."

"You described them just now as girls," Amanda said. "How old do you think they were?"

"Teenagers, maybe early twenties."

"Anything else you can tell us about them?" Trent asked.

"They were both blond. I could tell that when they went under the streetlights. Oh, their clothes were, uh, pretty tight and revealing."

Yet still, Justin hadn't seen anything suspicious about the fact a man was with them and headed toward an empty house.

"The girls were stumbling like they were drunk. The man took turns righting each of them," Justin volunteered. "They were laughing, though, like they were happy."

They were probably drugged. Just enough to make them compliant, but not incapacitated. A different dose of the same drug used on Fox? Or was the killer pulling from a medicine bag full of options? She hoped Jeffery could shed some light on that later today. She asked Justin, "Did you happen to notice if either of the girls had any tattoos?"

"No. Sorry. It was rather dark."

She nodded. Even if it had been light out, there's a good chance the tattoo would have been covered anyway. "What can you tell us about the man?"

"Not a lot. He was nice-looking, I guess. I'd definitely say he was older than the girls."

"Approximate age, if you were to guess?" she prompted.

"Late twenties, early thirties."

A little younger than the man that Chris Ingram had described, but age was so subjective. "What about hair color and build?"

"Brown hair, average size."

Generic, like the portrait Chris Ingram had painted. "How was he dressed?"

"All in black."

"Have you ever seen him or the girls in the neighborhood before?" Trent asked.

Justin looked at Trent and shook his head.

"So you saw them at midnight," Trent began, circling back toward the start of the conversation, it would seem. "Why were you up then?"

"Am I a suspect here?"

"Not at all," Amanda assured him. "But Trent's question is still valid."

Justin grimaced, seemingly not soothed by her response. "I was getting ready for bed, if you must know. I have a habit of making sure my doors are all locked, and when I do, I look out the windows. It was when I was at the front door that I saw the three of them."

It was probably a good time to ask the question Amanda had burning inside of her. "Why didn't you call the police?"

"I was exhausted and wanted to go to bed."

"But you knew the house was vacant, and he wasn't the real estate agent. Then there's the two young women appearing to be drunk off their feet. None of this seemed hinky to you?" she asked him, putting it out there as casually as possible.

"Honestly?" Justin sighed.

"That would be refreshing." Amanda gave him an encouraging smile.

"I didn't know what they were up to, and I didn't want the police showing up and it being something innocent that I had misinterpreted, making me look like a fool. And if it was something, and they were up to no good and found out that I'd snitched... I just didn't want to draw a target on my head."

A target? He'd probably read the article about Fox's mutilation. Her mind skipped to Malone's idea of a tip line. Would anyone call? She needed to stress the importance of speaking up. "We'll only grow stronger as a community if we look out for each other, Mr. Cooper."

"I appreciate that, but—" he shook his head "—I didn't want to get involved. As I said, I was tired and wanted to go to bed."

She mulled over what he'd told them so far and what else he might know that could help them, then landed on something. "Did you see what direction they came from?" If he had, they could backtrack the trio's steps and maybe get somewhere useful.

"Yeah. From that direction." Justin pointed a finger and indicated the west.

Stashing that fact away, she pulled out her business card and got to her feet. She extended it to Justin, who asked that she put it on his side table.

"Germs," he mumbled.

"May I suggest something, Mr. Cooper?" Amanda started. "Continue to lock your windows and doors, and if anyone comes to your door that you don't know, talk to them through the door. Don't let them in, no matter what. Even if they say they're a reporter or a cop, you call me."

Justin glanced at the card and then back to her. "Will do."

"Thank you." Amanda didn't want to frighten him, but she felt it necessary to warn him to be diligent. The killer they were after was unpredictable and looking for a reason to kill. Exhibit A: Shannon Fox. She didn't want to add Justin Cooper to the list of victims.

CHAPTER THIRTY-NINE

After leaving Justin Cooper's place, Amanda called Malone. He answered on the third ring. "Was just starting to wonder if you were going to answer."

"What do you need?"

Malone's sharp and pointed response surprised her. "Everything all right?" He seemed his normal self when she'd left him.

"Fine, but I'm really busy. You called me. What do you need?"

"Ah, Trent and I just finished talking to the eyewitness." She paused, expecting him to inquire how it went and whether they obtained any good leads, but he said nothing. She updated him anyhow, then added, "I need you to reach out to a sergeant from the uniformed officers division. Canvassing officers need to know that the witness saw a man and two young women coming from the west around midnight. They might want to extend their reach a few blocks in that direction. Even branch out onto some side streets."

"Sure. That all?"

What the heck is his issue?

"Detective?" he prompted.

She wanted to ask again if he was all right, but she knew better. "Ah, yeah. If the officers could submit their interviews to me and Trent as fast as possible, including the ones conducted with the people in the crowd, that would be great."

"That all?"

She considered asking how he'd made out with the real estate agent but thought he would have said if he had anything. "Yeah, that's—" And he hung up on her. She held out her phone to verify that, yes, he had, in fact, ended the call.

"What's up?" Trent asked.

"Good question. Malone's acting strange." At least toward her. His reputation around the department was that he was a little gruff, all business, and matter-of-fact, but he'd never shown that side to her before now.

"He's probably just coming to grips with the fact that Prince William County has a serial killer. Again." Trent added the later bit, and it stamped home the sad reality. Their poor county seemed to be a ripe poaching ground for psychopaths. Then again, they were close to Washington. Politics. Politicians. She would have found her train of thought amusing if it weren't for the fact two more people were dead, likely the young women Justin Cooper had seen.

She gestured for Trent to join her, and they started down the sidewalk, heading west. She didn't even know what she was looking for and hoped if there was something noteworthy to the case, she'd be able to pick it out. But sometimes the relevance didn't crystallize until later, once other factors entered in.

Her phone rang, and they stopped walking.

She expected caller ID to show *Malone*, that he was calling to explain why he'd been rather rude, but it showed as *Unknown*. "Detective Amanda Steele," she answered.

"This is Dr. Jeffery from the Office of the Chief Medical Examiner."

A quick look around confirmed no one else was within earshot. "One second. I'm going to put you on speaker." Amanda pulled her phone back and could hear Jeffery talking as if she hadn't heard Amanda. She clicked the button for speaker and then cut into Jeffery's speech. "Can you start again, please?"

There was an audible sigh. "I heard back from the lab about the drug used on Ms. Fox. It was a lethal dosage of ketamine, or Special K as it's called on the street."

"It's one of the most commonly used date-rape drugs out there," Amanda said. Her time on the job taught her that much. "Women wake up the next morning and may not remember anything, or if they do it's blurry and scattered." What she didn't verbalize was the drug also had an intoxicating effect. Her earlier suspicion—that the girls Justin Cooper saw weren't drunk but drugged—was gaining merit.

"Well, as you know, Fox wasn't raped, but I'd say the killer used the drug on her for two purposes. One, for sedation so that he could sever her tongue without resistance, and two, for the purpose of killing her."

Pleasant thoughts…

"You should know, Detective, that the drug actually has a practical use as well. It's used to treat depression and provide pain relief."

"But varying doses would have a different effect, correct?" Amanda asked, her mind on the way evil people manipulated the drug.

"Yes."

"Thank you." Amanda ended the call and turned to Trent. "The girls weren't drunk, they were drugged. Probably with Special K. Also, if we run with the assumption that the man Justin Cooper saw was our killer, then he brought the girls to 816 Clear Mountain Circle."

"Okay, but Ted Dixon recognized Ashley Lynch, having seen her around the house on Bill Drive. Was she squatting there, or had the killer taken her there?"

"Hard to say. Chris Ingram described a girl who could have been Ashley Lynch walking with a man on Bill Drive. Taking her to five thirty-two?" She shrugged. "I don't know. What I do know is if Lynch was drugged with ketamine like Fox, then that remains a constant in his MO. He might normally use it for its intoxicating effects but chose to switch it up with Fox."

"When will we know if Lynch was drugged?"

"Good question." She pulled out her phone and called Rideout. She met with his voicemail and left a message.

She resumed walking, soaking in how beautiful the day was. It was warm, but not blazing hot, and the sun was shining brightly with barely a cloud in sight. Yet no one was out walking, working in their yards, or sitting on their front steps or porches. The only people out of their homes seemed to be clustered across from the scene at 816.

She noted many vehicles in driveways, some on the street. A white van, marked with a decal on the door, pulled away. *The Pansy Shoppe.* They were out of Triangle, a small town about four minutes from Dumfries. She'd ordered her wedding flowers from them, and sometimes picked up arrangements for Kevin's and Lindsey's graves there.

The observation portrayed such a contrast. Death, murder, and mayhem steps away. Yet people went on with their lives, even beautifying them with fresh bouquets.

"Let's turn back and see if there's anything more the fire marshal can tell us. Maybe the anthropologist has arrived and—" Her phone rang, and she answered without consulting caller ID.

"Mandy, you're still coming for dinner, right? I know you're a busy girl. Don't know if you're caught up with investigating those murders that have hit the paper, but your family wants to see you." Her mother finally stopped to catch her breath.

The family Sunday dinners started when her mother was released on bail. In her mom's words, "I want to make the most of my time left as a free woman." There was no way Amanda wanted to let her down—she'd already done that enough for a lifetime and then some—but she had a serial killer to stop. "Yeah, they're my cases, Mom."

"Oh." The disappointment, the dejection… One of the teeniest words in the English language, and her mother had managed to wield it as a knife. "You do need to eat. Can't you just drop in for a quick bite? I promise I won't tie you down." Her mother's voice was grim, but her turn of phrase was macabre considering she'd restrained the man she murdered. Her mother cleared her throat and said, "Poor choice of words. But I won't be here forever, you know."

Amanda glanced at Trent, considered her mother's words and balanced it with the workload and urgency of this case. Her mother was right about Amanda needing to eat, though argument could be made that she often went hours without food when on a case. Her mother also had a point that the family dinners would soon come to an end. "What time will dinner be on the table?"

"Wonderful. That means you're coming? Say six? You can make it then?"

Amanda pulled back her phone and read the time. *2:20 PM.* "I'll do my best." There was a brief silence, which Amanda filled. "I love you, Mom."

"Oh you've made me so happy. Love you, Mandy Monkey."

Amanda ended the call.

"Mandy Monkey?" Trent said and started laughing.

She glared at him. "What the—"

"I, uh, overheard." He was snickering, probably doing all he could not to have a good old belly laugh.

No one was to call her Mandy Monkey outside of her family. She didn't even like them calling her that, but she tolerated it because of who they were. Trent might be her professional partner, even a friend, but for him to use her nickname was crossing a line. "Don't you ever call me that."

"I'm so… sorry." He bit back more laughter, and tears beaded in his eyes.

She shook her head. "Do what you must. Get it out of your system before we go back to the scene."

He instantly became silent, his spark gone like she'd put a hose on him. And thank goodness, because they needed to keep perspective if they were going to win this one.

*

There was a new vehicle at 816 when Amanda and Trent returned.

"The anthropologist has arrived, as you probably figured out," Mia announced.

If the van hadn't been a clue, Amanda could see three people working in the interior of the structure, which served as a stage for a sold-out macabre production, given the growing audience across the street. She turned to Trent and said, "Take pictures, please."

"Sure."

"I already took a lot at different points today," Mia said, almost sounding offended.

"I'm sure you did." Amanda smiled pleasantly. *Next subject...* "Are we any further along in knowing what was used to cause the fire?"

"Situations like this can take a while, but I'm considering bringing in some dogs trained to detect different accelerants."

"Excuse me—are you detectives?" A thirty-something man came toward them. He had been one of the three people working inside the rubble.

"Detective Amanda Steele," she said and gestured to her partner. "And Detective Trent Stenson."

"I am Leo. I work with Dr. Strickland. He is the anthropologist." He paused to indicate a man who was hunched down. "He asked that I give you an update." Leo talked like a programmed robot and seemed to have an aversion to contractions. "It will take some time to reconstruct the victims from what we have to work with. So far, he has found the remains of two distinct individuals. Both female, teenagers."

"Is there any way to tell if they were dead before the fire?" Amanda asked.

The tiniest of smiles formed and disappeared. "It all depends on what the bones tell Dr. Strickland."

Amanda nodded, supposing she could appreciate that. "Thank you for the update."

Leo dipped his head and returned to his boss. Mia had walked off, leaving Amanda alone with Trent.

"I think we should assume our killer strangled them before setting the fire." She at least hoped for that mercy to being incapacitated and left to burn alive. "We need to find out what took place between the time they'd headed into the backyard and the fire." She put her gaze on the burned structure, her mind compiling everything from the previous cases with what was before her. The killer had failed to destroy Lynch's body, making finding her identity easier. Had he intended to make that impossible with these two girls? Was he trying to disguise the fact his victims were involved in sex trafficking—if they had been? Justin Cooper had described the girls as wearing tight and revealing clothing. That could fit. But why had their killer targeted them? It was beyond time to find out, but she didn't know where to start. What she did know was she had to be on time for dinner with her family, and she had a few things she wanted to take care of first.

CHAPTER FORTY

Amanda managed to cross some to-dos off her list before heading over to her parents'. She got Mia's business card and confirmed with Malone that the real estate agent had a solid alibi. Malone was still acting curt, but she let it go. She was going to need as much emotional fortitude as she could gather just to be with her family. As nice as it was to be reunited with them, it still churned some unpleasant feelings—mostly of guilt for leaving their lives for the majority of the past six years.

She also reached Aiden Adkins at home, and it turned out he managed 816 Clear Mountain Circle. The only third-party people who crossed over between that house and 532 Bill Drive were the real estate agent, who they already knew about, and the estimator, who was on vacation. So they were back to square one.

Despite all that, Amanda managed to have a shower and to put on a change of clothes. She'd caked on makeup to hide the growing bags under her eyes and arrived on her parents' front step at six on the mark.

She rapped on the door and let herself in—and took a deep breath. Roast beef and onions... So much better than smoke, fire damage, and charred remains.

Her mother sandwiched Amanda's face with her hands and pulled her in for a hug. "Sweetheart, I'm so happy you made it!"

"Just here for dinner, Mom." Amanda backed out of the embrace.

"I know, I know… Come on, take off your shoes and stay a while."

Amanda shucked her shoes next to a bunch of others that belonged to her siblings, their mates, and their children. She'd identified a few of their vehicles in the driveway and along the street. When she parked behind her brother Kyle's pickup, she'd hesitated and considered just driving away. Ever since she'd been involved with arresting their mother, she was quite sure that Kyle blamed her. He hadn't said so much in words, but he was cool toward her and they used to be so close.

Voices were coming from the family room at the back of the house. It was past the kitchen and dining room.

"How did you make out after I left?" Amanda asked her mom, referring to the lawyer visit she had run out on a few days ago.

Her mother waved a hand. "I don't want to talk about that tonight, Mandy." She turned and went toward the kitchen. Amanda followed.

Her sisters Kristen and Emily were performing a type of choreographed dance as they worked around each other to take pans out of the oven, clear pots from the stove, and dish food into bowls.

Smiles, hellos, and waves were passed around.

Her twelve-year-old niece, Ava—Kristen's daughter—and Demi, her brother's daughter, were setting the table. They were good partners and had the rhythm down, but they should—this was a show on repeat every Sunday night. Nothing like a murder charge to bring a family together…

Ava set down the utensils and hugged her aunt. She was just a couple of years younger than Demi, an age when it was acceptable to still show affection.

"Hey, sweetie, how are you?" Amanda asked her.

"Doin' all right. Looking forward to summer break."

"That's still a long way out, but stay strong." Amanda smiled and latched eyes with Kyle. He was sitting in a comfy rocking chair that faced the dining room. She brightened her expression for him, but he looked away. That cut. And it had her taking a few seconds to compose herself.

"Hey, Aunt Amanda." It was Demi calling her name. She'd finished setting out the plates and was at Amanda's side.

"Hiya, sweetie." She hugged her niece. Maybe Demi wasn't too old, after all. And the grudge her brother held against her didn't seem to have passed along to his daughter.

Amanda took a deep breath and continued to the family room. It was full. Besides her brother, there was Kristen's husband, Erik; Emily's love interest of a few months, Rocco; Kyle's wife, Michelle; her sister Megan; and her father.

Missing was Megan's husband, Ray—though that was no surprise. He wasn't exactly into the whole "Sunday night dinner with the in-laws" thing and made no secret of it. Amanda sometimes wondered if Ray even liked them. His loss if not. Also missing was her baby sister, Sydney, and her boyfriend, Dylan; her nephew, Jake, who was her brother's son; and Emily's daughter, Katie. But teenagers could be excused.

Hugs had just been given all around, except for between her and Kyle, when her mother called out, "Dinner's ready. Get to the table."

Amanda had never seen people move as fast as her family did when one of their mother's meals was about to be served. The subsequent thought stung Amanda: who would take care of their dad after Mom went to prison? None of them could really tend to him like his wife had. Did her dad even know how to cook? Heating up a microwave meal didn't count.

He'd been spoiled—as they all were—by Mom's cooking. She wasn't fancy, but she did wholesome, home-cooked meals that would have made the pilgrims proud.

As Amanda munched on the most delectable and moist roast beef of her life, she listened, she absorbed, she observed. She was soaking all of this in. Family. What she had given up for so long. After Kevin and Lindsey had died, she'd pried herself away from them. Such a hard thing to comprehend now. And she couldn't help but feel responsible for what their future as a family looked like. Their mother would go to prison; it was just a question of for how long. So Amanda would enjoy this time with her family, even if it was a brief visit. Sometimes, though, she wondered if the continuous banter was how they distracted themselves from reality.

As everyone finished up, most eased back in their chairs with satisfied looks on their faces. Her father patted his stomach and was the first to praise his wife for the fantastic meal. The gratitude and compliments were echoed around the table and ended with Kyle, who belched his appreciation and received a "Dad, that's gross" from Demi.

"Your sister's sorry she couldn't make it for dinner." Her mother was sitting next to Amanda and took her hand. "Syd isn't able to get here until later, but you'll be running off. Am I right?" A little stab of a guilt—a weapon most mothers were skilled at wielding.

"No choice," Amanda said. "I'd stay if I could."

Her mother patted Amanda's arm. "I know."

When Amanda looked up from where her mother had touched her, she met Kyle's gaze. Again, he looked away.

Her sisters Kristen and Emily had kicked into action and were clearing the table, and Amanda went to get up to help.

"You stay right there," her mother directed.

"I should help," Amanda said.

"Stay," her mother said, then, "Kristen."

Their mother's tone had her thirty-three-year-old daughter moving faster. Why?—Amanda had no idea. Just like every other week, it would be tea and apple pie. But it was a brief glance from Kristen that told her they had something else planned.

"No. You didn't need to do anything," Amanda groaned and slid down her chair.

"Nonsense. It's your birthday," her mother said.

"Not until Tuesday."

"Now, now, this is the best time. And sit up before your back becomes a question mark." She rushed Amanda with waving hands.

Kristen brought in a large rectangular cake with white icing and, gratefully, no candles to serve as a visual testimony to her age.

"Vanilla with a strawberry filling, just how you like it." Her mother beamed at Amanda. "At least I hope you still like it that way. I should have asked, but then it wouldn't have been a surprise. You didn't think we weren't going to do anything for your birthday, I hope. Happy birthday to you, happy birth—" She stopped and leveled a glare at the rest of the family, and they all joined in singing to Amanda.

Off-pitch, off-key, off-tempo, but it was the most beautiful thing she'd heard in a long time. Tears sprung to her eyes, but she pressed her lips into a smile to stave off crying, while her heart ached. She had forgotten just how much her family meant to her and how much they were a part of not only her life, but her very essence.

CHAPTER FORTY-ONE

He had followed her home and waited outside, wanting to knock on her door and witness her reaction when she answered. But maybe his face would mean nothing to her. It would all depend on how smart and good she was at her job. He'd given her an opportunity to see him, but he was quite sure she'd looked through him, just like his mother often did.

Sure, she'd thanked him for getting the door for her that one day at the diner, but she didn't really *see* him. It had been nothing more than etiquette in action, practiced by rote.

But with his mind yapping tirelessly, he'd ended up missing his opportunity to surprise her—and what did he really want to do anyway? He still hadn't decided. Did he want to kill her or just make her realize how she was interfering in his plans and had strayed from his team?

She'd ended up coming out of her house, dressed differently than when she'd entered. When she drove off, he followed her across Dumfries. He kept at a distance but watched as she parked behind a pickup truck near a house with a large wraparound porch. It looked like there was a party going on with the full driveway and some other vehicles parked on the street.

He keyed the house's address into his phone and did a reverse search. *Nathan Steele.*

He grinned broadly. "I'll be," he said out loud to himself.

This was Amanda's parents' place, and all those vehicles had to belong to her siblings.

Her siblings…

Anger knotted in his chest, and he clenched his hands into fists on top of the steering wheel. She had a real, functioning family who did dinners together on Sunday. Idyllic. Fictional—in his experience.

He found himself hating the detective even more. He wanted to strip everything from her, let her know true pain when he killed every one of her siblings and her parents.

But he calmed as he remembered that Amanda didn't have a perfect life, the perfect family. She'd lost her husband and daughter, and her mother was a killer, just like him.

He felt a little warmth shoot through him. Amanda should understand him. The instinct to kill probably flowed through her veins, just like the woman who had given birth to her. And yet she wasn't on his team as he'd first thought. She was working against him to shut down his stories from getting out. She'd turned that newswoman away. He really couldn't forgive her for that.

She had to know that she was making herself an enemy. The severed tongue—how could he have been any clearer that he wanted no more interference? Had he messed up somehow, sent another message entirely? Or was the detective not as good as she was portrayed in the newspaper back in January? Another option, and this one sent rage through him, was that the detective had purposely done her part to ignore him and deny him satisfaction.

That possibility was worse than all else. She had seen him but chose to disregard him and assign him little value and importance.

What more could he do to make it evident that he was serious and that it was his time to be glorified? He deserved to be seen for what he was—someone who made a positive contribution to this world.

He was no longer that child doing whatever he could think of to make his parents pay attention to him. He'd found his path through his pain, and now he had his life mapped out. He knew what to do to make a difference in this world. And he was doing it.

The detective obviously didn't understand that, but she would. He would see to it.

CHAPTER FORTY-TWO

Amanda had eaten two pieces of cake before leaving her parents and hugging everyone goodbye. Kyle hugged her, but he had clearly done so because he'd caved under the pressure of everyone watching. He had whispered into her ear, "Mom may have forgiven you, but I haven't."

It had taken all her willpower not to cry then and there, but she made it to her car. She let the tears fall as she drove from her parents' to Central. Best she get the tears out of the way before she met up with Trent at seven thirty—something they'd arranged before they took a break for dinner.

Her phone rang, and *Jacob Briggs* popped up on the vehicle's onboard display. She answered immediately. "Tell me you have good news."

"Interesting way of answering your phone."

"I could just use some good news right about now."

There was silence on the other end.

"You're not calling with any," she surmised.

"You'd be right about that. Sorry."

"Nope. You would have done all you could." She had every confidence if there was a way to track the blocked number that had called Fraser Reyes, Jacob would have found it.

"I did. Wish it met with better results."

"Makes two of us. Thanks, though."

"You're welcome." Jacob ended the call.

She pulled into Central, and a message from Trent came in. She parked and read it.

Be there in about thirty minutes. Sorry.

Okay. she sent back and pocketed her phone. The time in the top left-hand corner of her phone told her it was seven thirty now.

She went to her desk and found a handwritten scribble on a sticky note that the canvassing officers' interviews from that day were already in the system, available to read.

"Good to know," she said to herself as she sat at her desk. If talking to oneself was the first sign of insanity, she was in trouble.

Before she went looking for the interviews, though, she logged into her email to see if anything useful would filter in. There were a couple. One from Detective Robbins and another from Mia Vaughn. Amanda opened the latter first.

Some pictures of the crowd. Sketches and photos of the house to follow.

They always seemed to take longer, but Amanda couldn't imagine them revealing much to her, given the condition of the structure. But at least she had something to work with. She printed the three image attachments in color, collected them from the printer on her desk, and closed the email.

Next, she opened Chester Robbins's email. Attached were the investigation files for Crystal Foster and Ashley Lynch. In the body, he provided a clear list of the top three suspects' names. At the sight of them, she knew what she had to do. Her father had placed a high value on intuition, that sixth sense as a cop, so she listened to hers and called Patty Glover.

"Detective Glover."

She had expected voicemail due to the time of night. "Ah, Patty, it's Amanda Steele."

"Hey there, what's up?" The cheeriness in Patty's voice made Amanda wish she'd been calling with good news.

"There was another fire, and two more young women were killed."

"Oh." One word, and Amanda felt the pang of hurt travel the line.

"That's four victims in…four days, three of them only teens."

"Were the most recent ones branded too?"

"No way of knowing. The fire destroyed their bodies, left only bones. All we have is an eyewitness who saw a man with two young women go into the backyard of the house."

There were a few seconds of silence.

Amanda went on. "We were able to ID the victim pulled from the first fire. Her name was Ashley Lynch, out of Washington. She was groomed on social media by someone claiming to be a boy from her high school. Obviously it wasn't. Ashley was spotted with another friend—who also ran away—talking with a woman."

"I wish I could help."

Amanda shifted straighter in her chair. "You might be able to, and I may be able to help you. I have a few names from the detective who investigated Ashley Lynch's disappearance. He cleared these people, but I was hoping you could take a look and see if any of them mean something to you. Might even give you a lead to shut these monsters down. Or at least make their lives hell." Amanda had amended her comment because Patty had told her before that it was near impossible to destroy these rings. They'd just reorganize and pick up business as usual.

"Sure, shoot the names over, and I'll take a look."

They wished each other a good night in spite of the darkness that had occupied their entire conversation.

Amanda's phone rang immediately.

"Just wanted to let you know that the tip line will be functional and broadcast on the eleven o'clock news." It was Malone, and he was to-the-point again.

"You got that set up fast."

"How I work."

She thought for a second he was going to hang up on her, but he said, "How are things going with the case?"

"Nothing more since we last spoke. Just about to dig back in now. I'll probably start with reviewing the interviews conducted by canvassing officers from today and see if any leads pop up there."

"Good. Keep me posted."

"You're sure everything's okay?"

"Four dead bodies in four days. Not really." He hung up.

Maybe he was just upset about the murders and his mood had nothing to do with her, after all.

"Heard you on the phone."

She turned to see Trent going to his desk.

"Was it Malone?" he asked.

"Yep. The tip line will be in place for the eleven o'clock news."

"That's good. Right?"

"Sure." She was for it when Malone had made the suggestion, had doubts about its effectiveness when talking to Justin Cooper, and now, with its inevitability, they had become stronger. Even if someone did decide to speak, would they come forward only to get themselves killed for doing so? She cleared her throat and told Trent about the memo she'd received on the yellow two-by-two square.

"I'll get started on reading the interviews." He no sooner finished speaking than he started clicking away on his keyboard.

"Ah, just a couple more things. I got an email from Mia, and she sent over some pictures of the crowd."

He looked over the partition, and she passed him the colored printouts.

He glanced at the pictures, then at his monitor, back at the pictures. His brow furled up. "Huh."

"What is it?"

"Well, it looks like…" His lips were moving, but no words were coming out.

"Trent," she prompted.

"There's a folder on the server labeled *Crowd Interviews*, but nothing from canvassing officers."

"Okay, well, start with what we have."

"No problem, but I just counted and there are fourteen interviews and, in this picture—" he held up one of the printout she'd given him "—there's fifteen people."

"You're sure?"

"Let me count again…" His lips started moving like before, then he nodded.

"All right, well, we'll just have to figure out who got missed."

CHAPTER FORTY-THREE

"How do we figure out who wasn't interviewed?" Trent left his desk and joined Amanda in her cubicle.

She could only think of one way. "We read through all the interviews—you do half, I'll do the other half. We'll pull background reports for everyone as we go and compare their DMV photos with the pictures of the crowd. It's likely most of them have a driver's license. We mark off every face as we go along. Make a copy of the picture and give one back to me."

Trent left for the copy room to do as she'd asked and returned seconds later. "Here."

"Thanks."

"No problem." Next thing she saw was the top of Trent's head from his cubicle as he looked down and pecked away on his keyboard.

She got to work on her half. She'd had to pull a lot more backgrounds at one time before. Seven were nothing. But still the hours passed. It was one fifteen in the morning when she had one more report to pull.

The interviewing officer recorded her name as Cindy Page.

Cindy... It wasn't a common name, but one she'd heard recently.

She typed Cindy Page into the system and... nada. She brought up a map of Dumfries in her mind, and the address Cindy gave during the interview was only a block over from the first fire. Then it suddenly sank in why Cindy was familiar. She was the young woman Amanda had spoken to, the one who had brought her boyfriend a coffee. Why wasn't she in the system, and what was she doing at the scene of the second fire?

"Trent, you finished over there? I need your photo to see who you marked off."

"Ah, yeah." Trent's marker squeaked across the page as he inflicted his final *X* before handing it to her.

She scratched off the faces on his that she had on hers. They were left with two—a dark-haired man and a blonde with teal highlights standing several people apart. "Okay, quite sure this is Cindy Page. I spoke to her and her boyfriend at the scene of the first fire. But that man is a mystery." She went digging through the image gallery on her phone, searching the photos of the gawkers from the first crime scene. She stared at one after the other, looking to see if she could find his face in the crowd there—and finally she found him.

"Look!" She pointed excitedly at his face on the screen and then to the one in the printed copy from the Clear Mountain Circle crime scene.

"He was at both fires."

"And so was Cindy…" Did that mean anything? Was she grasping for a clue so badly she was making them up now? After all, Cindy and the mystery man weren't standing together in any of the photos. There was nothing screaming that they knew each other. It could have just been a coincidence that they were both at the two scenes? But what about the morning of Fox's murder? Had they been in the crowd that day?

"Quick," she directed Trent, "look for them in the crowd across from Fox's house."

Trent rushed back to his desk, and shortly later, his printer came to life.

"Both the man and woman were there too." Trent bolted to his feet, snatched the paper off the tray, and handed it to her. He pointed out their faces. "Him, right there in the back, and her near the front."

What the hell is going on? Her heart raced, and her stomach tightened. "Okay, we pull all the crowd interviews—from the first fire and across from Fox's house. His name has to be there somewhere." As she heard herself rattling off directions, she realized she was getting ahead of herself. And if the man was the killer, would he have stuck around to be interviewed? By extension, if he was questioned, she couldn't imagine that he'd provide his real information. There was something they could try right now, though.

Amanda took out her notebook and confirmed the address was the same as the one Cindy's boyfriend had given her at the first fire. She got up from her chair and said, "Let's go."

"Where?"

"To visit Cindy Page, assuming we have her right address. I'd like to know why she was at all three crime scenes, and if she knows who he is." She pressed a fingertip to the man's face and felt a tug of recognition, but she couldn't really place from where. Maybe she had seen him in the crowds, but he hadn't really stood out to her. Though he did look a lot like that actor Tom Cruise.

CHAPTER FORTY-FOUR

Two in the morning was an advantageous time to show up at someone's door. It would probably throw Cindy Page and her boyfriend off guard and give Amanda and Trent the advantage.

Amanda knocked hard with one hand and rang the doorbell with the other. And she kept pounding until she felt a vibration reach the porch floorboards. Someone was coming. The outside light flicked on, and the door *whooshed* open.

The guy with the teal hair—Simon West—was standing there with a gun pointed at them.

Amanda and Trent drew their weapons.

"Prince William County PD. Put your gun down and your hands up," she barked.

"Hey, I didn't know who I'd be opening the door to at this hour." The guy held up his free hand and put his gun on the floor.

Trent collected it and proceeded to clear the magazine and chamber.

"We're not off to a very good start here, Simon," she said.

"What are you doing here?"

"Simon?" It was a female's voice, leery, small. She came up behind Simon. It was Cindy.

"You may not remember me, but I spoke to you on Thursday across from the house fire at five thirty-two Bill Drive. I'm Detective Steele, and this is Detective Stenson." She dropped their first names to stress this was anything but a social visit—as if the hour alone didn't say that much. "We need to ask you some questions." She gestured toward the inside of the house, implying that she was looking for the invitation to enter.

The couple backed into the house, allowing Amanda and Trent room to get in.

Trent closed the door behind them once they were all standing in the entry.

"Do you have someplace we could sit?" Amanda had intended to approach this visit calmly and rationally, but starting off with a gun in her face had her very guarded and vigilant.

Cindy covered a yawn with her hand while Simon's body sagged, and he led them down a short hall to a living room. The place could have used a good tidying. Dirty plates and a couple of empty beer bottles sat on a coffee table.

Simon dropped onto the couch, Cindy next to him, their hips touching.

Both of them looked like death warmed over, and Amanda would guess that she and Trent had woken them up. There were a few other chairs in the room. Trent sat in one, but Amanda remained standing.

"Cindy, why were you at the scene of the fire on Bill Drive the other day?" Amanda started.

"We told you," Simon jumped in. "We just heard the fire trucks and were curious."

Amanda gave him a corrective glare and said firmly, "I asked Cindy."

"What he said."

"Okay." Amanda had the photo of Cindy in the crowd across from Fox's house ready to pull up on her cell phone, and she did so now. "And we see that you were here the next day."

Cindy's cheeks flushed. "So?"

"Do you know where this picture was taken?" Amanda asked.

Cindy wet her lips and stared across the room for several seconds but said nothing. Then, "Also on Bill Drive."

"That's right. What were you doing there?"

"Just watching everything going on. That's all."

Amanda would play diplomat to start. "Did you know Shannon Fox?"

She shook her head and blinked slowly.

"What about him?" Amanda pointed to their mystery man's face.

Cindy looked closely at the picture. "He looks familiar. But I don't know him. I probably just saw him when I was there that day."

Amanda had a feeling that might have been the case but had to ask and see her reaction. It would seem she was telling the truth—she didn't know the guy. She pulled up the computer-rendered photo of Ashley Lynch and showed it to Cindy. Before she could ask, Cindy started trembling, and her chin quivered. Tears fell down her cheeks, and she gripped the fabric of her shirt over her heart.

Amanda had hit a bullseye. "You knew her."

Cindy sniffled. "She was... my best friend."

Amanda felt tingles run over her shoulders and down her arms. She hadn't expected that response, and it had her looking at Cindy in a different light. When she'd first met Cindy on Bill Drive, she pegged her in her twenties, but she had been wearing sunglasses. Now that Amanda was able to peer right into the girl's eyes, she saw she was much younger. Also, the words *best friend* kept circling in Amanda's mind, and she recalled the card at the memorial signed off "Always" followed by *C* and a doodle. "Did you leave a card at the memorial on Bill Drive with a dragonfly on the front?"

Cindy licked her lips, bit down on her bottom one, and nodded.

"And you love dragonflies?" The Fosters said their daughter did.

"Yeah. So?"

"Are you... Crystal Foster?" Amanda had a hard time getting the words past the lump in her throat.

Cindy—Crystal?—burrowed against Simon's side. She clung to him like she depended on him to protect and save her. Amanda looked with closer scrutiny at Simon. He had to be several years older.

Amanda scanned Crystal for any signs of branding, and any other red flags she knew about sex trafficking. Normally the girls were spoken for and never let out of their pimp's sight. Simon tended to do the former, but maybe it was just his personality or desire to shelter her. She had left Simon's side without supervision to get coffee the other day. It wouldn't seem Simon was controlling her in the obvious sense, and he gave Amanda the impression that he really cared about the girl. But did he know that she was only sixteen? The mother in Amanda wanted to react, slap cuffs on him, and put him in jail without hesitation. The cop in her cautioned that if she wanted Crystal, a.k.a. Cindy, to talk, she had to remain cool.

"Are you Crystal Foster?" Amanda repeated.

The girl's eyes connected with Amanda's, and eventually, she sluggishly nodded. "But not in a very long time."

"And the girl in the picture here... Who was she?" Amanda wanted further confirmation.

"Ashley Lynch." Crystal bit her bottom lip.

Amanda left the screen in Crystal's face. "Do you know who killed her?"

Crystal kept her eyes on the image.

"Your best friend, Ashley Lynch, was murdered." Putting it out there so bluntly to a young woman pierced Amanda's heart, but this girl needed to know there were consequences to striving for so-called freedom. Amanda also wasn't too certain of her innocence just yet. She let the image stay in front of Crystal for several seconds before she pocketed her phone and sat in a chair next to Trent's and across from the couch.

Crystal was sobbing, and Simon passed her a tissue. Considering their illegal union, she didn't give Amanda any obvious signs that she was there against her will. Then again, that was the power of a talented abuser: mind control. The restraints were there but not visible. Even if they considered themselves in love, it still came down to the fact that Simon was much older, and as such, could manipulate her.

"We need you to start talking to us, Crystal," Amanda said. "Did you know Ashley was inside that house?"

Crystal rubbed her arms. "I didn't know, but—" She stopped talking and let a fresh batch of tears fall in silence. She dabbed them with the tissue and continued. "I ran into Ash a couple of weeks ago at a vintage clothing store. I hadn't seen her in years." Pain riddled the young woman's expression, wrenching Amanda's heart.

"You ran away together, didn't you?" Not so much a question but a way to keep her talking.

"We did." She rubbed a cheek to a shoulder. "I left mostly for her. She met some guy online and was obsessed with him.

"Can you tell us about him?" Amanda asked. "Did you ever meet him?"

"No." Crystal played with the hem of her pajama top, seeming to search her mind for the words to express herself. "Ash was a little nervous. She'd only met him online, but he wanted to hook up in person. He told her to go the food court in City Center Mall. She asked that I go along with her. The guy wasn't there, but some woman was. She said that Riley sent her—that was Ash's crush—and he wanted her to go to Corner Pocket Billiards here in town." Crystal shivered, and Simon hugged her tighter.

"What happened then?" Amanda was curious how it had all unfolded.

"The woman gave us some cash—said it was a gift from Riley—and bought us bus tickets to Dumfries. I wanted to turn around and go home, but Ash said we'd come that far and it wasn't fair to bail on Riley now. She told me he must have a good reason for changing locations. That woman tagged along with us."

It was likely the woman that the kid from the burger place had described to Detective Robbins, but maybe Crystal could give her more. "Did she tell you her name?"

"Nah. Just that she was a friend of Riley's."

"What did she look like?"

"She was pretty. Blond, but had a large tattoo up the side of her neck." Crystal ran her hand over the left side of hers. "There was something really, ah…" A shudder tore through her. "She sort of looked like she could be someone's aunt or mother, all kind and pleasant to your face, but there was something so fake about her—and very dark. I still have nightmares about her."

"What happened when you got to Dumfries?"

Crystal took Simon's hand and squeezed it. "I had a really bad feeling, and I… I left Ash…" She let go of Simon and started sobbing. She sniffled and said, "That lady turned her over to some very nasty men. Ash confirmed I'd been right to leave. It doesn't mean I forgive myself for abandoning her."

Amanda wanted to reach out and offer Crystal comfort, but it wasn't her place. It was apparent that Crystal was well aware of Ashley's fate. Not surprising, but something else was. "How did you get away?"

"I told that woman I needed to use the restroom and snuck out a window in the stall."

Smart girl. Did Crystal have any idea how lucky she'd been? Or was she? Amanda glanced at Simon, wanting to broach the topic of their relationship, but there was still more they needed to know.

"Did Ashley sometimes sleep in the house that was set on fire?" Trent slipped in, beating Amanda to the question.

Crystal looked at him. "I don't know if she slept there. She sometimes escaped there for short pockets of time and got back before they noticed her missing. I don't know how she got out of where they were holding her, and don't ask me where it was. I went to the house on Bill Drive with her once or twice and hung out."

"But you were just reunited a couple of weeks ago?" Amanda asked. It was starting to sound as if they'd spent more time together than that.

"Uh-huh, but we chatted more than the one time." Crystal sniffled.

"And how did you arrange to meet up?"

Crystal looked at Amanda as if she were being interrogated. "When we bumped into each other, I gave Ash my address. She'd pop by here. Then we'd do whatever…"

Amanda nodded. "How much do you know about the place on Bill Drive, Crystal?"

"Please stop calling me Crystal. That life was so long ago." Her voice went shrill, and she returned to picking at the hem of her pajama top.

"Okay… *Cindy.*"

A few seconds ticked off.

"She just said she had some friends who squatted there. She talked of running away with them." Crystal licked her lips. "But she was so afraid her pimp would catch up with her."

Amanda wanted more specifics about their reunion. "What was the name of the vintage clothing store where you ran into Ashley?"

"Second Treasures."

Amanda was familiar with the store. It was in Dumfries. "That must have been emotional."

"There were lots of tears." As if on cue, more fell. "She felt so trapped, ya know? She wanted out but couldn't see a way. When we were at the store, there was this guy standing in the corner watching us, mainly Ash. He came over and broke us up and grabbed her arm. I've never seen such fear in a person's eyes in my life. She was terrified, but she pressed on this smile, ya know, for me, to make it look like everything was okay, but I knew it wasn't."

Maybe they'd concluded too soon that the sex ring wasn't behind Ashley Lynch's murder—but where was the motive? And how did Fox and the two recent victims fit in? Either way, there was a question Amanda needed to ask. "Can you remember what the man from Second Treasures looked like?"

"He had the face of the devil. The whites of his eyes were black."

"You're sure?" Amanda asked.

"I'll never forget his face. He was a monster, and he stank of cigarettes and had deep pockmarks in his neck."

"What about age, hair color, build?"

"I dunno… Average and blond."

Not the person described by eyewitnesses and not the mystery man in their photos. "I can understand why you were outside the house where you and Ashley spent some time, but what brought you to watch the scene unfold down the street where that woman was murdered?"

"As I said, curiosity." Crystal's voice trembled.

Amanda nodded. She'd been curious if Crystal would say something different when asked again. "And to the fire that happened on Clear Mountain Circle?"

"Curiosity."

"Again. Okay. How did you even know about it?"

Crystal glanced at Simon, then said, "We have a police radio scanner."

Those things should be banned. Amanda rested her gaze on Crystal's face again. So young to have been through so much. Her mind turned back to Ashley, and she asked Crystal, "Did you give Ashley your dragonfly pin?"

"How do you know about… You found that?" Her voice was small, more like a child's than ever. "Was it on her?"

"It was," Amanda confirmed gently.

"Can I get it back?"

"Maybe after the investigation is over."

"Please. I know it's worth a lot. I told her to pawn it or something, run far away."

She didn't want to lay any guilt or blame on Crystal, but she had other questions that needed answers. "Why didn't you do that a long time ago, and why not go home?"

"I thought of it, but that's when I met Simon and—" she touched his arm "—he made me feel safe and loved, more than my parents ever did."

"You've been together a long time?" Trent asked.

"For almost three years."

So he was the reason she didn't go home. "Your parents love you. They want you to go home. And, Simon, you should have encouraged her to."

"That was no home!" Crystal yelled. "My parents didn't even raise me—or know me. They had hired help for that. Mom and Dad loved their business far more than me."

There was still obvious hatred and hurt charged around the subject. Amanda raised her hand as a truce—for now. "Why didn't you and Ashley go to the police about her situation? She was able to sneak away for 'pockets at a time,' as you said."

"Ash was convinced they'd kill us both. And now—" Crystal sniffled and pinched the tip of her nose. "They killed her." She sobbed, and Simon hugged her tighter.

"If you thought that, why not come forward?" Amanda asked.

"You're kidding, right?" Crystal's brows knotted. "I was terrified for my life, for Simon's. I'm also terrified that *you're* going to rip us apart."

Amanda looked at Simon, and he stiffened.

"No!" Crystal cried out.

"She's sixteen years old, Simon." Amanda attempted to appeal to his maturity. "You are how old?"

"Twenty-four."

"You knew that she was, and still is, a minor," Amanda concluded.

He looked at Crystal and took her hand. He kissed the back of it.

"Time to go." Amanda gestured for Simon to get to his feet and cuffed him. "You're under arrest for kidnapping and multiple counts of statutory rape."

"No!" Crystal shouted again.

Amanda proceeded to read off his Miranda rights as Crystal went berserk, screaming and wailing.

The night had certainly taken a different turn than Amanda had planned, but that was life. Always tossing curveballs when you least expected.

CHAPTER FORTY-FIVE

Amanda pried her eyes open, and the clock on her nightstand told her it was just a few minutes after eight. It had been five in the morning when she'd finally arrived home after taking Crystal back to her parents in Washington. Amanda had even hung around a little for the reunion, and that had sapped more life from her. Crystal's mother, Leila, had collapsed into herself as she held her daughter tight. Henry had latched onto his wife and daughter and was even more outwardly emotional than Leila. He sobbed loudly, letting the tears stream down his face.

Amanda had made sure Simon West was booked for kidnapping and multiple counts of statutory rape. The cherry on top? Possession of an unregistered firearm, as it turned out.

All that in a day's work—technically *today's* work—from two thirty to five this morning.

She just wanted to burrow her head deeper into her pillow and pull the covers over her face… shut her eyes. But she had a killer to stop. She got out of bed, went through her morning routine, and was about to leave when there was a knock on her door.

Amanda froze, her heart thumping wildly. Was the killer standing on her front step ready to overpower her the second she opened the door? Did killers knock? She shook her crazy imaginings away but laid her hand over her hostler, ready to pull her Glock if needed.

She stood on her tiptoes to see out the high window in the door. Logan stood on the doorstep with flowers. She took a deep breath and opened the door. "Hello… What are you doing here?"

He smiled and extended the bouquet. "Thought I'd hand deliver these."

She took the flowers from him. "What are they for?"

"Your birthday. It is today?"

She sniffed the blooms appreciatively but shook her head. "It's tomorrow."

"Shoot! I thought for sure I had it right. Well, it's better early than late." He hugged her and tapped a quick kiss on her mouth.

She licked her lips and smiled. "I wish I could ask you in, but I have to be going." She touched his cheek, appreciating that his face was becoming familiar and trusted, even a comfort.

"No problem. I've got to get to a dentist appointment myself. Just figured I'd try to catch you. I swung by last night, but you weren't here." There was the enclosed question of her whereabouts, and she'd answer—this time.

"I'm working all hours right now. I actually didn't get in until after five."

"I don't know how you pull it off."

"Me either, honestly."

"Oh, not just the long hours, but still looking the way you do." He smiled. "You're beautiful."

"You caught me after I caked on makeup with a spatula, but I'll take the compliment." She grinned. She wanted to open up to him about the investigations that had her on the go at all hours, but why darken his day? She lifted the flowers. "Thank you for these."

"Don't mention it. But do call me. We're past due for some quality time."

"That we are." She remained at the door, appreciating the view as he walked off and got into his black Dodge Ram. Logan was one good-looking man, and she was grateful for his attention, but she was determined to keep a level head and not get too attached. She knew all too well that good things had a way of being taken away.

She put the bouquet in some water and headed out the door for Central. She grabbed a coffee at Hannah's Diner on the way. Then, she settled at her desk.

The first thing she did was send a copy of the mystery man's photo to CSI Blair asking if she could run it through facial recognition. Getting a hit there would mean their guy had a record. Next, she searched the internet for *white of eyes black*. She had enough time to read some results before Trent arrived.

"Mornin'." He put a to-go cup on her desk and smiled at her before heading to his cubicle.

She eyed the brown cup with the small, scripted *H* in a circle. It was from Hannah's Diner. "You have impeccable timing. I just finished the one I was working on."

"I know how much you love their coffee."

"They've got the best I've ever had."

"As you've said before." Trent laughed. "It's pretty good, but I think you might be stretching it a bit… or you need to get out more."

She narrowed her eyes at him. She couldn't get too angry at him though; he had brought her coffee—and she rather liked the frequency with which it was happening these days. "Just before you got here I googled what could make the whites of a person's eyes black. The guy could have a rare case of severe kidney or liver failure, wear black sclera contact lenses, or he had the whites of his eyes dyed."

Trent's jaw dropped, and he lowered into his chair. "Dyed. Are you kidding me?"

"Add it to the list of the strangest things I've ever heard. But it's called scleral tattooing. It's where a dye is injected between two layers of the eye and the color spreads out."

"Yikes. The thought sends shivers through me."

"Makes two of us. Unless he's wearing contacts, the black is a permanent feature of his appearance, so it should make this guy easily recognizable."

"That's true. So how did you make out last night?" Trent asked, then pressed his cup to his mouth.

She'd taken Crystal to Washington by herself and let Trent go home and get some rest. "It was an emotional night." She stopped there, impacted by the memory of Crystal's face upon seeing her parents. There was spite that had flicked across her eyes, and then there was sorrow. The teenager had ended up bawling as hard as her father.

"I can understand that. Did you tell the Fosters everything— about Ashley, and how Crystal might have something to offer our investigation?"

Before she'd taken Crystal back home, Amanda and Trent had discussed it might be useful if Crystal sat with a police sketch artist and have them draw the woman and the man with the black eyes. "I did. I gave them a heads-up that a police sketch artist might become necessary and gave them the very basics, saying that Crystal might be able to help the police. I recommended to the Fosters that they keep a close eye on Crystal for the next while I also called Detective Robbins to notify Lynch's family."

"Yeah, it seems we have no doubt it was Ashley Lynch now. But how did the Fosters handle everything?"

"About as well as can be expected. They just want to shelter their daughter now that she's back, and I can't blame them."

"Maybe it won't come to needing a sketch artist, but it would be nice to make a dent in this ring."

"You could say that again." Her gaze caught on an incoming email. It was from CSI Blair, subject: *Graveyard & Memorial Notes*.

Amanda opened it and read. The card from the memorial didn't have any useable evidence on it, but they knew its origin now. The note found at Lindsey's grave, along with the envelope, were clean of prints except for Amanda's. Blair said if they found a printer, she could confirm if it was the one used to print the label and message. She might as well have said "go find the needle in the haystack." The envelope itself had been a peel-and-stick, so no saliva mixed with the glue. Blair also said that she had a look at the photo Amanda had sent of the mystery man and could tell immediately that it wasn't of high-enough quality to run through facial recognition. Just one more dead end in trying to get the name for Tom Cruise's lookalike. She recapped everything for Trent.

"It was almost too much to hope for something," he said. "Just like trying to read this killer's mind is proving impossible."

"Challenging, sure, but not impossible."

"If we think of him as being mission-oriented, why these girls who are already victims? It's not like he's really cleaning up the world. If he wants to do that then he should kill the guy with the devil's eyes." Trent was getting himself worked up, but Amanda could empathize. It was frustrating not knowing exactly what was motivating their killer—or how to stop him from murdering more people. Trent added, "Our killer's actually targeting victims, and I'm not sure what to make of that."

"Maybe we should worry less about motive, and just follow the clues. Let's revisit the interviews conducted with people from the crowd. And maybe the ones from the door-to-door canvassing are in now too."

"Detective Steele!" Malone was rushing toward her, and he rarely moved fast.

She got to her feet, sensing there was real trouble. "What is it?"

"Got a lead. A good one."

She'd woken him up last night to fill him in on Crystal, how that went down, the man with the black eyes, and the as-of-yet unidentified man in the photo. "Let's have it."

"A lady here in Woodbridge called the tip line. She saw a man with two young women near her home on Saturday night. Said it looked like he forced them into the back of a van."

"Could be the same man and women from the Clear Mountain Circle crime scene. Trent and I will check it out."

CHAPTER FORTY-SIX

Janet Mills welcomed Amanda and Trent inside her house and told them to get comfortable in the dining room while she put on the kettle for tea. She was in her early sixties with a rotund body and a pleasant smile, though it came quickly and disappeared just as fast.

Amanda and Trent were seated at her dining table while the woman walked around, getting mugs from the cupboards and milk and sugar. It would have been nice to turn down the tea and crank up the urgency of their visit, but Amanda had the sense that, with a woman like Janet, hastiness would just clam her up. She was talking to the cops because she wanted to help, but in return, she expected respect.

"We just need to wait for it to steep." Janet poured the boiled water into an actual teapot and set it on the table. As much as Amanda's family loved tea, they were good with a bag in a cup.

Janet sat down, smoothing out the front of her yellow, floral-patterned dress as she did so. She'd apparently put some effort into beautifying herself for their visit. Her gray hair was bobby-pinned in tight pinwheels against her scalp. She had on red lipstick, which was half worn off due to her dry lips, and some color was outside the lines.

"Thank you for calling in about what you saw, Ms. Mills," Amanda started, and had her mouth open to continue when Janet proceeded to talk.

"Of course, dear. It's the least I could do after hearing about those two dead girls in the fire." She tsked and shook her head.

"You said that you saw a man with two young women getting into the van Saturday night?" Trent asked, leaning forward, his notepad nearby.

Janet slowly drew her eyes from Amanda to Trent. "I did, and I just got the feeling that something wasn't right. He *forced* them into that van, I tell you."

"Actually, before we get to the details of what you saw, what time was this?" Amanda asked, passing a soft glance at Trent.

"It was somewhere around eleven thirty."

Justin Cooper said that he saw the man and women around midnight, so that could fit. They would have had to drive from Woodbridge to Dumfries, park, and go from there. "Okay, so you saw them around eleven thirty... Did you see where they came from before getting to the van?"

"They came from that way." Janet pointed toward the front window, which was visible from where they were, and crooked her finger to the right.

Janet's house was in an area that was mixed residential and commercial. "Great. Did you see them coming out of a house or another building?"

"No, I'd remember that."

"Did you ever see them before?" Trent interjected.

"I don't think so. Now, if you look out my front window—" she gestured in its direction again "—you see that parking lot across the street?"

Amanda nodded.

"The van was parked over there," Janet said.

Amanda had seen the sign when they'd pulled up—the lot was attached to Gamble Insurance, quite a name given their business. But if they had surveillance cameras, their recorded footage might be useful to the investigation. They'd go over there after finishing with Janet. Now, an insurance company would likely be barren at night, let alone on the weekend, but Amanda asked, "Were any other vehicles parked there at the time?"

"Just that jalopy in the corner." Janet got up and walked to the window. Amanda joined her but noticed that Trent had removed the teabags from the pot and set them on a saucer, before following.

There was a rusted sedan with at least one deflated tire—the car sat on an angle, like it was depressed. It was at the edge of the lot, newer models all around it. Monday morning: everyone was at work now.

"Think it belongs to one of the owners," Janet started. "It's been there forever. Wish they'd move the bloody thing, though. It's such an eyesore."

"But there were no other vehicles or people around that you saw Saturday night?" Amanda just wanted to be sure.

"No. I would tell you." She flashed a pleasant smile.

Amanda returned her gaze out the window and across the street. There were streetlights around the edge of the lot. "Were you able to get a good look at the three of them?"

"Fairly, I suppose. As you see, there are lights, but only one works. The other is constantly flickering. Like it needs a swift kick."

Amanda laughed. Janet had spunk; she'd give her that.

"Where was the van parked?" Amanda swept the curtains back more to afford a wider view.

"A couple of spots away from the useless light, but he parked so the van was lengthwise to my house."

Staying in the darker area made sense, but why park lengthwise? For that matter, it had been brazen to bring the girls there and load them into his van where anyone could see. Had he been relying on the girls to be more cooperative and not give the impression of being coerced? Amanda wanted to know more about this van. "What—"

"Oh! The tea!" Janet exclaimed, arms flailing the air, as she hurried back to the dining table. "Sorry, but the bags need to come—" Her words stopped there as her gaze hit the plate where Trent had deposited the teabags. He was standing next to her, smiling. "You did this?" she asked him.

Trent nodded.

"Such a nice boy," Janet said, and he blushed.

Janet proceeded to pour the tea and distribute the cups. Everyone made up their tea the way they liked it and sat where they had been before the little trip to the window.

"Ms. Mills, as I was about to ask," Amanda began, "what can you tell us about the van? Its color, age, make and model?"

"It was a GMC Savana. Looked pretty new." Janet blew on her tea and took a sip. "It was white, but it had lettering on the front door. One of them magnet signs, I think."

Amanda sat straighter. She'd seen a white van with lettering recently, and it had been a couple of blocks away from the second fire. "What did it say?"

Janet chewed her bottom lip. "Sorry, but that I couldn't make out. It was black lettering, if that helps. Oh, and it was rather—" She swirled her left index finger in the air.

"A scrolly font?" Trent wagered a guess.

Janet smiled. "Yes, that's it."

The lettering used for the Pansy Shoppe would be considered a scrolly font. That was the business name on the van that Amanda had seen pulling away, and Janet's description, though vague, could fit. Had they finally received a solid lead on their killer? But why would he essentially advertise where to find him? And did the decals have anything to do with the reason he'd parked lengthwise? If so, it was like he wanted people to take notice.

"There were no windows on the side facing me, or on the back of the van," Janet added. "I noticed that when he had the door open, and later after he drove away."

"That's often the case with commercial vans." Amanda was still chewing over how this made sense. "Please run us through exactly what you saw."

"Sure. Ah, the three of them went to the van. One of the girls stopped and pointed at the lettering, and he swept up her arm and sort of corralled her and the other one to the rear door. He opened one side, and the girls seemed hesitant to go inside."

"Did they appear scared? Like they were pulling back or trying to get away?" Trent asked.

"They resisted by what I could tell, but they weren't steady on their feet. The man tried to keep them upright. One of the girls fell down, and he helped her to her feet and put her into the van. Then he lifted the other one inside too."

Amanda wasn't sure that exactly translated to *forced*, but it had obviously been enough of a spectacle to get the older woman's attention. "Then what happened?"

"He got into the driver's seat, and they drove off."

"Which way did they go?"

Janet pointed left this time—the opposite direction than she had earlier.

Amanda nodded. "Was he driving fast or slow or…?"

"Just at a normal speed."

If this was their killer and the two victims from the second fire, he was certainly calm and collected, like nothing unnerved him. Amanda wouldn't be getting any sleep until he was behind bars, and she was already running on fumes. She and Trent had to take a look at the Pansy Shoppe—especially now that it had come up twice. "Can you tell us what the man looked like?"

"He was wearing a dark sweater with black jeans, and he had brown hair."

They needed more than a man in black. "Did you see his face?'

"Not enough to make out any of his features. But I assume he had two eyes, a nose, a mouth." A small chuckle.

Amanda smiled. "How old would you say he was?"

"Hmm. Maybe thirty-something. Your age, possibly younger?" Janet flicked a hand toward Amanda.

"A woman never reveals her age." *Especially with another birthday around the corner.* "What was his build like? You said that he lifted the girls into the van. Did he appear strong, muscular?"

"Sure, I guess. He was probably about six feet tall."

She'd show Janet the picture of their mystery man, but if he turned out to be their killer, a skilled defense attorney would allege that Amanda had fed Janet their suspect. They were best to wait until they could add him to a photo spread. Better yet, an in-person lineup. "What about the girls? Could you describe each of them, please?"

"They were both young. Dressed like hookers, if you ask me. If my daughters ever tried to sneak out like that, I would have sent them back to their rooms for a wardrobe change."

Justin Cooper had commented on the provocative clothing, though he'd never made the "hooker" comment. Could be a generational thing. "Like hookers, huh? Can you elaborate?"

"Just tight leggings on the one and a low-cut shirt."

Low-cut shirt… "Did you happen to notice any markings on her chest?"

Janet raised her eyebrows. "Can't say I was looking."

"The other one?" Trent asked.

"A short skirt, well above the knees, and a skintight shirt that left little to the imagination. She was big chested, that one. Both had heels taller than they could manage."

"How old would you say they were?" Amanda twisted her teacup but didn't lift it for a drink.

"Mid-teens, I would guess, but I could be wrong. It's so hard to tell people's ages these days. Or it's just me."

"And you never saw any of these people, or the van in this area before?" She thought she'd ask again.

Janet shook her head. "Never. And when I heard about the two girls on the news, I got this horrible feeling it might have been them. Do you think it was?"

"We're here because of what you saw, but it's too soon to say." Amanda was taking the neutral route, but her intuition was screaming, *Hell, yes, it was them!* "Why didn't you call the police at the time?"

"By the time I thought to, well, it was too late. They were gone. And I didn't feel like getting into it with the cops that late at night. I just imagined them grilling me for hours. But if they were the girls on the news, I may never forgive myself."

Amanda tapped the back of Janet's hand. "None of us can see the future, Ms. Mills, but thank you for calling the tip line."

Janet squeezed her eyes shut for a moment and dipped her head. "I hope I've been of help."

"More than you know. Here—" Amanda pulled her card and handed it to Janet "—call me if you remember anything else."

"I will."

Amanda and Trent saw themselves out. She stopped at the driver's-side door, leaning against it and crossing her arms. He stood in front of her, hands on hips.

"I saw a van like that a block away from the second fire," he said. "The Pansy Shoppe."

"Yep. Me too."

"You think someone from there is our killer?"

"We can't dismiss the possibility, though it doesn't make much sense he'd want to draw attention to himself in such a blatant manner. It's a lead we need to follow, but it seems too easy."

"I get that. Doesn't make much sense either why our killer would murder a woman to silence her, then drive around in a van with lettering on the side."

"Exactly. And to park lengthwise... it was like he wanted someone to see the lettering on the van. I'm going to get officers over to the Pansy Shoppe to make the inquiries. We'll also need to check if the interviews are in yet from canvassing officers in the neighborhood of the second fire. Maybe someone mentioned the van or, even better, noticed the license plate."

"Good idea."

She pulled her phone out and made a call to Malone. He sounded cool again. She was driving herself crazy trying to figure out if it had to do with her or just the case. She put some distance between herself and Trent and turned her back on him. "Are you upset with me for some reason?"

There was silence, but the line felt electrically charged.

"You are," she concluded.

"Don't want to talk about it now, but we will. Why did you call?"

She filled him in on their conversation with Janet Mills, ending with the Pansy Shoppe and the van. "Could you have officers ask if they have a white GMC van in their fleet. Then, if they do, ask if it had any business being near Clear Mountain Circle Sunday morning, or near Ms. Mills's home Saturday night."

"Sure."

"Oh, and one other thing, could you get officers reviewing the interviews from the residents on Clear Mountain Circle? Trent and I saw the van a couple of blocks over from eight sixteen. I'd like to know if anyone commented on seeing a white van in the area, maybe parked or lingering nearby. Someone might have even seen a license plate."

"Consider that done too."

"Thanks."

Malone hung up, and Amanda turned to Trent.

"Malone's getting officers on everything we just talked about, including the interviews. That frees us up to take a look around. We'll start there." She pointed to the insurance company and headed over. It only took a few minutes to dash the hope that a surveillance camera could have captured their killer. She stood back, her hands on her hips, and looked around. "All right, time for a walk. If we're lucky we'll figure out where the man and the girls came from." She retraced the direction from which Janet said the trio had originated. Just more houses, much like Janet's, for a few blocks.

She was about to say something to Trent when she saw through the backyard of a corner lot on her right. It was banked by a chain-link fence, and on the other side was a two-story building. The backside of a motel, if Amanda remembered correctly. She could vaguely recall the roadside sign but couldn't pin down the name.

Working on the assumption that the two new victims had also been caught up in sex trafficking, a motel could make sense. The girls could have been delivered to the motel, and then the killer had taken them from there.

"Come with me." She picked up her speed and ducked up the side street toward the motel. With each step, she felt like they were getting that much closer to their killer.

CHAPTER FORTY-SEVEN

Amanda could have been seeing things where there was nothing to see, a link, a connection, and tugging at loose threads with no consequence. But she had to follow her gut. Her father had taught her that.

Trent was tagging along behind her. Her focus was on the motel. It looked like every second room had a rear exit. She walked to the front of the place and saw the sign.

Sunny Motel. All in its bright-yellow glory, but it brought the past hurtling back. Sunny Motel had been one of the first dive motels where she'd had a one-night stand.

She went into the lobby and found a forty-something man sitting with his legs crossed and reading a newspaper behind a counter. He set it down, uncrossed his legs, and leaned forward. "Hourly or for the night?" He drew his half-mast, lazy eyes from Amanda over to Trent.

Trent held up his badge, beating her to doing the same thing by a few seconds. "Prince William County PD, Homicide," he said.

"Detectives Steele and Stenson," Amanda added. "We have some questions about a guest who might have rented a room Saturday night."

"I can't answer those type of questions without a warrant." He picked up his paper.

"Maybe you could tell us if you saw this man before." She brought up the picture of their mystery man on her phone and held it toward him. She felt fine about showing this to the clerk, as she was just making a simple inquiry at this point.

Time ticked off. Slowly, the paper was lowered again. He rolled closer to the counter and squinted at the screen. "Tom Cruise?" Only one of his eyebrows arched up.

"Someone who looks like him."

"Tom Cruise's doppelgänger is wanted by the police?" His eyes sparkled, and he chuckled. "Now I've heard everything."

She shrugged. "You could just say he's a person of interest. What's your name?"

"Roy Marble, but you can call me Roy."

"Okay, Roy, have you seen this guy?" She looked at her phone to draw his attention back to the photo.

He rubbed his jaw. "I think I need a warrant."

She bobbed her head. "Sure, I can understand if you'd prefer one, but for me to get that approved, I need a little help from you." She held her fingers to within a half inch of touching.

"Sounds like your problem," he muttered, then volunteered, "My aunt Judy was murdered. You said you were with Homicide?" He looked at Trent to answer.

"Uh-huh," he confirmed.

"Sorry about your aunt," Amanda offered sincerely, but she also saw a way to use this knowledge to their advantage.

He waved a hand of dismissal. "It was years ago now, but it really tore up my mom. It was her sister."

"A horrible thing to be sure," she said and put her phone away. "Murder of a loved one really cuts deep. My partner and I are just trying to bring some solace and closure to the friends and family of two recent victims."

"Huh. I see what you're trying to do here. You're empathizing with me, so I feel sorry for you and open my mouth."

Actually, you brought up your aunt...

"What's the worst that can happen?" That came from Trent, and it had her looking at him. He met her gaze, and his eyes lit up like he was pleased with himself.

"I could lose my job, pal," Roy said.

"Is it really that great of a job?" Trent made a show of gesturing around the ancient lobby and the pine—so much pine.

"That's a low blow."

"I mean, in light of what your help could do for bringing closure to the victims' loved ones." Trent applied one more twist of Roy's arm.

"Very well," Roy mumbled. "Yeah, I saw your Tom Cruise."

A buzz jolted through Amanda's body. He was no longer just a nameless face in a photo; he was most likely their killer. She wanted to pepper Roy with questions but feared shutting him down. She let seconds pass, giving Roy the opportunity to speak first, to give him a sense of control. It worked, because Roy eventually went on.

"He rented two rooms—seven and eight—for the night. He insisted, and I mean *really* insisted, that he have those specific rooms."

"Did he say why?" Amanda asked.

"Said they were his lucky numbers. Whatever. Not that I really gave a crap what rooms he had as long as they were vacant."

"How did he pay?" she inquired.

"Cash. Pretty much everyone pays cash here."

She nodded. "Did he give you any ID?"

"Defeats the purpose of paying cash, don't it?" He squared his shoulders, a bit on the defensive.

She could make an issue out of this, but Roy would probably show them the door. That would set the investigation back. "Anyone else rent those rooms since him?"

"Nope."

"What about security surveillance?" she began. "Any cameras around here?"

"We got 'em, but I'm not giving you the footage without a warrant. The boss would have my ass."

She nodded. "We'll get a warrant. Right now, though, we'd like to see rooms seven and eight."

"Sure. The hourly rate is affordable. See the sign." He pointed to a sheet pressed into a laminate holder on the counter.

"We won't touch a thing; you'll never know we were there." Amanda stopped talking as she observed his body language was still rigid. "You can come with us."

Roy huffed. "Fine. But don't make me regret this. I've gotten along fine all these years minding my own damn business, then the likes of you come around..." He was still grumbling while he grabbed the keys for both rooms from a pegboard. "Let's go." He held the lobby door open for them.

They followed him to room seven, and he unlocked the door. Inside, the place was furnished with dated furniture and had a worn, burnt-orange carpet. Just as she remembered it from years ago. There was a strange odor to the air that Amanda couldn't quite place and wasn't sure if it was must, mildew, human, rodent—or a combination.

"This is it," Roy announced, opening his arms. "Quite the Ritz." He smirked at Trent and went to a door in the middle of the room and unlocked it. "Voila! There you have it—adjoining rooms."

Amanda and Trent walked into the room and through the door to the next. Room eight was a mirror of seven, but it had a rear exit. She put on a pair of gloves, unlatched the bolt, and ducked her head outside.

"Hey, you said you wouldn't touch anything."

She held up her gloved hands.

"Ah, so you go all *CSI* on me, and I'm supposed to be good with it?"

"You asked for that warrant, Roy, and I'm going to oblige. But there's no harm in us having a quick look now. Was the man alone, or did he have company?"

Roy's face became shadows. "I really shouldn't say anymore." He fidgeted with the keys in his hands.

"And why's that?" she asked.

Roy rubbed his jaw, slid it left and right, and scanned the room. "Two girls were dropped off and joined him."

Amanda's stomach tossed. Sometimes she hated it when her instincts turned out to be right. Those young women had been sex-trafficking victims.

CHAPTER FORTY-EIGHT

Amanda could only imagine how terrified those girls must have been every time they were delivered to a john. "Did you see who dropped them off?"

"I didn't exactly get his name."

"No need for sarcasm, Roy. And not really an answer to my question."

He met her gaze but was the first to break eye contact. "I don't think I'm comfortable saying much more."

"You know what's going on at the motel, then?" Amanda angled her head. "I'm going to guess it's a regular thing by the way you're acting. That would mean that you're facilitating sex crimes."

"I didn't do anything to those girls."

"Indirectly you did. Silence is what these lowlifes prey on. By not doing anything to help, *you* are a part of the problem." Amanda paced a few steps. "I can have this entire place put under surveillance, and then you know what will happen?" She would be anyway, but he didn't need to know that.

"What?"

She stopped moving. "You'll be looking for a new job, possibly living out your life behind bars."

"I didn't do anything, and if I start talking, I'm good as dead."

"Just continue cooperating with us, and I can get you protection if it comes to that."

Roy narrowed his eyes and said, "I don't like being strong-armed."

"Look, it's up to you how it goes from here," she said. "Keep talking to us, and you're aiding the police. We're on your side. Clam up and—"

"Fine," he spat. "I'll talk, but I might take you up on that protection."

"Okay. Why don't we start from the top?" She figured if they backtracked and focused on the mystery man's movements first, by the time they reached the point when the girls showed up, he'd be a little more relaxed.

"The guy rented the rooms."

"Uh-huh, and what was he driving?" she asked.

"He arrived on foot."

Not surprising. He probably left his van in the insurance company's parking lot and walked over. "Okay, keep going."

"He got the rooms, went into them, then about an hour after, these two girls were dropped off."

"What time was this?"

"Say, ten thirty."

She nodded. That would have given the killer time to drug the girls and wait for it to set in before escorting them to the van around eleven thirty, when Janet had spotted them. He could have had the girls long gone before their handler even clued in. "What did the girls look like?"

"I dunno. Young, I guess. Pretty, blond. They wore sexy clothing."

"Did you happen to notice if they had any tattoos?" she asked.

"Nope. Didn't notice."

"Okay, they were dropped off. Then what?"

"The girls knocked on his door, and he let them in."

"Which door did they go to?" she asked.

"Seven."

That was the one without the back door... So the killer had the girls delivered to room seven, and then unbeknownst to their handler, the girls were likely shuffled into room eight and taken out the back door. "Did the person who brought them leave or...?"

Roy licked his lips and pushed out, "He stayed out front in the car he'd brought them in."

Now that Roy was opening up, Amanda slipped in her earlier question. "Did you get a good look at him?"

He met her gaze. "He had the driver's window down, and he was smoking. Oh, and he was playing country music. Just loud enough to sort of pick up, but not booming or anything. But gah, I hate the stuff."

"Did he ever get out of the car?" Amanda was pressuring now, but she felt the effort would pay off. After all, Roy didn't bring up protection because he didn't get a good look at the girls' handler.

Roy's eyes went dark, and he stared across the room. "Yeah."

She might need to wait a little yet before getting some description on the guy. "And what did he do?"

"He banged on the door of room seven."

"What time was this?" Trent asked.

"About one in the morning. When no one answered, the guy stomped into the office and demanded I give him a key to the room." He paused there, and his body was visibly trembling.

"You're doing good." Amanda was trying to keep calm herself. Roy would have gotten a real good look at the guy. "Keep going," she encouraged.

"I told him I couldn't give him a key."

Trent winced. "And how did that go over?"

"He kicked down the room's door." Roy hitched a thumb over his shoulder. "We got it fixed up yesterday."

"Guessing you didn't call the police about any of this," she said.

"Nope. I called Kirk, that's the owner, and he said to just let it be."

That was interesting… But even if police had been called to the motel for property damage, the handler would have been long gone by the time they'd arrived. But there was one possible way to track him down. "Did you get a plate on this guy's vehicle?"

There was a pregnant pause, then, "Yeah, I have it." It felt like Roy had more to say, but he didn't.

"We'll get that from you in a minute," she said. "Now can you tell us what he looked like?"

"Rather thin, dark hair, sunken cheekbones, but it was his eyes that were the real creep show."

Amanda angled her head. "What about them?"

"The whites… They were black."

The skin tightened on the back of her neck. She briefly glanced at Trent, whose eyebrows were raised. He was thinking the same thing. Was this the same man from Second Treasures who had been tailing Ashley Lynch? It had to be, because what were the chances that someone else in the area had these eyes? "You're sure they were black?"

"Definitely. Guy looked like quite the freak."

"Okay," Amanda said. "You're doing great. About how old?"

"Say mid-to-late thirties."

"Has this guy been here before or since?" she asked.

"I don't know if I should say."

That's a yes… "If you see him again, call the police. You can even call me directly." She pulled her business cards from a back pocket and handed him one. She was quaking with anger. People like Roy were why sex traffickers got away with their crimes.

He took it but didn't put it any of his pockets, and Amanda imagined it would be crumpled up and tossed into a wastebasket the first chance he got.

She mulled over what had transpired here, and there was no reason why everything couldn't have played out much the same way with Ashley Lynch. And Roy had just confirmed that the black-eyed man had been there before. She took out her phone, brought up the photo of Ashley and showed it to Roy. "Does she look familiar to you?"

He cupped his hand over hers to steady the phone and leaned in. "Ah, no."

"You're positive? Sometimes it can be a little tricky to recognize people when it's a computer-rendered graphic." She angled her head and studied his face as he took a long, hard look.

He let go of her hand and the phone. "Nope. Never seen her."

"All right. You can lock up here and go back to the office. My partner and I will catch up with you in a minute."

They all shuffled outside. Roy returned to the office, and Amanda and Trent huddled.

"He was here," she said. "That means Crime Scene needs to be called in to sweep the rooms, see if they can find anything useful. Prints, etcetera. We also need approval to collect the video footage."

"I get that."

"We'll need a verbal warrant, so that can get started ASAP. You ever get one of those before? I can give you the name of a friendly judge."

"I can figure it out."

"Good." Amanda pulled out her phone and shot a contact over to Trent. "That's Judge Armstrong's info."

He looked at his screen and nodded. "Got it."

"Tell him that you're my partner. He'll approve it right away."

"Okay."

"I'm going to call Malone, let him know there's been another sighting of our suspect here, and have him get officers out to similar motels in the area. My bet is if our killer had his latest victims delivered to this place, he probably had Ashley Lynch dropped off somewhere similar and pulled the same stunt. Oh. They'll need to get a photo array done first. Then the officers can show it as they do their rounds."

Trent put his phone to his ear and stepped away to make his call, while she made hers.

Malone answered on the second ring, and she rushed ahead. "Pretty sure we're getting close to this guy, boss, but there's a few more t's to cross. That's where I need your help."

"Already have been helpin'." His tone was still cool, but not arctic like it had been recently. He went on. "By the way, I was about to call you. Officers visited the Pansy Shoppe, inquired about the white GMC Savana. They have one delivery van, but it's a Ford."

Not surprising, but it still left the reason for the use of the decal unresolved. "Did they ask about any deliveries in the area of the second fire?"

"Yes. And there were none."

"Just confirms it. This guy is our prime suspect."

"This guy?"

"The mystery man from the crowd photos," she reminded him. She had filled him in already about the face without a name. Though it had been in the wee hours of Sunday morning before taking Crystal Foster home to Washington.

"Right."

"Well, he was at all three crime scenes, and we just spoke to the clerk at the Sunny Motel. The man rented adjoining rooms and had two young girls delivered to one of them. Blond, young like Ashley Lynch, and fitting the descriptions given to us by our two eyewitnesses—Mills and Cooper."

"Let me guess, no ID collected by the motel?"

"Nope. Paid cash too. Now, the girls were dropped off by a man the clerk said had black eyes. Crystal Foster told us a man who looked like that had grabbed Ashley Lynch by the arm in a vintage clothing store."

"I remember you telling me about that. So this guy must be a handler."

"I'd say so. We believe our killer drugged the girls, then gave the handler the slip and took the girls out the back door of the neighboring room, where he proceeded to walk with them to his van. He'd parked it across from Janet Mills's house, which was a few blocks away. That's where she saw the man with the girls. Good news is the motel has working security cameras. I've got Trent on a warrant for the footage. And, apparently, the clerk here at Sunny's has the handler's plate number."

"Good breaks."

"It's a start." She'd reserve her optimism for a little longer. "Sarge, we need to consider that our suspect ran with the same MO on the first vic. He probably had her dropped off at a motel and snuck off with her. We need to have officers show Ashley Lynch's photo to every dump like the Sunny Motel in Prince William County to see if anyone saw her. We also need to get a photo array made up that includes our suspect and have the officers show that around. I'll fire his picture over to you."

"Sure, but hold up. There has to be a lot of motels that fit that description."

"I don't see what else we can do at this point."

There was more silence on Malone's end.

"Is there something I should know about?" She just got this tingling sensation. "Is the LT on your back about all this?"

Malone sighed heavily. "She's not letting up. When I went to her about the tip line, well, she wasn't too happy to hear there were two more victims."

"Let me guess—and I'm to blame."

"You and I know you're not."

"Huh, but she thinks I am. We'll see what she has to say when I find this bastard and bring him in."

"Keep positive like that. It works."

For the trace of a moment, she felt whatever had been bothering Malone was gone, like he was on her side again. "Thanks."

"Keep me posted."

He beat her to hanging up, and that bittersweet feeling returned. There was something niggling at him besides Sherry Hill. Now, if only she could figure out what.

CHAPTER FORTY-NINE

Amanda forwarded Malone the photo of their mystery man as Trent was putting his phone away.

"Judge Armstrong gave me the go-ahead," he said. "We need to follow up with the proper paperwork and get it signed."

"Standard procedure. But at least we can get started. You call Crime Scene?"

"Yeah."

She filled Trent in on her call to Malone and nudged her head toward the motel office. "Let's join Roy."

They entered the lobby to find Roy behind the counter, his nose buried in the newspaper again.

He didn't move the paper but spoke. "I've said too much already. I should have just kept my mouth shut. As I said before, it's served me well."

"We'll get you protection if you're truly concerned about your safety, but it's very important that we get that license plate, as well as the make and model of the car that man drove."

He took one hand off the newspaper to hand her a yellow sticky note. She reached for it, but he pulled it back. "You're telling me the truth about getting me protection?"

"I will do all in my power to make it happen." That was as close as she could come to making a promise. She'd have to run this by Malone, and then the decision would be his, but Roy had a legitimate reason to be afraid. After all, the sex-trafficking ring wouldn't take too well to a rat and likely seek some form of retaliation.

Two cruisers pulled into the lot, and Roy got up. "I see the cavalry's here."

"It's how it works."

"Hmph."

"What would your aunt Judy tell you to do?" A low blow, but it was effective. Roy handed the sticky note to Trent.

"It's the license number. The car was a silver Nissan Sentra. I'd say a few years old."

"Terrific. Thank you," Trent said.

"Uh-huh. Let's just hope I live to see another day."

"You're doing the right thing by helping," she assured him. "Just a heads-up. We have a warrant to search rooms seven and eight."

"Sure. Can I see it?" Roy held out an open hand, presumably for her phone.

"It's a verbal one for now, but we could get Judge Armstrong on the line."

Roy squinted. "Convenient," he said sarcastically.

"Seriously. I can call him now if you'd like."

"Don't worry about it."

"We're also going to need to speak to whoever cleaned the rooms." She'd love for forensics to find something to tie them to their suspect, but she wasn't sure what that might be. If he had used a syringe to administer the drugs to the girls like he had Shannon Fox, it's not like he would have tossed it in the trash for the maid to find. And would he have used a needle with two girls present? He could have if he'd been discreet, but it was more likely that he'd add the drug to their drinks. Less chance of a struggle or altercation.

"Her name is Mariam," Roy said. "She's already gone for the day."

"We'll need her home address and a phone number." Amanda pulled her notepad out to write them down. "Ready when you are," she prompted when Roy hadn't said anything for a while.

He sighed but handed over the information.

"Thank you." She returned the book to her pocket. "And I'll be in touch about the protection."

"Uh-huh."

It was obvious that Roy had seen through her, that she hadn't exactly promised him anything, but she would do what was within her power.

Amanda and Trent went outside and approached the closest uniformed officer. It turned out to be Tucker from the Fox crime scene. He walked around the hood of his cruiser.

She flashed her badge in case he didn't remember her. "Detective Steele."

He smiled. "Yeah, I know who you are. How's it goin'?"

"Don't have a lot of time to chat, but it's goin'. We need a plate run. I'm sure you can help us."

"Ah, sure." Tucker hoisted up his pants, a habit that so many young officers had at the beginning. Not just because they hadn't literally grown into their uniforms yet, but because they were adjusting to the weight of the holster, gun, radio, baton, and Taser. It was like they didn't trust their belt to hold up their pants. He walked to the driver's door of his cruiser and sat inside, leaving the door open. "What's the plate?"

Trent rattled it off, and Tucker keyed the digits into the onboard computer.

"It's attached to a Kia. Sound right?"

"Nope." She glanced back at the motel office. "We were told it was on a silver Nissan Sentra. Who is the plate registered to?"

A few key clicks, then, "A Dorothy McKee."

"Stolen plate," she muttered. She should have known better than to hope it would lead them to the sex-trafficking ring. "Get officers to pay her a visit, but my guess is someone took her plates. Also, we need a BOLO issued for a few-years-old silver Nissan Sentra. We might not have a valid plate, but we'll use what we do have."

"Right away." Tucker handled his radio, ready to talk, but Amanda slipped her card into his hand and told him to keep her posted on everything that transpired at the motel. She also asked that he communicate with the CSIs when they arrived. She made special mention of the rear door of room eight. Maybe the investigators would get lucky and find prints that would prove useful.

She turned to Trent. "Let's go talk to the maid."

The two of them walked back to the department vehicle that they'd left out front of Janet Mills's house.

"I think we're getting close to catching this guy," Trent said.

"Would be nice. This guy is taking girls from a sex-trafficking ring—that doesn't seem like it's even a question anymore." After all, they had Ashley's tattoo and the handler with the two girls. She added, "I'd say that our suspect knows the people he's dealing with. He parked away from the motel and walked. He didn't want the handler—or the motel clerk—seeing his van. He had the girls delivered to the Sunny Motel with the intention of taking them out the back door. That's why he insisted on rooms seven and eight—adjoining rooms. Then he moved the girls from Woodbridge to a house in Dumfries. He was doing what he could to elude the handler."

"But how did he get the girls to go with him? We could assume he drugged them—they were described as acting drunk—but still, those girls would have to know that if they left, and were ever found, there'd be hell to pay. I can't imagine the people in these rings take very well to their—and I hate to put it this way—merchandise going missing."

Trent's words reminded her of what Patty had alluded to days ago. "We've got to find our mystery man before the people from the sex-trafficking ring. We just want to put him behind bars; they'd want to kill him."

CHAPTER FIFTY

The fact their murder suspect had a knowledge of how sex-trafficking rings worked made Amanda want to know how he'd gained his insights. From research on the internet or first-hand experience? She couldn't shake what Brandon Fisher had said about the possibility that their killer had been personally affected at a young age. Had he been exposed to sex trafficking, or had someone he loved fallen prey to it? Any of these things could have given him understanding as to how they worked, but that still didn't explain why he was targeting the girls. Rape hadn't been on his agenda with Ashley Lynch or Shannon Fox. They'd never know with the two girls in the most recent fire, but she'd wager not.

Trent pulled into the lot for the apartment building where the maid from the Sunny Motel lived. It was in Woodbridge and only a few minutes from the motel. Her name was Mariam Ruiz, and she was in unit 328.

It was an unsecured building, and they saw themselves up to the third floor and knocked on her door.

"Just a second," a woman called out from inside, followed by the sound of footsteps padding toward the door. "Who is it?"

"Prince William County Police, ma'am." Amanda held up her badge to the peephole.

The deadbolt *clunked*, and the chain slid across. The door opened.

A woman in her thirties was standing there. Chestnut hair pulled back into a high, long ponytail. Brown eyes. Tan complexion. Large cross on a gold chain around her neck. She wore jeans and a white tank with a pink-plaid, long-sleeve shirt unbuttoned over it. She was beautiful until she frowned and crossed her arms.

"Are you Mariam Ruiz?" Amanda asked.

"Yeah, but you can call me Mitzi. Who are you?" Her gaze skipped over Amanda to Trent.

"I'm Detective Trent Stenson," he said.

"And I'm Detective Amanda Steele. We need to ask you some questions about two rooms you would have cleaned yesterday morning at the Sunny Motel." She added the last bit, just in case she had another cleaning job.

"You 'spect me to remember?"

"We're hoping you can. We're following a lead in an open murder investigation," Amanda explained.

She didn't say anything, just backed up to let them enter.

The apartment was compact and modestly furnished. It was clean and tidy.

"What do you want to know exactly?" Mitzi asked.

"Rooms seven and eight were rented out Saturday night to a man," Amanda started.

"If you say so."

"Yes, I say so." Amanda gave her a tight smile. "Do you remember cleaning those rooms on Sunday morning?"

"Well, I would have cleaned them, yes."

"Do you remember the state of the rooms?" She'd start there.

"Ah, *sí*, both beds were made. Found that unusual. Very unusual. I stripped and remade them anyway. You know, just in case people had done the nasty and pulled the sheets back."

"Was there any evidence that the person who rented the rooms had sex in them?" Trent asked. "Maybe used condoms in the trash?"

Mitzi shook her head. "The garbage cans were empty."

So what did the guy do? And how could nothing in the room have been touched? Surely even the girls would have come in and sat on the bed. There was a table and two chairs in each room, though. "Did anything in the room looked used?"

"*Sí*. Two glasses. Smelled like whiskey maybe?" Mitzi didn't sound like she was confident in that conclusion. "They would have been washed and put back in the room."

Amanda sighed. Just as she had feared. That made them of no use to the investigation, just like this interview was proving to be. "Thank you for talking with us, Ms. Ruiz."

"You're very welcome."

They reached the hall, and no sooner had the door closed than Mitzi secured the lock and chain.

"Too much to hope we'd have gotten something from her," Trent lamented as they headed back to the car.

"We had to talk to her."

"What's our next step? Revisiting the interviews and seeing if we can somehow turn up an ID on Tom Cruise?"

They got into the car, Trent driving.

"Unless you have a better idea." But their killer wasn't going to hand over his ID and address. Besides, he likely left before the interviews were started, as she'd thought earlier. "We can also dig more into closed cases that are similar to the ones we're working."

"We only reached a dead end with that before."

"Well, if you have any suggestions, spit 'em out," she snapped, and felt instant remorse. "I'm sorry. I'm just tired of banging my head against a brick wall."

"Me too."

Her stomach growled. "How about we grab something to eat before heading back to the station? It's not quite five, but better to grab something while we can."

"Not going to argue."

Her phone rang, and the caller ID told her it was Malone. She answered on speaker.

"Good news. We got a plate on the GMC Savana van, but it was reported stolen."

She groaned. "Figures."

"Wish I had more for you."

"Makes two of us. Oh…" She went on to tell him about Roy Marble at the Sunny Motel requiring protection. "He took quite a risk talking to us," she stressed.

"I'll take care of him."

"All I can ask. Thank you."

Malone ended the call just as Trent pulled into the lot of a burger place.

He pointed to the drive-thru, and she nodded her approval, then said, "A double patty with cheese and extra onion, please. Also, a small soda." She fished a twenty-dollar bill out of a pocket and handed it to Trent. "Get what you want. My treat."

"Thanks." He took the money and rolled up to the order window. He had the same thing, plus a small order of fries.

A few minutes later, they had their food.

"Why don't you just park? We'll eat in the lot," she suggested.

Trent pulled into a free spot and let the car run.

She took a large bite and savored every bit of it before swallowing. Prior to having a partner, she'd often find herself in a parking lot eating her lunch or dinner and thinking. It was actually quite conducive to brainstorming.

Right now, her mind kept going to the signage on the white van. Why any at all, and why the Pansy Shoppe? Did their killer have a vendetta against the place or the owners, or had they been chosen completely at random?

If only she could get into the killer's mind…

She tore off another mouthful and turned to Trent. "What do you think the significance is of him having the Pansy Shoppe decals on his van?"

Trent took a draw of his drink, through a paper straw, and lowered the cup.

Before he could respond, she tossed more questions at him. "Do you think there's a connection between the killer and the flower shop? If so, what? Or is there something there he wants to draw our attention to?"

Trent's brow tightened with concentration. "I think the Pansy Shoppe's an avenue we should explore. Then again, the magnets could also be a diversion. Something to distract us."

"I'm afraid of that. Let's pull some backgrounds on the people from the florist's, though." She took a few more bites of her burger, polishing it off. "And to switch tracks a bit, something triggered him." She glanced thoughtfully at Trent. "He said we're on the same team." She chewed on that, tossed it around, then an idea struck. "He *was* injured by sex trafficking somehow. But as a victim himself, or was a loved one?"

"Still doesn't explain his hatred for the victims."

"But what if it does? What if a loved one became a victim, but he blames them?"

Trent shifted in his seat, so he was more directly facing her.

She went on. "He was deeply hurt, and as much as the girls are victims, he wants to punish them for whatever had happened in his personal life." She could hear her words coming back to her ears and could hardly believe she was theorizing all this. "And then there's the cleansing aspect of fire."

"Sure… but maybe it's just to recreate something from his past or to destroy the bodies and the evidence."

"Could be. And how long has he been killing? Are we aware of all his victims? What if the article about my rescuing those girls triggered him?" She was finding it hard to stop the flow of questions.

"You can't blame yourself for this guy."

She wished she could accept that. "Maybe that's why he left me that note? Not just to say we're on the same team, but also as acknowledgment, like a thank-you to me for setting him on this path."

"Then he feels like killing is his calling and purpose in life. Why isn't that comforting?" Trent stuck some fries into his mouth.

"Probably because if he loves what he's doing, he's not going to stop unless we make him. And we haven't had much luck so far."

CHAPTER FIFTY-ONE

Trent was eating from a bag of chips and swigging back coffee when Amanda returned to her desk with her own refreshed mug. They hadn't really hit pay dirt before by searching the CCRE, so they decided to go at things from another angle. Latching onto the possibility that their suspect was affected by sex trafficking, they took to the internet. It was at their fingertips and didn't require getting the FBI involved. She and Trent had been searching for several hours and weren't getting anywhere.

"There are more instances of crimes and murders related to sex trafficking than I would have guessed," Trent said.

"Sad fact."

"What if... and I hate to even say this... but what if our suspect's story isn't out there to find? At least not how we're looking for it."

"Oh, my God. I officially have a headache." She massaged her temple.

Another few hours passed with no forward progress. She might be better off directing her attention to the Pansy Shoppe, if for nothing but a change of pace.

"Steele, Stenson." It was Malone headed their way, and she was surprised to see him here so late. But they were dealing with an ugly case. He was just outside her cubicle. "I heard back from the uniformed division sergeant. Our suspect and Ashley Lynch were at the Ritter Motel in Dumfries. Same trick. Adjoining rooms. Paid in cash."

"Dumfries... Woodbridge," she mulled over out loud. "He really is doing all he can to evade the sex-trafficking people."

"And went from ordering one girl to two," Trent pointed out. "Just another way to cover his tracks. They wouldn't think it was the same person ordering the girls, even if the type was the same."

"Uh-huh," Malone said. "Obviously, the room at Ritter's is no good to us for processing, with that being five nights ago."

"That's all? Feels much longer ago than that." She rubbed her head again. Time to call in help. She took an ibuprofen from her desk drawer and swallowed it with a swig of water.

"Got a call from the CSIs who processed rooms at the Sunny Motel," Malone went on. "The only forensic trace they deemed to be evidence was a palm print they lifted from the back door of room eight. But, before you get excited, there was no hit in the system."

"Hardly even worth mentioning," she mumbled, feeling extremely discouraged with the lack of progress on this case.

Malone snapped his jaw shut. There was anger in his eyes. "I believe in open communication, Detective. Along those lines, you should know video was collected from the Sunny Motel, and stills of both our murder suspect and the handler are being run through facial recognition programs."

Hopefully, they were of better quality than the photo Amanda had sent of their suspect in the crowd across from 532 Bill Drive. The good news was that since they had the Devil's picture now, there was no need for Crystal Foster to sit down with a police sketch artist. She could just start getting on with her life. But hearing about the stills also made her think of something else. "Can we expect to get a copy of the photo array that includes our prime suspect?" There would be one out there, as the officers would have used it when asking around at motels.

"I'll make sure it gets to you."

"And it probably wouldn't hurt to get copies of the stills from the video."

"I told CSI Blair to send those along."

Amanda would be checking her email as soon as Malone left.

Malone nudged his head toward their desks. "What are you doing now?"

"Searching older, similar cases. And having no luck so far. I was actually just about to take a break from that and look into the Pansy Shoppe," she said. "We know the van wasn't theirs, but why would our suspect put their logo on his van? Maybe he's pointing us there for some reason."

"Could be. All right, carry on, but don't spend the night here. Cut out no later than midnight. Neither of you are any good to me dead on your feet."

Amanda glanced at the clock on the wall. *9:45 PM*. After a couple of nights of little sleep, she'd happily go home and crawl into bed now. "You got it."

"Just a word, Amanda, before I leave." He motioned for her to follow him to his office.

He closed the door behind them. "You asked me if I'm all right lately. I'm not. And it's not entirely to do with the LT." He gestured to the chair across from his desk and dropped into his. "It's come to my attention that you may have received correspondence from the killer early on in this case."

Her heart thumped rapidly. This had to be about the note at the cemetery. She sat down. "I meant to tell you."

"I don't want to hear excuses, Amanda. I want you to talk to me. How can you expect me to help you if you don't?"

"But..." She considered how to word what she had to say next. "I wasn't needing your help. I didn't even know what to make of it myself."

"But you took it to CSI Blair to have it processed. You must have 'made enough' of it to do that."

She felt her cheeks heat with the betrayal. She should have known that CSI Blair would say something to Malone. She thought back to his chilly demeanor, and it had started around the time of the second fire. Blair must have told him then, but Amanda asked anyway. "When did she tell you?"

"That doesn't matter. You should have told me." His tone was more hurt than anger, and it caused remorse to set in.

"Yeah, I should have. I'm sorry."

"Don't let things like that fall through the cracks again."

"I just didn't want you to take me off the case."

He regarded her, his face all bunched up. "Don't you know me at all?"

"You're telling me you wouldn't have? Hill's breathing down your neck."

"You let me handle her." He was so tight-lipped he could have been a ventriloquist.

She'd apologize again if it didn't make her feel like she was playing on repeat.

Malone got up with a heave. He reached the door and told her, "Night."

"Night."

She returned to her desk, her mind lingering on her conversation with Malone and his words, *"You let me handle her."* He had always proven to her that he had her back, so why would she ever think that would change?

She sank into her chair and opened her email. There was one from CSI Blair with two attachments. The still of their suspect and one of the Devil. It was certainly understandable why he gave people the creeps.

She quickly sent the Devil's photo and a note about the Sunny Motel, Second Treasures, and Ritter Motel in Dumfries over to Patty Glover.

Then she proceeded to key in a business search for the Pansy Shoppe and found the names of the business partners—a man and woman, different last name.

She pulled their backgrounds. Neither had a criminal record. Both were single, lived separately, and held mortgages. Nothing was glaringly wrong with them, but what about their employees—past and present? She'd need to wait until morning as the place would have long been closed for the day. They'd probably also want a court order to part with their employee names.

She got the paperwork together to subpoena that information and sent it over to the judge on call. By the time she came in tomorrow, she should have the approval she needed and be able to march right to the Pansy Shoppe.

She got up and stretched her arms overhead. The clock told her it was now half past ten. "Let's call it, Trent."

CHAPTER FIFTY-TWO

Amanda had arrived at Central the next day to find the approved subpoena for the Pansy Shoppe employees in her email inbox. There was a card on her desk as well. Probably for her birthday and signed by everyone in the station. She didn't resent getting older; if anything she was thankful. But she left the envelope unopened and headed for the flower boutique.

She called Trent from their parking lot to let him know where she was, and he told her that he'd just pick up where he'd left off last night.

She got out of the car and went inside. A bell rang when she entered, and Bonnie Pratt, who Amanda recognized as one of the owners, greeted her with a pleasant smile.

"What can I get together for you?" Bonnie asked.

Amanda hated to wipe the grin off the woman's face, but she was there on business. She held up her badge. "I'm not here for flowers today."

"Oh. All right, then. What can I help you with? I'm guessing this has something to do with that guy putting our name on his van? But I told the officer who came by that wasn't us."

"It's in regard to that case, yes," Amanda admitted. "But I'm going to need a list of your current and former employees. I have a warrant." She pulled it up on her phone and showed Bonnie.

Bonnie's lips moved as she read, then she met Amanda's gaze and walked to the counter. She went behind it and clicked on the computer. Shortly after, a printer was humming to life. She snatched a sheet off the tray and handed it to Amanda.

There were fifteen employees listed with addresses and phone numbers. "That's all?"

"We're a small shop, and we don't have much turnover in staff."

Amanda held up the piece of paper and said, "Thank you."

"Uh-huh."

Amanda left, hating how she'd entered Bonnie's life as a gray cloud over her otherwise sunny morning, but she had no choice.

*

By the time Amanda was walking to her desk at Central, it was ten o'clock. Trent looked up, appearing haggard.

"You all right there?" she asked him.

"I think so, but I'm still not getting anywhere."

"Keep looking. I'm going to dig into this." She held up the page she'd retrieved from Bonnie. "It's the employee list from the Pansy Shoppe."

"All right." Trent returned his gaze to his monitor.

She sat down and got to work, focusing on the male employees. The last one on her list was a former employee named Randy Hart. She pulled his background. No record, but his DMV photo had her blood running cold. "Trent, come here."

"Ah, yeah." He sounded like she woke him up.

"Get over here."

He made quick work of it; he must have sensed the urgency in her voice.

"Look." She pressed a finger to her screen.

"The Devil."

"Yep."

"Okay, but how does a sex-trafficking guy wind up working at a flower shop? And can you imagine this guy behind the counter, or at your door with a delivery? I'm guessing the Pansy Shoppe kept him working in the back."

"Well, he was a former employee…" She looked at the list, which included hire and leave dates. "Looks like he left nine years ago."

"Maybe before the black eyes and the sex trafficking."

"Probably." And she hoped so. She hated to think that the flower shop was caught up with the sex-trafficking ring somehow.

"I'm still stuck on why our killer pointed us to him in the first place. Does he hold Randy Hart responsible for whatever happened in the past? If so, why not just kill him?"

"He could be biding his— Oh. Maybe he's just trying to protect his own ass? He could view Hart as a threat." She met her partner's gaze, feeling confident in this suggestion.

"We did discuss that the sex-trafficking people would be interested in exacting revenge for the stolen girls."

"We've got to move." She jumped to her feet and went down the hall, Trent behind her. She stopped at Malone's office, rapped her knuckles on the door.

"Yeah?"

She entered with Trent and filled him in about Hart.

"Hold up." Malone sat back in his chair and swiveled slowly. "Do we think he's working with the killer?"

Amanda glanced at Trent, back at Malone. "We have no reason to believe that, but our killer wanted us to find him. At least I believe so. Hart should be brought in and questioned as soon as possible. It might shed light on everything."

"Not disagreeing with you there."

"Good." She spun to leave.

"Detective Steele," Malone said.

She turned back around. "Yes?"

"You could go in there and really muck things up—" he held up a hand to stave off her defense "—not intentionally, of course, but this man could be the key to bringing more down in the sex-trafficking operation. I'd contact Sex Crimes. Let that department handle Hart."

She felt like a balloon deflated of air. "But… Sarge—"

"No, I feel strongly about this, and I know you wouldn't want to jeopardize justice being brought to those girls—and the countless others still out there."

"Never."

"Okay, then. Call Sex Crimes. Pass this along."

"Wait," she blurted out.

Malone angled his head. "I'm listening."

"Let us at least stake out this guy, track his movements. It's the best thing we have going right now. And, yes, I see your point about Sex Crimes. Trent and I won't move in. We'll just see where he goes, keep a distance. But here's what I'm thinking: he's in charge of watching the girls. If our guy orders another one or two, we'll be in the vicinity to follow him. Hart might lead us to our killer *and* where the girls are being held."

Malone stared at her, thinking it through. "Huh. You'll stay back, observe only? Call in Sex Crimes if—and when—it comes to that?"

"I promise, and I'll call Detective Glover when I leave this room, just to give her a heads-up." She'd already sent Randy's picture, but now they had his name.

"All right, then. Do it."

Amanda and Trent didn't waste time leaving his office and heading to the lot.

"If there's something personal there, between our killer and this Hart guy, why not just kill him then? He obviously knows where to find him." Trent looked her in the eye and the validity of his question caused her mind to go blank.

"Yeah, I don't know."

"Suppose whatever the reason, it would serve to get us off the killer's back and onto Hart's."

Amanda could agree that was the simplified version, but she had a feeling there was something more there between their killer and Hart. Just what was it?

She called Patty while Trent signed out a car, and they got on the road. When Patty answered, Amanda said, "I sent you a picture of a man with black eyes, the suspected handler." Though it was fact—not suspicion—in Amanda's head. "I've got a name now."

"You work fast," Patty said, a smile lighting her voice.

"Things came together, but I need to let you know that my partner and I will be tracking this guy's moves for the next while and seeing what he does."

"Okay, just observe, if you can help it. I'd rather see where he can lead us."

"That's the plan, I assure you. I want us to have the best shot at bringing down the ring, not just a single player."

"Good luck on this guy leading you to your killer too."

"Thanks." Amanda pocketed her phone and hated how the words "good luck" seemed to hover overhead like thunderclouds.

CHAPTER FIFTY-THREE

It was inching close to noon when Amanda had Trent park a few houses down from Randy Hart's duplex. The department car was unmarked, but bad guys had a way of spotting cops.

"Hard to say if he's home," Trent said. "No sign of his Nissan."

No sign of any *vehicle…* And the curtains were closed tight like it was the middle of the night. "We'll sit here for a bit and see if he shows up."

"Good thing I have a bladder like a camel."

She wasn't sure she'd heard him right at first, then looked over at him, and he was laughing, and she started up. "You're certifiably crazy."

"In good company, then. Oooh."

She narrowed her eyes at him.

"Hey, normal's boring," he said.

"What is normal anyway?" She smiled at him and then sought to get comfortable. She reclined the chair a bit and clasped her hands in her lap. "Just shutting my eyes for a few seconds. You got this?" She looked at him with one eye open, one shut, and smirked. "I'm just kidding." Just then her phone rang, and it showed *Alibi.* Even though it was Logan, she answered formally because he liked it. "Detective Steele."

"Well, hello there." It was a man's voice, but it wasn't Logan's. Dread pricked at her skin. "Who is this?"

"I'm pretty sure you know who it is. I really thought we were on the same team, Detective, but I've been wrong before."

She sat up and pointed at her phone, her eyes wide. Her heart was racing so fast she couldn't see right. "Where are you?"

He cackled. "You don't really think I'd tell you that, do you?"

"What do you want?"

"Now, see, that's a better question. I thought I'd give you a call just in case you didn't get my card today. Happy Birthday, Detective."

She detected a smile travel the line, and shivers ran down her spine. *How does he know it's my birthday?* But he mentioned a card. Was it the one currently sitting on her desk that she'd thought was from her coworkers? How had he walked right into Central without anyone stopping him?

"I bet you're trying to figure me out or trace the call. I just want you to back off. You let me do what I do, and you look the other way."

"You know I can't do that. I... We found Randy Hart."

"Bravo. He's the real criminal, not me. But in case you don't believe me, I have an insurance plan."

There was scuffling on the other end of the line.

"Amanda?" It was Logan.

"Are you—"

"Now, now." It was the killer again. "As I told you, all I want is for you to back off and your boyfriend doesn't need to get hurt."

She looked around fervently. *Can he see me now? Where is that son of a bitch?*

"You kill innocent girls," she said, hoping for a part of him that remained human and compassionate.

"They are not innocent. No one is innocent. Back off or your boyfriend dies, and I'm sure you don't want to lose another man in your life."

The line went dead.

She felt numb, cold, angry as hell, and terrified. She clutched her stomach and rocked.

Trent put a hand on her shoulder. "What did he say?"

"He… He has Logan." Tears welled in her eyes, but it was like they were frozen there. She was catapulted into the past to a time when the heartbreak was all-encompassing. Logan was new to her life, yes, but she had feelings for him, and their relationship held promise of becoming something great. She couldn't survive another loss. "We have to save him."

Trent didn't move, didn't say anything.

"Hurry. Get us back to the station." She called Malone and told him about the situation. As she was running through it with him, she felt like she was telling a story outside of herself, like she had no connection or involvement.

Trent flipped the lights and gunned it to the station. She was pretty sure the car hadn't come to a full standstill when she jumped out at Central.

She went right for her desk and the card. Malone was already waiting. Trent was behind her, and he nudged her gently aside.

"Gloves," he said, and pulled a pair from his pants pocket and handed them to her.

She put them on and opened the envelope. She pulled out a birthday card. A piece of paper had been taped inside with a typed message, same font that was used on the note left at Lindsey's grave. She took a steadying breath and read it. "'You think I'm the bad guy here, but I'm really not. So STOP trying to stop me, or I'll have no choice but to kill him.'"

She choked back a sob. Malone reached out to console her, but she withdrew and shook her head. "No, I'm not… *not* giving in. We're going to save him." She stood tall, squared her shoulders, and met Trent's gaze, feeling fierce determination.

He took the card and envelope from her, also in gloved hands, and peered inside the envelope.

"Is there something else in—" Amanda's words froze on her tongue when she had her answer.

Trent had removed something. He held it for her to see. A colored print of Logan. He was tied up and gagged, his back against a wood-planked wall. Next to him was a gas can, and a flame on the tip of a lighter was in the bottom right-hand corner.

She gasped.

Trent put a hand on her shoulder. "He's just trying to bully you. Remember, you got this card before you talked to Logan. He's still alive. We have time to save—"

"We're going to, Trent." She was screaming in her head. She couldn't lose Logan now, not when her life was just starting to resemble something close to a new normal. But the guilt pierced through her just at the thought. This wasn't about her. Logan's life was the one at risk.

"Is there anything I can do?" Malone asked.

"Yeah. Find out how he got in here," Amanda said. "How did no one notice?"

"I'm on it." Malone took one step, and Trent spoke.

"We'll need officers watching Hart's place in case he shows up."

Malone made a finger gun, fired, and walked toward the front desk.

She paced, mumbling, and then it hit! She faced her partner. "He's trying to tell us he's not the bad guy. The clue to finding him needs to be in that. Somewhere. Damn it!"

CHAPTER FIFTY-FOUR

Detective Steele said they *had* Randy Hart. Did that mean he'd been arrested? He'd taken a risk by pointing the police Randy's way, but it served a few purposes. His primary intention was to occupy the police's attention with a little detour, but it also protected his ass from the sex-trafficking ring. Surely they'd be too busy trying to avoid the police themselves to come after him—The Merciful. He also held Randy accountable for the course of his life, though in a different way than his parents had. In part, due to Randy, he'd become even more invisible to his parents than ever before.

All Mom and Dad could talk about was their little "Tina"— especially after her death. She was their star child, the one born with a tiara on her head, while he had a crown of thorns. He really hoped Christina had suffered excruciating pain before she succumbed to that fire. He hoped she'd smelled her flesh burning as it cracked, curled, and blackened, like a roasting pig on a spit.

Just as he had received a taste of that horror at a young age— because of her. He laid a hand over his abdomen, thinking of the scar tissue there. He could feel the heat of the fire on his face, on his arms, on his torso. He recalled the fire crawling up his pajamas, eating at the fabric and his flesh like a starved, deranged lunatic.

A firefighter had saved him. He'd rolled him on the ground, but the damage had been done. Third-degree burns. All that at the age of thirteen.

Christina had come into his room in the loft and lifted his kerosene lantern over her head. The flame was flickering. "Tell me later how it felt." She cackled and smashed it to the floor. He couldn't get out of bed fast enough.

His suffering didn't matter to their parents. His father wouldn't even look at him afterwards, and his mother blamed him for the fire. Christina got away with everything. They idolized her, their sweet Tina. They just couldn't see that she was the very embodiment of evil.

His sister, the devil. Himself, the angel of mercy. The Merciful.

He looked over at the blond man, ankles and wrists tied, his mouth re-gagged after the phone call. Pathetic.

"We'll see just how much you actually mean to her," he said and left the man alone in the dark room, feeling the burden of the man's fate was in the detective's hands, not his.

He returned to the living area of his loft. He knew that the sex-trafficking ring had to be noticing their girls disappearing. Even with Hart presumably out of commission, someone else from the ring would probably come looking for him. It might be time to leave the area. But he had to know what Detective Steele had meant by "We have Hart."

He'd order another girl—just one more before moving on. He'd see if Randy showed up or another handler. He found himself wishing for Hart. Maybe he'd been too merciful, essentially gifting Randy to the police. Yes, if he got the chance, he'd take him out himself. He could handle that now.

He went to the internet and logged on to the dark web. He selected a girl from the list named Amber. Her real name had probably been something more American red, white, and blue. Something like Susie or Jane. Simple, naive, boring. She may even have been born into a home with doting parents she didn't appreciate. Could have had a brother or sister who always came in second to her as well.

He clenched his hands at his sides, his gaze in the direction of his screen, but his focus was somewhere distant, his mind in the past. His vindictive sister was why he could kill without remorse. He saw her reflected in the eyes of the girls he strangled. Tonight, he wouldn't waste one second feeling merciful toward anyone.

CHAPTER FIFTY-FIVE

The call to Amanda's phone had been untraceable. The front desk was managed by a mix of officers and civilians, but it had been one of the latter who told Malone that a man had dropped off the card with her. She was the one who had put it on Amanda's desk. Still, a brazen move that the killer had showed his face in a police station.

Amanda kept repeating the words in the card like a chant. "Not the bad guy." Finally, an epiphany struck. "Our killer doesn't think he's a bad person, hasn't from the start. He sent me that note—the one at Lindsey's grave—saying we're on the same team. I lock up bad guys. He sees himself as being to that level with what he's doing. He sees himself... as what?" She locked her gaze with Trent's and snapped her fingers. "He sees himself as a victim. He suffered because of sex trafficking, and he pointed us to Randy Hart. I don't think it was an act of self-preservation. There's more to Hart. His background gave us nothing... google his name."

Trent stepped in front of her to use her computer, brought up an internet browser, and entered *Randy Hart*. There were several hits.

"Narrow it down," Amanda said. "Add the words 'suspect' and 'sex trafficking.'"

Trent proceeded to do that, and she watched as articles popped up.

Arson Killed Young Woman.

Young Woman from House Fire Identified.

Arson Suspect Questioned & Released.

Prince William County—A Stalking Ground for Human Traffickers?

Trent said, "These results link to articles dating back seven years."

"Pick the second one." She jabbed a finger toward the screen, and Trent clicked on the link. He read, "'The remains of a young woman were pulled from a house fire three weeks ago today.'"

"The article title alludes to the fact she was identified. Her name?"

Trent drew a finger down the screen. "Christina Ross of Haymarket, eighteen."

Haymarket was a forty-five-minute drive northeast of Dumfries, with a population under two thousand, and still part of Prince William County.

Trent resumed looking at the article. "From what I can tell, Christina disappeared from a horse show when she was eleven." He looked over his shoulder at her.

"She'd been kidnapped and held for seven years before her death." Amanda clutched her stomach.

"And here's her picture at age eleven." Trent flicked a finger toward the screen.

"Even considering the age difference the resemblance to Ashley Lynch is still uncanny."

"That's one word for it. So what's the killer doing? Targeting her lookalikes for some reason?"

She hitched her shoulders and nudged her head toward the monitor. "Does this article say anything about Randy Hart?" Sometimes Google produced results that didn't include all the search words.

"Ah, let me see." Trent scrolled down. "Actually, it's not looking like it. Let me try another one." He duplicated that page in a new internet tab and returned to the search results. He opened the "Suspect Questioned" piece.

Right there in the second paragraph was Randy Hart's name. She read to herself and picked up that Hart had been questioned about his involvement in sex trafficking and the death of the young girl—Christina Ross. Suspicion was dropped when his alibi was confirmed. The house that had been set on fire was believed to have been a holding house—otherwise known as a weigh station—for trafficking victims. The property was registered to a numbered company that law enforcement had no luck in tracking down. Then another interesting tidbit ... "It was an anonymous phone call that tipped off police about Hart," she said, tingles running down her arms. "We need to find out who made that call."

"Thought it says *anonymous*..."

"Yeah, nothing's anonymous. But first, let's find Christina's family."

He searched *Obit Christina Ross*. "She was laid to rest at Eagle Cemetery."

"That's where—" Amanda cleared her throat. "That's where Kevin and Lindsey are buried. Continue," she encouraged.

"Looks like she left behind her parents and a brother."

"Bring up their backgrounds."

"Just a minute..." Trent clicked away on the keyboard, then scribbled on a blank page of a notepad she had on her desk.

She was tapping her foot. All she could think about was Logan. She had to save him. There was no other option. "Trent?" she prompted.

"I've got their names. Just bringing up the individual backgrounds." One filled in on the screen. "Christina's father... it looks like he died five years ago."

"What about the mother?"

Trent brought up her report. "Also deceased, just before Christmas last year."

"Tell me about the brother."

"Name's Daniel Ross." He typed on the keyboard. "He's still alive. Twenty-eight. Currently lives in Dumfries. He would have only been fourteen when his sister was taken."

"Young enough to be greatly impacted. Let's take a look at his photo."

Trent clicked on it, then sat back. "Look familiar?"

"The mystery man's ID solved."

"Yep. Meet Daniel Ross, our killer. He could have read the articles on Randy Hart and felt there was an injustice. That could be why he pointed us to Hart."

"Not sure about that. It's like he's killed his sister repeatedly through the girls he targets. If he's directing our attention to Hart, is he also trying to avenge her death? Brandon said our killer could have murdered before. Maybe he didn't like his parents either. I want to know how they died and if their deaths were suspicious."

Trent reached for the phone. She held out a hand to stop him.

"Tell me more about Daniel Ross. Where does he work?"

Trent went to the employment section of the report. "He's an estimator with Star Properties."

"Where did Woodbridge Bank's estimator work?"

Trent did a quick search. "Same place. Ross must have found out about the vacant properties through work."

"We need unis over at Star Properties, but start with bringing in SWAT. I want this done right, so this man goes away for life!"

One of the Strategic Weapons and Tactical Unit's responsibilities was to clear and secure a scene when apprehending suspects considered extremely dangerous or when there was a hostage situation.

"You got it," Trent said, lifting his phone's handset.

She left him to make the necessary calls and went down the hall to Malone's office. She found him on the phone. He waved for her to enter, and she did, closing the door behind her. She dropped into the chair across from his desk and waited.

Malone placed the telephone handset in its cradle.

"We found him." She'd imagined saying the words would bring more relief, some excitement, but she felt tapped out, drained dry.

"You...?"

"The suspect's name is Daniel Ross, and he lives in a quiet Dumfries neighborhood." She filled him in on all they knew. "Trent's calling in SWAT. We're going to do this all above board. I want him to rot in prison for what he's done." She heard the vindictiveness in her voice, and maybe she was being rash judging the man so harshly, but all she could think about were those girls and Logan.

"He will if I have a say."

"Trent's also sending officers to his place of work."

Malone rubbed the top of his head and let out a long sigh. "You okay?"

"Don't even know how to answer that." She couldn't pin down exactly how she was feeling—couldn't limit it to one thing anyway. She was numb, in shock, scared for Logan, for herself, and sad, to name a few.

"I can't imagine what you're going through right now... with Logan being held by this man." He didn't say it, but Amanda imagined the words *and at his mercy* being added to the end of that sentence. He proceeded with an even softer tone. "You might think that you have everyone fooled, Amanda. Fooled into thinking that you have it all together. But I know you better than that." He paused there like he expected her to interject with something, but she was too distracted to concentrate on compiling words. "And I hope you know by now that you don't ever have to go it alone. You do know that?"

All she could do was bob her head, trying not to cry.

CHAPTER FIFTY-SIX

It took time for SWAT to do their thing. They had to plan and strategize approach. Search, breach, and arrest warrants needed to be obtained. If they decided to hit later at night, that would involve another type of warrant. Amanda hated the waiting and not knowing if Logan was still okay.

An officer had called from Star Properties, and Daniel Ross had called in sick. *He is that…* Other unis were placed at a discreet distance from Ross's house to keep an eye on things there.

Eventually it came back that SWAT would be striking at eight o'clock that night, but that left hours to kill. She pressed on, trying to silence her thoughts and stay focused. She and Trent would use the time to dig more into the Ross family. Her phone rang at around four thirty, and it was Patty.

"Glad I got you. Randy Hart's bad news, Amanda."

"Yeah, we discovered that. He was investigated seven years ago for involvement in sex trafficking."

"That's right. How did you find that out?"

Amanda brought her up to speed, including mentioning that they had a murder suspect now. She left out Logan's abduction.

"You have your killer."

"Should." She hated the need to stay grounded, but she wasn't getting burnt by raised hopes. "How did you find out about Hart's past?" The background Amanda had pulled on him had showed nada.

"One of the old dogs in the unit saw his picture on my computer when he was walking by my desk. He's the one who interrogated Hart when the allegations were originally made. He said he couldn't get anything to stick, but he had this strong suspicion he was guilty as hell."

"Apparently he's got good instinct. This might be a long shot, but I don't suppose there's any way you can find out where the tip originated from?"

"A woman, the way the old dog tells it."

A woman… Tingles ran down Amanda's arms. *Could it have been one of his victims?* "The old dog have a name?"

"Detective David Melbourne. He's one of the good ones."

"Can you look into tracking the call?"

"That will be a dead end after all these years."

"Was afraid you'd say that. I have a favor to ask, and it might be a leap, but maybe Christina Ross is on the data chip we recovered from the bracelet a couple of months ago. Could you take a look and see if you can find her? I know she won't be listed by name but…"

"I'll see what I can find."

"Thanks." She ended the call, and Trent looked at her over the divider.

"I have the details on the parents' deaths. The father died of liver failure, and the mother, Lori Ross, died of an overdose of ketamine and fluoxetine. Apparently, she was prescribed both to help her deal with medical depression."

"Both deaths could have been aided along. We just assumed Ashley Lynch was his first victim." Her gaze drifted down to the plastic evidence bag on her desk that contained Logan's photo. She ran her fingertips over his face, wishing she could touch him in person, that he wasn't holed up with some lunatic.

"Maybe we were wrong to do so."

"I don't know, but I think we could have found out how Daniel got his hands on the ketamine. It's not a stretch that his mother left some behind." She looked again at Logan's face, peered closer into his eyes. They were riddled with fear. Failing to save him wasn't an option. He was counting on her.

She must have stayed lost in her thoughts for awhile. The next thing she knew it was time to hit Ross's residence.

*

Everyone was in position who needed to be. Ross's townhouse was in a low-key area of Dumfries. SWAT would move in, clear, and secure the location. Also, hopefully, free Logan. Amanda and Trent were hanging close by to make the arrest. At least that was the plan.

At 8:15 PM, the SWAT team leader approached Amanda, Trent, and Malone.

She stepped forward. "Did you find Logan?"

The SWAT guy shook his head. "No sign of him or Ross, but we'll be executing the rights of the search warrant. We'll keep you posted on what we find."

"No sign of—" She clamped her mouth shut and swallowed hard. Maybe they were too late to save Logan? Maybe they shouldn't have waited on SWAT and just moved in themselves...

"Could we take a look inside?" Trent asked.

"Sure. That's fine."

She followed Trent into the house and noted immediately how tidy and organized it was—everything had its place.

She went over to the coffeemaker, gloved up, and opened the filter section. It was empty. She checked the garbage bin, also empty. Was he living or staying somewhere else?

She looked over for Trent but couldn't see him. "Trent?" She walked down a hallway.

"In here," he called out.

She joined him in a bedroom. "I don't think Ross has been here in the last day or two."

"Longer than that." He pointed toward the dresser where an alarm clock was flashing. "The power went out last Wednesday."

"He might have just left it to blink?"

Trent shook his head. "No. His crimes tell us he's organized."

"Suppose that's true and, if anything, this would drive him mad." She tried to keep calm, but it was impossible. "Where are they, Trent? Are we sure this is the only property registered to Ross?"

"All that I found."

"We look again. He has to be holding Logan somewhere else." She could hear the pleading in her voice, but he had to still be alive. She pulled the bagged photo of Logan she'd brought with her and took in the wood boards behind him. "Look," she said, pointing it out to Trent. "It looks rustic." With the word, it seemed like everything started to tumble into place. She paced and spoke. "The Ross family was from Haymarket. It's more rural there. They could have lived in a farmhouse or log cabin."

"Okay, but there were no other properties under Daniel's name, and his family is all dead."

"All dead," she repeated and headed straight for their department car with Trent tagging along. "You said the mother just died around Christmas, right?"

"Ah, yeah. So?"

"*So...* maybe the property's held up in probate. Daniel could still have access to it."

They got into the vehicle, and Trent did a search for properties under the name of Lori Ross. "She had a place out on Logmill Road."

That was about as rural as a place got around here, and it was in Haymarket. "Let's go." She pointed to the ignition button.

"What? No, we can't go. We need to inform Malone, get SWAT together again."

She took a few deep breaths. Daniel's warning had been clear: stop coming for him or Logan was dead. What if he knew they'd just stormed his house? "I'm serious, Trent. You either start driving or get out of the car. We can't wait for SWAT again. Logan might not have that amount of time."

He looked at her for a long moment, and his cheeks flushed. She was about to state her case again, when he turned on the car and pulled away from the curb.

"Screw it," he said. "A man's life is at stake, right? We can't wait."

CHAPTER FIFTY-SEVEN

"This it?" Amanda looked out the passenger window as Trent slowed the department car to a crawl, then a stop, in front of a driveway.

A gate sat open and crooked on its hinges, and a rusted trailer sat sentinel just inside the entrance, listing to its left side and disappearing into a thicket of grass. Down the driveway, through and around more overgrown grass, thick bushes, and mature trees, she could make out the peak of a barn. The wood was gray and weathered in the moonlight. The property must have suffered from neglect long before Lori Ross had died.

"Right address," Trent said. "Should I pull in?"

She didn't see a white van, and aside from the opened gate there was nothing to indicate that someone might be on the property. "Drive up there and park." She flicked her finger toward a small curve in the road that was shielded by a row of mature trees.

Trent crept them ahead and cut the engine. "Now what?"

She already had her arm extended for her door handle. "We take a look around. If we spot anything suspicious, we'll call it in. Promise." She wasn't going to tell Trent that her desire to nail Daniel Ross had slid down her list of priorities beneath saving Logan. She got out of the car, noticing that with the headlights off, it was pitch dark. She turned on her phone's flashlight.

The air felt like rain, and thunder rumbled in the distance. She looked up at the sky. Heavy cloud cover.

"We approach slowly, and we stick together," she cautioned.

"Don't have to tell me twice. Last time I ran off ahead after a serial killer, I was shot."

They kept their flashlights aimed right in front of them to keep their beams small and pointed. Less chance of it tipping Daniel off they were there, and less chance of them stumbling on the uneven ground.

They passed the trailer and stuck to the edge of the drive, close to the high grass. Maybe it had been a bad and impulsive idea to come here—but she shucked it aside. In life, seconds mattered, and she wouldn't waste any more getting to Logan.

The barn was on the left of the driveway. A white fence banked the property on the other side of the barn.

"This used to be a horse farm," she concluded.

"Think you're right."

They were passing the barn now, and a side door was open to the driveway. She held out her arm for him to stop. She strained to listen but didn't hear anything. And she didn't see any lights inside. If Daniel was in there, he was in the dark.

Creep—

Her cell phone trilled out into the night air.

She jumped!

Then she rushed to silence the thing and stepped into the grass and tucked down, motioning for Trent to follow her lead. She rejected the call, cursing. It had been Malone. She turned her phone to silent instead of turning it off completely. That way Malone could track her whereabouts if he got antsy.

"Mute your ringer too," she whispered to Trent, and he did as she told him.

They stayed in their hidey-hole a bit longer. Amanda's heart was racing and thumping in her ears.

She got up and went back onto the driveway. They walked for a little and came to a small farmhouse. It would have been glorious in its day. Now, the roofline bowed, and the place begged for maintenance and fresh paint.

The front porch groaned loudly when Amanda stepped onto it. *Why am I always slinking around at night?*

She studied her surroundings and kept her hand not far from her holster, ready to draw her gun, if needed. She tiptoed across the deck and peeked into a window. There was a faint light on in a room at the back. It spilled across the floor.

She turned to Trent. "Someone's in there. We're going to knock, act like everything's normal." That sounded like a sane option. She knocked on the door, and it swung open. She took that as an invitation and stepped inside while calling out, "Prince William County PD."

It was a much different approach than the "armed to the teeth" move used by SWAT, and Amanda couldn't help but feel vulnerable and exposed.

She repeated the callout. Still not a sound.

The front door entered into a small mud room, and to the right was a modest kitchen. Outdated décor, but it appeared functional.

Trent touched a countertop and lifted his hand, held it under his flashlight. "Coated in dust, but that looks almost brand new." He pointed out a K-Cup machine, gloved up, and opened the unit. He pulled out a used pod. "Not warm, but I'd say recent."

"He's been here. Still may be."

"But there's no van."

"He's playing us now. We're on his chessboard." She moved through the house, going cautiously toward the light—trying to dismiss the connotation. She certainly wasn't ready to die.

The light ended up being from a small lamp on a table next to a rocking chair. Most of the place was dusty like the kitchen counter, but the chair seemed to glisten. On the floor beside it was a satchel overflowing with balls of yarn.

"It's like Lori Ross just got up to use the washroom," Trent said and shivered. "Also feels like her ghost's here."

Goosebumps rose on the back of her neck and slithered down her arms. "Nothing creepy about that…" But it was starting to feel like the walls had eyes.

They went through the rest of the house together and methodically. None of the rooms looked like the background in the photo of Logan. They did find prescription bottles of ketamine in the bathroom medicine cabinet issued to Lori Ross.

"Looks like you were right," Trent said.

"Don't sound so surprised. But where are Logan and Daniel?"

They returned outside. From the porch, the moon could be seen peeking out from behind the clouds. Its light reflected off something metal to the side of the driveway…

She hurried toward it and realized it was a wooden carport that had been overtaken by nature like the rest of the yard. She angled her flashlight into the void—

Could it be?

She motioned for Trent to come closer. "Help me clear this." She started pulling away small branches and twigs as spits of cold rain hit her exposed skin and had her shivering.

It took them little time to reveal their find.

"Hart's Nissan?" Trent said. "Does that mean Daniel's got another girl? And I don't see the white van. I think it's time to call for backup, Amanda."

She heard him but didn't respond and walked to the back of the car. She stopped next to the trunk. It was ajar. She gloved up and opened it the rest of the way. Trent's flashlight hit the interior at the same time as hers.

Randy Hart's body—one bullet hole between his black, devilish eyes, and another in his chest.

Trent stumbled back, and Amanda reached out and helped him catch his balance. He was pecking away on his phone, but she stopped him.

"He's dead. He's not going anywhere. But we can still save Logan. If everyone starts storming up here with their sirens, who knows how things will turn out? Please, just wait a few min—" She sniffed the air. "Smoke—" She stepped out from under the carport and saw a flicker of orange flame in an upper window of the barn. "Fire."

CHAPTER FIFTY-EIGHT

Amanda could wait for the fire department, or she could take the power into her own hands. And Logan needed her. She'd never forgive herself if he was in there, and she never even tried to save him.

The smell of burning wood was only getting stronger and more smoke was rising into the air.

She turned to Trent. "You make the call for backup. I'm going in."

"What? No you can't—"

"I am, and I mean it. Stay out here. If the shit hits the fan, you don't want to get buried in it any more than you already are." She started into a run toward the barn, unable to get her legs to move as fast as she wanted. Her entire focus was on getting to Logan. Surely he had to be inside.

The flames were starting to dance wildly in the upper-story window. But the rain had fully arrived, and Amanda was thankful as she felt fat raindrops pelt her skin. The heat from the fire was intense the closer she got to the barn.

She entered, moving past stalls, and started hacking on the smoke. She covered her mouth with her arm and kept moving, head down. She kept one hand poised over her weapon. She could draw and fire in seconds. Though she was wilting under the heat, and it was getting harder to breathe.

Timber creaked overhead and ash and sparks rained down. She looked at the old straw in the stables. It would just take one to spark to ignite, and she'd be trapped in here.

There was a door at the other end of the barn, straight ahead of her. She pushed through and opened it.

It was pouring even harder now, and there was a thunderous crack that had her jumping and turning around. A beam had crashed through the ceiling from the floor above.

She was left with two options. One, go out the door she'd just opened to safety. Two, go up a staircase that ran along the wall.

If Daniel Ross had set the fire, his MO usually meant there was a body to hide. But could she live with herself if Logan were still alive and she hadn't tried to save him?

She coughed and watched as the fire lavishly danced across the fallen beam like it was putting on a show for money.

More crackling wood. The fire was growing rapidly and taking on more power.

She should just leave and let the firefighters do their job. *They could be too late*, kept playing in her head.

Then she heard it over the din of the blaze. A voice. Faint at first, then a bit louder. A scream? A call for help? But where was it coming from?

She coughed. The smoke was curling around her face in long tendrils and wreaking havoc on her lungs.

The person shouted again, and this time, she could discern it was coming from upstairs.

Amanda put her hand on her gun and headed up, taking each step slowly, her back against the wall.

A couple of steps from the top, she could see into the loft—though only a few feet ahead of her, as the smoke was thick. The fire itself seemed mostly contained to the right of where she was. Two forms were struggling, but it was hard to make out faces.

Daniel and Logan? Had Logan gotten free? And who was crying out for help?

She breathed shallow, trying not to cough and reveal her position before she was ready, and crept up one more stair. She drew her gun. "Prince William—" She coughed, and both people stopped and appeared to be facing her. "Police!"

They lunged toward her, their steps moving in close unison and eating up floorboards. They were approaching as a front against her, but that wouldn't make any sense if one of them was Logan. She fired a high warning shot, but that didn't stop either of them from advancing on her. She stumbled, lost her footing, and felt herself falling backward. Her heart jackhammered—but she caught her balance.

Her gun, though, had slipped from her wet palm and clattered down the staircase. She hurried to retrieve it, sensing impending danger, and found her Glock a few steps down. She turned again to face the loft area. The pair was still coming toward her—still working as a team. It was clear now that neither of them was Logan. In fact, one of them was a woman.

"Stop right there!" Amanda barked, but they paid her no attention.

She squeezed the trigger again, but her aim faltered. Torso hit. Red spray cut through the smoke, and a body fell toward her and tumbled down the stairs. The woman's.

A quick glance behind her—at the unnatural position of the body—told her the woman was probably dead.

Amanda turned around to look up into the loft again, but the other person was gone from sight.

The smart thing to do would be retreat. Breathing was getting harder. Her body and clothing were drenched with sweat. She turned to leave but stopped at another cry for help.

She couldn't just ignore it—even with the other man still in the loft and posing a threat to her. She rushed up the stairs and stumbled around through the haze. The place was finished and furnished like an apartment. She had to stop to cough, but eventually made it to a closed door. She banged on it and called out, and a voice came from within. A girl's voice.

She reached for the doorknob, stopping just shy of contact. It would be scalding. She covered her hand with the base of her shirt and—

She was grabbed from behind and thrown to the floor. Her gun flew out of her hand and down the stairs to the floor below. Her skull hit wood, and her vision flashed white.

Daniel Ross shadowed over her. "You came."

He was holding something in his hand, and Amanda used all her energy to kick his arm. The object skittered across the floor, and he went after it. This gave Amanda the precious seconds needed to spring to her feet. But Daniel turned on her, and swept out a leg, brushing both of hers out from beneath her.

She flew forward and smacked her chin on the floor. She scrambled to get upright. She could sense Daniel coming at her, but she didn't want to look back. She just wanted to move. She had to. She couldn't give in to the paralyzing power of fear.

Her hair was yanked from behind, and she was flipped to her back. Daniel pinned her to the floor, and his hands went for her neck and squeezed hard. She fought against him, but she could feel her strength quickly fading away. Her eyes rolled back, and her arms reached out, her fingertips searching—and then she felt something! Was it what Daniel had been holding? She worked her fingers around it—a knife.

She raised it and thrust it into his side with all the force she could muster.

His eyes widened—the anger in them melting away and softening to relief. "You see me." Daniel's voice was barely above a whisper in the din of the fire's roaring, but there was the hint of a smile on his lips. His grip weakened, and his body sagged and fell to the side of Amanda.

She let go of the knife and lay there, struggling to catch her breath. She considered giving in to the darkness when there was another scream.

She had more than herself to think about. She scrambled to her feet and returned to the door, covered her hand with her shirt, and twisted the handle. It was locked. She choked on smoke, and a violent coughing fit erupted from her lungs. She lifted her shirt to cover her mouth and turned to search for something to bust the knob. She thought of the knife. It had felt large in her hands.

She made her way back to it and realized it was probably the Bowie knife he'd used on Fox. She returned to the door, pierced the blade into the door jamb, and wormed the door latch from its hole. She blinked away tears from the smoke as she opened the door.

Inside, there was no sign of Logan, but there was a teenage girl with red hair. No longer screaming, she was curled into a ball on the floor. Amanda was too late and considered resigning to death herself. The burning in her lungs was surreal. But when the girl coughed weakly, Amanda was compelled to action.

She helped the girl to her feet, even though Amanda could barely stand herself. She had to get them down the stairs and out the door as fast as possible.

Stay strong for a few more minutes, she coached herself.

She hooked the girl's arm over her shoulder, and they staggered toward the stairs and started going down. She could feel the heat of the fire kissing her skin, and the stalls at the side where she'd entered the barn were completely engulfed in flames.

She passed the woman and glanced at her motionless body. Her gaze landed on a vine tattoo crawling up the woman's neck. Was she the one who had lured Ashley and Crystal to Dumfries? What was she doing here?

The observation and thoughts were made in milliseconds as Amanda and the girl rushed by. Amanda got them out the side door and into the night air. She took them a safe distance away and collapsed. She could feel the cold rain beating down like ice pellets on her hot flesh.

Amanda closed her eyes, and she had two final thoughts before her world turned to black. *Where the hell is Logan? And who is that woman?*

CHAPTER FIFTY-NINE

When Amanda came to, she was lying on a stretcher in the back of a medic's vehicle. An oxygen mask was in place over on her face, though breathing still felt like an effort.

"There she is," the medic said, smiling.

"I feel like—" Her head swooned, and she tugged at the mask.

"No, please leave that on." The medic fought her, and for a second, she didn't have enough strength to argue. Then she saw Logan's face in her mind.

"Where's Logan? Did we find him?"

"I…" The medic's brow screwed up like he was confused. She bolted upright to a seated position, and her head felt like she'd drunk a few martinis—from what she remembered when she did drink. She tore the mask off and coughed. "And the girl…" Images were coming back to her in pieces.

"The girl should be fine. She's been taken to the hospital."

The medic's response barely sank in, and she flung her legs over the side of the gurney.

"I'd advise that you stay—"

"There was a man…being held hostage." She realized she was talking in fragments but couldn't help herself. Her lungs were burning, and she was having a hard time catching her breath. But she slid to the floor until her feet found purchase and stood. Her head spun, but she had to move… Logan. She stepped out of the vehicle and saw that she was still at the Ross property.

The sky was dark, but the rain had stopped, and the fire was out. Smoke clung stubbornly in a low-lying haze. The place was teeming with emergency responders. The lights from their vehicles gave the entire area a glow.

She got off the bumper and stumbled across the driveway. She spotted Trent among the throng. At least he'd stayed outside like she'd told him to; he looked fine. She took a step toward him, but Malone cut her off before she could reach him.

"It's best you don't talk to him." His voice was gruff, but his eyes were soft, like he wasn't sure if he should be mad or relieved. "There's going to be shit to pay for this, Detective."

She bristled at the formal address. She glanced again at Trent, but he had turned away. She said, "I saved a girl. That has to count for something." She coughed again and gripped her chest.

"Might not be enough, and you could use a doctor." Malone looked at her firmly.

"Did we find Logan?" The question cut from her throat, and when Malone shook his head, her knees buckled.

He helped hold her up and nudged his head toward the medic's van. "You really need to take care of yourself, Amanda."

He was certainly torn between which hat to wear—the professional or the personal.

"Logan has to be here somewhere," she pleaded.

"He doesn't have to be, but people are searching."

"Let me. Please. If I could just…" Her voice disappeared to nothing, and she reached inside her pocket and pulled out the bagged photo and removed it to get a better look. "He's against a wood-paneled wall."

"Amanda, please, just leave it to the rest of us to find him."

But she couldn't just let it go. She returned her focus to the photo, following it around the edges, and she saw something. "Look." She pointed and showed the photo to Malone. "The ceiling looks like packed dirt, and there are beams." She met his gaze, and they both spoke at the same time.

"It's a storm cellar."

"Spread out," Malone bellowed to anyone within hearing range. "We're looking for a storm cellar! Our hostage may be in there."

She started toward the house.

"Nuh-uh. I'm sticking right to your side." Malone hustled to catch up with her.

She was dizzy and panting for breath, but she would push through for as long as she could.

She went to the west side of the house and traced around the building, shining the flashlight from her phone ahead of her. "There!"

Barely visible was a door practically buried in the grass, but there had been some recent foot traffic that had flattened some blades.

She bent over to open it and swooned.

"Let me get it," Malone huffed out.

He threw the door open, and she shone her light into the hole. She couldn't see anything from the entrance, and slowly proceeded down some wood steps. She reached the bottom and put her flashlight around the space. Wood-planked walls just like in the photo.

"Logan?" she called out hoarsely.

She heard mumbling and followed in its direction. It took her around a large shelving unit full of canned goods.

Logan was there, and he widened his eyes at the sight of her. Fear replaced by relief.

She hurried to him, pulled the gag from his mouth, and freed his wrists and ankles.

"What happened to you?" He pressed the pads of his thumbs to her cheeks and held them for her to see. They were black.

Soot. Of all the things for him to say first… "Never mind me. You okay?"

"I've been better."

She put her arms around him and squeezed tight, but she was the first to pull away. Her chest felt heavy, but there was also something she wanted to do. "Logan Hunter, this is Scott Malone. He's my sergeant and also a family friend."

"Hey," Logan said, "we spoke on the phone before."

Malone glanced at her, and she shrank under his gaze. The time Logan had referred to was when he'd provided Amanda's alibi.

"Nice to meet you," Malone said. "Now, I don't want to come across as an ass, but you both need medical attention."

She and Malone helped Logan out of the bunker and summoned for a stretcher.

It wasn't until he was loaded and on his way to the hospital that Malone turned to her. "Why am I still looking at you? Shouldn't you be in an ambulance yourself?"

"I'll be fine." It took all her power to suppress another cough.

"Nope. You're out of here." Malone signaled to another paramedic to come over.

"Fine, I'll go, but..." She was almost hesitant to ask her next question in case she'd fabricated all of it.

"But?" he prompted.

"Who was—" she coughed, no longer able to hold it back "—that woman?" If she was real—and not imagined, that is—Amanda needed to know her identity.

Malone held up his hand to stay the paramedic, who came to a standstill about thirty feet away.

"I should say ask her yourself," Malone said, "but then you'd go do it. She was taken to the hospital for treatment. Again, something I recommend that you do."

"She survived?"

"No thanks to you, I'm guessing?"

"That woman tried to kill me."

"Can't say I'm surprised."

"Are you going to tell me who she was?"

Malone blew out a big breath. "We believe she was hired by the DC sex-trafficking ring to take out Daniel Ross because he was killing their girls."

"Trent and I thought that might happ—" She silenced under his glare. No one liked being interrupted. "Sorry."

"Uh-huh. Well, Ross's van was found near a dive motel in Dumfries—where Hart was shot." He held up a hand, and she shut her mouth. He continued. "We have an eyewitness who saw the entire thing, and his descriptions line up. Hart was shot by the woman and stuffed in the trunk of his Nissan by her and Daniel. There was also a young girl in the car."

"The one I pulled from the barn."

"I'd assume."

"Okay, but if the woman was hired to take out Daniel, why didn't she shoot him when she shot Hart? And why did Daniel help put Hart's body in the trunk?"

"She had Daniel at gunpoint. But why she didn't just kill him then, too, I don't know."

"Do we know the woman's name?"

"This part you might do better sitting down for."

"Tell me, and I'll go to the hospital." She'd prepared her mind to anyway, but Malone didn't have to know that.

"She let it slip that Daniel was her brother."

Her mind was murky, but eventually the name surfaced. "Christina Ross? But how? She's dead."

"She was ID'd incorrectly. Sometimes it happens…"

Malone had been right when he'd suggested it would have been best for her to be sitting for that news. Wow. Christina Ross was back from the dead—and she'd returned to kill her own brother. So many questions, starting with: what had happened to turn Christina from sex-trafficking victim into one of the perpetrators?

CHAPTER SIXTY

Five days later, Sunday

Amanda hadn't slept very well since the fire. The screams, the smoke, the heat, the feeling of being strangled. Every time she closed her eyes, she was back in the barn about to die, and she'd wake up drenched in sweat, the sheets soaking wet.

She'd survived, but she hadn't gotten away completely unscathed. She'd hit her chin really hard in that loft, as well as her knee when she'd fallen down the stairs—not that she'd noticed until much later thanks to the adrenaline coursing through her veins—and she'd inhaled more than her fair share of smoke. But she was grateful there were no burns. Her doctor said she was lucky and told her to get some rest and pop ibuprofen as needed to ease the pain.

The "lucky" part was debatable, and certainly not how she felt at the moment. Malone had forced her to take sick leave until her fate with Lieutenant Hill was decided.

But Amanda had her reasons for doing what she had. At least the girl was going to be fine—though it would be a long road ahead. They discovered her name was Abigail Butler, only fifteen years old. And Logan, who Daniel had taken from his home Monday night, had been dehydrated and starved for over twenty-four hours. He had recovered physically, but Amanda could tell he'd been mentally scarred by his experience—not that he was admitting as much to her. But she hadn't talked to him a lot in the past week, and every time she did, he had a reason for cutting the conversation short.

She grabbed a coffee from her kitchen and got as comfortable as she could manage on her couch. She normally loved tucking her legs beneath her, but that was not on the agenda for the time being with her blasted knee. She grabbed a folder from the side table.

Malone had come by yesterday and delivered it to her. She really was living a waking nightmare. Not only had she disappointed him by "going rogue," as he put it, but she hadn't been able to question Christina Ross at all. It had been Cougar who got the job, along with Patty Glover in Sex Crimes. Malone didn't want Trent to touch the case anymore either. Her partner was just one more casualty for how everything went down. Malone had strongly cautioned her not to speak with Trent until after her meeting with the lieutenant. She'd ignored his advice—apparently, she was in a rebellious phase—and was happy she had. Trent told her he didn't hold any of what had happened, or what would, against her. As he'd said, "I'm a big boy, Amanda, and more than capable of handling whatever's coming my way." She hoped he was right.

She opened the folder and gleaned the takeaway points again. Daniel Ross had died in that barn from the stab wound she'd inflicted. Finding this out hadn't filled her with regret. He wouldn't face his day in court and be held accountable by the justice system, but it was assured that no one would suffer at his hands again.

It was not getting full closure as to motive that gnawed on her, but some cases never got neatly wrapped up. While they'd never hear what had driven Daniel directly from him, she suspected he had been desperate for attention. His final words, "You see me," sort of clinched that for her.

And it would seem he'd hated his sister. They were struggling in that loft, after all. How far back did the sibling animosity go? Had Daniel's parents always favored the daughter, and then when she went missing and was declared dead, had they become consumed by grief and neglected Daniel completely? If so, maybe Daniel's young mind had placed the blame for that on Christina's shoulders. It could be that every time he killed, he saw his sister's face and was really killing her. As for what had triggered him, that answer, too, was taken with him to the grave.

Another thing that may be buried forever were the identities of the victims of the Clear Mountain Circle fire. At least they weren't without justice. But one day, Amanda hoped to bring their families closure.

Mia Vaughn confirmed that the second fire was the result of a propane tank explosion, though she couldn't narrow down exactly what had been used to start the fire that ignited the gas.

Forensic results from the murder cases had finally come back too. The tox panel on Ashley Lynch had confirmed that she had ketamine in her system. The epithelia under Fox's nails, and the palm print lifted from the Sunny Motel matched to Daniel.

She checked the time on her phone and realized she had to get going. She was meeting a friend for a long overdue coffee and hoping for some updates. It was still playing on her mind how Christina had gone from victim to perpetrator.

*

Amanda entered Hannah's Diner, and May pulled her in for a hug and squeezed tight.

"There's my girl. Let me get ya a coffee and muffin. I'll be right back with it." She nudged her head to a corner booth. "Your friend's already here."

May hustled off, and Amanda headed toward a woman who could easily have been a model. Athletic build, with a dark, smooth complexion. Her skin seemed to glow, testifying to regular exercise and a healthy diet. Her brown hair was all tight, springy curls, and didn't reach the top of her shoulders. But what Amanda really noticed were her sparkling eyes, and the second they met each other's gaze, the two of them grinned.

"Is that actually Detective Amanda Steele in the flesh?" Patty beamed.

"Only if you're Detective Patty Glover." Amanda had imagined Patty to be older, but seeing her now, she realized they were probably about the same age.

Patty held out her hand and gave Amanda's a robust shake. "Please, sit." She gestured across from her, and May returned with the coffee and the snack.

Amanda lifted her cup to take a sip, and Patty rushed to lift hers, holding it toward Amanda's in a toast gesture. "To the beginning of an amazing friendship."

Amanda smiled and clinked her cup to Patty's, and both women took sips of their drinks.

"Okay, now, maybe I'll get down to business…" Patty angled her head. She had such a harmless mischievousness to her in person. Not a real surprise, as it did travel across the phone line. In person, though, her entire face lit up with the delivery. "I don't even know where to start."

"Christina Ross." Amanda had heard that Christina was expected to make a full recovery.

"All right. You know she's going to be just fine and that I've interviewed her?"

Amanda nodded.

"She confessed to setting that fire seven years ago. She was eighteen at the time and saw it as her way out."

"Brave. She must have been terrified."

"No doubt, and desperate. She's not remorseful that one of the girls died, though. Something's gotten screwed up in her mind—not that that's a surprise, given all she's been through."

That brought up another chilling thought. "Someone else was laid to rest under Christina's headstone. Did she know who died in that fire?"

Patty shook her head. "She didn't give me anything, no matter how hard I pressed. There's an order underway to exhume the remains, but it might be a long time before we ever get a name. If we ever do. No idea where Christina's been living, but I did find her on the data chip. Her nickname had been *Fresh off the Farm*. Sickening."

Amanda took a deep breath, her coffee still mostly untouched. "I really need you to help me understand something. What turned Christina Ross into one of them?"

"Short answer. Survival. She told me that she'd reported Randy Hart all those years ago."

"The nine-one-one call."

"That's right. She was hoping police would dissemble the ring, but instead the ring caught up with her. She felt she had to make herself valuable to them if they were going to let her live. So that's what she did."

"But isn't that unusual?" Amanda had heard of Stockholm syndrome. Was it something similar that had messed up Christina's mind?

Patty pressed her lips and shook her head. "I wish I could say it was. You'll be surprised—and shocked—to know that nearly forty percent of the people involved with sex trafficking are women. Many were formerly victims."

"Wow."

"Yep. As I said, it's about survival. And the leaders in these rings need some women on their side. A young girl's more likely to trust a woman than a man."

"I get that." Though the concept pierced Amanda's heart. "And she was sent to kill her brother?"

"Yep, and she had no qualms about doing so. When she'd volunteered to take out the person killing the girls, she hadn't known it was Daniel, but she was committed to seeing it through. She and her brother were never close."

"I suspected as much, but I'm curious why she didn't just shoot Daniel at the motel where she killed Hart. Did you ask her about that?"

Patty nodded. "Uh-huh. She wanted to toy with him and had him take them to their old farm. She thought it would be poetic to kill him there. She said she always hated the place. But apparently Daniel got the upper hand and managed to disarm her."

"They were fighting in the loft when I arrived," Amanda conceded. She didn't remember seeing another gun and wondered if Christina's had ever been recovered. Amanda knew her Glock was brought in as evidence, and she hadn't been issued a replacement with her being on sick leave. "Were you able to get anywhere with who Christina was sold to?"

"The money trail seems to lead to somewhere in DC. Still working to narrow that down."

Was the ring's name, DC, unoriginal and purely based on location? Amanda had this niggling feeling there was more to it. Maybe one day she'd find out what. "Let's hope it ends up getting us closer to the ringleader."

"We can wish upon a star. Now, I've got more updates for you. Where do you want me to go from here?"

"With anyone who's going to prison." Amanda smiled at her new friend. It was so nice to finally be with her in person.

"Very well. The owners of the Sunny Motel and Ritter's Motel are facing jailtime. They were facilitators—enabling the ring to solicit the girls at their motels. We've accessed their financials and see large and regular deposits going into the bank accounts."

No wonder the owner of the Sunny Motel didn't want Roy to call the cops. "Can you track those?"

"Uh-uh. I did, and we've got some names. Arrests will be made." Another beautiful smile from Patty.

"That's fantastic. Are the motel owners saying anything? Do they know who's behind the DC ring?" Amanda leaned across the table.

"They both offered to turn state's evidence in exchange for protective custody. They have some names, but don't know the person at the top. All they know about them is that they are extremely powerful and believe it might be a prominent politician, or someone in law enforcement."

"Scary thought."

"Sadly, only to be expected in that world. Now, I'm still working on Second Treasures. The people there claim they had no idea that these girls have been shopping in their store. I subpoenaed their financials, and there's nothing untoward that's been found. The owners and employees there might be innocent, but at least we now know about it and can keep the place under surveillance."

For all that Patty was offering, Amanda felt bad asking for more. "Anything useful turn up on those suspects I forwarded from the initial investigation into Lynch's disappearance?"

"No dice, I'm afraid."

Amanda twisted her cup and looked down into the coffee, one more question coming to mind. "Did Randy Hart lead you anywhere?"

"Unfortunately, no. We checked his home and came up empty. We also spoke with his former employer, Bonnie Pratt, at the Pansy Shoppe. She only had nice things to say about him."

"Do you think the flower place is mixed up in any of this?"

"Involved in the ring? No way."

Amanda was relieved to hear that and overwhelmed with gratitude. She made eye contact with Patty. "You've just done so much. It's fantastic."

"Don't mention it. This job is my work and my passion. It's also why I had to meet you, Amanda."

"*It* being?"

"You're like me and have a strong desire to find justice. You really care, and that's—I'm sad to say—harder to find in the department than it used to be."

Amanda smiled, so thankful that their paths had crossed, though sad at why they had. But there would be a lot of really bad men and women out there who would be hoping Amanda and Patty never joined forces. They may not know it yet, but their day of reckoning was coming.

CHAPTER SIXTY-ONE

The following day...

Amanda was sitting outside Hill's office with Malone and her lawyer. What a horrible way to start the week.

Hill's assistant, Lily, kept smiling awkwardly at her. If needing the lawyer wasn't enough of a bad sign, this was another one.

The phone beeped on Lily's desk, and then a voice came over its speaker. "Send them in."

Hill sounded sour, and Amanda couldn't help quaking internally. This case had rocked her emotionally, mentally, and physically, and it felt like she still had a long way to go before she healed. But she took a deep breath and stood tall. She had no reason for regrets. And she had saved two people. She went through the doorway first, her lawyer and Malone behind her.

Hill was perched at her desk, her beady eyes fixed on Amanda. The LT didn't smile, but her eyes brightened. "Close the door, Detective."

"I've got it." Malone stepped in and did as Hill had requested of Amanda.

Hill got up, rounded her desk, and said to Amanda, "Please, sit."

Amanda recognized the LT's intended power play immediately. With her sitting and the lieutenant standing, it was an intimidation tactic. Sadly, it was working.

"I'm not the type to mince words, Detective Steele, and I'm quite sure you know why I've called for this meeting."

Amanda didn't say a word. On previous advice from her lawyer, she was to limit her responses to "yes" or "no."

"Do you know why I called this meeting?" Hill leaned against the edge of her desk, sitting but still above Amanda.

"No."

"Not sure I buy that."

Amanda shrugged, kept silent.

"I see how this is going to go." She stood again. "Did you request backup to accompany you to the Logmill Road property?"

"No." She balled her hand tight but released it before it rigored in a fist.

"Did you enter the property anyway?"

"Yes." She stared straight ahead.

"Did you put the lives of yourself and others in jeopardy?"

"Yes."

"Including that of your own partner?"

She hadn't directly but things could have taken a dark turn. For that she had to answer, "Yes."

Her lawyer gently nudged her arm, but Amanda didn't look at her.

"Did you enter the barn while it was on fire?"

"Yes."

"Did you convince your partner to join you?"

She stumbled with that one too. Self-imposed guilt was a bitch. She certainly hadn't made him go along with her, but she hadn't discouraged him either. The only right call she made was telling him to stay out of the barn.

"If you're worried that I will hold him accountable for your poor leadership, I won't. I'll ask again—"

"No." One word, two letters, and she felt like she betrayed Trent.

Hill's lips rose in a subtle smile. "Did you ignore a call from your supervisor, Sergeant Malone, when he called for your whereabouts?"

Amanda's lawyer touched her forearm. "Don't answer that." She turned to Hill. "There's no way she could read his mind to know the reason for his call."

Hill steepled her fingers. "Right. Because she ignored it. Is that right, Detective Steele? Did you ignore a call from Sergeant Malone when you were on the Ross property?"

"Yes."

Hill smiled and dipped her head at the lawyer, then met Amanda's gaze. "I believe I've allowed you a long leash, Detective."

A ball of rage knotted in Amanda's gut, but she clamped her mouth shut.

"You've wasted department time and taxpayers' money on the interrogation of a suspect, a Samuel Booth, who turned out to be absolutely innocent."

"Is there a question in there?" Amanda's lawyer asked.

Hill quirked an eyebrow and addressed Amanda again. "And while you had Mr. Booth in custody, did you miss following vital clues that led to the death of two more women?"

Another one she struggled with. Her conscience would find her guilty, but there was no way to be certain. "No. We followed the evidence we had at the—"

Her lawyer urged her to stop talking.

Hill looked over the room. "I really think we've all heard enough. I'm suspending you without pay for thirty days and will be asking for your badge to be taken away for good."

Amanda met Malone's gaze. He pressed his lips down, but otherwise tried to infuse encouragement into his eyes. He'd told her before he had her back, and she believed it, but right now, she was floating in the ocean without a life raft. If she was going to survive, she'd have to swim. She cleared her throat. "What about Trent?"

"That's really between me, Detective Stenson, his lawyer, and his sergeant, but I'm going to request that he be relegated to desk duties for thirty days."

"I thought you said he wouldn't be in trouble," Amanda burst out, and her lawyer set a hand on her forearm.

"I said I wouldn't hold him accountable for *your* actions. He could have refused to go with you, and he could have called for backup long before he did. He chose not to."

"He didn't because of me. I'm the senior detective."

The lawyer put a hand on Amanda's arm again, applying more pressure this time, but Amanda had more to say.

"You do realize that if we didn't move when we did, that girl would have been dead. And Logan."

Hill's smile was twisted. "You a fortune teller now? And how dare you defend your actions by claiming that you saved two people? Do you forget that one is in the morgue because of you? Another recovering in the hospital from a gunshot?"

Both of them were killers, but that didn't seem to matter to Hill. Any outburst would be a waste of energy. Hill had made up her mind about Amanda a long time ago.

Amanda got to her feet, took her badge and cuffs from her pocket and put them on Hill's desk.

She looked down at what had been her life since she was twenty-one years old. She could accept that part of her life may be over and move forward—or she could fight. She wasn't one to succumb to bullying, and if the last six years had taught her anything, it was just how formidable she was and how she could overcome anything. This setback included. And no matter how much Hill hated her or fought against her, her opinion didn't have a bearing on Amanda's value as a person or as a cop. If only Daniel had realized that his self-worth wasn't reliant on other people's approval. He might have never killed anyone.

But Amanda saved lives. She worked for justice. That was in her blood.

This was just a blip on her journey. She'd be back, and when she rose, Hill would most certainly fall.

A LETTER FROM CAROLYN

Dear reader,

I want to say a huge thank you for choosing to read *Stolen Daughters*. If you enjoyed it and would like to be notified about new releases in the Detective Amanda Steele series, just sign up at the following link. Your email address will never be shared, and you can unsubscribe at any time.

www.bookouture.com/carolyn-arnold

I never planned to write about human trafficking, but sadly, it's a disease that's infected the world. With tens of millions of victims and countless perpetrators, it's not something that we can ignore. Silence is what gives these monsters power, and how great it would be to strip it completely from them. I suppose writing about this horrible atrocity is my way of shedding light on the darkness, and showing love, compassion, and understanding for the victims.

This was a challenging book in many respects and required research into fire investigations and tapping into the mind of a killer who was especially conflicted and complex. It took a lot of effort to untangle his psyche. And fire… well, I have a heightened respect for firefighters! I quickly found out there's often no simple, black-and-white answer, and there are so many things that factor into putting out a blaze.

If you loved *Stolen Daughters*, I would be incredibly grateful if you would write a brief, honest review. Also, if you'd like to continue investigating murder, you'll be happy to know there will be more Detective Amanda Steele books. But I also offer several other international bestselling series and have over thirty published books for you to enjoy in everything from crime fiction, to cozy mysteries, to thrillers and action adventures. One of these series features Detective Madison Knight, another female kick-ass detective, who will risk her life, her badge—whatever it takes—to find justice for murder victims.

Hopefully, you also enjoyed meeting FBI Special Agent Brandon Fisher. He has a series by his own name, and those books are heart-pounding thrillers for readers fascinated with the psychology of serial killers. Each instalment is a new case with a fresh bloody trail to follow. Hunt with the FBI's Behavioral Analysis Unit and profile some of the most devious and darkest minds on the planet.

I love hearing from my readers. You can follow me on Facebook and Twitter, or drop by my website. These are good ways to stay notified of all my new releases. You can also reach out to me via email at Carolyn@CarolynArnold.net.

Wishing you a thrill a word!
Carolyn Arnold

🖥 carolynarnold.net

🐦 Carolyn_Arnold

📘 AuthorCarolynArnold

ACKNOWLEDGMENTS

This book wouldn't be the same without the assistance and support of certain people. To start, I thank my husband, who has been my cheerleader for over twenty years and by my side from the start of my writing career. He's never let me down, and I suspect never will.

Gratitude goes to my editor Emily Gowers at Bookouture for her unwavering faith in my writing and Detective Amanda Steele. I also am thankful for the team at Bookouture—the numerous editors, those in marketing and social media, audiobook production, design and formatting, and countless others who work behind the scenes to make it all come together.

I'd also like to thank Janet Fix, who had a part in polishing this book to a shine. Sorry that I gave your name to a rather quirky character, but think of it this way, she's memorable.

In this book, I wrote about fires for the first time, and I needed insight into how this would be handled from an investigative standpoint. Thank you to David Glinski with the Dumfries Triangle Volunteer Fire Department for his time answering my questions. If I got some facts wrong, I hope he forgives me.

Again, the patience of Yvonne Van Gaasbeck, a former coroner in Georgia, is appreciated. She's always ready and willing to share her knowledge. For this book, she specifically helped me understand that hyoid bones are not as easily broken as one might be led to believe—and not necessarily as readily detectable.

A thank you goes out to lawyer Addie King for her willingness to share her expertise in criminal defense. Her continued insights will no doubt prove even more helpful as the series moves forward, along with Julie Steele's criminal trial. Addie is also a paranormal/fantasy author.

As with the first instalment in this series, help received from local law enforcement in Prince William County, Virginia, has been extremely valuable.

And speaking of Prince William County... If you're familiar with the area, including Dumfries, Woodbridge, and Haymarket, you probably noticed that I took some creative license—including assigning fictional names to some streets. But, hey, that's what authors often do.

Lastly, but not least, a shoutout goes to all first responders—the police, firefighters, paramedics, and medics. And let's not forget others on the front line at hospitals and clinics who help save lives, while putting theirs on the line. Thank you for all that you do.

Made in the USA
Las Vegas, NV
16 June 2022